BROKEN WING

Judith James

D0291192

Jewel Imprint: Sapphire
Medallion Press, Inc.
Printed in USA

DEDICATION:

This book is dedicated to the lost boys. God bless them. May they all find a place to belong, and someone to love them as they deserve.

Published 2008 by Medallion Press, Inc.

The MEDALLION PRESS LOGO
is a registered trademark of Medallion Press, Inc.

Typeset in Adobe Caslon Pro
Printed in the United States of America

ISBN: 9781933836447

10 9 8 7 6 5 4 3 2 1
First Edition

ACKNOWLEDGMENTS

I'm one of those lucky people who have a family you can count on through thick and thin, and are also a great joy to be around. I'd like to thank my three best friends and beta readers, my wonderful, literate, talented sisters, Cindy, Linda, and Sandy. Without their insights and always constructive criticisms, and more importantly their enthusiastic support, this book would never have been finished. I'd like to thank my Mom and Dad who didn't blink an eye when I quit a nicely pensioned day job to try my hand at writing, but said good for you, you can do it. They've always been that way. I'd like to thank Karen, who helped me brainstorm at a pivotal moment, and along with Geraldine, graciously changed her itinerary in Europe so I could visit Paris and do a little research. Thanks ladies. A special thanks to winemaker extraordinaire and captain of The Irish Rover, Nick Dubois, who (with some help from his Mom) helped me with my French. Any faux pas that remain are mine.

Thanks also to my ever-patient agent, Bob Diforio, who took a chance on an unknown unpublished author with an unconventional book, and Pat Thomas for listening and for her help with the early editing when I didn't know anything at all. Special thanks go to the Medallion team, who are so supportive and such a pleasure to work with, from Christy, my copy editor to Jim and Adam and company in the art department. I don't think there could be a better experience for someone launching their first book. People told me how scary it could be, but these folks made it fun. In particular I'd like to thank Kerry Estevez for all her help, and for saying just the right thing at just the right moment; Helen Rosburg for taking a chance on a first novel that doesn't quite fit the mold; incredible artist Arturo Delgado and everyone else involved in producing a gorgeous cover, and my editor Janet Bank for her enthusiastic support, always constructive guidance, and for "getting it" and helping me write the book I wanted.

Last, but most important, I'd like to thank my beautiful talented daughter Danielle. A couple of years ago she gave me a very special leather bound journal inscribed with the words. "Whatever journey you choose to embark on in the coming years, here is a place to recount it. I hope it brings you luck." It was there I wrote the first chapters of Broken Wing, and she is all the luck I'll ever need.

PROLOGUE

Wearing a new suit, shoes pinching, blinking from the searing sun, his eyes are riveted on the door, black and menacing. The knocker, a grinning gargoyle, watches him, knowing eyes alive with malicious glee. This is bad! A bad place! He whimpers with dread as the door opens. They mean to leave him here. He knows it. Sorry, sorry, sorry! Whatever he's done, he won't do it again. Not ever! Please! I don't like it here! But they push him forward and he's powerless to resist. "Pretty child!" he hears as the black maw opens. They reach for him, greedy grasping hands pulling him inside.

He's running as fast as he can down endless twisting corridors, past open doors, afraid to look inside. He catches glimpses, angry red faces, leering smiles, whips and chains and naked flesh, and something grunting. He hears moans, sibilant whispers, ugly cries of pleasure and of pain as he tries frantically to find a way out. Something horrible, evil, is right behind, reaching for him, grabbing at his heel,

1

plucking at his shirt. He dodges and twists, too terrified to turn or look. If he did, it would be upon him, and he'd be lost.

No door, no escape, and still he runs, breath straining and heaving, heart hammering and rattling in his chest. Up ahead, the figure of a woman turns toward him, beckoning. Hope. If only he can reach her, take her hand, she'll lead him from this place. A burst of speed, hand outstretched. He's jerked back savagely, his ankle caught in a grip that burns his flesh and freezes his soul. Still he fights, fingers scrabbling, gripping the carpet, tearing gouges in the floor as he's dragged inexorably back into the seething, gaping maw. Soundlessly he screams and screams and screams.

Gabriel crouched on bended knee, hunched against cold stone above an ancient alley fetid with the smell of piss and vomit and cooked sausage. A door slammed in the distance. The sound of cursing, a man's and then a woman's, was followed by slaps, screams, and then silence. Far away, the sound of a guitar drifted to him, melancholy in the cold night air. There were sounds from the building behind him, closer, but muffled through stone and mortar and thick brick walls. He tilted his head back and took a long swallow from the decanter beside him, as he gazed, unfocused, into the distant heavens.

Once, years ago, before all sense of wonder had been beaten out of him, he'd climbed up here on a crisp, late, August night, and stumbled into an enchanted fairy-land. Magical lights had danced overhead, streaming across the sky, leaving arching trails of color and fire in their wake. He'd made wishes upon them, one after the other, and dreamt for a short time that they might come true. *Stupid child!*

This night's sky was black, cold and uncaring; re-lieved only by the glittering shards of harsh and distant suns so far from his reach they offered no warmth, no illumination, and no comfort. Desperate to escape the nightmares that chased him through his sleep, he ca-ressed the blade held tight between his fingers, wincing as cold steel slid delicately through tender flesh. There was a little frisson of pain, almost pleasure, as crim-son life oozed in a delicate band, slowly encircling his wrist. Again and again, steel kissed flesh. Not too deep. Not now. Not yet. Dead inside, lifeless and empty, the crimson bracelets offered a needed proof that for now at least, he was still of this world.

Holding his arms out, he turned them experimen-tally, left, right, his wrists barely visible in the pallid light, though his eyes had long since grown accus-tomed to the dark. The blood had thickened, slowed, almost stopped. Angry dark lines mingled with pa-per-thin silver and white ones, in an intricate pattern of defiance and despair. He allowed himself another

3

swallow, a solitary pleasure, a small comfort on a cold and cavernous night. He sensed the dampness in the shifting wind as it lifted a strand of his hair and fluttered against his cheek. It was a cold caress that chilled him to the bone. Looking up, he saw clouds scudding and scurrying across the night, like frightened little creatures scrambling to escape some implacable, hungry beast.

Slumping down out of the wind, he rolled onto his back, fingering the blade. He drew it gently across his cheek, back and forth. His lips curved in a jaded smile. He knew he wouldn't do it. He had no skills but those of a whore. No assets, nothing of value but his body and his face, and while he lived he needed them, treacherous and degraded though they were. As for death, well . . . there was the boy to consider. He didn't understand it really, how he'd left himself vulnerable this way. There had been a plan, money hoarded and hidden, a goal, and always there had been some small measure of control. He could refuse a thing if he wanted. They would punish him, yes. Make him pay and try to make him regret it, but they *were* running a business and he was valuable, and they never went too far.

Then the child had come, and something inside him, something weak and treacherous, had betrayed him. He'd wanted . . . needed . . . to protect the boy, to keep him safe and innocent. Well, as innocent as a child could be this close to the brimstone, he reflected, with a grin and another swallow. They'd found it amusing, but more importantly, they had found it profitable, and so it was allowed, because Gabriel would do anything to protect the boy. And so he had, anything and everything.

He pulled himself up, sitting with one leg bent. Tucking the blade in a coat sleeve, he wrapped his arms around his knee and rested his chin. A chill had seized him. His task was almost done. It seemed the boy had a family. He supposed all stupid lost little boys dreamed of a family that would come to find them, moving heaven and earth until they were safe again at home. It never happened, though. But this time, against all odds, it appeared to be true.

Wee little Jamie, well, James, now, he supposed, had a family who'd been searching for him these past five years, and they'd found him, or the runners had. There were two of them now, posted in front of Madame's establishment to make sure that the child would not be lost again. They were coming for him, this family of his, a man and a woman, all the way from England. They would arrive before the week was out.

Good! He was glad for the boy. He couldn't have kept him safe much longer. He was a pretty child, fast growing succulent and sweet. There had been a close call already. He would soon be worth more than Gabriel's obedience, and then he would be lost. Now he could scamper home, safe and sound, singed by the flames perhaps, but not consumed.

As for himself, well, the sooner the brat was gone, the better. He would be free at last. Free to leave, to look to his own best interests . . . Ah, Christ! Why bother pretending? Hooking the decanter with two fingers, he tipped it up again, draining the last few drops before hurling it to the cobblestones below. He chortled in drunken glee at the sound it made as it shattered and scattered into thousands of tiny pieces. Take your enjoyment where you can, boy. You're naught but a catamite, and a whore. There's nothing to live for, no one who cares, and your pleasures are few and far between.

He settled back again with a grin. He was as stupid as any of them. He'd let himself pretend that Jamie Boy was his family. It had given him reason to go on from one day to the next, and though he was glad, truly glad, and deeply relieved that the boy would soon be gone, he dreaded it, as well. It was a bone-deep dread, a stomach-clenching terror of returning to the desolate, lonely void where he'd lived most of his life.

Maybe, once the boy was gone, he'd find the courage to give himself some peace. Not here, though. No. He had a distant recollection of being by the ocean, skin pricking, the smell, and taste of salt. It was the only peaceful reminiscence he owned. He guarded it jealously, embellishing it with memories borrowed from books and other people's stories until it took on a luster and familiarity that felt like home. That's where he'd go when the time came. He would journey to the ocean, lay himself down, and let the water wash him clean. He was so damn tired. Oh, Christ! He wasn't crying, was he?

As if to mock him, a drop of rain, fat and gelid, splattered against his cheek, mingling with his own hot bitter tears. It was followed by another, and then another. Clouds were racing overhead now, and thunder moaned and grumbled in the distance. Good God, but drink could turn a fellow into a maudlin fool! Needing to piss, tired of self-pity, tired to the bone, he dragged himself stiffly to his feet.

Taking one last look at the angry sky, he sketched an elegant, mocking bow to whichever almighty sadist ruled the universe. Crossing his arms over his chest, shirt wet with blood, rain, and tears, he made his way back toward the sounds of shrill laughter, and the soft moans of men and women in pleasure and in pain. Opening the door, he stepped inside. Moist and seething, it smelled of whiskey and rum, tobacco and semen. It smelled like sex and desperation. He grinned. It smelled like home.

CHAPTER 1

Sarah, Lady Munroe, was also known as the Gypsy Countess, a moniker given her on account of her unfortunate parentage and her even more unfortunate behavior. Less than five years ago, the polite world had been shocked and titillated when she left her elderly husband only a week after her nuptials. It was widely rumored since that she dressed as a man, consorted with pirates, and counted among her numerous lovers her own half brother, Ross. All but the last charge were true.

She glanced at her brother now, in commiseration. Their plush, well-appointed carriage jolted and shimmied, rattling teeth and bone, as they made their hurried approach to Paris. Just ten years ago, the streets of this city had run red with blood as its citizenry turned on their betters in an excess of patriotism and democratic fervor, hacking many of them to pieces. Now, poised on the cusp of a new century, these bloodthirsty idealists, finally sated and shocked by the efforts of that ravenous matriarch, Madame Guillotine, looked for reassurance and order. Their attention had been drawn to a sallow young Corsican, Napoleon Bonaparte. Brilliant, charismatic, and politically astute, he was fast becoming a force to be reckoned with on the Continent, and a cause of great concern to Britain.

None of this had any negative impact on the commerce and custom of the finer Parisian brothels. Uncertainty, danger, and war were aphrodisiacs, and brothels were operating to capacity, catering to the well-heeled and providing delicious diversions to suit any need, regardless of political orientation, or sexual preference. It was to just such a place, Madame Etienne's, *Maison de Joie*, that Ross and Sarah now hurried in hopes of finding their younger brother.

"Oh, God, Ross, do you really think it's him? Could it be after all these years?" Sarah closed her eyes, desperately wanting to believe it, and desperately afraid of what it meant if it was true. The thought of the innocent child she'd played tag and soldiers with, living in such a place these past five years, filled her with horror.

Ross reached across, patting her hand. "I have very good reason to expect that it is, my dear. Our agents have done a thorough job of investigating. This child is the right age and coloring, and they indicate there's a striking family resemblance. They've been able to trace his route from London to the Continent. He arrived at Madame Etienne's a month after James disappeared."

He glanced out the window, troubled and far more aware than Sarah of what that meant. "We must be prepared, Sarah. He's not likely to recognize us, and he'll not be the child you remember. He has doubtless been through an ordeal. He may be . . . damaged in ways that—"

"Shhh," she interrupted, gripping his hand. "Think of it, Ross! After all this time, we've found him. If he doesn't remember, then we'll remind him. If he's hurt we'll heal him, and by God, we will bring him home!"

Leaning back into the cushions, Ross nodded in agreement, some of his anxiety subsiding. She would have made an excellent commander, he reflected. She had the ability to look at a complex situation and find its heart. He thought about what she'd said and prayed to God it would be that simple.

The warm spring day gave way to the cooler shadows of late afternoon as they wended their way through the city, silent, lost in thought. It was a city of contrasts. Beautiful boulevards verdant with spring buds were lined with stately homes girdled with black wrought-iron fences and window boxes riotous with color. Scattered among them were abandoned dwellings, defaced and looted, with broken gates and tumbled walls, the detritus of revolution and civil strife.

As they approached the city center, they passed narrow alleys crammed with tanners and fishmongers. The stench that escaped them joined the clatter of carts and the screeching of merchants in a noxious tumult of smell and noise that left Sarah feeling nauseated. The congestion grew heavier as they advanced through bustling neighborhoods lined with shops and restaurants, crowded with the scent of flowers, freshly baked bread, and the pungent odors of tobacco, coffee, and perfume. Everywhere, swelling crowds argued, haggled, and socialized. It all reminded her of some great, rushing, bellicose beast. This beast had swallowed her brother.

It was well past four in the afternoon, and the city had quieted as its inhabitants sought their dinner, when they finally arrived at Madame Etienne's. The elegant town house, with its cream brick façade and rose-trimmed windows, perched on a corner on top of a hill, as if guarding the warren of alleys and narrow streets below. There was a large balcony on the second floor and a smaller one on the third. A liveried doorman stood at attention. A knocker in the form of a grotesque gargoyle was the only hint that the house was anything other than a benign and sober, private domicile.

Sarah shivered. "How innocuous it looks," she mused aloud. It should look more foreboding, ominous and dark with crenulated towers, like a witch's house, or an evil castle from a fairy tale. Her palms itched, and she had to concentrate to breathe. Ross, his face grim, helped her down from the carriage.

A diminutive redheaded man stepped forward to shake Ross's hand. "Mr. Giles, of Bow Street, sir. My partner, Mr. Smythe, is inside with the boy."

Sarah's cousin and Ross's best friend, known to his intimates as Gypsy Davey, had arranged the paperwork they needed to travel to France, and it was he who had first suggested they try the services of the Bow Street Runners. A relatively new development in the world of law enforcement, the runners were known to take private commissions and their reputation was excellent. The investment had been well worthwhile. In four short months they had produced results where the past four years had proved barren.

"Mr. Giles, may I present my sister, Lady Munroe?"

"An honor, ma'am," Mr. Giles said with a bow. "It's not that many would bother bringing a lad home from a place like this."

Sarah stiffened. "Why ever not, sir?"

"No offense, milady, just speaking the God's truth."

"How is the lad?" Ross cut in before Sarah could respond.

"He seems surprisingly well, sir, under the circumstances. Not the best-mannered little jackanapes, but the lad has spunk. He doesn't appear to be much the worse for wear." Blushing, he cast a glance in Sarah's direction. "Begging your pardon, ma'am. Shall we go in, sir? Ma'am? He's waiting in the drawing room with Mr. Smythe. The old harridan, Madame Etienne, is in the library."

A sour-faced majordomo, stiff, formal, and elegantly attired, ushered them into a spacious entrance hall with a lofty ceiling and black and white marble-tiled floors. The walls were hung with paintings featuring some of the more notorious scenes from classical myth. They followed him through a sumptuous salon decorated in silk wallpaper, depicting men engaged in amatory acrobatics with a variety of partners, both male and female. The overall impression was one of opulent debauchery.

The library was a welcome relief from the calculated lasciviousness of the rest of the house. Paneled in oak, it contained book-lined walls, an imposing fireplace, and furniture comfortably appointed in rich brocades and plush velvets. There was a large desk, and behind it sat a tiny, steely-eyed, silver-haired woman who, if not for the gleam of avarice and contempt in her eyes, might have been mistaken for someone's dowager auntie. She didn't bother to rise, but motioned regally for Ross and Sarah to be seated.

"Tea? Brandy, perhaps?"

"We did not come here to socialize, Madame Etienne," Ross said.

"No? Well, then, to business. You wish to see the boy. First, let me tell you this matter has been a great nuisance and I shall expect compensation, whether the boy is related to you or not. You should also know he has cost a pretty penny to feed, to clothe, and . . . to train."

Ross stiffened slightly, and leaned forward. "Be very careful, Madame," he warned softly. "If this boy *is* my brother, it means you have kidnapped, and held imprisoned, the heir to an English peerage. You will hand him over to me immediately, without question, and my sister and I will take him home, or I give you my word, I will most certainly see you . . . compensated."

Momentarily nonplussed, Madame Etienne drew back, blinked, and then rallied, her malicious smirk replaced by a look of wounded innocence. "But, monsieur, this is ridiculous! I did not kidnap the boy. I rescued him! I did not imprison him. I gave him a home! You make such threats! To me, who has nursed and cared for the poppet, fed and clothed him when he had no family to turn to. Of course, if he is your brother, you must take him. I have only meant well by the boy."

"We wish to see him, Madame. Now!"

Madame Etienne motioned to the servant standing silently at attention by the door. "Bring the boy, Henri," she snapped.

An uncomfortable silence followed, relieved only by the monotonous ticking of the clock and the distant sounds of Paris. All eyes turned when the door opened with a slight click, and a young boy, delicate featured, towheaded, and slight of stature, stepped hesitantly into the room. He was accompanied by a beefy dark-haired man who looked like he'd be more comfortable in a boxing ring. "Good evening, Governor, milady.

Mr. Smythe, at your service. May I present young James here?" he said, encouraging the boy forward with a reassuring hand on his shoulder.

Sarah and Ross rose as one, stunned the moment had finally come. There was no question. He was taller and his face had lost its childish roundness, but the brilliant green eyes and hint of freckles were unchanged. A handsome child, he was the spitting image of their father.

Eyes narrowed with hostility, the boy glared at the bawd before turning to examine the strangers who had sent for him. His gaze was direct and self-assured, and he eyed them with a mixture of suspicion and curiosity.

Ross noted with relief, and some degree of surprise, that there was nothing servile about the lad, no hint of depravity. There was caution and distrust, but no fear. Mr. Giles was correct. Somehow, remarkably, the boy seemed undamaged. "Good afternoon, James. Do you know who we are, and why we are here?" he asked, breaking the silence.

"Gabriel says you're my parents and you've come to take me home," Jamie answered with a hint of challenge.

"We are not your parents, James, but we *are* your family. My name is Ross. I'm your half brother and the Earl of Huntington. This is your sister, Sarah, Lady Munroe, and we've been looking for you for a very long time."

"It took you long enough to find me," Jamie said, unimpressed.

"Yes, Jamie, we know," Sarah interrupted. "Do you remember me? We used to play soldiers together a long time ago." The boy looked at her with a gleam of interest but shook his head, no. Sarah stepped forward impulsively, enveloping him in her arms. "Well, I remember you, Jamie, and I'm so glad we've found you at last."

Jamie's face turned crimson, and after a moment's surrender, he pulled away.

Ross clapped him on the shoulder. "I know we seem like strangers now, lad, but that will change soon enough. Give it a bit of time. We are family, and you're safe now. That's all that matters at the moment. We shall all be well acquainted by the time we get you home. Mr. Smythe? Please inform Mr. Giles, and ask him to alert the coachmen."

"What about Gabriel?"

"Gabriel?"

"I'm not leaving unless he comes, too, and I've not had my dinner," the boy stated emphatically. His lips took on a mulish cast as he prepared himself for battle.

Sarah reached out a hand to ruffle his hair but he pushed it away. "Calm down now," she said in a soothing voice. "Who is Gabriel, Jamie?"

Madame, who had been watching everything with calculating eyes, answered for him. "He is one of my prize employees, highly sought after by the men and women who frequent this establishment."

The boy glanced her way warily.

"Leave us now, Madame," Sarah commanded. "We would speak in private. My brother is hungry. See that a meal is prepared for him."

Sputtering in indignation at being ordered from her own library, the old bawd complied, certain there was money to be made here, despite his high and mighty lordship's threats.

"Now then, Jamie," Sarah said, "tell us about Gabriel. Is he another boy who lives here, a friend of yours?"

"Gabriel's not a boy he's a man. *He's* my big brother. He takes care of me and teaches me things."

Ross crouched down so that he and Jamie were eye to eye, and clasped him by the shoulder. "How does he take care of you, James? What does he teach you? Has he ever hurt you?"

The boy snorted in disgust and jerked from Ross's grasp, angry now. "Gabriel wouldn't hurt me. He's my friend! He doesn't let anyone hurt me. When the German tried he . . . never mind."

Sarah stepped in, giving Ross a warning look. "You're very lucky, Jamie, to have such a good friend."

"I know." Jamie said, his bottom lip quivering.

"What's wrong?" she asked gently.

"Nothing," he blurted. "Just sometimes I get in trouble. They hurt him instead of me when I make a mistake or make someone angry. He says that's all right because he's bigger than me and he doesn't mind and I shouldn't worry 'cause it's not my fault . . . but I think . . . mostly it is

18

my fault." His voice was only a whisper now, the ticking clock a counterpoint. "He never cries, though. He says I shouldn't, either."

"Oh, Jamie!" Sarah gathered him into a hug, her heart breaking. "It's all right to cry. Sometimes it's good for you."

Ross, distinctly uncomfortable, cleared his throat and rose stiffly to his feet, grateful and content to let Sarah steer the way through these unfamiliar and dangerous shoals.

A maid poked her head into the room. "Is the boy to have his dinner, then?"

"No!" Ross barked. "We shall be leaving the premises immediately."

"I'm not going without Gabriel. You can't make me."

Ross gritted his teeth and refrained from telling him that, indeed, he could. He was sick of this place, desperate to remove the boy as quickly as possible and take him back to the good clean air of Cornwall. "You're a good lad, Jamie, and it's to your credit that you hold by your friends, but Gabriel has his life here, and yours is with us now," he said patiently.

"He says that, too. But I *won't* go. Not without him."

Mr. Smythe interrupted with a knock. "Your pardon, my lord, but a meal's been laid in the parlor for the young master. I should be pleased to accompany him, if you wish."

Jamie looked eagerly toward the door, his stomach

growling. "I'm hungry," he informed them.

"Yes I can hear. You won't run away, James?"

"No, 'course not! You're here to take me home. Gabriel said to go with you so I will . . . if he comes too."

"I see . . . Well then . . . Mr. Smythe will accompany you while your sister and I discuss your . . . friend. You will be perfectly safe with him."

Ross eyed Sarah ruefully as Jamie left the room. "Gabriel says, Gabriel thinks, Gabriel, Gabriel, Gabriel. It's a bit of a tangle. I don't want to upset the boy, but good Lord! We can hardly bring home a fully grown male prostitute, no matter how good a friend he's been."

"Why can't we?"

"I beg your pardon?"

"Why can't we? You've seen Jamie, Ross. He's still innocent, untouched. It's miraculous! When I think of what might have happened—" A sob tore from her throat, and Ross awkwardly patted her back and passed her a handkerchief. She blinked and smiled, dabbing her eyes. "Sorry, that's not at all like me, but I confess to feeling somewhat overwrought. Ross, this man, Gabriel, prostitute or not, was here for Jamie when we couldn't be. He's guarded him and protected him, at no small cost to himself. It's due to him alone Jamie has been allowed to remain a child; that he's been spared the horrors we most feared."

"Your point is well taken, Sarah." Ross patted her hand. "Of course I'm grateful, and he will be handsomely rewarded. Well enough that he can choose to live as he pleases."

"Jamie wants us to bring him home, Ross. What harm can it do? If he's looked after him these past five years, he's hardly going to harm him now."

"Think, Sarah! This isn't a boy we're talking about. He's a fully grown man. I can assure you he'll not be an innocent. For heaven's sake, my dear, the madam has all but said he's a catamite and a whore!"

"He is Jamie's friend and rescuer," she insisted stubbornly. "The least we can do is meet him."

"Very well," Ross grunted, "but I promise you it will do no good. The bawd will not wish to release him, and even if she will, he's not likely to want to come with us."

"Perhaps so, Ross, but then it will be this Gabriel who refuses, rather than you, and that will be easier for Jamie to accept."

Madame Etienne sailed regally into the library several minutes later. Reestablishing herself behind her desk, she favored Ross with a sour look. "Well, monsieur, I trust you have made yourself at home? The only thing you've not made claim to is one of my ladies. Perhaps one of my gentlemen would be more to your taste. Your young heir, he *is* your heir, is he not? His friend, Gabriel, might suit . . . for either of you," she smirked, "or both. *Non? C'est bien.*"

"Madame, if you know what is wise, you will close your foul mouth and never speak of my brother again, except to make arrangements for his immediate departure. You will also set a price on this man Gabriel, and bring him to us now."

"I will be happy to let you have Gabriel, for a price. You may have him for the evening. He is highly skilled and very versatile, I assure you. He is much sought after by our clients, male or female, no matter their tastes."

Ross replied coolly, each word clearly enunciated, "Madame Etienne, my patience wears thin. How much to release this man from whatever obligation he has to you?"

"I am not prepared to release him, monsieur. He brings a great deal of money to this establishment."

"If that is so, Madame, then any obligations must be long since settled," Ross replied silkily.

"*Au contraire*, monsieur." Her smile was vicious; her voice sweet. "How do you think he protected your precious heir? Every time someone wished to whip or pet the child, Gabriel paid the house for him to be left alone. He should be glad to see the brat gone. Now he'll become rich."

Ross rose to his feet. "I warned you not to speak of my brother again. This has become a matter for the *gendarmes*."

"No, no, monsieur, surely not! I apologize. I will guard my tongue and you will reflect on the embarrassment your heir would suffer should his circumstances be made public. I am certain we can come to a satisfactory arrangement. Ten thousand pounds, monsieur, and you may have him."

"You're joking, woman!"

"I assure you, Lord Huntington, I am not. An evening's pleasure does not come cheaply here. Why it's hardly more than Gabriel has spent over the past few years keeping your precious little brother pure and untouched."

"Very well," he said tightly, "but he is not to know. I can't imagine he'd appreciate being haggled over, bought, and sold, like a bloody piece of meat."

"Oh, he's used to it, I assure you, monsieur. Yet, I fear, we shall both be disappointed. He will certainly refuse. Henri! Go and find Monsieur Gabriel. Tell him *les Anglais sont ici*, and wish to meet him."

CHAPTER
2

Gabriel was confused and resentful; surprised Jamie's family would ask to see him. He would not have expected them to know anything about him, or to care, if they did. He supposed Jamie must have said something. He supposed they were curious, this English lord and his lady. He had hoped to be spared any leave-taking. He resented being paraded like some zoo animal for their titillation and edification, but he was curious, as well, to see what kind of people came across the ocean to claim a little boy, what sort of people lost one in the first place.

He was expecting clients this evening and was already well begun on the brandy, the alcohol thickening him, distancing him, making it all just a little more bearable. It never inhibited his performance. If anything, it enhanced it, gracing him with a charming insouciance of demeanor he was well-known and well-paid for. It was better to work tonight, anything to fill the void widening at an alarming rate inside him. He hated them, without seeing them, for taking the boy away. He hated them for what he feared most, that they would make him see Jamie one last time, and he would betray the boy and what little pride he had left by begging his indifferent Creator to make them leave the child behind.

He took a deep breath, preparing himself, then pushed open the door and stepped into the room. The bitch regarded him with gleeful eyes. She expected entertainment. My lord, tall and elegant in the severe way characteristic of certain military men, was rising, his eyes showing his alarm, a polite smile of welcome pasted on his face. Gabriel favored him with a feral grin.

Milady had also risen. He regarded her knowingly. Unfashionably tall, unfashionably dressed, a somewhat mannish creature with an air of health and vitality, she'd forgone corset and powder, and her chestnut hair tumbled loose in riotous curls. A cast to her smile, and a set to her eyes, suggested intelligence, and hinted at kindness and good humor. With amber-colored cat's eyes and a light dusting of freckles, she was an exceedingly handsome woman. It caused a small flare of genuine interest, but she stared at him like all women did, and many men. Mercifully, there was no sign of the boy.

Ignoring Ross's proffered hand, he moved to stand against the far wall. Striking a negligent pose, pale face impassive, his exotic kohl-lidded eyes flicked over each of them in turn, looking with bitter calculation and unconcealed contempt as he arranged the bountiful folds of lace at his wrists.

Riveted, Sarah studied him carefully. This was the man Jamie thought of as family, who'd sheltered him at considerable cost, and for reasons of his own, these past five years. It was difficult to imagine this hard-eyed glittering stranger showing kindness to anyone, let alone a child, and impossible to imagine that they might take him home.

Her eyes traveled his length. Broad-shouldered, he was tall and lean, and despite his languid posture and elegant clothing, there was something infinitely hard and cold, almost wolfish about him. He wore a black silk coat, edged in a peacock motif of blue and gold. His legs were encased in tight-fitting trousers and soft leather boots. Blushing, Sarah lifted her gaze and flitted to his waistcoat. Its gold brocade and silk buttons matched the etching on his coat. Lace spilled from his cuffs, framing long, beautiful hands, and skillful-looking fingers a musician might envy.

He wore no stock and his linen shirt was open, exposing the elegant line of his collarbone, and the strong column of his neck and throat. Coffee-colored hair fell past his shoulders. Tangled with strands of cinnamon and caramel, it framed high-sculpted cheekbones and a full sullen mouth. His eyes were dark chocolate, bruised, alive with intelligence, and framed by full, sweeping lashes. A proud straight nose and a firm jaw, rescued him from a too feminine beauty. The overall affect was one of sensuality and danger. He was breathtaking.

Heart pounding, short of breath, her reaction stunned her. Tearing her eyes away, she focused on slowing her breathing, trying to master herself. Pressing her feet firmly into the floor, welcoming its solid bulk beneath her, she turned toward Ross, forcing her way back into the room, back into the conversation. To her astonishment, no appreciable length of time had passed. She ventured a quick glance back. He watched her with eyes that saw everything, eyes that knew too much. The look he gave her was cold, contemptuous, and just a little triumphant. Ah, well. It had been extremely rude to stare, though in truth she'd been incapable of doing anything else. Clearly, caught with her hand in the pastries, she gave a slight shrug of her shoulders and flashed him a rueful grin, missing the pulse of surprise in his eyes as she returned to the business at hand.

Gabriel tore his attention away from the girl, slightly disconcerted. The witch was cackling about something, and introduction of sorts he supposed. They were all staring at him now, waiting for some kind of response. "Well," he drawled, "I'm here. What is it you want with me? My time is valuable, monsieur, madame. Get to the point, please." He spoke with the barest hint of an accent and his voice, deep, cool, and slightly exotic, was as seductive as the rest of him.

Ross, his inbred habit of courtesy seriously tested by the fellow's pointed lack of civility, refused to be rushed. "Yes, of course. I do beg your pardon. I am Lord Huntington, and this is Lady Munroe. James is my brother."

"Yes, yes, of course, and you have come to take him home, *non*? Very good. We have all heard the story. It has been the *on-dit* here for days. Now, if you will excuse me, I've pressing matters to attend to."

"Wait, monsieur, there is more." Ross plowed ahead despite reservations that had been growing louder ever since this unsettling creature had entered the room. "James has become very fond of you. Indeed, he speaks of little else. He has requested that you come with us. We are hoping you will agree."

Gabriel was stunned. It was the last thing he'd expected. He steeled himself instinctively, crushing a sudden stab of hope. Other than a blink, no trace of his struggle showed on his impassive features. Taking his hands from his pockets, he crossed them over his chest and cocked his head to one side. His reply was cool, amused. "You don't look like a sodomite, my lord. But then . . . one can never tell. Or perhaps you are thinking of your lady wife, yes? I am very skilled in such matters of course, and can pleasure you singly, or together. Perhaps—"

Ross stood, openmouthed with astonishment, and Sarah burst into startled laughter. "Well, Ross . . . I dare say we've been put smartly in our place! Your mouth is agape."

Ross snapped his mouth shut, no longer inclined to courtesy. "Sarah, it is past time for us to leave."

Madame Etienne watched with undisguised amusement. Eying the English milady with new appreciation, she poured herself a drink. It was all very entertaining, but she had a business to run. There didn't look to be any profit here. She'd leave it to Gabriel to sort out lord and lady English. "I've other matters to attend to," she muttered, as she rose to leave, glass in hand. "The brat will be on his way. Ring for Henri when you are ready to go."

Gabriel started toward the door, as well, but Sarah moved to block his path. "A moment more of your time, monsieur, *s'il vous plait*. Our business is not yet concluded. Lord Huntington and I are brother and sister, not husband and wife. I assure you we have no improper designs upon your person, either singly or together, as I'm sure you're well aware. It is a simple matter, really. Jamie has made it clear to us you have acted as his protector, and he considers you his dearest friend. Naturally, we are very grateful. He has also made it clear he'll not leave this place without you."

That surprised him. She noted it in the sudden clenching of his hands and a slight flush to his cheeks.

She really must stop staring at the man! It was unfor-givably rude. "We could force the issue, of course," she continued, "but I am certain you can understand why we are loath to do so." She moved closer to him, her voice becoming husky, soft and pleading. "Surely, monsieur, as someone who's taken Jamie's interests to heart, someone who has sheltered and protected him, you would consider coming with us, at least to help him through this transition."

Gabriel's breath stilled in his chest. Miraculously, he was being offered another chance, and despite his best efforts to strangle it, hope was born again. He knew he shouldn't trust it. Vile temptress, she betrayed him every time, leaving him weak and wounded in ways too cruel to endure without the familiar palliatives of brandy and blood. He also knew, deep in his soul, if he refused her now, the offer would not come again.

He met her gaze directly, his eyes intense, uncer-tain, and in that moment Sarah saw past kohl, artifice, and carefully constructed defenses, to a heartbreaking vulnerability. Careful not to show it, she struggled to give him what he needed, something he could trust.

"We would pay you, of course," she said brightly.

His eyes sparked with sudden interest. Leaning toward her, he murmured in a sinful whisper, "And what are my services worth to you, *ma belle*?"

"Eh!" Ross started.

"Ten thousand pounds, monsieur," she respond-ed, taking a step back. The man's sensuality was a potent force!

"Indeed," Ross grunted, deciding he'd best take command now, before the situation got worse. Ten thousand pounds, to a glittering catamite, an accomplished whore, because Sarah and James wished it. On top of that, Sarah meant to take him home, make him part of the motley gathering of rogues and eccentrics she called family. Well the man *had* placed himself between James and those who would have devoured him. Sarah was seldom wrong about people, he acknowledged, and the man was owed that much and more. It was a small price to pay for his guardianship, however unconventional, of young James over the past five years.

The creature was studying him, eyes hooded, lips curled in a cynical smile, anticipating his outrage and refusal. Insolent pup! He had a good deal to learn. "Ten thousand pounds for a year's employment, half now, the rest upon termination in one year's time. You will be employed as James's companion and treated as a gentleman in my home, as long as you comport yourself as one. I will expect from you, at minimum, the respect and deference a guest should show his host."

Gabriel hesitated. It was a considerable sum. Enough to buy a comfortable home, to travel to all the places he'd read about, to leave his life at Madame's and never return. "Am I not a little old and . . . experienced, my lord, to be companion to a ten-year-old boy?"

"You are, indeed," Ross said. "As my sister has

explained to you, monsieur, we are mostly concerned with sparing James any unnecessary worry or fear after all he's been through. He feels safe with you. Your presence will reassure him as he adjusts to being home. We require nothing more from you than that."

"And this agreement, Lord Huntington, it will be in writing, signed and witnessed?"

"Yes, of course." As Ross spoke, Monsieur Henri arrived with Jamie and Mr. Smythe.

"Gabriel!" Jamie hurtled into the room, oblivious to his new brother and sister, chattering excitedly about Bow Street runners, Mr. Smythe, and oh, yes, his new family, which had come to take him home. Sarah and Ross watched in amazement as the elegant, cynical, debauchee they had just invited into their home transformed before them.

A genuine, sweet smile lit his features as he crouched down to the boy's level and ruffled his hair, saying with a gentle laugh, "Calm yourself *mon vieux*. It is generally useful to the art of conversation to take a breath now and then, *non*?"

Obediently Jamie drew a deep breath before rattling on, "I told my brother, that's him there, and that's my sister, Sarah, and he's a my lord and she's a my lady, I told them you have to come, too, Gabriel, so you'll be coming with us." He looked expectantly at Ross and Sarah. "He *is* coming with us, isn't he? Gabriel, you will come?"

Sighing, Gabriel straightened and rose, squeezing

Jamie's shoulder with a graceful fine-fingered hand. He looked past the boy to meet Ross's gaze, his own somewhat amused, and slightly defiant. "Why, yes, Jamie. I suppose I will. It should prove to be an adventure."

CHAPTER
3

They came to pick Gabriel up the next morning. Sarah was relieved he hadn't changed his mind. She'd been almost certain that he would. Ross was relieved at his appearance. His unadorned suit was elegant, but simple. The kohl and the extravagant profusion of lace were gone, and his hair was tied neatly in a queue.

Jamie, energized and excited, had been to a restaurant, breakfasted in a café, stayed in a hotel, and tried lemonade and hot chocolate for the very first time. Thrilled at the idea of setting out to sea, he insisted on regaling Gabriel with all the details and observations he could manage, as Ross produced a contract and laid it on the desk.

"I apologize, monsieur. I neglected to inquire as to your surname. If you will provide it, I will enter it into our contract now."

"St. Croix will do as well as any, Huntington," Gabriel said with a shrug. He grinned, equal parts mischief and malice. "It is the name of the street on which I was abandoned as a child."

"St. Croix, it is, then." Ross added the name and affixed his signature, passing the pen to Gabriel, who signed it with a flourish. Mr. Smythe and Mr. Giles, who would be accompanying them on horseback and taking passage aboard his lordship's schooner, were pressed into service as witnesses. If they saw anything strange in their patron bringing home a denizen of a notorious Paris brothel as the young lord's paid companion, they were careful not to show it.

The journey to Calais took most of the day. It was dusty and hot, and after the initial jostling for seats, there was little to say. Gabriel's presence was not an easy one. Brooding and magnetic, his attempt to subdue his appearance only made him more attractive, as his cheekbones and full mouth appeared more pronounced with his hair tied back off his face. Sarah found herself unaccustomedly self-conscious. She tried to think of something to say, but there appeared to be little in common between them except for Jamie, and the circumstances of the last five years was hardly a topic for light conversation. Her attempts at discussing the weather or their destination met with a polite but unenthusiastic response. She wondered if he was having second thoughts, and tried to imagine how she would feel in a similar situation. Like an outsider she thought, awkward, defensive, and decidedly uncomfortable.

For much of the journey he appeared to be sleeping, or at least trying. Jamie had elected to sit beside him, elbowing him frequently as he clambered over him trying to see out the window, and constantly jostling him awake. Always patient and good humored with the boy, he would retreat as soon as he was able into a private space of his own. If not for Jamie's constant observations and questions to the three of them, there would have been no conversation at all.

It was a relief for everyone when they arrived in Calais and could extricate themselves from quarters grown suffocatingly close. Once on board, the irrepressible Jamie begged to be shown the workings of the ship. Gabriel accompanied him as they toured the vessel, paying close attention to the answers the boy received from the captain and crew as he peppered them with questions. For the next couple of days, he appeared to be as fascinated as Jamie was by the sprightly little schooner.

Gabriel took to the sea as if he were born to it. He had no trouble keeping his footing, or the contents of his stomach as the ship rolled and pitched beneath him. When rough weather approached, he found his way up on deck, turning his face into the wind as it whipped spray over the bulwark and onto the deck, soaking his clothes and hair and splashing his hands and face. The wind was sweet as music to him, making the little ship sing as it whistled and shrieked through the rigging, setting off a wild staccato of flags and pennants flapping madly overhead. He felt at home, in his element. The ocean called to him, and something resonated deep inside.

Turning around, he was taken aback to find Sarah on deck, clutching the rail. As soon as he saw her, he turned to leave.

"Please don't go on my account, monsieur. I would enjoy the company. It's magnificent, is it not?" she asked with a brilliant smile, almost shouting, straining to be heard over the din. "I feel so alive when it's like this, as if I'm a part of it. I feel like I could fly."

"I am surprised, mademoiselle, that your brother, or the captain, allow it," he said sourly.

She grinned and brushed away a stray lock of hair. "Oh, Ross knows better than to forbid me, and I'm well acquainted with the ocean. Is this your first time at sea?"

"Yes, mademoiselle," he allowed.

"Please, call me Sarah."

"No, mademoiselle."

"Well, stop calling me mademoiselle at any rate, Gabriel, because I am, in fact, a widow."

"I am sorry, madam," he said with a courtly bow, impressive given the pitching deck. "Might I remark that you seem a rather merry type of widow to me?"

"Well," she said, "in truth I didn't care for Lord Munroe very much, and although I didn't wish him dead, I would be a hypocrite to say it causes me any undue sorrow." Leaning into the rail, she closed her eyes and raised her face to the spray.

He couldn't help but notice that the damp was making her dress cling in an interesting fashion. It fueled a flicker of hunger that alarmed him. It would not do to allow any interest. Used to controlling his responses, he took a deep breath and suppressed it. If she really was a lady, she would not appreciate or reciprocate the attentions of a prostitute. If she wasn't, she would find that he'd not left Madame Etienne's to be a whore, for her, or for anyone else. "I believe I was brought here to entertain your brother, madam, not you. If you will excuse me, I am done with taking the air." Turning on his heel, he left.

"Well!" Sarah said to herself with a snort and a blink, momentarily annoyed by his rudeness. Nevertheless, it really was a magnificent day and as the storm whipped, howled, and tugged at her hair, she forgot the annoying Monsieur St. Croix. Letting her head fall back, she laughed into the wind.

Turning for a last look, Gabriel stood riveted. He'd thought her handsome, rather than beautiful, but at that moment she appeared elemental, like some ancient goddess of the sea, and he felt something dangerous stir within.

With the storm, the journey from Paris to Falmouth

took a little over five days. As Gabriel approached his new home, he felt a growing sense of wonder. The large, two-story manor house stood on a bluff, nestled along a wild stretch of coast above cliffs that fell sheer to the pale sands and rocky shore below. It looked out across the channel, with banks of windows throughout to capture the ocean vista and the rising and setting of the sun. It took full advantage of its aspect, with terraces and gardens surrounding the house, and broad balconies abutting the second floor. He noted numerous well-worn paths along the cliff edge leading down to the wild beach. Creamy-flowered magnolia trees and the tangy musk of pine and sea joined in a heady fragrance that reminded him, somehow, of Lady Munroe. He supposed he was as close to heaven as he was ever likely to get.

He was given a well-appointed room next to Jamie's, and introduced as "Monsieur St Croix, a friend of the family from France." Jamie came to the rescue again as they toured the house, acting as a much needed buffer, pulling Gabriel along by the hand, chattering excitedly about his room and asking questions of all three of them. It was a warm and comfortable house. The main floor had an airy open design consisting of a long gallery with interconnecting rooms. With the doors open, one could move freely from music room to library to salon. The furnishings were sturdy and inviting, made for relaxation and set in conversational groupings to provide a quiet refuge and placed to enjoy

Judith James

the view. The overall effect was open, eclectic, and unusual, not unlike its inhabitants.

Sarah found herself watching Gabriel curiously, trying to gauge his reactions, indeed she had made somewhat of a game of it. He had blinked several times during Ross's lecture on plumbing and indoor heating, signaling she thought, a keen interest. He seemed to have little interest in the music room, looking polite and bored as she showed them the various instruments, but when she bent to help Jamie return a violin to its case, she saw him from the corner of her eye, his fingers poised over the keyboard with what might have been a wistful look.

Caught up in her study of their enigmatic new friend, Sarah was finally rewarded in the library. Gabriel walked slowly along the shelves of books, his index finger tracing covers and spines as he searched the titles, interest sparking, then flaring in his eyes. She watched as his face relaxed into a slight smile, and ventured to address him. "It's an impressive collection is it not?"

He turned to her with an excited smile that made her heart flutter. "It is indeed mademoiselle. I am permitted to make use of it?"

"But of course! This is your home now. You are welcome to use the library whenever you wish. Perhaps you'd like to take some books to keep in your room."

His smile widened into a grin that pierced her to the quick. "Thank you, mademoiselle, I should be delighted."

40

She decided not to correct him. If he wished to smile at her, he could call her madam, or mademoiselle, or whatever he damned well pleased.

Sarah's hopes that their conversation in the library signaled a more comfortable relation between them were quickly dashed. Jamie grew in size and confidence as spring changed decisively to summer. He was a delightful child, quick of wit and curious, and the combination of good clean air, plentiful food, exercise, and safety, helped him adapt quickly to his new surroundings. He showed little visible effect from the years he'd been away, his recuperative powers astonishing, but Gabriel struggled to adjust.

He had no complaint about his treatment. Sarah seemed to harbor no animosity in regard to his rudeness aboard ship. Her smile was friendly, and she continued to make efforts to include him in conversation. He found himself watching her when she didn't know he was looking, noting with some degree of surprise that she often wore men's clothing, and sometimes went barefoot. No one seemed to remark upon it, not even her brother.

He remained a solitary character, avoiding company, though Jamie often sought his. He was generous with his time with the boy. They went exploring together, learning to fish, climbing cliffs, and exploring the many caves that dotted the shoreline, but he ate alone in his room unless Ross insisted he join them. His manners were impeccable, but he remained withdrawn and ventured nothing in conversation. When asked a direct question, his responses were cold and clipped, and though he had a clever wit, he used it to distance rather than endear himself.

The truth was that, at Madame's, he rarely spoke unless spoken to. He hadn't been paid to give his opinion, and except for the boy, he'd kept his thoughts to himself. His social interactions had revolved around the rites of seduction and the negotiation of payment. They had not prepared him for dinner hour with the Huntingtons and he was finding it difficult to relate to the relaxed banter and lighthearted discussion they indulged in at meals. The more he was surrounded by this unaccustomed wholesomeness, the more lost and angry he became, until he was barely civil to anyone but Jamie. There were moments he felt despair equal to his worst nights at Madame's as he realized that he didn't belong anywhere, anymore.

Over the next several weeks the rhythm of the house became familiar to him. He knew the minute the lights would come on, and when the fire would be lit. Huntington and his sister settled in the library most evenings to talk and compare their days and some nights, bored and lonely, unable to sleep, he would sit on the wide veranda, watching the sky and hugging himself against the cool night air as he listened to the buzz and hum of distant conversation. They'd invited him to join them, of course, several times; they were nothing if not polite, but he had no desire to perch, awkward and sullen, an ugly cuckoo soiling their nest, spoiling the intimacy of their evening. He much preferred sitting in the dark, listening to the soft murmur of voices and laughter. It warmed him somehow, like sitting by a fire on a cold night. Long after they left, long after the last embers had died in the fire, he remained, rocking silently back and forth in the darkness, cold as stone.

CHAPTER
4

Ross and Sarah sat in the library, enjoying an aged brandy and talking companionably over the chessboard. "Jamie is doing remarkably well, don't you think, my dear?"

"Oh, yes, Ross! I swear he's grown three inches since he's been home. He's a delightful boy, curious, eager, and full of energy and good humor. I wish Mother and Father could see him."

Ross flinched, uncomfortable with the topic. "Who knows, Sarah? Perhaps they can. I hope, at least, they may rest easy, knowing he's returned home."

Sarah smiled. "Having him back is a blessing and a miracle. Seeing him whole and happy is . . . Oh, Ross, we owe Gabriel so much!"

Ross grunted at that, but didn't deny it. "He is not behaving as I expected. Indeed, I suppose I had no idea what to expect."

"What do you mean?"

"Well, for one thing, it appears he's not tumbling

the maids . . . or the stable boys."

"Good God, Ross! That was cruel and uncalled for! You might be speaking of Jamie, if not for him!"

"I'm sorry, my dear," Ross said, somewhat chagrined. "He's so surly with me I act like an ass at times. Still one didn't expect him to become a monk, or a recluse. It's been over three months, Sarah. He doesn't seem happy here. One cannot say he's adjusting. What do you make of him?"

"Gabriel? I think he's magnificent, achingly beautiful, and so very lost. I don't know how to reach him. It breaks my heart."

Ross patted her hand, somewhat alarmed. Despite her brief marriage, Sarah's experience with men was rather limited, and she was sometimes too tenderhearted for her own good. Regardless of what the man had done for James, there'd been something calculating and cold in his gaze when they'd first met that reminded Ross of the eyes of a mercenary. "I know you're grateful, my girl, as am I. He *has* been Jamie's guardian angel. You must be careful, though, not to romanticize him. He is, I'm afraid, a very hard, and a very dangerous, young man."

Later that night, Sarah tossed and turned, restless

in the oppressive heat. The day had been sultry and the night offered little relief. Despite open doors and windows, there was no hint of a breeze and the water lay still as glass. Flinging off her covers, she rose and stepped out onto the balcony. The night was bejeweled, the stars glittering and sparkling overhead, reflected by the flat-mirrored surface of the ocean below. She gasped in delight and imagined herself in a magnificent, celestial ballroom. Lost in fancy, she began to sway to a haunting otherworldly melody that hung in the air, enticing, entrancing, and magical. Fairy music, Davey would call it. Her reverie was broken, with a start as she realized the music, faint and delicate, was real.

Hastily donning a nightgown and a wrapper, she started down the stairs. Ethereal whispers of sound took on substance and immediacy as she descended. It was coming from the music room, where she could see a spill of light from under the door. She wondered who could be playing. Ross was skilled with guitar and lute, but he'd never taken to the keyboard, and Davey was not expected back for another month. Realizing he must have returned early, a smile of welcome lit her face as she pushed open the door. She stopped in astonishment; her mouth rounded into an *O* of surprise. Gabriel was bent over the keyboard, eyes closed in concentration, his beautiful fingers stroking the keys with delicate artistry as he swayed to the music.

He was disheveled and barefoot, his shirt and coat open. Long strands of hair clung to his shoulders in the sticky heat. A bottle of brandy perched precariously on the piano's edge. He seemed unaware of her, and she watched the play of muscle along his collarbone and shoulders with fascination, as his clever fingers created magic, weaving it into the still night air. He tossed his head suddenly, and looked straight at her. His face was unguarded, his eyes yearning, and distant, as if he were half there and half in some faraway place, listening to a melody from beyond this world. She was mesmerized, moved in a way she could not have described. Her arrested eyes watched his for several moments before she tore them away.

"I'm sorry. I didn't mean to interrupt. I heard the music and thought . . . Gabriel, you play beautifully!"

Ignoring her, he turned his attention back to the keyboard, taking a sip of brandy with one hand as the other continued to caress the ivories, coaxing a haunting melody.

"Where . . . how did you learn to play so exquisitely?"

Continuing to play, he regarded her through hooded eyes. Angry with her for the intrusion, wanting to shock her, to drive her away, he decided to tell her the truth.

"When I was about fourteen, mignonne, I was sold to a very rich patron, a nobleman, Monsieur Le Comte de Sevigny. I was sent to amuse him, and tend to his needs." He gifted her with a slight, sardonic smile. "Do you understand my meaning, mademoiselle?" His voice was smooth and even, and his fingers continued weaving their magic as he spoke. "*Non*? Let me explain. He taught me how to please him. There are many ways a boy can pleasure a man, with hands and with . . . well . . . suffice to say, I learned them all. I wanted to. It was better there than at Madame Etienne's, and there was only him to please. He presented me as his page, and had me educated as he imagined a page should be. It amused him to see I was given a fine livery, taught proper manners, to read and write, to dance, even to ride. I was given a music master. I had a small modicum of talent, as it happens. I was taught the violin, the keyboard, and the guitar, so that I might divert my master . . . through all his senses. Surprisingly, I still find myself almost grateful for that." His fingers moved across the keyboard in an elegant flourish.

Sarah gulped, shocked, not sure what to say, but hypnotized as she watched him play. "You weren't there long though, were you? Not long enough to acquire such skill."

"No," he said with a soft laugh. "Two years. Long enough to learn the fundamentals, sexual, musical, literary, things that Madame had neglected, though it increased my value to her, no doubt." This was followed by a flourish of notes, and a feral grin. "As I grew older, it seems I lost some of my charm," he looked at her with a dead smile, "and I did something that annoyed him terribly."

"What?" she asked, breathless.

"I ran away," he said, his voice as cold and distant as his smile. "It was terribly rude and unappreciative of me. He punished me, of course. He caned my hands until they were so swollen I thought I would never play again. He knew how much it meant to me. I think he wanted to break my fingers," he added lightly, "but he was too afraid of what Madame would charge him for that. She had use for my hands, even if he no longer did." He picked up the tempo, a sprightly melody now. "He beat me, of course, whipped my ass until it was bleeding and raw, and then he passed me to his friends before sending me . . . home . . . where Madame taught me to please ladies as well as gentlemen."

His voice, throughout the recitation, remained deceptively soft and cool, dripping with practiced seduction, but his eyes were bleak. It chilled her. She gasped, horrified, trying not to imagine that lonely, desperate youth, and trying not to imagine the fate that had been stalking Jamie, if not for this man. The notes continued, plaintive, heartrending, and then trickled to a stop. She had no words for him. Sorry she'd asked. Sorry she'd opened old wounds.

He glanced up at her as he took a swallow of brandy. "Do I make you uncomfortable, mignonne?" he whispered into the silence.

"Yes! Very!"

"Ah, you are shocked, yes? You must learn to be careful what you ask for, *chère*." He returned to playing, a gentle, pensive tune.

"You never stopped playing, though," she observed.

He shrugged. "There were instruments to play at Madame's. It afforded some small amusement."

"What of . . .?"

"I am very tired, Lady Munroe."

"Sarah, please."

He hesitated. "Sarah, I am sorry if I disturbed your slumber. Forgive me if I go seek mine." He rose, hooking the brandy bottle between his fingers, preparing to leave.

"No," she blurted. "I disturbed *you*. I apologize. Please don't stop on my account." Moving to the door, she turned to look back. He might have been an angel, cold, remote, unearthly in his beauty.

When he was certain she was gone, he bent his head over the keyboard again. She could still hear the lovely, lonely notes as they hung in the air, haunting her as she ascended to her room.

CHAPTER
5

The next morning broke crisp and clear, the cooler winds of autumn nascent on the late summer breeze. Gabriel approached the breakfast room, uncomfortable and angry with himself. He had meant to shock her, punish her for the intrusion, and warn her away. Instead, he'd stripped himself bare in front of her. He knew she must be disgusted. Taking a deep breath, he pushed open the door.

"You look well this morning," she said. Her eyes were warm and welcoming.

Surprised, he couldn't suppress the slight smile that raised the corner of his mouth.

Sarah cleared her throat. His smiles, rare as they were, left her feeling lightheaded and short of breath. "I did wish to apologize for interrupting you last evening, Gabriel. I should have knocked, but it was so beautiful I . . . well, I . . ." Flustered, she shook out her paper and raised it in front of her face. After a moment, she inquired politely from behind it, "Would you care for a section?"

"No, thank you." The room was so quiet that the clock on the sideboard could be heard ticking away, imperious and demanding. "Do you play an instrument, Sarah?"

Putting down the paper, she rewarded him with a stunning smile. "Yes, I love to play. My mother was part Gypsy, you know. She was a virtuoso on the violin, and my father loved to play, as well. I make no claim to great skill, but I vow I'm not lacking in enthusiasm. Perhaps you'd allow me to join you sometime. Ross is too busy, more often than not, and I so enjoy playing with someone else."

He nodded, unwilling to play the churl, and made a bit more effort than usual at conversation, awkwardly commenting on the weather and recounting one of his and Jamie's adventures, much to her delight.

He escaped to the beach as soon as he was able, trying to make sense of the past twenty-four hours. He had revealed himself to her, at least in part, and she had responded unexpectedly. Shocked, yes, but apparently unchastened, she'd greeted him this morning as if nothing had happened. He'd noticed her interest before. Far more subtle than what he was used to, it was real, nonetheless, and very familiar. She was a widow, after all. She'd likely been without a man a good while. Doubtless, she wanted him the way other women had. That explained why she'd chosen to ignore the sordid history he'd shared with her last evening. Relieved at being able to characterize her motives, he determined to keep her at a distance. If he was to make any sort of life for himself, he needed the money Huntington had promised him, and the last thing he needed was any sort of entanglement with the man's sister.

After breakfast, Sarah went to the stables and saddled her stallion. He fussed and stamped his feet, and blew out his belly. "Oh stop it," she snapped, digging a sharp elbow into his side as he tried to press her up against the wall. Grunting, he surrendered, allowing her to tighten the girth and put on the bridle. She mounted, and let him dance and snort for a few moments. He was a male, after all, and that sort of thing seemed important to him. Once that was out of his system, she loosed the reins and leaned forward, urging him into a full gallop.

She thought about Gabriel. She'd been astonished by his artistry. He played like an angel, with a passion and melancholy genius that no amount of training could instill. He had shocked her last night. She'd had some sense of his background, of course, but she'd never thought about it too deeply, for the same reasons one refused to pursue most unpleasant thoughts she supposed, because it made her feel uncomfortable.

Last night, he had made her starkly aware of the evil some men inflict upon the innocent, the evil forced upon him, and the fate that had awaited Jamie. He'd compelled her to acknowledge it, to feel it, and it had made her heart freeze. She imagined how lonely he must feel with all those terrible memories that no one wanted to hear, trapped inside him. Gabriel had talked to her last night, though, and he'd been almost civil to her this morning. She'd been trying to reach him for over three months, ever since they'd brought him and Jamie home in early May, and last night, finally, he'd opened a door. She was determined not to let him close it.

Whether by fortune, misfortune, or fate, Gabriel's life was destined to intersect with Sarah's again before the night was out. Ross had insisted he attend dinner. Having listened with marked tolerance, as Jamie waxed eloquent about the finer points of gunnery and naval tactics, he'd pled a headache at the first opportunity, and excused himself. Deciding to stop for a moment in the music room, he turned to find himself squarely in the path of the increasingly vexing . . . and fetching, Lady Munroe.

"Why do you follow me, madam? Surely you should be at supper with your family."

Sarah blinked in consternation. He was as curt and cold as ever. It was as if their conversation last evening and this morning had never occurred. "I wanted to apologize again, monsieur. I hope you will continue to make use of the music room. I'll not interrupt you again, I promise."

"But you are doing so now, Lady Munroe," he said coolly.

"I . . ." She blinked, flustered. "I'm sorry, I didn't realize."

"Your apologies aren't necessary," he insisted brusquely. "I pray you disregard the whole affair. If you will pardon me?" He moved to pass her.

"A moment, monsieur," she pleaded, clasping his forearm. "I've upset you. I don't mean to. I worry that you're not happy here."

He sprang erect at her touch, his manhood hungry and bold. Christ! Her brother should insist she dress as a woman. Those long shapely legs, encased in tight breeches, could drive a man to distraction. "I'm not happy anywhere, mignonne," he replied bitterly, trying to edge away from her. "What concern is it of yours?"

"Is there naught we can do, Gabriel, to make you feel more welcome?"

She was going to ruin everything. He wanted her, even though he was so sated and weary of sex that he usually had to distance himself from his body in order to allow any arousal at all. He wanted her badly, in ways he'd never expected, and he hated her for it. "You can stop following me. You act like a bitch in heat," he grated, suddenly incensed. Seizing her wrist in one hand and her throat with the other, he pinned her body hard against the wall with his own, grinding his hips, his throbbing cock hard against her stomach. "Is this what you want, mignonne?" She stood rigid, shocked, gasping for breath. Realizing he held her by the throat, he moved his hand to grasp her jaw, forcing her mouth to his in a brutal, passionless, punishing kiss. "It *is* what you want. You're no different from the others. I can smell it."

Leaning into her, he loosened his grip and whispered in her ear, "I'm a whore, dearling, and you're certainly paying me well enough. I'm as skilled at pleasing a woman as I am at pleasing a man. Some say better." He teased her lobe with hot breath and fluttering tongue. "Are you wet for me, mignonne? Shall I show you what pleasure truly means?" Forcing her hand down, he rubbed it against the bulge in his breeches, stifling a groan. "I'm ready for you, *chére*. Feel me," he crooned. "Shall we go to my room, or yours? Or perhaps right here, with your brothers just a shout away. Does that excite you?"

He was right, damn him! She did want him. But not like this! God knew she'd thrilled to the feel of his body pressed hard against hers; his sex, potent and probing; his soft whispers and skillful tongue. To her shame and horror, she *was* wet for him. She hated him at that moment. She jerked her arm as if suddenly released from a relentless force, and pulled her hand away.

He loosened his grip, steadying her so she wouldn't fall, and let her go. He stepped back, breathing as heavily as she was. She looked at him, her hair disheveled and her mouth bruised from his kiss. Her eyes, full of unshed tears, were angry and unmistakably hurt, and he felt a brief stab of regret.

"I was only trying to help," she said coldly. Gathering her dignity, and what was left of her wits, she turned to climb the stairs.

"Then stay the fuck away from me," he rasped to her departing back. "Fuck! Fuck! Fuck!" He entered the music room and leaned against the door. Closing it behind him, he slid to the floor. Why couldn't she leave well enough alone? Why did she have to plague him? She would tell her brother now. Huntington would make him leave, and make him pay. It would be best to go now, immediately. But where? There was no past he could bring himself to return to, no future he could possibly imagine.

Climbing wearily to his feet, he helped himself to the brandy he'd left the night before, and made his way listlessly back to his room. A fire crackled in the hearth, bringing light and warmth to ease the late night chill. Tipping back his head, he took a healthy swig, hoping to warm himself inside. It couldn't numb his pain, though. It didn't even touch it. It remained raw and sore and throbbing, like his cock. He stroked himself, striving for comfort and release, trying to imagine her lying beneath him, warm and soft with welcome, but all he could see were her eyes, hurt and angry, and he felt sick with shame.

Denied any release from alcohol or sex, he hurled the bottle against the wall, watching it shatter into myriad pieces of crystal, each one catching the glow of the fire, sparking scarlet and crimson with its own internal flame. Fascinated, he rose from the bed. Replacing the sacrificial brandy with a bottle of whiskey from the liquor cabinet, heedless of the crystal crunching under his bare feet, he crossed the room and picked up a shard, examining it, holding it to the light, admiring its shape and the feel of it between his fingertips.

He sat cross-legged in front of the fire, grimacing only slightly, a half smile on his face as he pressed the razor-thin glass against his wrist until the blood welled ruby red. Carefully he drew a line, and then stopped for a swallow of whiskey, another line, another swallow, continuing until something eased inside him, allowing the whiskey and brandy to do their job, allowing him, finally, to escape into nightmares and a troubled sleep.

Cold rough hands stroked him awake. "Réveille toi mon ange." An icy, amused whisper. He was running, running as fast as he could, down twisting corridors. Ancient doors yawned open as he hurtled past, hissing voices calling him, arms reaching out to grab him, voices grunting with twisted passion and sick promise as he searched frantically for the door that would let him out, but he couldn't find it. There was no escape from the terrible, hungry thing closing in on him. He saw her up ahead, drawing away, preparing to leave. He shouted and she turned to look, her eyes cold, condemning, and he knew he was damned. A frigid vice closed around his ankle, dragging him screaming and kicking, down, down, down . . .

CHAPTER
6

Gabriel rose late the next morning, bleary and sick, grateful someone had come and cleared away all traces of last night's excess. He was almost relieved when, late in the afternoon, a servant came to tell him his presence was required in Lord Huntington's study. He'd known she would tell her brother. He'd assaulted her, held her by the throat in her own home just steps away from her family. He'd been waiting for it all day. He was about to be exiled from a home where he'd never belonged in the first place.

Unaccustomedly nervous, fighting to armor himself for what was to come, he took several deep breaths before knocking and entering the study. The room was hung with seascapes, maps, and charts. There were several models of ships of various types on display, as well as a magnificent globe. Ross stood behind his desk, framed by the window and the late afternoon sun. He held a whip in one hand. Gabriel swallowed and concentrated on breathing. He didn't know if he could accept it. Not from this man, not from any man ever again, but he knew he deserved it. He was seized for a moment by a wild hope. Perhaps the punishment would suffice. Perhaps he would not be sent away. Wordlessly he removed his coat.

Ross was stunned, speechless. Surely to God the fellow didn't think he had called him here for . . . to . . . Good God! What kind of depraved creature had he let into his home? He clutched the whip convulsively in his hand, and it was only then he understood. The lad had seen the whip and thought he'd been called for punishment. Relieved and horribly embarrassed, he quickly tossed it onto the desk and spoke in his sternest voice, "Your pardon, young man. I have business to discuss with you, and though I am aware that everyone in this household takes a slapdash attitude toward dress and deportment, I feel it is reasonable of me to expect a degree of formality in what *is* in effect, my place of business. Kindly put your coat back on and take a seat. When we are done, you may gambol about the halls, dressed as you please."

Seating himself, he added sourly, "Frankly, Gabriel, I had not expected *you* to be learning bad habits from my sister." He was aware he sounded like a pompous ass, but really, it was the best he could manage under the circumstances. He wondered fleetingly what misdeed the fellow had committed that he imagined warranted a whipping, but chose not to pursue it.

Gabriel, whose face had been white and drawn,

now flushed a bright pink as he sank slowly into a chair. *She hadn't told him. She hadn't said a thing!*

Having rescued them both from a great embarrassment, Ross felt more than entitled to a stiff drink. Pouring two glasses of his best port, he handed one to Gabriel and settled back into his chair, watching and wincing as the lad threw it back as though it were water, with no respect for pedigree or vintage. "Good God, man! That's sublime and complex ambrosia! Show it some respect. It is meant to be sipped and savored, not carelessly tossed."

"What do you want with me, Huntington?"

"I've decided, after much thought, that James has adjusted well enough to his new circumstances for me to consider sending him to school. He's an extremely bright boy, eager to learn, and as you will appreciate, he has not had the opportunity to make appropriate friends. It is apparent he will quickly outstrip his tutor. How is it, by the way, that he has learned to read and write so well in English and in French?"

Hands tightening around his now empty glass, Gabriel's stomach clenched and roiled. So he was to be sent away after all. He shrugged. "It amused me to teach him. As you said, he learns quickly." In fact, he'd loved teaching Jamie. It had made him feel useful and important, and he'd shared vicariously in the boy's wonder and excitement. Books were familiar accoutrements to Madame's' clients, and her library had been well stocked. To her they were props, used to create a mood of welcome and comfort for those who wanted a piece of the familiar served with their vice. To Gabriel they were life and death, a door through which he could escape to ideas and adventures, other lands and places, converse with great minds and play with grand ideas. It was the only place that offered him any escape. Jamie's constant barrage of questions had driven him there repeatedly in search of answers, and as he taught him in French, Gabriel's skill in English had developed apace.

Ross nodded thoughtfully. The man had hidden depths, no doubt about it. They owed him a great deal. "I am debating letting him try the fall term. He is eager to do so. He wants to meet other boys his age, and I believe it might be for the best. He is my heir, and he has lands of his own passed to him by my parents. He must learn to take his place. I'll not force it, though." He leaned back, fingers drumming on the desktop. "I am cognizant that you know him better than I do. What is your opinion on the matter?"

Gabriel blinked, truly startled. With the exception of Jamie's constant questions, no one had ever asked his opinion about anything before he came to this strange and unpredictable house. He took his time, striving to answer as honestly as he could. "I think he's lost his chance to be a child, and there's nothing you or your sister, can do to change that, but he can still be a normal boy. Let him do what other boys his age do if that's his wish. He's a pretty child, though, Huntington, and he's been protected." He gave Ross a challenging look, but the older man only nodded and gestured for him to continue.

"One hears things about some of these places. It would be a pity to have him escape the whorehouse intact, only to be buggered at school."

Ross shifted uncomfortably. He'd spent time at school himself. Big for his age, and well schooled in self-defense, he'd managed well enough, but he knew what Gabriel meant. "What do you suggest, then?"

"It seems simple enough, Huntington. Find him somewhere safe and close to home. Make your presence felt and let him know that he can leave at any time he wishes." Gabriel tossed back the remainder of his drink and rose to leave. "If that is all?"

"No, it's not. Sit, please."

"I prefer to stand." It was said without rancor.

"I also wished to discuss your situation, Gabriel."

"That will not be necessary," he replied, voice clipped. "With Jamie in school, you will have no need of me here. I agree it's for the best. Pay me a third of what we agreed. It will suffice."

"Are you so eager to leave us?" Ross asked, much to his own surprise. "Has anyone mistreated you here? Offended you in anyway?"

"No."

"Then sit down . . . *please*, and let me be clear. My brother, provided I can find him a situation of the nature you suggest, will be home every fortnight as well as over the holidays. He will be expecting to see you here, and, well . . . one hates to be indelicate, but I must remind you that our written agreement is for one full year. If you choose to end it prematurely, I am not required to pay you anything at all. Come now, lad," Ross relented, "surely you can put up with us a while longer, for young James's sake."

Gabriel nodded stiffly, knowing he'd been deftly manipulated into doing exactly what he wanted most. "You and your sister have a great deal in common," he observed coolly.

Ross grinned and raised his glass in salute. "Why, thank you. Now back to business. It is my intention that you continue your education as a gentleman." He raised his hand for silence before Gabriel could protest. "I mean no offense. You are being presented as a friend of the family. It is assumed you are a distant relative, ergo you must have the necessary skills and training. It is clear you have exquisite manners when you choose to use them, and James's tutor tells me you have a classical education at least the equal of most of the young fops passing for gentlemen these days. It is my understanding that you are largely self-taught. This is much to your credit, given your circumstances. My sister tells me you're an accomplished musician, another noteworthy achievement. She's quite skilled herself, and assures me there's nothing a local music master could teach you. One cannot help but wonder what you would have accomplished if your upbringing had been more orthodox. Now then," he said, drumming his fingers, "do you dance?"

"Yes, it was part of my training."

"Mmm, quite. Ride?"

"I have . . . I did . . . It's been a few years."

"Any good at it?"

"I was."

"Excellent! It's not the sort of thing one forgets. We'll head to the stables after our meeting and find you a suitable mount. Can you defend yourself? Have you any training in boxing or fencing, any experience with sword or pistol?"

"I can use my fists, and a dagger," he answered grimly.

A slight inflection in his voice made Ross give him a sharp look. "Indeed?"

Gabriel returned his look with the same cold stare Ross remembered from their first meeting. A decorated military man, sea captain, and adventurer, he'd seen that look many times before. The fellow knew how to kill, no mistake about it. A dangerous man, this young lad. Best not forget it. He wondered, not for the first time, why he allowed him near his sister, his little brother. Still, he was no hypocrite. Only a dangerous man could have kept James safe in that hellhole he'd been plucked from.

When it was clear there was no explanation forthcoming, Ross continued, "Well, yes, of course. Ahem . . . I should like, however, to see you trained in the arts of gentlemanly combat, as well. I have a dear friend, a partner and business associate, Gypsy Davey. He's currently at sea but we expect him home any day now. He'll be staying with us over the fall and winter. This is a most fortuitous circumstance for you, young man, as there are few, if any, men alive who could best him with sword or pistol. He is also skilled in hand-to-hand combat and, er . . . dagger.

"I will ask him to assess your skill and train you if he's so inclined. You will, I hope, be appreciative of his time and show him the utmost respect. If all goes well, and you're interested, he may even teach you seamanship. The sea can be good to a man if he has daring and ability. Captain Jenkins was favorably impressed with you on the crossing. He remarked upon your interest and felt you might have an aptitude. Do you know, he asked me about having you as a midshipman? In any case, you will want some form of useful career suitable to a gentleman, and I can't picture you in the clergy," he said with a chuckle.

Gabriel hadn't known. As far as he was aware, he'd never been noticed for anything, other than his body and his face. He'd never been praised for anything, other than that, or his skill with his hands, his mouth, or his prick. Hearing Huntington listing his accomplishments and planning his future when he'd come expecting anger and retribution, left him feeling buffeted and bewildered. He could make no sense of this new world, no matter how hard he tried. He had no map, no compass, no idea of what to expect next. He'd awoken this morning feeling shame and self-loathing, expecting punishment and exile. It seemed that Sarah had chosen mercy, and now her brother was offering gifts. He knew the dangers of easy acceptance and self-delusion, but he was unable to refuse. None of it showed on his face. "Yes, sir. Of course. Thank you."

Ross nodded, startled and pleased. He recognized that the honorific and appreciation were not trivial things, coming from this man. He was beginning to appreciate what Sarah saw in their prickly young friend. There was enormous potential within him, the makings of something fine. He knew, though, far better than Sarah could, what cruelty, violence, and lust could do to a man, how unlikely it was the lad would ever be able to free himself. Still, he was owed the opportunity for what he'd done for James, and Ross was a man who always paid his debts.

Several hours later, Gabriel turned his mount around and headed back to the house. Leaning forward, he gave the horse his head and thundered down the beach. He felt an intense exhilaration, a rough, unfamiliar joy, and he reveled in the feel of freedom and power as the ground passed beneath him. He slowed the big animal to a walk as he neared the house. The tide was coming in now, as was the night. Reluctantly, he returned the horse to the stable, removed the saddle, and bedded him down.

He felt somewhat guilty for missing supper again. After Huntington's generosity he should have reciprocated with a show of good manners at least, but he'd wanted to take the horse, and he'd wanted to avoid Sarah. As his thoughts turned to last night's debacle, his ebullient mood was punctured and his pleasure fell flat. He couldn't avoid her forever, but he didn't know how to face her, either. He wasn't a vicious man, but last night with her, he had been, and she hadn't deserved it. He didn't understand why she'd kept it to herself, but he was grateful. He knew, instinctively, that if she were going to tell Ross, she would have done so already. Last night was between the two of them, and so it would remain.

CHAPTER
7

Though the days were still sultry, the end of August was approaching and the nights foreshadowed the coming season. The air had turned cool, and the night had crept in by the time Gabriel made it back to the house. He could hear the sound of the rising surf breaking against the cliff, crashing and booming against the rocks below. He sat for a while on the cliff's edge, legs dangling down, feeling the power beneath him. Lying back, he closed his eyes and let his mind wander, listening to the ebb and flow of the waves, content, for once, in his life; at peace.

He didn't know how long he remained there before hunger and cold drove him to his feet. Looking up, he could see that the lights had been dimmed or extinguished throughout the house. It was quiet, most of the staff and family having gone to bed. His disinclination for company and constant struggle to sleep had left him no stranger to nocturnal ramblings.

The kitchen, the library, the music room, he had no trouble finding his way in the dark.

Having missed supper, he headed for the kitchen, stomach growling, only to stop dead at the entrance. His nemesis sat at the table, coffee mug in hand, dressed in a shapeless frilled monstrosity, with a shawl draped about her shoulders. He wanted to run away. He wanted to tell her he was sorry, to beg her forgiveness and thank her for her forbearance. Instead, he offered her a mocking bow. "Mademoiselle, as always, is the height of fashion I see." She grinned and chuckled appreciatively, the only woman he'd met without a trace of vanity.

"Yes, I know. I must look a fright. But I'm nice and comfortable and warm. You missed supper."

Nice and comfortable and warm. Yes, she was that, he mused, and yet so powerfully unsettling. "I was riding. I lost track of time."

"Ah, well, you're in luck, I think. There's ham, pie, and apples, on the counter. I won't keep you from your meal."

She gathered her cup, preparing to leave, and he found himself desperate to stop her.

"And you?"

"Me?"

"Can you not sleep? I hadn't expected to find any-one here at this hour."

"Oh, no, it's not that. I was sleeping until a half hour ago. I woke myself up and came down to gather my star-gazing supplies."

"Star gazing?"

"Yes!" she said. Her face lit up and she almost danced with excitement. "There's going to be a meteor shower over the next few nights. It comes this time every year and tonight will be especially grand because there's hardly any moonlight. There'll be shooting stars hurtling across the sky. Hundreds of them! I'm gathering supplies so I can watch the show in comfort," she said smugly. "It's best just before dawn." She'd been trying her best to remain as cool and distant as he was, determined not to intrude on his privacy and not above punishing him for his behavior last night. She simply wasn't very good at it.

Looking into her shining eyes, Gabriel felt his heart flip and flutter in his chest. She really was the most singular female he'd ever encountered.

"Would you like to see?" she asked impulsively. "We could watch them together." She regretted the words as soon as she'd said them.

"Where?" he rasped.

"From my room. I have a telescope and a small observatory on my balcony," she said proudly. "The view is magnificent."

He wondered at her invitation, especially after last night. He'd found her here, waiting for him. She hadn't told her brother about what had happened, and now she was inviting him to her room in the middle of the night. Understanding dawned, and he felt a sharp pang of disappointment. She meant to take him up on his offer. It seemed she hadn't minded his rough treatment. He knew some women liked it, but he hadn't expected it from her. Well, what had he expected? He was a whore, after all, and he'd asked for this. He'd deliberately shown her what he was, and he could hardly blame her for accepting what he'd so baldly offered. And he wanted her. He would give her whatever she wanted, and take whatever she'd allow.

"Well?" She was still waiting for his answer.

He gave her a mocking bow. "I follow where my lady leads."

She grinned again. "Excellent! I like to be prepared so I can settle in and really enjoy it. Ross says if you're going to do a thing, do it well. I know he means duties and responsibilities and such, but I believe it applies equally well to pleasures and enjoyments, don't you?"

"Indubitably, mignonne."

"Hold out your arms."

Recognizing the voice of command, he obligingly held out his arms, wondering what pleasures and enjoyments she had in mind, what orders she would give him this night, and why it should make him feel so . . . sad. His thoughts were rudely interrupted by a large serving plate.

"Steady, don't drop it. Do pay attention, Gabriel!"

Bemused now, he watched as she piled it high, a knife and spoons, a half leg of ham, the pie and apples she'd spied earlier, a chunk of cheese, and after a bit of rummaging, a bowl of trifle.

"How are you managing? Can you carry it all?"

Refusing to fail in his first commission, he grunted and nodded.

"All right, this should do us handsomely. Let's be off." She hefted a jug of wine that had been sitting under the table. Speaking in a hushed voice, almost a whisper, she lifted a lamp in her free hand. "Follow me."

He did, mouth watering as he watched the vague outline of her bottom swaying under her shapeless gown as she climbed the stairs in front of him. If he hadn't been carrying the tray he would have grabbed her hips and pulled her tight against him, rubbing his swollen sex against her round backside. His hands itched and his cock twitched in anticipation.

"One more flight," she whispered, as they reached the first floor.

One more flight. It had been far too long since he'd had a woman. He felt a brief flicker of regret to be breaking Huntington's trust so soon after it was given, but the man deserved it. He was a fool to let a jaded whore anywhere near his sister, and a bigger fool if he couldn't see that she was far from being the innocent she appeared.

"Here we are." A door opened, spilling soft light into the dark hall.

Gabriel followed her in, looking curiously about him. A fire blazed cheerfully in the hearth, dispelling the chill and adding light to the room. There were several lamps and candles, some of them lit. There were bookcases and a fiddle, a small black statue of what looked to be some ancient goddess, shells, and stones, and feathers, and oddly shaped pieces of dry wood. He noted a writing table, and several curio cabinets he would have liked to explore if he hadn't had other things on his mind.

The furniture was solid, sturdy, and exuded comfort. Soft carpet and colorful tapestries blended it all together, creating an impression of warmth and welcome. It was the kind of room where a man might relax and stay a while. A large bed on the far wall, parallel to a recessed window seat, captured his attention. Strewn with pillows, books, and discarded clothes, its velvet coverlet was thrown back, exposing what appeared to be silk sheets. It looked comfortable and inviting. He imagined he could still see the imprint of her body in the sheets, and his body tightened in expectation.

Sarah motioned him to place the tray on a low table. "There will be fine, for now." Stretching to reach, she opened the doors to a large armoire, pulling out a soft wool blanket.

His nerve endings hummed with expectation as his body came exquisitely alive. His nostrils flared, capturing her scent, clean, musky, with hints of smoke, salt, and spice. He was intensely aware of his clothing, caressing and constraining, his erection heavy and turgid, twitching and swollen against his breeches. Without conscious awareness he changed, metamorphosed, his manner becoming languid, seductive, his eyes hooded and heavy with sensuality, his lips parted, full and inviting.

Sarah was trying to open the doors to the balcony, struggling with the blanket and almost tripping over her shapeless nightgown, somewhat annoyed that he was standing there, doltish, rather than aiding her. "Bring the tray if you please, Gabriel." Goodness, what was wrong with him? Couldn't he see she needed help?

Distracted, he did as he was told. He'd been hoping for the bed, but he would service her anywhere, and any way, she pleased, standing, sitting, or lying on cold stone. Stepping out onto the balcony, he stopped suddenly, turning his head in amazement. He'd read somewhere of how homeowners in Arabic lands would turn their rooftops into delightful gardens, fantastical, private oases, open to the sky. He imagined they might look something like this.

The balcony was wide and solid and ran the length of her room. It seemed to float out over the ocean, like the prow of a ship, and he imagined he could feel the swell and pitch of the waves beneath them. An ancient oak loomed in the darkness on the northern edge to his left, its branches shading the second floor and towering above the roof. The balustrade was fitted at regular intervals with oil lamps in the shape of widemouthed brass bowls. Some of them were lit now, providing a soft, unobtrusive, glow. There were shrubs, herbs, and exotic potted plants along the wall and in the corners, mingling with the breeze in a heady aroma that re-minded him of her. Stone benches fitted with padded cushions lined the seaward edge here and there, and what appeared to be a swing sat almost dead center.

Wordlessly, Sarah stepped forward and took the tray from his unresisting grasp, setting it on a low stone table next to the swing as he continued to marvel at the magical little world he'd stepped into. Turn-ing his face up to the heavens, his skin pricked with superstitious awe. The vaulted ceiling above him spar-kled and glittered, pulsing with an ancient beauty, stirring something deep, and atavistic, within. The enchanted little space from where he watched wasn't dwarfed or diminished by the night's majesty, but somehow enhanced, fragile, warm, human, and all the more precious because of it. The overall effect was one of floating, as if they were part of the night, sailing amongst the stars.

He turned to look at her, his eyes filled with won-der, and then moved to examine an instrument set out on a jutting platform. It looked like the muzzle of a small cannon set on a tripod. Reaching a hand out tentatively, he looked back at her. She smiled and nodded, and reverently he felt the barrel, trailing his hands along its length, examining the focusing mech-anism, tubes, mirrors, and mounting. "Is it real? Does it work?"

His eyes gleamed with boyish excitement, and her heart skipped a beat. "Yes, it works. Have you used one before?"

"No, I've read about them, though."

"Here, then, let me show you. Let's start with the moon." Careful not to touch him, Sarah showed him how to focus and align the instrument with the thin sliver of the moon. Standing by his shoulder, she explained that this was a twenty-four-inch reflecting telescope, made by Mr. James Short, of Scotland. She was about to regale him with the advantages and disadvantages of reflecting versus refracting telescopes when she realized he was far too engrossed in what he was doing to pay her any attention.

She contented herself with watching him. It was the first time she'd seen him completely stripped of mask or artifice. He was boyish and eager in his enthusiasm, enraptured with the wonders revealed through the lens, and she saw past all the walls that hurt and cruelty, abandonment and betrayal had built around him, to the lively, sensitive, spirit within, and realized she was in danger of falling quite hopelessly in love.

Gabriel was caught up in an excitement of discovery unlike anything he'd ever known. To learn from books was one thing, but to actually see, with one's own eyes! The moon had taken on a character now. It was a place. It had mountains and valleys! He had seen them clearly, stark against the shadow that obscured all but the crescent edge. He wondered what it would look like full. He must ask her to show him. Surely she'd let him look again. Might he be able to find Mars, the red planet? He began to realign the telescope, beginning his search, when she spoke over his shoulder.

"Come, Gabriel. It's time."

"But I want—"

"You'll miss the shooting stars. They've started. You have to watch the whole sky now, or you'll miss them." Forgetting her promise not to touch him, she took hold of his hand, pulling him away. "You can come back to use it, Gabriel, on any clear night, but these only come once a year. No one else ever watches except Davey."

Who *was* Davey? Gabriel wondered, not for the first time.

"Please, Gabe! I want someone else to see it with me, to know."

He recognized her plea on a level so intimate he almost gasped. How many times had he looked to the sky in awe and appreciation, only to find the beauty diminished and hollow as it echoed, lost inside him, with no one to share it with? He understood her invitation now. She had brought him here to share her treasure, to fashion it into a gift for someone else . . . for him.

He sat beside her on the swing, close, but not touching, and she spread the woolen blanket over their legs. Munching an apple and doing justice to the excellent local cheese, he happily accepted the wine jug she passed him. Leaning back contentedly, he used one leg to push the swing back and forth as he scanned the sky, eager to take it all in. They stayed like that for hours, in a companionable silence, broken by short sharp bursts of excitement.

"Did you see that? Did you see it?"

"God, yes! It was amazing!"

Finally, gathering his courage, he said what he needed to say, asked her what he needed to know. "You didn't say anything to your brother, about last night."

"Why would I tell Ross about a private matter between you and me?"

"Christ, Sarah! I assaulted you!"

"Well I would hardly call it that. Oh, my God! Look! From the west, did you see?" She tugged urgently at his elbow.

"Why, Sarah? Why didn't you tell him?"

She turned to look at him. "Because he didn't need to know, and he wouldn't have understood. He would have overreacted, and as I've told you, I didn't consider it any of his business."

Her gaze met his, steady and clear, and he wanted desperately to kiss her.

"Sarah, I . . . I've been wanting to tell you how sorry I am." Damn but this was hard! He felt exposed and vulnerable, and he hated it. "I acted like an animal, and you didn't deserve it. You should have told him and had me thrown out of the fucking house."

Exasperated, she glared at him, digging a sharp elbow into his ribs. "Gabriel, we're missing the best part, and you shouldn't use such language! You're making much too big a fuss. You grabbed me and kissed me and I'm sorry to tell you, you weren't very good at it despite all your boasting. You caused me no harm. None at all, except to my pride." Her eyes softened and her voice gentled. "I'm sorry, too. I provoked you. I'm forever poking my nose where it doesn't belong. I didn't mean to cause you any distress."

He realized she was holding his hand, or he hers, and the ache that went through him spread from his chest to his loins. At a loss for words, tears pricking the corner of his eyes, he was tremendously relieved when she gasped in amazement.

"Oh, my Lord!"

Turning to follow her gaze, his eyes lit with wonder as a fireball trailing plumes of blue, yellow, and green streaked across the sky. They turned to look at each other, still holding hands, grinning in awe and excitement. It was the most beautiful moment of his life. It was something that he'd never done, never even imagined possible, sitting under the stars with a young lady, hand in hand. It was something that lovers, sweethearts, people who cared for each other, did. Her hand was soft, strong, cool, and he stroked her wrist with the pad of his thumb, unconsciously sensual. Delicately tracing her knuckles, he gave her hand a soft squeeze and she turned, smiling, and gently squeezed him back.

He felt it when she drifted off to sleep, her head

coming to rest against his shoulder, her body, soft and warm, pressed against his side. Shifting to make room for her, he eased his arm around her shoulders and contented himself with holding her, as the dawn made its first ascent in the eastern sky. She slumbered, a contented smile on her lips. Tracing the line of her jaw with his knuckles, not quite touching her, he bent and stole a featherlight kiss, grinning as her nose wrinkled in sleepy protest.

Hooking an arm gently under her knees, he gathered her into his arms as the house began to wake. Cradling her close against his chest, relishing the feel of her, he buried his face in her hair and carried her carefully to her room, laying her down on the big bed with a rueful grin. This wasn't at all how he'd imagined their evening ending, when he'd first laid eyes on those rumpled sheets. He tucked the blanket around her, allowing his fingers to trail through the wisps of chestnut curls at her brow. Retreating to the balcony he closed the doors behind him. Sliding easily to the ground with the aid of the great oak, he made his way back to the stables, surprised to find himself whistling. He hadn't known he knew how.

CHAPTER
8

Gabriel met Ross at breakfast, relieved he could face him with a clean conscience. Well, somewhat at least. He didn't suppose the earl would be delighted to know about his nighttime visit to his sister's bedchamber. Still, the evening had ended innocently enough. Innocence—it was a new and heady flavor, and he liked it tremendously.

He spent most of the next two weeks in Jamie's company. Lord Sidney, a distant neighbor with two boys of his own, was hosting an Oxford tutor of some renown. Jamie had been invited to attend, along with Sidney's nephews, and Ross hoped it would help gauge his readiness for formal schooling.

Something inside Gabriel had eased since his afternoon in Ross's study, and his night with Sarah. He joined them at meals, was a polite and amusing dinner companion, and even joined them in the music room one night, accompanying them effortlessly, on the piano. Huntington played the guitar like a Gypsy, and Sarah coaxed unearthly delights from her violin. He was surprised at how much pleasure it gave him to join them in point and counterpoint, trading notes and rhythm into something greater than the sum of its parts. He hadn't returned to Sarah's room, but he thought he might, when the moon was full, to look through her telescope.

At week's end, he accompanied Ross and Jamie to Lord Sidney's. Accepted for what he appeared to be, a distant relative visiting from abroad, he caused a stir amongst the young ladies of the household and an inquiry from Sidney, as to his prospects. He watched with a wistful smile as Jamie joined in quick alliance with Sidney's brood, fretting impatiently to be free of the adults and off on his own adventures. Gabriel had never known friends growing up, and it filled him with satisfaction to know things would be different for Jamie. Still . . . he was going to miss him.

They made some attempt at conversation on the ride back, but without Jamie's enthusiastic chatter, they soon settled into a companionable silence. Gabriel felt unsettled leaving the boy behind. His guardianship of Jamie had been the most important thing in his life, the only important thing for the past several years. He'd built his life around protecting him. Jamie had anchored him, keeping him from drifting any farther toward self-destruction. He'd been a little dismayed at how easily the boy had said good-bye, clearly impatient and eager to return to his new friends. Sighing, he shook his head, earning a quick glance from Ross.

"Ungrateful little bugger practically tossed us out on our ears. Couldn't wait to be shed of us, eh?"

Both men burst into laughter and Gabriel felt a warm rush of appreciation. One had to admit that for a pompous ass, Huntington wasn't a bad sort at all. In better spirits as they neared home, he noticed a large three-masted sloop in the harbor below. "Is that one of yours, Huntington?"

"Eh? What? Be damned! It's that rogue, Davey, home at last! I'll wager he's already up at the house cozening Sarah with gifts and tales of derring-do."

Gabriel stiffened in his saddle, causing his horse to dance and snort in protest.

"Come along, lad, you're in for a treat," Ross said, grinning, as he urged his horse into a gallop.

The house was awhirl with excitement, all of it centered on a large charismatic fellow holding court in the library, as the servants and Sarah crowded around him. Broad-shouldered, merry-eyed, with braided, coal black hair, he had a broken nose and a dashing scar that scored him from jaw to cheekbone. He was a wildly romantic figure. Dressed all in black, with leather boots and breeches, he looked every inch the pirate.

"Well, if it isn't Gypsy Davey, returned from the sea, and turning my household upside down."

"Ross!" the dark-haired giant boomed, striding across the room, and throwing his arms around him, lifting him up off the floor.

Laughing, Huntington enthusiastically returned the other man's embrace. "You took your time, you canny bastard! I was beginning to fear you were swinging from a rope somewhere, you old pirate!"

The man they called Gypsy Davey placed a finger against his lips and winked. "Shhh, my darling. Not in front of the children, and it's privateer, if you please." Turning to look at Gabriel, he grinned and bowed. "And who's this pretty child, Huntington?"

Gabriel returned the bow, replying before Ross was able, eyes hard, voice cold and dangerous, "Why do you ask, my dear? Do you fancy a tumble?"

"Oh, ho! What's this? Huntington, the cub has teeth!"

"Aye, that he does, Davey. That he does." Quickly stepping next to Gabriel, Ross gave his shoulder a friendly squeeze. "I'm hoping you can teach him how to use them."

Cocking his head to one side, Davey looked at Gabriel again, assessing him. "Well, it appears you've some spirit, at least. If you've any ability, I might consider teaching you a thing or two, to please my old friend here. What would you say to that?"

Gabriel wanted to tell him to go fuck himself, and it showed clearly in his eyes, but he wouldn't embarrass Sarah, or Ross, by insulting a friend in their home. Remembering what Ross had said about this man, he struggled to contain the rage his careless comment, and more to the point, his obvious interest in Sarah, had engendered. "I would say, monsieur, that I would hope to show myself most appreciative of anything you might care to teach me."

Davey regarded him with renewed interest, a speculative gleam in his eyes. "Your name?"

"Gabriel, monsieur."

"Ah, a fellow Frenchman, yes? *Et bien*, Gabriel, I'll be staying on my ship for now. Make yourself available in the morning and we'll see if you're worth my while." Turning to Sarah, he bowed gallantly. "Sarah, my darling, I must do my duty by your brother. If you'll excuse me, I'll continue my tale at supper."

Ross and Davey retreated to the study, leaving Sarah alone with Gabriel for the first time in over two weeks. She'd been a little surprised to wake snug in her bed after the meteor shower. He must have carried her there, and the thought of it made her blush. She rather regretted she hadn't been awake to enjoy the experience. He'd seemed hesitant, almost shy in her company since then, but that was a vast improvement over cold and surly, she thought with a grin.

Something fundamental had shifted between them since their rough encounter in the hall. She'd appreciated his apology, though she'd never really feared he would harm her. His coldness and contempt were what had wounded her, and that had disappeared since his visit to her balcony. They had shared something magical that night, and it had sown the seeds of a fragile but budding friendship. They had been careful with each other since, neither of them wanting to presume or impose.

Having acquired the habit of studying him, Sarah hadn't missed Gabriel's angry reaction to Davey's careless comment. She knew, better than most, how it would have stung. It couldn't have been easy for him to see Jamie off, either, she reflected. With a smile of sympathy, she walked over to thread her arm through his. "You mustn't mind Davey. He's a little wild and tends to say whatever he pleases, but he has a heart of gold and there's no truer friend. Come, walk with me, and tell me what happened at Sidney's. Will Jamie be happy there, do you think?"

He answered her questions as best he could, soothed by her touch. As they walked, he realized he had many questions of his own. How did this man they called Gypsy Davey fit with Sarah and her family? How had they lost Jamie in the first place, and why had it taken so long to find him? Had she really been married before? Conditioned to acceptance of whatever fate sent his way, he'd taught himself to be incurious unless a matter was likely to affect him directly. Now he was realizing there were many things he needed to know. "Who is he, Sarah? This man? What is he to your family? Everyone speaks of him."

"Davey?"

"Yes."

"Well, he's been a part of my life for as long as I

can remember. He's of Huguenot descent, a second cousin on my mother's side. His family left France for Ireland when the persecutions started. His parents were killed in some futile border skirmish and he came to live with us. I remember him being great fun, and wickedly adventurous. He was like an older brother to me, but he was rather wild, always off with the Gypsies, or getting into some scrape or another. We had some grand adventures together growing up, and of course, he and Ross connected immediately."

Gabriel snorted, "That's a little hard to believe, mignonne."

"Oh, but it's true! They were closer than brothers. They still are. They used to sail and adventure together all the time, but Ross has settled somewhat over the past few years. I don't know that Davey ever will. He's disgusted with politics and religion and sick of what he's seen done to the Irish and his own people. He's called Gypsy Davey for his childhood adventures, and because he's always restless and moving from place to place. He's quite proud to call himself a man without country or religion." She grinned. "That's terribly convenient for a privateer and a smuggler, you know, as he feels free to take commissions where, and as, he pleases. My brother is seriously worried that he's becoming too bold. He wasn't joking about seeing him swing from the neck."

Gabriel tried to picture the reserved, immaculate Lord Huntington engaged in pillage and high seas adventure, with little success. "And he lives with you? When he's not at sea?"

"He lives with us when he pleases. We are his family, and he is ours."

Emboldened, he managed one more question before they were summoned to dinner. "I've been meaning to thank you, mademoiselle, for sharing your observatory with me. It was a night I shall never forget. I was wondering if I might visit you again, when the moon is full, to view it with your telescope."

"Of course," she said with a bright smile. "As I've told you before, you're welcome to come whenever you wish."

"Thank you, mademoiselle"

"Sarah, please."

"Thank you, Sarah."

Feeling in charity with the world, he went in to dinner. Putting aside his fears for Jamie and his alarm at Sarah's obvious admiration for her handsome cousin, he relaxed and enjoyed the good cheer, ready wit, and fine wine, enthralled as Davey regaled them with tales of battle and adventure, exotic ports, and narrow escapes on the high seas.

Plagued by a growing restlessness for several days

now, Gabriel was already waiting for Davey, idly fishing off the dock, when the sun rose the next morning. He was set to work hauling rope, pumping bilges, cleaning decks, and doing other menial labor. Davey's motley crew greeted him with whistles and catcalls, smirking and blowing kisses. He had no difficulty ignoring them. It wasn't his habit to concern himself with what others thought. The crew's opinion meant nothing to him. It wasn't Davey's comment that had angered him last night. Under other circumstances, he might have found it amusing. But he'd made it in front of Sarah, and for better or worse, her opinion *did* matter. Somehow, it had come to matter very much.

It was midday before Davey came and tapped him on the shoulder, sending him on his way. The crew, faced with his complete and utter indifference, had long since abandoned their harassment. Muscles aching, weary and hungry, he returned to his room. Sleep still eluded him. It came to him that night, though, and so did the dreams.

The boy is lost, somewhere in the big house, lost and calling for him. He searches frantically, racing down endless corridors, tearing open doors, hunting from room to room, sick with dread. He finds him, whimpering, terrified, cowering

before a grunting, red-faced satyr. He knows him well. The German. Enraged, he reaches for his dagger, stabbing and stabbing, sharp blade into yielding flesh, plunging through cartilage and tissue, grinding against bone, over and over as the boy sobs in terror and blood gushes and spurts and pools on the floor.

He looks around. The boy has disappeared. There's blood on his hands, but the urgency and rage are fading. He's calmer now, floating, detached. He sees the bed. Luxurious, opulent, red silk and satin, a woman on it, beautiful and coarse, wearing only stockings, legs splayed wide in invitation, her busy fingers tugging, sticky with her own juices. "Come," she tells him, command, not invitation.

Waking with a groan, his heart pounding with rage and fear, Gabriel heaved himself from the bed and prowled restlessly about the room. He stopped by the window, leaning his forehead against the cool pane, his body still shaking. Letting loose a gasp that was half sob, half laughter, he fumbled about until he found his brandy. He'd been drinking less these past weeks, but he always made sure he had a ready supply, close to hand. One never knew. He padded to the fire, stirring it and adding another log, trying to ward off the sudden chill that seized him.

It seemed the longer he went without sleep, the more vivid his nightmares became, and the worse they became, the more he avoided sleep. He'd hoped that hours of strenuous labor would purchase some dreamless slumber, but he couldn't seem to escape the vicious cycle that robbed his nights of rest or peace. He was grateful for it in a strange way. He'd been forgetting himself lately, caught up in a fantasy world, pretending he had a place here. It was foolish, and dangerous. The dream had served as a much-needed reminder of who he was and where he came from. He smacked his fist into the wall, abrading his knuckles, the sharp shock of pain helping him collect himself. This place was the fantasy, only the dreams were real. Best not forget it.

Knowing he'd sleep no more this night, he donned a pair of breeches. Neglecting to put on boots or fasten his shirt, he made his way outside and down the steep cliff face to the beach. Still shaken, the dream had been so damn real, he began applying himself to the bottle in earnest. Wind whipping his hair and shirttails around him, grim and weary, he looked up toward the house. It was quiet and cold tonight, retaining none of the warmth and cheer that had been there earlier in the day. It had passed through, evaporating, as if it had never been.

Nursing the bottle, he noticed with dull surprise that the moon was almost full. It reflected off the surface of the still water, a brilliant, beautiful, ghostly highway, beckoning unwary travelers to a haunted world of mystery and imagination. Duplicitous bitch! He shuddered and raised his bottle in salute before starting back, not really aware of how he managed the steep path in the state he was in, not really aware of where he was or what he was doing, until he found himself standing under the tall oak, looking up at her room.

Well, she'd promised him the moon, he told himself with a drunken chuckle. Barefoot, with a bottle in one hand, he managed to pull himself onto the lower branches. In short order, he leveraged himself over the balustrade and onto her balcony, without spilling a drop. Her door was open to the breeze, and he nudged it wider, standing there for several moments framed in the moonlight, watching her sleep.

Well this was damned disappointing! If a wench was going to give a fellow an invitation, the least she could do was stay awake and wait for him. Overall she was a good girl though, he thought charitably. She'd let him use her Mr. James Short telescope; she wasn't a telltale, and she always smelled very nice, indeed. He moved closer to the bed, until he was standing over her.

Her skin glowed alabaster in the moonlight, and she smiled in her sleep, soft and innocent. Her breasts, though, full and rounded like . . . melons, juicy and succulent, meant to quench a fellow's thirst, rising and falling with her breath, inviting a man to caress them, kiss them... now they were downright sinful! He held out an unsteady hand, and then drew it back. Best not to wake her, best to leave, but he was exhausted and cold, chilled bone deep, and he wasn't too drunk to fear what he might do if he was alone this night. Sighing, he let himself slide to the floor, knowing he shouldn't be there, but unable to bring himself to leave.

Waking from a dream, Sarah moved in an instant from drowsy to wide-awake. There was someone in her room! She raised herself cautiously on her elbow, straining to see. A tiny flame licked in the grate, casting more shadow than light. Gabriel was sitting on the floor beside her bed. One knee was drawn up to his chest and he had a bottle in one hand, resting on his lap.

She studied him carefully. Shirt open, he was bare-chested and disheveled, his hair in wild tangles about his shoulders. His eyes were unfocused, gazing inward. He seemed lost in a trance, contemplating some long-ago sorrow, the hurt clearly visible in his face. She wanted to be angry with him. He had clearly been drinking and he'd given her a fright, but he looked so tired and lost. She felt an odd combination of pity, lust, and the desire to comfort.

When he finally realized she was awake and watching him, he acknowledged her with a sad, crooked smile, and an unsteady salute.

"You're drunk!"

"Completely foxed," he agreed with a genial grin.

"How did you get in here?"

He crooked a finger toward the balcony. "Tree."

"You climbed that tree in this state?"

"Mmm," he agreed. "The tree, the cliff, the stairs. As long as I'm drunk, what does it matter?"

"You're an idiot! You might have been killed!"

"And you, mignonne, are very astute." His head was beginning to clear. The more he drank, the more it took to put him under and keep him there. "I shouldn't have come."

"Why did you, Gabe? What's wrong?" she asked gently.

"A bad dream," he said tiredly. "Nothing more."

"Well, now that you're here, why don't you tell me about it? It might help you sleep."

"Christ, woman, I came here for some peace, to escape it, not to wallow in it!" He pulled himself to his feet. This had clearly been a mistake.

"You don't honestly think you can escape it by ignoring it, or running away, do you?"

No, he'd never thought that. Only hoped. He'd hoped he might escape for a while, by running to her, and hoping was the thing that would destroy him in the end. He knew it. He turned, glaring at her in the dark. "Shall I tell you then, Sarah? Do you really want to know? Would you like to know what I was doing the night before you and your saintly brother arrived at Madame Etienne's?"

Her silence drove him on.

"I was auctioned off that night, my services for the evening, to the highest bidder. I did my best to appeal, as half the proceeds were mine to keep. I was a very valuable asset there, you know. I'm surprised she released me."

He stalked toward her, his body tense, vibrating. His voice became cooler, deliberately seductive and compelling. "It was a husband and wife, or a man and his mistress, a playful pair. I was the wicked footman"—despite his obvious tension, his voice sounded amused—"burning with lust for my haughty countess. I was . . . tasting her, pleasuring her, a thing I'm very good at, when her husband arrived, catching us in the act. Naturally, he was furious and determined to punish us both. I, the insolent servant, was taught to regret my impertinence by being bound to the bed and whipped by his lordship as his lady knelt between his legs, vigorously sucking his cock. Fortunately, she was thorough enough that he was not inclined to complete his amorous designs upon my person."

Silence. It continued unabated, except for their breathing. He knew he'd shocked her, had strangled something delicate that had been growing between them, and he wasn't done yet. "And do you know what else, my dear?" he asked, his voice mocking. "I thoroughly enjoyed it." He wasn't sure what he expected from her—horror, condemnation, and disgust, certainly not a reply as cool and detached as his own.

"Well, now, if you'd enjoyed it, it wouldn't be giving you nightmares, would it?"

Rage blasted through him, demolishing years of

hard-won control. The bottle flew from his hand, shattering in the corner as a distant part of his brain noted that broken glass was becoming a habit, a different form of comfort. Damn her! Damn her! He took a ragged breath, then another, clenching his fists, refusing to look at her lest she provoke him to further violence. Stiffly he turned toward the balcony and disappeared into the night.

CHAPTER 9

Gabriel spent the rest of the night walking the sand. The surging waves resonated with the turmoil inside him, allowing him to reassert some measure of balance to his shattered nerves. Sleepless nights were nothing new to him, and well before dawn he made his way to Davey's, spending several hours scrubbing decks and climbing rigging, grateful for any activity, the more strenuous the better. Numbing his mind, he channeled his dismay and confusion into physical exertion, until Davey called him down and sent him on his way.

He cringed at the thought of seeing Sarah, again. He'd been stripped naked before, in many ways, but nothing had made him feel as skin-crawlingly vulnerable and exposed as she had last night. If he could take it back, he would. He would have stayed in his room and played with glass or steel, and then gone about his business. Now she knew far too much, and when he looked in her eyes, he'd see his real self reflected back. It was almost too much to bear.

He'd intended to go to his room, not wanting to face her, but his body, starved and demanding to be fed, betrayed him. Well, he thought with bleak humor, nothing new about that. In any case, he couldn't avoid her forever. Steeling himself, he went to the breakfast room. Naturally, she was there. She offered no greeting when he came in, and he avoided her eyes. He moved stone-faced to the sideboard and piled his plate. His spirits might be deadened, but the hours aboard Davey's ship had left his body ravenous. He took his time, hoping she would get up and leave so he wouldn't have to join her at the table.

"Why, Gabriel, do hurry up. It's not like you to be so delicate around your food. Or perhaps you are, how does Davey put it . . . green about the gills from an excess of bacchanal?"

"I'm not hung over, *chère*."

"Good, and you didn't fall and crack your head on the rocks descending from my balcony?" she asked sweetly.

"Not unless this is hell, and you are one of Lucifer's minions."

"Perhaps this is heaven, and I am an angel," she said with a wry grin.

"No, mignonne, they would never allow *me* in there."

"Hmm, perhaps not. Davey says all the most

interesting people are bound to go to hell. I would like to ask your help with something, if I might."

He dared to look at her then. Her eyes were clear and guileless, shining with barely suppressed excitement. He blinked, bewildered, and wondered if he'd dreamt last evening. Perhaps it had never happened.

"Gabriel? Are you daydreaming? If you're too tired, that's fine. I'll get Mr. Simmons to help me."

"Help with what, Sarah?" he asked, bringing his plate to the table and sitting across from her.

Leaning across the table, she gripped his forearm in excitement, her touch an exquisite ache, teasing his abraded nerves. "I've arranged a surprise for my brother, a Barbary stallion and two fine mares. Davey brought them with him. I was hoping to collect them today. I can manage the stallion, or the mares, but not both. Davey has promised to keep Ross busy so I can slip them into the stables."

He let his eyes feast a moment on the cleft of her bosom as she leaned across the table. He imagined burying his face there, enveloped in her warmth and her scent, his hands cupping her breasts, his fingers and thumbs—

"Gabriel? Are you all right?" She pressed the back of her hand, smooth and cool, against his forehead, feeling his temperature.

He bit back a groan and gently removed it. "A slight *megrim*," he lied as his erection strained painfully against his breeches. "Nothing a coffee and breakfast won't cure."

"You might consider . . . cutting back a little, on the alcohol," she said carefully.

"Sarah," his voice held a note of warning. "Would you like my help, or not?"

"Yes, please," she said meekly.

"Fine, give me a moment to finish my coffee. Go ahead if you like. I'll catch up shortly. I need to ah . . . use the necessary."

"Oh, yes, of course. Well, then, I'll go on ahead and you catch up."

She jumped to her feet and he realized she'd been as nervous about this encounter as he was, as uncertain of his reaction as he was of hers. Not sure what to make of it, he watched her leave the room, shifting in his seat as her fetching bottom shifted pertly in her tight breeches.

Gabriel prided himself on his control. He'd learned how to produce an erection at will, as well as how to suppress one. It wasn't working very well around Sarah, though, he noted sourly. Once she was gone, he left the table, returning to his room. Throwing himself on the bed, he freed his throbbing organ. Swollen with need, stroking, and pumping, imagining her lying wanton and willing beneath him, he brought himself to release.

Sarah waited for him on the cliff edge, leaning back on her elbows, legs dangling over the side, thinking about last night. After he'd left, she'd lain in her bed too shaken to move, shocked by what he'd told her, and stunned by the depth of his rage. She'd sensed that she wasn't the cause of his anger, but she'd certainly been the catalyst. She regretted how she'd handled it, bungled it really, driving him back into the night when he'd clearly come to her looking for some kind of comfort.

She wanted to help him. At first, it was because of what he'd done for Jamie, but that had soon changed. The more she came to know him, the more she was drawn to him, until he invaded her thoughts, day and night. She was already more than half in love. Seeing him last night, lonely and lost on the floor by her bed, she'd wanted nothing more than to take him in her arms and hold him tight. Perhaps she should have, instead of asking questions. Why must it be so complicated? She'd worried about him the rest of the night, and she'd been tremendously relieved to see him safe, and in one piece, this morning.

It took him just over a quarter of an hour to catch up with her. She turned her head to watch his approach. His stride was long and he moved with the same fluid grace that had so fascinated her when she'd first seen him in Paris. He awakened an intense sensuality in her she'd never once suspected she possessed. At breakfast, she'd been studying his lips, for heaven's sake! Closing her eyes for a moment, she heard his voice again, cool, seductive, *I was tasting her, pleasuring her, I'm very good at it*. Feeling a stab of guilt and shame, she jumped to her feet, determinedly banishing the memory, and her reactions to it.

"Well, Gabriel, I must say, you look a good deal improved."

"Yes, I feel much better, thank you. The coffee," he said with a hint of a smile. They continued down the path together, an awkward silence between them. "I suppose I should apologize, Sarah, for my behavior last night. It seems I've acted the brute again."

She stopped walking and turned to face him. "More like a bloody big fool, I'd say."

"I'm really very sorry."

"And so you should be. It took me half an hour to clean up that mess, and I cut my thumb doing it." She held up her abused digit for his perusal.

"It won't . . . it won't happen again." He would make sure of it. These visits to her room were too dangerous for his equilibrium. They would have to stop.

"Well, whether it does or not, I won't clean up after you again. You make a mess, Gabriel, you should stay to clean it up."

He looked down at his fists. "I know. I just . . ."

"Yes," she sighed, "I know. I upset you terribly and you had to leave. I have to learn not to go blundering about in other people's private affairs. I apologize for that. Again. I didn't mean to. It seems we both keep repeating the same mistakes."

Meeting her gaze, he saw the worry and concern in her eyes. It wasn't what he'd been expecting, but that shouldn't be a surprise, when everything about Sarah was so . . . unexpected.

"Friends?" She held out her hand to him, an expectant look on her face.

Her invitation almost unmanned him. Unaccountably, he wanted to cry. He stood there in the middle of the path, doltish and inept, with no idea how to proceed.

Grinning, and playfully raising her brows, Sarah spoke slowly and carefully, as if to a simpleton, "Gabriel, this is where *you* say friends, and we exchange a hearty handshake, leaving all last night's unpleasantness behind us."

He blinked, then smiled in gratitude and relief, taking her hand and bowing gallantly. "Friends."

As his mood eased and the tension between them evaporated, the boyish grin he gave her was so genuine and so beautiful it curled her toes, and made her glow all over. Vastly pleased with each other, they continued the rest of the way to Davey's, chattering about horses and composers, and telescopes and the moon.

Friends. It was such a simple word. She was the only one who'd ever cared to know any more about him than what they could see. The only one who'd ever asked, and in response, he'd told her things he'd

105

never told anyone else. He realized that he'd *wanted* to tell her about his dream. He'd needed to know if she would still welcome him, still accept him, if she knew, really knew, what his life had been like. He'd allowed her a glimpse into the dark horror of his past, and foolish girl, wise in all ways but this, she'd extended her hand in friendship. She knew what it meant, as much as anyone could, but she couldn't possibly have known what it meant to him. There had never been anyone to share thoughts or ideas with, hopes and dreams, fears or hurts or sorrows. Until Sarah, no one had cared.

He waited three days, afraid to test the boundaries of this new friendship, afraid to make a mistake, but on the fourth night he went to her, drawn like a moth to the flame.

CHAPTER
10

Sarah was asleep when he arrived, and something was different. It took a moment before he realized the window seat was strewn with cushions, furs, and blankets. A leather wine flask had been left, as well. The gesture offered comfort and invited him to stay and take his ease. He wasn't used to anyone caring for his comfort, and it convinced him that her offer of friendship, and the welcome he'd seen in her eyes, was genuine. Choosing not to wake her, he settled in between the furs, falling into a deep, dreamless, and much needed sleep, and left silently with the dawn.

He came often after that, no longer hesitant of her welcome. He stayed for hours on her balcony, watching the stately dance of constellations as they spun slowly overhead. It struck him that there had always been other worlds surrounding him, just outside his reach, unexpected and unseen. They were opening to him now. Sarah was opening them. They spoke long into the night, their voices joining in easy laughter and lively debate. For the first time, Gabriel shared his opinions and ideas. They discussed the philosophers, Voltaire and Hobbes, Locke, and Rousseau. They discussed composers, Haydn, and the prodigious Mozart, and Sarah discovered, much to her delight, that Gabriel was as talented with violin and guitar as he was with the piano.

Gabriel felt intoxicated, as if he'd stepped through some fairy-tale mirror into an enchanted world. He knew he was in love with her, deeply, sweetly, madly in love. His world had been dark and colorless before she'd come into his life, devoid of any strong emotion, except hatred, despair, or fear. She'd opened his eyes to wonder, had welcomed him into her home as warmly as she did her brothers, or Davey. She filled his every waking thought and his heated-longing dreams, keeping the nightmares at bay and giving him a reason to welcome sleep, rather than dread it. He was always respectful, careful never to jeopardize the bond growing between them, and he was truly happy for the first time in his life.

The next few months went by in a blur of activity. His days were spent under Davey's tutelage. A hard taskmaster, Davey insisted that Gabriel learn his way about the ship, sending him aloft, clambering up the shrouds with the topsmen over a hundred and fifty feet above the deck until he was at ease skylarking in the rigging. He learned how to set, reef, and furl a sail, edging out along the swaying yardarms with only footropes for support, each roll of the ship whirling him about in dizzying circles.

Balancing on heaving deck and narrow rail, he practiced with short sword, cutlass, rapier, and a curved sword Davey called a *katana*. The long weeks of strenuous physical activity hardened and honed his body, sculpting him into an engine of muscle and sinew and fluid grace. His early experiences had taught him to distrust his body, to distance himself from it, divorcing mind and sensation. Now, his training with Davey forced him to meld mind and body—focused, present, and aware. As his training continued, he became more comfortable and at ease within himself. He enjoyed the gentle ache that drugged his arms and legs after a long session. He enjoyed the way his body responded and moved, as quick as thought, and he found himself running, jumping, and climbing, for the sheer joy of it.

The focus that had allowed him to survive his disastrous childhood, now helped him to be one with his weapon, as Davey taught him to channel his anger and passion into the blade in a living, breathing dance of beauty, steel, and death. A natural athlete and thirsty to learn, he poured himself into the rhythm of sea and ship and sword, until they were an extension of himself, as natural to him as breathing. He exulted in it, and despite his late start, he soon excelled.

Gabriel was as susceptible to Davey's roguish

charm as were Sarah and Ross. He valued the man's opinion, understood what Davey expected of him, and found himself able to fit in with the assorted collection of misfits and eccentrics that made up Davey's crew, in a way that eluded him in other settings. He knew he excelled at the things Davey taught him, and the man's irreverent good humor and world-weary cynicism struck a chord that resonated deeply within. Davey was enough of the outlaw that Gabriel felt comfortable, on occasion, sharing some small part of his past. Davey greeted these revelations with humor at times, but never shock.

His relationship with Davey was far easier and more relaxed than the one he had with Ross, who had undertaken to instruct him in estate matters, and matters of trade and investment. He suspected the older man was trying to prepare him to make the most of his ten thousand pounds when their bargain was complete, and the thought made him distinctly uncomfortable. He also felt that he was being measured against some standard he didn't understand, couldn't relate to, and could never achieve. It never occurred to him that these feelings of being judged and found lacking might involve his own interest in Ross's sister. He respected, admired, even liked Ross, but he never felt completely at ease in his company, and it amazed him that the two men, who seemed so different in temperament, were such close friends.

As much as Gabriel's days were filled with challenge,

hard work, and physical effort, his nights were filled with magic. Some evenings they would all join on the lower terrace. Davey would come with one or two of his ragged crew, or Gypsy friends from across the river. They would sing and play throughout the night, drinking whiskey and wine and raising their voices in laughter, conversation, and song. Trading words and melodies, challenging each other with whatever the moment, the mood, or their imagination allowed; they made wild and beautiful music against a background of sea and sky, in a warm and wonderful communion that left Gabriel feeling exhausted, happy, and replete.

Most nights he waited, breathless and excited, for the sun to set, the moon to rise, and the house to settle for the night. Then he'd climb the oak to her room, to watch the sky and talk, listening to her voice, husky with excitement, watching in fascination as her eyes flashed with passion, lit from within, and watching in envy as the evening breeze caressed her cheeks, ruffling her hair and playing with the tendrils as he longed to do.

On cooler nights, he settled himself in the place she'd made for him on her window seat. He told her more about his time at the château. How he'd loved the stables and the horses, and what it had meant to him to discover music and learn to read and write. In time, hesitant and careful, he told her more of de Sevigny, how he would have done anything in his power to please him so that he might stay, how he'd tried to escape, and how in both ways, mired in shame and confusion, he was an active participant in his own ruination. He told her how badly it had hurt, how much he'd hated both de Sevigny and himself, and how much he'd hated going back to Madame's.

Sarah seldom said much as he told her these stories, just lay in the dark listening, a soft comment now and then. "You loved him because he made those things possible, the books and the music. He gave you the only pleasure you'd ever known."

"Yes."

"But he didn't care for you. Not at all. You were just a thing to him. Something to use. And he let you do those things, let you ride and play and learn, to make you a more valuable thing."

"Yes," he rasped.

"And so? You took what you could, what you wanted and needed, and then you left. Or you tried to, at least. You survived him. What else could you have done, Gabriel?"

He shook his head in the dark, uncertain, never having thought about it quite that way before. "I don't know." He fell asleep there, more often than not, warm and peaceful in her cozy room. He imagined it possessed some powerful, protective enchantment, because the nightmares could never seem to find him there, not even when he opened the door to bitter memories.

As the days grew shorter, and the first frost covered

the ground, he found himself climbing the big oak almost every night. One night, when the wind was whipping cold spray and early sleet against the window behind him, she invited him to share one side of the big bed. Breathless, careful not to misconstrue, he accepted, lying gingerly beside her above the covers, an arm's length away. In this intimate and rarified atmosphere, he told her that Davey was in love with her, and she called him a muddle-headed fool. He complained of her arrogant older brother, and he described with enthusiasm the feeling he got from the bloody and controlled dance of violence, metal, and mind Davey was teaching him. One night he asked about her husband.

"Were you really married, Sarah? I have trouble imagining it."

"So do I," she said with a shudder.

"You told me, on the ship, that you didn't care for him very much."

"I . . . I didn't care for him at all."

"I wouldn't think . . . I'm surprised that Ross, or your parents, would force you to marry someone you disliked."

"No . . . it wasn't like that, Gabriel. It's . . . it's rather a long, complicated story."

"I'm sorry, mignonne. I didn't mean to intrude."

As the silence stretched between them it struck her how difficult it was to reveal painful memories to someone else. She didn't want to tell him about it. It made her feel exposed in a way she didn't like, and she truly appreciated, for the first time, what it must cost him to answer all her questions. "It's not an easy thing, to talk about one's past, is it?" she said quietly.

"No, mignonne, it's not."

Reaching across the space that divided them, she found his hand and squeezed it tight, making his heart thud wildly in his chest. "It happened so quickly," she offered, "and lasted barely a week. I was sixteen years old. My parents . . . their ship foundered. They . . . they were drowned. When it happened, Davey was away at sea, looking for Ross. Ross had been reported dead, a casualty of war, over a year before, but Davey wouldn't accept it." The swift sharp wave of pain surprised her, bringing tears to her eyes. She'd thought it long since eased. She'd never talked about this, any of it. It made Ross uncomfortable, and even Davey closed himself off if she brought it up. She hadn't realized how close it hovered to the surface of her being.

"I'm not sure if you're aware, but Ross is my half brother. His mother was my father's first wife. She came from a very powerful family, as did my father. I don't know what she was like. Ross . . . well, he doesn't really speak of her, although he told me once he remembered her as being very cold. I don't think they were very close. In any event, after she died, my father met my mother. She was from Bohemia, they fell madly in love, and they married.

"My father's family was furious. She was a foreigner

and had some Gypsy blood, and they felt her far beneath him. She told me once, that I was named after Kali Sara, the Romany goddess. Nobody would have cared. I was only a female. Jamie was a different matter, but at least Ross was heir, and that suited everyone. When Ross was declared dead . . ." She took a deep breath. "When Ross was declared dead and Jamie became my father's heir it enraged them. They called him the Gypsy brat. My uncle was furious, and when my parents died... he became Jamie's guardian, and mine, as well. He wanted me out of the way as quickly as possible, I suppose, so he could have full control over Jamie and no interference. He married me to an old crony of his, Lord Munroe. I hate the name. I hated him."

"He . . . What was he like?"

"He was sixty-two years old, mean, vicious, smelly and sour, with rotting teeth. When he tried to kiss me, I gagged."

"Your first experience, then, was not what you would have wished."

"No, Gabe, it was not." She was embarrassed to discuss it with him, but after all he'd shared with her, she couldn't very well refuse. "It was damned unpleasant. He came to my room, drunk as a soldier, dragged me onto the bed and jumped on top of me. He was a very big man and I could hardly breathe. When I tried to protest he slapped me, and when he . . . well, suffice to say it was painful, and messy, and terribly embarrassing, and I cannot say I was eager to repeat it."

"Did you?"

"Yes, three times, each time worse than the last, although from what I've gathered since, I was being very melodramatic. It seems to be the general way of things between husbands and wives."

"No wonder I never lacked for clients." It was a thoughtless remark and he regretted it the instant he said it, desperately seeking some way to take it back, but her startled laughter was genuine, and she looked at him in fond amusement. His heart eased as he realized that apparently, inadvertently, he'd done something right, or at least he hadn't done anything wrong. "What happened then, Sarah? How did he die? How did you come to leave him?"

"My uncle came. He called to tell me that Jamie had disappeared on his way to boarding school. I didn't believe it. I . . . Oh, God, Gabriel! We'd been so happy together, my parents, Ross, Jamie, Davey, and I. We loved each other so much, and in a year they were all gone!" Tears were streaming down her cheeks now.

Unaccustomed to offering comfort, Gabriel resorted to the methods that had worked with Jamie. "I'm sorry, mignonne," he offered, awkwardly rubbing her back and patting her shoulder.

"It was a very dark time. I . . . I think in my grief for my parents, and for Ross, I let myself go numb. I stopped caring, stopped paying attention. Poor Jamie, he needed me and I let him down. If I'd been thinking

. . . If only I'd—"

"Shhh, mignonne, it wasn't your fault," he said gently, putting his arms around her. Sobbing, no longer able to contain the guilt and pain she'd been holding in for so long, she didn't resist as he pulled her into his lap, rocking her back and forth. He held her like that for several minutes, letting her cry, stroking her hair and patting her back as she soaked his shirt with her tears. Suddenly becoming aware of her in a different way, warm, soft, and vibrant, he groaned and changed position, praying she wouldn't notice his rampant arousal. Christ, he was an animal! Carefully shifting her back onto her side of the bed, he used his shirttail to wipe her tears and then ruffled her hair, much as he used to do with Jamie. "Better now?"

"Yes, I'm sorry. I'm not usually so . . ."

"I know, mignonne. It's not like you at all," he said with a grin.

"Gabriel, I don't know if I've ever really thanked you. If I've ever actually said it. Told you how grateful I am for what you did for Jamie."

He hushed her, embarrassed and uncomfortable. "Shhh, Sarah, stop it, please. It's not necessary. Your brother helped me as much as I helped him."

"No, Gabe," she said, hugging herself. "You may not want to hear it, but I need to say it. When my uncle came, when he told me that Jamie was gone, I woke up from the daze I was in, but it was too late. I knew he was behind it. I escaped my husband by dressing as a stable boy and stealing a horse. I came back here to hide and wait for Davey. I sailed with him for two years, you know, as we searched for Ross and Jamie, and every day I felt sick with fear, and sorrow, and guilt. We found Ross, thank God. And then we had news of Jamie after five long years. I couldn't believe it. I thanked all the gods and all the angels. I wept with joy. And then they told us where he'd been. I was sick with fear, Gabriel."

She looked directly into his eyes. "I couldn't stop imagining the horrors he must have been through. I thought about it, and dreamt about it, and I knew it was my fault. I knew that however he might be wounded, it was because I'd failed him. Failed to protect him when he had no one else in the world."

"Sarah, no! You were just a child yourself, an unmarried female. You would never have been allowed to be his guardian, and you couldn't have kept him safe."

"I could have run away with him, hidden him."

"Why would you do such a thing? Take a boy who'd just lost his parents and live as a fugitive, forsaking his inheritance, putting him at risk? You had no way of knowing your uncle was capable of such a thing."

She had no answer for that. She needed time to think about it. "I do know this, Gabriel. You did what I couldn't do. As soon as I saw him, healthy and curious and proud, I knew that something, *someone*, had intervened, had protected him and kept him safe from harm. It was unbelievable, a miracle. You did that, Gabriel. And I have never been so grateful to anyone in my life."

"So . . . that's why you brought me here."

"If you mean here to Cornwall, then yes. That's why. You saved my brother. That makes you family. Ross or Davey will never tell you, but I know they feel the same."

"What other here is there?" he asked quietly.

She looked surprised, flustered. "Why... here in my room, of course."

It begged the question. "And why did you bring me here, to your room, Sarah?"

"I really don't know, Gabriel. I didn't mean to. It just seemed to . . . happen."

Hesitant to push, he decided to let it rest. "Tell me the rest, mignonne. What happened to your husband and your uncle?"

"They died."

"Sarah . . ."

"When we found Ross, he was being held as a prisoner of war. He might have been ransomed if . . . well, it appears that my uncle had known all along. He was quite likely complicit in my parents' death, as well. They . . . they were wrecked off the coast, not that far from here, and there's no doubt he was responsible for what happened to Jamie. It was said that highwaymen waylaid him, that he angered them somehow, or they were particularly vicious. In any case, they took him from his coach and hung him from a tree, leaving his purse dangling round his neck. It did a great service to the local gentlemen of the road, as their victims were very polite and quick to hand over their purses for many months after. I'm certain it was Ross, or Davey, or both of them. They refuse to discuss it with me, even though I'm the one who was here while it all happened. It used to make me so angry. I felt I had a right to know."

Gabriel grunted, realizing there was a great deal about Huntington he didn't know, had never suspected. "You did, mignonne, you do," he said, soothing her. "They think they protect you. They don't understand."

"I know," she sighed. "I'm so tired of it all now. I don't suppose I really care anymore. My husband died of natural causes a few weeks after I left him, leaving me the title of countess, and two small estates. I was out to sea with Davey and didn't hear of it for several months. I'm convinced he was killed by a combination of bitterness, bile, and apoplexy, but according to his family and polite society, it was shame and a broken heart brought on by my scandalous behavior that did him in."

"Naughty child," he whispered with a grin.

She smiled back at him. "There was some good that came out of it, though."

"And how is that, chère?"

"Well, it horrified everyone. Not what my husband or my uncle did to me, but what I did to them. I became a social outcast, and in an odd way, it set me free."

"Free?" He was finding it hard to follow her

words, when most of his being was focused on her hand, smooth and warm in his.

"Yes, free. Think of it, Gabe!" She turned to face him, eager to share this new idea. He tightened his grip on her hand, not eager to have it escape him. "People like us, people who've been forced out of the world they know by habit or by birth, pushed or shoved or maybe just allowed to walk into new ones, they get to see that the rules of those worlds have no intrinsic meaning, hold no fundamental truth. Once you recognize that, you're free. Free to choose what makes sense, free to be yourself instead of what others expect you to be. Instead of knowing your place, you can get to know yourself!"

He tilted his head back, caught by the idea, considering for some time before responding. "But what if the self you find is someone you don't like, mignonne?"

She gave a low, husky laugh that sent a sweet thrill up his spine.

"Are you speaking of yourself, Gabriel?" she drawled, sleep clawing at her. "Because if you are, I would have to disagree. I may be a poor judge of character, but I find I like you very much." She punctuated that astonishing statement with a little sigh, wrinkling her nose and falling asleep.

Weary himself, he lay beside her, savoring her words, *I find I like you very much*, and savoring the feel of her hand in his, as his thumb traced patterns across her knuckles. It amazed him to think that

121

only six months ago, he'd been dead inside, alone and friendless, trading his body for money and favors, and dreading the coming of tomorrow. Now here he was, lying comfortably in the bed of a lovely woman, holding hands like lovers, talking and chatting like old friends, and falling asleep together like a happy and contented old couple.

A sudden bolt of fear seized him, twisting his vitals, and clamping tight around his throat. It couldn't be real. Such a life was never meant for him. Certainly, not such a woman. She was clean and sweet, kind and wholesome, everything he was not. He needed to take stock, to slow this headlong rush toward destruction. He concentrated on breathing until his panic receded. If he were careful, he might keep her as a friend. But he had to be careful not to reach too high, not to want too much, or he'd lose it all.

CHAPTER

11

Despite Gabriel's best intentions, it was growing increasingly difficult for him to stay within the bounds of friendship. As novel and as rewarding as the intimacy of friendship was for him, he was a healthy male in the prime of life, and in peak condition. He was also a deeply sensual man, a thing he had found to be a curse as he responded repeatedly to sensations and situations he neither welcomed nor enjoyed. In response, he had learned to detach and distance himself, so that sex became a dark mechanical exercise, a performance he could summon at will, and dismiss just as easily. He had realized early in life that it was the only thing he was wanted for, all that he had of value to anyone, other than Jamie. It had become his main form of relating to others, and it left him feeling angry, ashamed, and utterly alone.

Sarah expected more from him, wanted his company in ways no one else ever had. He had wanted to be listened to, wanted someone to care about what he thought, what he did, and who he was, and she offered him all of these things. She saw him as something better than he was, not as damaged goods or some bitter, jaded whore. There were times when he saw himself through her eyes and he knew she thought him brave, strong, and kind, because of her brother. She had no idea that his rescue of Jamie had been largely a selfish act, as necessary to his own survival as it had been to the boy's. But when she looked at him that way, he found himself wanting to be that man.

What would she think if she knew what he did to her in his dreams, how he made her cry out, made her forget her loathsome husband, made her forget herself. She would be disgusted and disappointed if she knew. He realized, belatedly, that by allowing himself to dream about her, waking or asleep, he was only making things worse. Determined to cut back his visits until he'd reasserted some control, his resolve lasted two days, and then he found himself mooning like some lost puppy below her balcony again. Bewitched and bedeviled, prepared to sabotage everything he'd built in his life over the past half year, in defiance of all his own rules, he decided to do what he'd been dreaming of doing for the past several months. He decided he was going to kiss her. A part of him clamored in alarm, shouting that he was about to make the biggest mistake of his life, but as he took the familiar path into the starlit night, he ignored it, promising himself if it *was* a mistake, she would forgive him.

Sarah waited for him, snug in her bed, hidden beneath a mound of blankets and books, and her ugly nightgown. A fire was lit against the November chill. She watched uncertainly as he approached. There was something unusual about him this evening. His eyes glittered and he seemed edgy, restless, as he stopped beside her bed. She'd not seen him the worse for drink for several weeks now. Not since he'd told her of his nightmare, and though he seemed somewhat unsteady, different somehow, he didn't appear to have been drinking.

"May I, mignonne?" he asked, gesturing to the bed.

"Of course." She drew up her legs and moved her books and cushions, making a space for him. "I didn't think you'd be coming." It was a question as much as a statement.

Choosing to ignore it, he settled his length beside her. "What are you reading, *chère?*" he asked, his voice soft and beguiling.

She shivered at his tone. It struck her suddenly that she'd been playing a dangerous game inviting this man to her room, to her bed. Except it hadn't been a game. It had seemed natural and right, and somehow innocent. But the man beside her now was no innocent, and he watched her with eyes that were hot and hungry. He reached out his hand and she held her breath as he plucked the book from her frozen fingers, and tossed it to the floor. He held her captive with his

Judith James

eyes, intent and predatory, and his lips curved in a slow smile as he drew a path along the curve of her arm with his fingertip, gently skimming her skin through the thin material of her gown. Sensuous, unhurried, his wicked fingers traced the contours of her body, barely brushing her elbow, her shoulder, the curve of a breast, leaving delicious thrills of pleasure and anticipation in their wake.

Stunned, unable to move, she knew she was seeing a part of him she'd never seen before. She'd guessed at it, the first night they met in Madame's library; she'd seen a flash of it when he'd wanted to punish her and warn her away, but this was something else, *someone* else, and though she searched his familiar face, there was no trace of the man she'd come to know. She was bedazzled, unable to turn away as he shifted his body, moving closer, his fingers tracing her neckline now, stroking gently back and forth, hooking and tugging at her gown as her heart thudded in her chest and her body strained and ached, longing for his touch. She closed her eyes, fighting back tears as his clever fingers lightly brushed the swell of her breast, and then tightened around its bud. She gasped. Released from his spell and frightened by her own reactions, she tried to push him away. "No, Gabriel, stop!"

Lost in sensation, he was only dimly aware of her struggle, and it took him a moment to collect himself. When he did, lust was replaced by anger. What had she expected, inviting him to her bed? What had

126

he expected, that she'd welcome him? He'd known she'd be disgusted, but it wounded him, nonetheless. Well, he'd come for a kiss, and a kiss he'd have. Pulling her roughly beneath him, he held her hands above her head and plundered her mouth, claiming the prize he'd come for. Letting her go abruptly, he sat up, his back to her, and fought to master himself. He knew he should apologize. He knew he should leave. But at that moment, he was afraid to look at her and he was incapable of speech. They sat there for what seemed an eternity, lost in a sea of silence.

Finally she spoke, "One would think, with all your vast experience, you would make a better job of it."

He turned to look at her, and replied with a voice as cool as her own. "This is the second time you've complained of my kisses, mignonne. I shall be certain not to trouble you with them again." Rising from the bed, he moved toward the balcony, hesitated, and turned instead to sprawl on the window seat. Reaching for the wine flask, he took a swallow, grimaced, and leaned back tiredly, resting his head against the wall. She was still talking to him at least. He might as well wait until she threw him out.

Sarah noted with some satisfaction that this time he hadn't run away. She decided to reward him. "It wasn't the kiss I objected to, Gabriel. It was the manner in which it was delivered."

"What do you expect, mignonne? I *am* a prostitute, though we both choose to forget it at times."

127

"You *were* one," she allowed. "What does that have to do with it?"

He lifted his gaze to hers, overwhelmed by her innocence and saddened at the enormity of the gulf between them. "I am very fluent when it comes to sex, my dear, believe me." Looking away, he continued, "But kissing, well, it's something that lovers do, sweethearts, husbands and wives, not whores and their clients. It's far too intimate and personal, you see." He glanced her way again, with a hint of a smile. "You are, in fact, mignonne, the only woman I have ever kissed. I trust it was memorable at least. My apologies, mademoiselle," he sketched a mocking bow, "for botching the job."

Something sweet and painful pierced her breast. She looked at him, dissolute, debauched, and achingly beautiful. Vulnerable and alone, he challenged her with his humor and his pride. She thought him magnificent. Tears welled at the back of her eyes and she fought to contain them. He wouldn't appreciate her pity. "I'm honored," she said, ignoring his mockery.

Gabriel watched with puzzlement, then mounting alarm, as she threw back the covers and made her way across the icy floor, stopping an arm's length away. She reached out her fingers, lightly touching his jaw, and he hissed on indrawn breath. "Don't, mignonne," he pleaded. He grasped her hand gently, pushing it away. "No, Sarah," he whispered hoarsely.

"Then how will you learn to kiss me properly?" she

coaxed. "Let me show you, Gabe. It's just a kiss." Giving in to the hot urges and wild imaginings that plagued her every time she looked at his beautiful mouth, she took another step toward where he sat, splayed like some great jungle cat on her window seat.

Mesmerized, he made no further protest, no move to stop her.

Slowly, deliberately, she placed one hand on his shoulder to steady herself, and lifted her gown with the other, high enough to allow her to swing her leg to straddle him as she settled on his lap.

White-hot need shot through him, chasing away every trace of fatigue, every lingering doubt, or warning thought. His body jerked awake and he moaned low in his throat as he reached for her hips.

"Shhh," she quieted him, taking his hands and placing them on either side of the seat, "this is a kissing lesson, Gabriel. Will you promise to remember?"

"I will try, mignonne," he managed, but it felt more like torture, as he used his trembling hands to brace himself.

She shifted her weight in his lap, making him throb with blissful pain, his swollen member aching as she raised her hands from his shoulders to tangle them in his hair. "You have such beautiful hair," she murmured. "Like chocolate and honey, toffee, and cinnamon. When I first saw you, I thought of candy, and I wanted to taste you." He moaned in anticipation as she continued to stroke his hair, the back of his neck, nuzzling him with her lips, breathing soft against his cheek. Softly, gently, she kissed his brow. "Close your eyes, Gabriel."

He did, and felt her fingertips delicately tracing his face, his brow, his cheeks and jaw, the column of his throat. Her soft lips followed her gentle fingers, exquisite torture. Nibbling, nuzzling, they tugged on his ear and a bolt of desire, sharp as a knife, stabbed through his vitals as he rasped for breath. Christ! No one had ever . . . he'd had no idea . . . she had no idea what she was doing to him.

Unaccustomed to being hugged or kissed in tenderness, starved for affection, desperate to hold her closer, he tried to shift her, to move her beneath him, but she gripped his shoulders, pushing him back. "No, Gabriel, just kissing. You promised. Stay still, and let me kiss you." Her voice was warm, humming in his ear, interspersed with soft, moist kisses. It robbed him of breath and curled his toes. "Just enjoy it. You don't have to do anything. You don't have to go anywhere. Just relax."

Her voice bewitched him. Her tongue swirled hot in his ear and she nibbled his lobe, making him groan, but he did as she said, her kisses, her fingers, drugging him into a sweet surrender. He forgot where he was. Everything around him receded until there was only her whisper, her touch, her tender, aching kisses. After an eternity of intoxication and mad desire, her fingers bracketed his mouth and she finally, mercifully, brought her lips to his. Sobbing with relief and hunger, he clutched her wildly, his strong, skilled hands shaking as he pulled her closer, plundering her mouth, drinking her scent, and tasting her, sweet as sin. He plunged his tongue deep into her mouth, seeking her, finding her. They thrust and parried, the movement of lips, and tongue, and mouth, matched by that of their hips, grinding and rocking together.

He slowed then, and gentled. Not much experienced with kissing, he was nevertheless a sensual man. He'd thought it a curse until this moment. Now he surrendered to it, trusted it, softening his kiss as he stroked her lips with his tongue, dragging his full firm mouth back and forth across hers, gentle and slow, then hard and deep. Mouth, tongue, soft whispers and tender caresses, they continued long into the night, drugged and lost in each other.

It was Sarah who finally broke the spell. Pulling away with a shaky laugh, she laid her head against his shoulder and hugged him close. He gathered her tight in his arms and pulled her back against his chest, deep into the window seat with him, cradling her, warm under the blankets. "Sweet heaven . . . I . . . What was that?"

He had no words with which to answer her. He didn't know any more than she did. He'd never experienced anything as powerful in his entire life. All he knew was that his world had just been turned upside down and inside out, and nothing would ever be the same again. As the dawn broke over the horizon,

Sarah eased off him, slightly embarrassed, and though his hands were firm and gentle, supporting and guiding her as she stood upright in the morning gloom, he was unable to meet her eyes.

He rose to his feet, his legs so weak he could barely stand. "The sun's almost up," he said, cursing himself for being unable to find anything better to say, after receiving such a gift. "I . . . Davey will be waiting."

Her breath caught in her throat. He was blushing, awkward and vulnerable and clearly bewildered, not sure what he was supposed to do. How *did* you end a night like this? She didn't know herself. Impulsively she moved into his unresisting arms and hugged him fiercely, planting a firm kiss on his cheek. "Best you go then, Gabe. Thank you, for last night. I'm sorry about what I said before. You kiss like an angel!"

Ducking his head in embarrassment, absurdly pleased by her words, he managed a grunt and a slight squeeze in return, before beating a hasty retreat, back to the world of violence, flashing steel, and iron-hard control, back to somewhere safe.

Late that afternoon, tired from a sleepless night, muscles aching from a particularly grueling session with Davey, Gabriel hurtled down the beach, his horse's hoofs pounding through the surf, the damp cold invigorating him and clearing his head. Stopping by a large outcropping of rock, slick and accessible at low tide, he dismounted, and made his way over barnacles and shells to perch on the edge.

As the wind buffeted him, he closed his eyes and opened his senses. He listened to the dull rumble of the waves as they advanced and receded, hissing and sizzling and whispering deep secrets, and for the first time that day, he allowed himself to think of last night. His lips curled in a blissful smile. He felt like dancing, like singing. He felt as if he could fly. He thought of Sarah, and her laughing eyes, her welcoming smile, and her gentle touch. Her generosity astonished him. Everything he'd asked of her, she'd given freely, with openness and kindness. Kind, yes, but God, those kisses! They were the kind of kisses a woman gave her sweetheart. For the first time, he allowed himself to hope that maybe, as unlikely as it seemed, she was beginning to care for him in the same way he cared for her.

When he was younger, he used to pretend he'd been left at Madame's by accident, and pray that someone was looking for him, would come to find him soon and take him home. He'd learned the way of things quickly enough, and soon nothing could shock him. He'd stopped pretending, and he'd stopped praying after that. He'd looked for no mercy and held no expectations. Now he thanked a merciful God for sending him something so achingly sweet and beautiful as Sarah and her kisses, and he prayed earnestly that she would allow him to kiss her again.

She did. He kissed her often after that, every chance he got, slow, sweet kisses stolen under the moon and stars; hot, breathy kisses when he greeted her; and quick and furtive kisses in the kitchen, the stables, and on the stairs. He fully employed his talent for sensuality and seduction to master this new art, to fashion with slow hands and sweet mouth, a heady intoxicating communion each time his lips touched hers. He knew he pleased her, and it thrilled him when she moaned and clung to him, returning his passion with her own. It was joyous, innocent, a first for both of them, and each kiss became a memory, untarnished and pure, belonging only to them.

CHAPTER
12

Sarah watched Gabriel move as he practiced with Ross thrusting and parrying as the wind whipping his hair round his shoulders. The months of working with Davey had sculpted him. Powerful and lean, his body was corded, sleek with muscle and sinew, his stomach ridged and hard. He moved like a dancer, lithe, graceful, and deadly, and as she watched him, mesmerized, she unconsciously licked her lips.

"You like what you see, little cousin?" Davey whispered in her ear, startling her. Growling at him, her face a deep crimson, she didn't answer. With a knowing smile, he tugged on her hair and made to leave.

"Wait! Davey?"

"Yes, *querida*?"

"Do you . . . do *you* like him?"

He smiled sweetly. "Why, yes, cousin. I like him. I like him very much. But not as much as you do, I think." Giving her a wink, he moved away.

Over the next few weeks, the house filled with noise and laughter as Jamie returned home to celebrate Christmas. Cheerful and enthusiastic, he regaled them with stories of adventures with his new chums, pranks played on the stodgy schoolmaster, and the foolish escapades of Sidney's silly daughters. He'd grown in size and confidence over the past four months, and while he was clearly delighted to be home, there was a new reserve in his manner, reflecting his growing sense of himself as a young man, rather than a boy. Inclined to forget a past that had no place in his new life, caught up in the excitement, short memory, and endless joy of youth, the immediate was all that existed for him. He had friends his own age now, and for the moment at least, they were far more exciting to him than Gabriel, Ross, or Sarah.

Gabriel couldn't fail to note that Jamie no longer sought him out as he used to, and he wondered if he was becoming an embarrassment to the boy, an unwelcome remembrance of dark times. It reminded him that he was neither a guest nor a member of the family, but a paid employee whose services would not be required much longer. Stubbornly determined to enjoy whatever time he had with Sarah to the fullest, he buried all such hurts and fears, and let none of his worry show.

Over the course of the Yule, the house was decorated with greenery, and there were feasts, visits, dances, and much merrymaking with the townsfolk and the local gentry. Gabriel was surprised, embarrassed, and deeply moved when Ross and Davey presented him with the gift of a fine Toledo blade, made to match his height and reach. He was speechless when Sarah gave him a beautiful violin made by an old Gypsy fiddle master. He was embarrassed that he didn't have any gifts to give in return. He'd never celebrated any holiday before, hadn't known what to expect, and he'd certainly never been given gifts.

Sarah eased his discomfort by claiming he had given them the gift of music, and so it was that he found himself the center of attention at soirees and dances throughout the holidays, delighting family and guests with his artistry and skill. Not used to attention or applause, he found it distinctly discomfiting at first, but soon learned to manage a gracious, if somewhat terse reply, to the congratulations and admiring comments.

When Ross hosted a gathering of friends and neighbors for Twelfth Night, Gabriel was eagerly sought after by the local young ladies, much to his chagrin, and the household's amusement. Good-natured and polite, he danced with several country misses, providing more than one with fodder for dreams for years to come. He was, nevertheless, uncomfortable in such gatherings, and relieved when the season wound down and he could resume his training with Davey, his sparring with Ross, and his evenings with Sarah. His only regret was Jamie's return to Sidney's.

The quiet was welcome to everyone after the bustle of the holidays, and Davey and Ross sat enjoying a brandy in the library. Ross could see Gabriel and Sarah through the open door across the hall, heads bent close together as they played a duet on the violin. He couldn't fail but notice they were practically inseparable these days. Only half-attending one of Davey's scandalous stories, his glance flicked from his sister to his protégé.

To his credit, Gabriel appeared to be behaving like a gentleman, somewhat surprising under the circumstances. He was clearly considerate and respectful of her, and doubtless head over heels in love. As for Sarah, she practically glowed whenever he was in the vicinity. Ross sighed and rubbed his temples. The lad was badly damaged, entirely unsuitable, and he didn't want to see her hurt.

"They make a pretty pair, don't they? He's mad for your sister. You realize that, don't you, Ross?"

Ross blinked, giving Davey a sour look. He'd forgotten he was in the room. "He pants after her."

"Well, at least you know he's not a catamite."

"Blast you, man; that's not amusing!"

"It is to me. You're as ruffled and missish as some ancient spinster. She's been alone a long time, Ross. She's not found a man to interest her since that travesty of a marriage five years ago."

"I had thought, at one time, that perhaps you and she . . ."

"Ah, yes, well . . . these things happen. A man waits too long, you see, and some other fellow seizes the prize. She only has eyes for him. You're no more blind than I am."

Ross sighed. "I've feared it."

"Why? What's to fear? He's a likely lad, treats her well enough from what I can see."

"The thing is, Davey . . . he's not exactly what he seems. His circumstances, his background, through no fault of his own, have been horrendous. I fear he's been damaged . . . badly."

"Aye, well, so have we all, my friend. Life does that. What of it?"

"Christ, man, we found him in a brothel! He grew up there and he wasn't employed as the potboy or the cook. He'd been looking out for James, and Sarah insisted we bring him home with us."

"And so? The girl has good instincts and you've never been one to judge a man by what he can't help and had no part in creating. Or was he happy there?"

"No, I think not. I believe he stayed to protect Jamie."

"Hmm, so you owe him a significant debt, hence his welcome to your home."

"But not to my sister! I don't fault him for it, Davey, but if you knew the things he's been through . . . what he's done."

"Maybe I do; maybe I don't." Davey shrugged and poured himself another brandy, offering one to Ross. "What's your point?"

"I'm afraid he's damaged in ways that can't be mended, and that she'll have her heart broken trying."

"She's a woman, my friend, not a child, and a widow at that. It's for her to decide, isn't it?"

"I'm fairly certain that he's killed before."

"Well, heavens, Ross! So have we! It will certainly help with his training."

"You've had him for just over four months now. What do you make of him? Do you like him?"

"Aye, well enough, old friend. He's a good lad. Sharp as any I've trained. Hungry, curious, agile as a cat, and very quick to learn. I'd as lief have him at my back as any of my crew."

Ross's eyebrows raised in surprise. "High praise, indeed, Davey! He's that good?"

"Aye, brother, as good as you were at that age, and I reckon he'll be better than both of us before too long. I'll tell you something else. I know strength when I see it, Ross, and that boy has a core of steel. He seems decent enough to me, and not only because of what he did for Jamie. We've both seen lads no older than he is, born to fortune and privilege, given every opportunity, and what do they do with it? They debase themselves and others. Why? Because they're spoiled and bored. Because they can. Gabriel may have grown up in a hellhole, but I'll measure a man by how he's dealt with adversity, and from what I can see he's done all right for himself. He's a decent lad, Ross. More so than many I've met. If living a life like you say didn't destroy that, I can't imagine anything will."

Ross let out deep sigh. "You're right, Davey. I like the lad, too. It's just hard . . . one's sister. I daresay it would have alarmed me equally if she'd set her cap for you."

Davey threw back his head and roared with laughter. "Blast it, man! We need to find you a woman before you turn into a crotchety old crone. I swear! I am here to rescue you. Come, let us hie ourselves off to the widow Creswell's and lose ourselves in skirts and liquor."

"Aye, let's, but there's a matter I'd like to discuss first. It's come to my attention that there've been several smuggling runs recently."

"Indeed? And how did that come to your attention? Might it be the wine we had at dinner? Your afternoon tea? Or is it that cigar you're smoking?"

"I'm serious, Davey. I'm aware you've been taking

Gabriel with you, and I would rather you didn't."

"What? You've given him to me to train and you don't want me to take him to sea?"

Ross laughed. "You want to take him to sea? You mean you want to turn him into a smuggler, Davey, and introduce him to piracy, as well, no doubt."

"Tsk-tsk! Privateering, child. Do make an effort to get it right."

"Regardless, Davey, I didn't bring him here to have his head end up in a noose."

"The lad's learned a lot, Ross. He needs a chance to put it into practice. It won't hurt him to learn seamanship. He's not likely to be one of those pretty, puffed-up courtiers you see in London, prancing about with a sword dangling between their legs pretending it's their prick, sticking themselves with it and tangling it in the ladies' dresses. He'll be wanting a trade, and I can promise you he's not suited to being a bloody bookkeeper, or somebody's bailiff!"

"I say again, smuggling and piracy are not options."

"Well I'm sorry to hear you say that, and it's *privateering*, mind. The lad loves the water. He's at home on a ship, and he's an able seaman. I've a mind to promote him to midshipman soon. If he continues as he's begun he'll be a captain one day. You know as well as I what a nice prize can do to help a young fellow get a good start in life."

"Do you know, I've never quite understood exactly what kind of privateer you are, Davey. British?

French? American?"

"Well, now, that depends, doesn't it, Ross? When I'm down in the Americas . . . well, you don't want to know about that. If things become uncomfortable here, I may head back to the Mediterranean. It's proven to be a highly lucrative hunting ground in the past, and I've a letter of marquee against the French. Since the Corsican appears to have abandoned his fleet there in search of glory closer to home, it should prove an excellent time to pluck a juicy French prize or two. You should join me, Ross. It would do you good. You're reminding me more and more of my old spinster auntie these days."

"I'm done with all that, Davey. I've lost my taste for mayhem. It's a dangerous game you play, and you've no right to bring Gabriel into it. Lieutenant Brey is scouring the coast with the *Hind*, looking to make a name for himself. He intends to put an end to smuggling in this area, particularly since the murder of one of his men. You are well connected. If you were taken you might walk away, but the lad would be hung or transported. Leave off the smuggling for now. Take him with you when you're on legitimate business. Perhaps we can make him a merchant captain."

"If you would have my aid, I suggest you don't insult me. That popinjay, Brey, and his slovenly scow are no match for the *L'Espérance*, and well you know it. I'll be hoping to pluck a juicy French pullet or two come spring, but in the meantime, the free trade with

Guernsey is fat and lucrative enough to pay my men and fund their retirements. You're doing well enough by it yourself. The lad's of age and he has no wish to be beholden, Ross, and as much as I value your opinion, I will do my training as I see fit."

"Times are changing, Davey. You weren't here last year when those fools on the *Lottery* murdered a customs officer. It was a bad business, soured things all the way around. Those who used to turn a blind eye, or take their cut took it personally. I've met this fellow, Brey. He's no fool, and you'd be wise not to underestimate him."

"Ross, my boy, let's not argue. I promise you I'll think on it, but for now, what say we put it aside in favor of a warm woman and a cold beer."

"Aye. A man has needs. Give me a moment to finish this cigar and I'll join you."

"Fair enough. I'll check on the children, shall I?" Davey wandered out to the music room to join Sarah and Gabriel while he waited.

Ross watched them thoughtfully through the open door. His thoroughly unconventional widowed innocent of a sister was deep in conversation with a beautiful, doe-eyed and deadly ex-prostitute, and a charming, roguish, undeniably attractive sea-captain-cum-smuggler-cum-pirate. Ah, well. He shrugged his shoulders, readying himself to leave. If anyone tried to harm her, they'd be filleted and fried before they hit the ground, and with that, he must be content.

CHAPTER 13

Whatever notice Davey took of Ross's warnings, it didn't stop him from the lucrative free trading that kept his ship at the ready and his crew content. Gabriel had been out to sea several times now. On occasion they were gone for several days, flitting back and forth across the channel running wool from England to France, stealing back from Guernsey under cover of night with shipments of brandy, gin, and tobacco. He'd grown familiar with the system of caves and tunnels that made this stretch of coast a smuggler's paradise, and a nightmare to the many ships that foundered on her reefs. His cool head, quick wit, and willingness to lend a hand won him the respect of Davey and the crew, and promotion to midshipman, and his lessons now included navigation, nautical astronomy, and trigonometry. As his lessons in seamanship and swordplay continued apace, he found himself responding to the approval in Davey's eyes with a growing sense of accomplishment and pride.

Bright and teasing, ferocious and deadly, cobalt, silver, or phosphorescent green, Gabriel loved the ocean in all her changing facets, but Sarah claimed his soul. She was never far from his thoughts, and the adventures that fueled his days came truly alive when he was able to share them with her. Having spent almost two years with Davey and his men, Sarah had her own stories to tell of exotic ports and wild nights of music and dancing on faraway shores. Although she loved the ocean as much as Gabriel did, she'd known little joy at the time, consumed in those dark days by guilt, her grief for her parents and Ross, and her fears for Jamie. As she listened to Gabriel tell his stories, she found the old longing and excitement return, and it didn't take much for him to convince her to accompany them on some of their shorter jaunts, much to the delight of Davey and his crew.

Training, sailing, kissing and talking with Sarah, everything seemed to be going well for Gabriel as winter edged to spring. He was at a loss to understand why his dreams, which for several months now had receded to the odd or occasional nightmare, had returned to haunt him with a vengeance. He dreamt of de Sevigny, cold and terrible in his anger, waking him from his sleep, *Réveille toi, mon ange,* determined to punish him, mark him, debase him for daring to leave, then passing him to his friends as a thing of no value. He dreamt of cruel hands holding him down, strong arms binding him tight, and brutal invasion. He dreamt of blood and savage hatred, and once he dreamt he was walking on the moon and could see the earth, impossibly beautiful, bright with warmth and light, far in the distance, beyond his reach as he wandered a stark landscape, frigid and completely alone.

Some nights he didn't dream at all, but lay in bed awake, contemplating his future, sick dread knotted in his chest. With the coming of spring his contract with Ross would be complete and there'd be no reason for him to stay. Jamie had adjusted to his new circumstances so well no one would ever have guessed he hadn't been raised in them. He didn't need Gabriel anymore. In truth, they hadn't spent more than a few hours together over the past six months.

He knew he should be making plans regarding where he would go and what he'd do with his money, but thinking about it made him decidedly uncomfortable. He didn't discuss it with Ross, fearing to remind him, worried it might hasten his departure, something he was finding increasingly difficult to imagine. He'd come to feel he belonged here, but he wasn't some distant relation or a friend of the family, and it would soon be time for him to go. He was being handsomely paid and he'd be able to

Judith James

arrange his life as he pleased. He should consider himself fortunate, but all he wanted was to stay with Sarah.

February turned into March and he became taciturn and withdrawn, much as he'd been upon his arrival. As restless nights continued taking their toll, Sarah asked him repeatedly if there was anything wrong but he denied it, unwilling to have his nightmares and worries intrude on the time they had left.

Despite his denials, Sarah *was* worried. He had a bruised and haunted look she was seeing more frequently. Tonight, when he'd come to her room, pulling her down beside him on the window seat, his delicious kiss had been extravagant and lush, tasting of brandy and tobacco. He had that fragile, bitter edge she'd noted before when he drank to excess, something he seemed to be doing more often after a period of relative abstinence. "Tell me what's bothering you, Gabriel," she pleaded. "I know there's something. You're so quiet these days, and you seem so far away."

"I'm sorry, mignonne. It's nothing… really. I'm merely tired, and a little stiff and sore." He shifted, easing his back and twisting his neck.

"Here, let me." Moving to stand behind him, she began a gentle, rhythmic stroking.

Startled, his first instinct was to resist, but it felt too damn good, and he found himself leaning back into her touch.

"Is Davey overworking you, Gabe? Perhaps Ross should speak to him?"

"*Non*, mignonne . . . Jesus, that feels good!"

She deepened her strokes, her deft fingers kneading and soothing, relaxing taut muscles. He groaned with pleasure as she moved her hands from his neck to his shoulders. "Perhaps you're spending too much time here and not getting enough sleep. Maybe you should take to your bed early for a few nights."

"Christ, no!" he said, twisting away from her. "This is the only place I find any peace at night, *chère*."

He offered no resistance as she reached for his shoulders and drew him back against her, her hands resuming their magic. The silence continued for several minutes, punctuated by occasional blissful groans of pleasure as muscles, stiff from hard work, eased and loosened. After a time, she wrapped her arms around his shoulders and leaned her chin atop his head. "Now, tell me what's bothering you," she coaxed.

Eyes closed, Gabriel savored the feeling as she traced his cheekbones with her fingertips. Ignoring the question, he turned his face into her palm, kissing her fingers, catching them with his lips as he drew them one by one into his mouth, sucking and teasing with his hot, wet tongue. Shivers went through her, and she leaned into him, soft and feverish. He opened his eyes, heavy-lidded, and looked at her with raw hunger. Moaning, she sought his lips, tugging at his loose shirt, trying to pull it off his shoulders, wanting the feel of his skin. Unthinking, white-hot with need, drunk with alcohol and desire, he helped her.

Sarah gasped with shock and pity. A distant part of her brain noted with dull surprise that she'd never before seen him without a shirt on. Now she understood why. His back was laced with scars from whippings, beatings, cuts, and burns. She raised her eyes to his and they glittered back, cold, angry, and very dangerous. He stood without a word, reaching for his shirt and jerking it from her hands, and then she saw his wrists.

"Oh, my God, Gabriel! What happened to you? And what have you done to yourself?" She reached for his arm but he twisted away. His wrists were criss-crossed with scars, most of them old and long-healed, but there was an angry red line on his right wrist that must have been put there recently, perhaps this very evening. Shocked at the depths of despair that might drive a man to mutilate himself that way, she considered, for the first time, that he might really be beyond her reach, that he was far more dangerous than she'd imagined, and needed far more help than she could offer.

Gabriel felt as if he was going to be sick. Shame and humiliation twisted his guts. He'd never meant her to know, taken care that she wouldn't see. He'd always worn a shirt, covering his back and wrists on even the hottest of days. She'd made him forget himself, and her reaction had been everything he'd feared: horror, pity, and disgust. As he fought to control himself, he felt a rush of cold rage against everyone who had ever used him, against a god indifferent to his fate, and against her.

An icy calm enveloped him. "Come now, mignonne," he drawled. "I thought you knew. Did I neglect to tell you? Perhaps I did. It was one of the more unsavory parts of a childhood we both like to pretend I never had."

"Tell me," she whispered hoarsely.

He reached for the flagon of wine she kept by the window seat and downed half of it, wiped his lips on the back of his hand, then sat, cross-legged, insouciant, and dangerous, on the edge of her bed. "What do you want to know, my dear? Shall I tell you there are those who take pleasure from another's pain and humiliation, those who will pay to watch it, or to inflict it themselves? I was a whipping boy, my dear, before I was a whore. And surely I told you about de Sevigny, how angry I made him."

"I . . . I didn't know. I didn't realize . . . I had no idea."

He stood up and began to walk toward her, an air of menace surrounding him. He stopped in front of her, eyes glazed, muscles rigid, breath harsh and shallow. "Did you take a good look, mignonne? I confess I was caught up in the moment, and forgot what an innocent you are. To most of my clients, such marks add a certain . . . spice, to the proceedings. Certainly none of them seemed to mind. You didn't know? You didn't realize? You had no idea? Then it's past time you did. I've certainly tried to tell you, but as you're so slow to comprehend, let me be perfectly clear. I've been trained to please a man or a woman, with mouth, and hands, and tongue, anyway they might desire. I've been taken and used in every way imaginable."

He grabbed her wrist and pulled her close, whispering soft and husky in her ear. "I've dressed as a woman, mignonne. I can make myself appear as pretty and desirable as you." He nibbled on her earlobe as she stood frozen in place, and then nipped hard, making her jerk against him. Grasping her hand, he forced her fingernails to cut a jagged scratch across his heaving chest "I can also take pain, and turn it into pleasure,"

Freed from whatever spell she'd been under, she fought to pull away. He released her abruptly and she stumbled back, massaging her wrist.

"*Voilà*," he said, spreading his arms out wide. Do you understand *now*? *This* is what I am, mignonne. This is *who* I am. Now you know. Neither of us should ever forget it."

"And what of those, Gabriel?" she asked him, pointing to his wrists. "No one did *that* to you. You made those marks yourself, didn't you? Why? Why would you do such a thing?"

He blinked and stumbled. "Damn you, Lady Munroe! Why must you be such an interfering bitch? You can never leave well enough alone. What will you do when I leave? Who will you have to torture?" He reached for the abandoned wineskin and sketched an elaborate bow. *"Au revoir, ma belle.* Sleep well. May flights of angels sing thee to thy rest, et cetera, et cetera."

She had no words for him, shocked and confused, stunned by his barely controlled violence and shaken by the scars on his wrists. She was sorry she had asked, sorry she had opened old wounds, and sorry he had told her. He left, as he'd come, over the balcony and out into the night, and all she felt was relief.

CHAPTER
14

Gabriel made his way down to the beach, drinking from the wineskin with no expectation of relief. He was hollow inside, and the wine did nothing to fill his emptiness. It had little power over him now, did nothing to soothe the ragged edges of his soul. What does a man do when his medicine no longer works, when nothing eases his pain?

The tide was coming in, and the surf sizzled wildly, matching the wildness in his heart. The wind caught at his hair, whipping long strands against his cheeks and mouth. The sky glittered overhead, and the moonlight shone across the bay, bathing the night in an opalescent, silver glow, making it appear as beautiful and empty as the face of a porcelain doll. It reminded him of the night, almost a year ago, when he'd awaited her arrival.

Well, here he was now, by the sea, as he'd always wanted. The boy was safe and happy. It was past time to leave. What kind of idiot had he been to imagine, even for a moment, that there was any other way? Moving from a back alley, to a brothel, to a country estate, didn't change what he was, but God curse it, why did he have to tell her? What sick, sad compulsion had driven him to reveal any of it?

Because you're lonely, he answered himself. So damned tired of being alone. Well, he'd guaranteed it now. Milady sunshine, Sarah, had been suitably shocked, and in fairness, one had to admit she didn't shock easily. At least now she knew. There were no more illusions left for either of them.

Tilting back his head with a bitter laugh, he tipped the bottle and let the remainder of the wine drain down his throat before abandoning the empty container in the sand. The wind had picked up. Clouds studded the sky and moonlight illuminated the jagged rocks along the shore. His skin pricked with excitement, and he was filled with a curious elation. Bending down to remove his boots, he continued along the beach, closer and closer to the water until he stood in it, knee-deep. The cold seared him, sharp as a knife. He winced in pain before deliberately closing his eyes and submitting to it, waiting until he could feel the sensual pull of the surf as it tugged at his ankles, caressing and coaxing, drawing him farther, one step, then another.

Caught in its spell, he swayed with the waves, embraced by the cold sea and the cool night air. Looking out, he could see clouds of phosphor and foam. He took another step forward, wanting to be a part of the great mystery frothing and humming around him. He wanted to swim, as far and as long as he could, half-convinced that if he had the courage, if he was strong enough and swam far enough, he might reach some distant shore where he'd find welcome and peace.

"Gabe? Gabriel?" Her voice floated above the water, insistent and concerned. "Gabe?" a little sharper now, cutting clearly through the hiss and swoosh of surf on sand. He turned slowly in her direction, swaying with the force of the water, confused, as if he didn't recognize her.

"It's beautiful, isn't it? Grander than any cathedral."

He answered her with a bemused nod.

Barefoot, holding her ridiculous nightgown above the waves as best she could, she stepped into the water, hissing with pain. She held out her hand. "Come. Let's go for a walk."

He watched her in silence, his haunted eyes distant and confused.

"Gabriel, please come. I'm freezing!"

He extended his hand slowly, until the tips of his fingers brushed hers. A frisson pulsed through him, starting his heart pounding.

Entwining her fingers through his, Sarah took him in a firm grip and tugged him toward the shore. "Let's walk," she said again.

He looked into her eyes, startled, focused now, and managed a sardonic salute with his free hand. "As my lady commands."

She smiled as he stepped from the water, and something strung bow-tight inside her, eased. He was back. Back from whatever dark and faraway place had tried to claim him. She didn't release her grip on his hand as they walked back toward the house, not even as he bent to retrieve his boots.

"You followed me, mignonne?"

"No, Gabriel. I felt like a stroll and a quick dip in my bedclothes on a freezing night. Of course, I followed you, you dolt! You're lucky you didn't break your neck coming down here drunk as a—"

"Why?" he rasped.

"You frightened me," she said simply. "I didn't like the way you looked, as if you were lost, not really there. I was worried about you. I also wanted to apologize. I had no right to pry, Gabe. I keep saying I'm going to stop, yet somehow I never do. I *am* sorry."

"Don't," he pleaded. "Please, Sarah, don't . . . I . . ." he struggled to find words, to let her know how grateful he was that she'd cared enough to come after him. No one, except Jamie, had ever given a damn if he lived or died. It meant everything.

Sarah squeezed his hand, then wound her arm through his and pulled him closer. "You're shivering. Let's get you back before you catch your death." Leaning into him, she tried to share what little warmth she had. She could feel the rapid beat of his heart, the blood pulsing through his arm, vibrant and alive, but his skin was clammy and cold. He smelled of wind and sea and she wanted to kiss him, to slap and shake him. Impulsively, she stopped and flung her arms around his neck, pulling his head down into a scorching kiss, before pushing him away. "Fool! Idiot! Stupid, stupid man! What were you thinking? Don't ever frighten me that way again! Promise me!"

"I promise," he whispered, soft against her lips. He returned to her room, by the stairs this time, lips blue, and shivering with cold. Businesslike and efficient, she tossed him a blanket and turned to stoke the fire, briskly ordering him to remove his wet clothes and get into the bed. He did as he was told, climbing onto her bed with the blanket wrapped around him for modesty's sake as she spread his wet clothes in front of the fire.

"Under the covers, Gabe," she said, pulling the blankets back and plumping the pillows. Warming a glass of brandy in her hands, she came to sit beside him on the bed. "Drink this." Her fingers soothed his brow.

Gabriel was chilled to the bone, and shudders racked his body, but he was enjoying the novel experience of being taken care of. He swallowed the fiery liquid and settled into the nest she'd made for him, turning onto his side, and closing his eyes to avoid her gaze.

Concerned that his shivering continued unabated, Sarah dropped her sodden nightdress on the floor and crawled under the blankets to warm him. With only the sheet between them, she pulled him tight against her, vigorously rubbing his shoulders, arms, and back, as his body shivered with cold and delayed shock.

She'd been relieved when he'd left her chamber, overwhelmed by his pain and frightened by the anger and the barely controlled violence that simmered beneath his surface. She'd also glimpsed the desolation in his eyes, and had been terrified at the thought of what he might do, alone and lost, this night. She clutched him tighter, her nose pressed into his damp hair, glad she'd followed her instincts, glad to have him close and safe beside her, feeling as if she'd won some battle, snatched him back from the hands of some unseen, malevolent, and utterly merciless foe.

Gabriel relaxed against her as the room warmed, and the brandy and her heat began to chase the chill from his body. Speaking into the silence, he answered the question she'd asked him a lifetime ago. "Sometimes I feel nothing at all, Sarah. Sometimes I feel so empty I think I'm dead. When I feel the pain, when I see the blood, I know that I'm alive."

Hugging him tight, she answered, sweet and husky in his ear, "If you feel like that ... *When* you feel like that, come and see me, and I'll give you a kiss that will curl your toes and you'll know damn well you're alive, Gabe."

With a soft laugh, he pulled her hand to his lips and kissed it, and then placed it snug against his heart.

"What did you mean, earlier? When you said you were leaving?"

He shifted uncomfortably, and sighed. "I'll be gone from here in two months, mignonne, a little less."

Alarmed, she pulled herself up, leaning over him, trying to read his face in the dim light. "Gone? Why would you leave? Where would you go? I thought you liked it here. I thought you were happy."

He did. He was. "I don't know yet, Sarah. I haven't given it much thought. London, perhaps."

"I don't understand. Why do you want to leave us, Gabe?"

"I don't."

"Then why would you?" she asked, resting her hand on his shoulder.

"I signed an agreement with your brother, Sarah. It's March already, and our agreement ends in May. He'll not want me here after that. That's always been understood."

"By who? I want you here," she said, relaxing and giving him a hug as she settled back against him, "and you're wrong about Ross. He wants you here, too. He can be a little high-handed, and I don't suppose he felt the need to discuss it with you. He just assumed you'd learn to like it and would want to stay. He and Davey have great plans for you. Davey wants you to be a privateering adventurer, and Ross would have you a respectable merchant sea captain. They bicker over you like little old ladies."

"Really?" he asked, startled.

"Oh, yes. It's quite comical. Oh, Gabriel! Is that what's been bothering you? I'm so sorry! I thought you knew."

"I had no idea," he whispered.

Drawing him closer, she murmured in his ear, "This is your home now, Gabriel. We're your family now. Don't run away from us."

Warm in her arms, warmed by her words, he fell into a deep and healing sleep. He awoke the next morning, naked and snug in her bed. His arms were wrapped around her, their limbs were tangled together, and his face was buried in her hair. Disoriented, he tried desperately to trace the route that had placed him there. When memory flooded him, his face turned hot with embarrassment. His sex stirred, turgid and aching, and he fought the urge to rub it, rock-hard, against her bottom. It would be a poor return for her care of him last night. He gritted his teeth and carefully extricated himself, trying not to wake her.

It was the first good sleep he'd had in weeks. Yawning and stretching in the chill morning air, he reached for his clothes. He looked back at her fondly as he pulled them on. She looked like a lost waif, curled in the big bed by herself. Despite his embarrassment, a heavy weight had been lifted from him, and he had no idea how to thank her.

When Sarah awoke an hour later, she smiled to see that he'd lit a fire for her, and fetched her night-gown from where she'd left it to dry. He had truly frightened her last night. He might have drowned in those frigid waters, accidentally, or on purpose. She'd been too much the coward to ask. All she'd wanted was to bring him back and keep him safe. Now she wondered what to do. Common sense, warred with instinct and desire, telling her that by allowing Gabriel into her room, into her bed, she was risking more than discovery and the good opinion of people she cared about; she risked breaking both their hearts.

She knew he was falling in love with her. He'd known little of pleasure, nothing of kindness, and he had a heartbreakingly distorted view of himself. He was likely to fall in love with anyone who showed him warmth and acceptance, because he didn't know or understand his own worth. Trying to be honest, she admitted she'd wanted him from the first moment she'd seen him in Madame Etienne's library. His kisses melted her inside and out, leaving her hot and heavy and wanting more, but he'd known a surfeit of lust and sex, was intimately familiar with it, and she worried it wasn't a lover he needed; it was a friend.

He was so vulnerable, had taken so many chances

by opening up to her. Well, damn it! Who else would take the time to know him, to appreciate and value all that he was? Who would have a greater care for his heart than she did? She had grown to care for him far too much, and he had grown to trust her. The depths of his hurt and anger frightened her at times, as did the depths of her feelings for him, but she'd gone much too far to pull back now, not without wounding him terribly. For better or worse, they were embarked on a journey together. Her heart refused to abandon him, and her instincts told her he was worth any risk. There was nowhere to go, but forward.

CHAPTER
15

When Gabriel came, hesitant to her room the next night, he made for the window seat as was his habit of late, but Sarah patted the bed beside her. Needing no encouragement, he eased himself alongside her, gathering her into his arms and kissing her soundly. Last night hadn't been a dream then. She knew more about him than anyone did, and here he was, back in her bed, back in her arms, kissing her. Shifting position to pull her underneath him, he let out an involuntary groan as a spasm of pain seized his back. He'd been practicing like a demon over the past few months, partly to hone his skill, but mostly because it allowed him to escape from his worries, and his fears.

"You've been overdoing things, Gabriel," Sarah chided, pushing him away. "You'll do yourself a serious injury, if you're not more careful."

"Nonsense, my sweet. It's all your fault. You're aging me before my time."

Sitting up, she tugged at his collar. "Take off your

shirt. I can help you like I did last night."

"I'm fine, *chère*, and last night, as I recall, was rather a mixed blessing."

"Fine, have it your way. If you'd rather be stiff and sore than let me help you, that's your choice."

He supposed there was some lesson she meant him to learn, but he wasn't in a mood to be schooled. Nevertheless, after several minutes of pointed silence, he sat up suddenly and tore off his shirt. "*There*, woman, are you happy now? Have a good look." He lay down again, on his stomach as she'd asked, sullen, his back clearly exposed to her view as it hadn't been last night.

He flinched and stiffened as her fingertips traced his scars, brushing gently down his back. She worked slowly, easing knotted muscle with deep, smooth strokes, pulling and pushing to release the tension gathered there. She moved her hands lower as she felt him begin to relax, working the muscles in his lower back, her movements slow and sure as she allowed her fingers to feel him, to tell the difference between, and respond carefully to, the tension in his muscles, and that in his soul.

As her fingers worked their magic, something deep inside Gabriel loosened and relaxed. Her touch was calming, healing, and it lulled him gently into sleep.

He woke to an empty bed. She was sitting on the window seat, legs curled under her, head bent toward the candlelight, lost in one of her books. He allowed himself the pleasure of watching her as she bit her lip in concentration and tapped her fingers impatiently. Something she read was annoying her, he thought with a grin. He watched her fingers, fascinated as they turned the pages, gentle fingers, skillful fingers. He remembered them trailing down his back, and closed his eyes, imagining them circling his waist, stroking his belly. His body tensed again, this time with hunger. Shivering, he drew a ragged breath and opened his eyes, meeting her gaze.

She greeted him with a sunny smile. "Welcome back, Gabe."

He allowed himself a grunt, unwilling to turn over or to speak, the evidence of his arousal pronounced and unmistakable.

"Feeling better?"

He twisted his neck and shoulders, and then stretched from his head to his toes, ending with a groan of pleasure. Her fingers were magic. His aches were gone and he felt peaceful and content. He reached for a pillow to plump beside him before turning to face her. "Much better, mignonne. I swear you must be a witch, no, a goddess, like your namesake."

She closed her book and moved back to the bed, climbing under the covers to get warm. He pulled her into his arms and kissed her, the layers of blankets, covers, and clothes between them giving them both a sense of innocence, allowing them to indulge their senses.

Much later, breathless and dizzy, Sarah ventured

a question, "Gabe?"

"Mmmm?"

"Is there anything else you need to tell me?"

After a moment's silence, he sighed and rolled over on his back. "You know most of it, mignonne, more than anyone else."

"I just want to be sure you know you can tell me anything."

Silence stretched between them, the void filled with the sound of the surf, crashing against the rocks below. "What if I told you I'd killed a man?"

"It wouldn't make you different from many other men I know."

"What if I said I cut his throat and left him to die in an alley?"

"I would want to know why. Ross has killed before, several times, but he won't talk about it. He was a soldier, of course, and I told you about my uncle." She leaned into him, resting her arm on his chest, absently tracing his collarbone with her fingertips. "Davey's killed and he *does* talk about it. If it troubles you, you might want to discuss it with him."

He looked at her in amazement. "Does nothing shock you, Sarah?"

"Yes, of course! I'm shocked at what some people will do to children, to the helpless . . . Whom did you kill, Gabriel, and why?"

Gripping her hand, he clenched it tight against his chest, suddenly awash with memories. The taste and scent of fear and blood were acrid in his nostrils, coppery and dank on his tongue. His heart drummed faster as memories of ice-cold rage and bloodlust washed through him. "It was just a few months before you came for your brother. He was a German, a wealthy merchant from Brest." His voice was flat, devoid of emotion, but he gripped her hand like a vise, bringing tears to her eyes. "He was one of de Sevigny's cronies. He frequented Madame's when he was in Paris. He started coming more and more often. I was with him one night, in the salon when Jamie walked in looking for me."

Sarah gasped.

"We weren't . . . we were just talking. I chased Jamie out, but it was too late. I could see it, the interest and the hunger. He started asking questions, making offers to Madame. I could see her weighing it. What cost this? What cost that? He kept coming, asking. You don't want to know this, Sarah."

"Gabriel, tell me!" she said, frantic and sick with dread. "What happened? What happened to Jamie? I have to know!"

"Shhh," he released her hand and gathered her close, stroking her back, his voice colored by emotion again as he tried to soothe her. "Nothing happened to him, Sarah. He had a fright. That's all. I was going to my room and I heard noises. I thought I heard Jamie's voice. I went to check on him, and that piece of shit was there with his hands on him."

"Oh, God!"

Gabriel hugged her tighter. "He was too fucking drunk to do anything but scare him, mignonne. That's all. I swear. I got there in time. I . . . I was in the habit of carrying a knife. I don't know, something came over me . . . a rage . . . I put my hand over his mouth and dragged him out into the alley and cut his throat, Sarah, without a second thought. I didn't want Jamie to see, but he followed me, he saw the body. He knew what I'd done. I think that shocked him more than anything else. I can still see it. His eyes were huge and he couldn't stop shaking. As for the rest of it, I don't think he really understood what was going on, thank God."

They clung together, taking comfort from one another, as he continued, "I took care of things. It's not hard to dispose of a body in Paris at night, and I made Jamie promise never to tell. I told him it would be my head, if he did. I'm sorry, mignonne. If Jamie carries scars from Madame Etienne's, they're because of me."

"No! He was very lucky to have you, Gabriel."

"I didn't have to kill him. I could have left him in the alley, guarded Jamie more carefully, but I wanted to. I knew he'd keep coming. I . . . I enjoyed it, Sarah."

"Good! I would have done the same! You did well, as far as I'm concerned, and I pray you never lose sleep over it again."

Ruffling her hair, he gave her shoulder a little

push. "*Bon Dieu*, what a bloodthirsty wench you are! Remind me not to cross you. But it's not that easy, *chère*, to kill a man. One thinks about it a great deal more after the fact, than when it happens."

"I don't doubt it, Gabe. Talk to Davey; it will help."

"Thank you, mignonne, perhaps I will." Letting go of her, he rose and stretched, twisting, and adjusting his neck and shoulders as the rosy glow of dawn crept tentatively into the room. He was surprised at how good he felt. The aches and pains of his body had succumbed to her magic fingers, and those of his heart . . . well, confession was said to be good for the soul. Turning to take his leave, he was struck by how pale she looked. Crouching down by the bed, he stroked her hair. "Are you all right, Sarah? *Merde!* I need to learn to keep my mouth shut. Not all secrets need to be told."

Smiling she reached out and touched his cheek, his lips. "The dark ones do, Gabe. They keep people apart, and it's only by telling that they lose their power."

He realized he had no secrets left from her. She'd taken them from him, claiming them one by one, and then she'd claimed him, giving him everything he'd ever dreamed of, a home, a family, a friend . . . someone to love. His heart filled to overflowing. Taking her hands in both of his, he leaned in and kissed her tenderly. "I love you, Sarah," he whispered. He hadn't been thinking, or he'd never have risked it, but she didn't turn away.

With a radiant smile and eyes full of tenderness, she threw her arms around him, hugging him fiercely, and said words no one had ever spoken to him before. "Oh, Gabriel! I love *you!*"

He knelt there by her bed as she rocked him in her arms. Overcome by emotion, they didn't speak, they didn't kiss, they just held one another, neither of them wanting to let go, but too soon they had no choice. The day was almost upon them, and the house was beginning to stir.

"God, Sarah! I don't know if I can leave you," he said, his voice unsteady. "There's so much I want to say to you . . . to tell you . . . I—"

"Shhh," she whispered, kissing his lips. "You can tell me tonight." Her eyes were warm and full of promise.

His lit with hope and joy. "Yes, mignonne. We'll talk . . . I'll tell you . . . tonight." Exultant, Gabriel left her room, seeking out Davey, seeking out something, anything, to pass the hours until he was warm in her arms again.

Sarah lay in bed, eyes wide open, long after he left. She felt a connection with him so deep it transcended anything she'd ever known. She loved him. She had always loved him. At some level she had recognized it, and she had recognized him, the moment she'd first seen him standing, proud and wounded, in Madame

Etienne's library. She felt frightened and exhilarated, as if she stood on a cliff edge, poised to fly. She didn't know what would happen next, but she knew that things would never be the same.

She thought about what he'd told her last night, still horrified at how close Jamie had come to something vile, to being changed forever, his innocence stolen, his trust in the world, and himself, destroyed. But he'd had a protector. At last, she fully understood, viscerally, in her stomach, and her heart and her lungs, what Gabriel had tried so hard to tell her. "Oh, my God!" she moaned aloud, hugging herself. For him there had been no protector, no one to save him, not ever.

She cried for him, for the childhood he'd never had, and the pain and sorrow he'd endured, alone and friendless. She cried out of pity she knew he wouldn't thank her for, and with gratitude, that somehow, through some source of inner strength, he'd managed to survive it and become the decent, sensitive, remarkable man she'd fallen in love with. She vowed he would never find himself alone or friendless again.

Later that afternoon, exhausted from his labors, his body clamoring for sleep after all the restless nights he'd spent worrying about leaving, Gabriel excused himself from his duties, and crawled into his own neglected bed for an uncharacteristic afternoon's sleep. He dreamed, of course, of the German, of blood-bursting veins and white-hot rage, of the guilt when he saw himself, savage and half-mad, reflected in the stricken eyes of a small boy. In the midst of it she came. She stood behind him and wrapped her arms around him, whispering to him and drawing out his pain, lifting him effortlessly from the blood-splattered alley, and carrying him away with her to a deep and peaceful sleep.

CHAPTER
16

Gabriel awoke refreshed and eager for nightfall. Sarah had said she loved him. There was little about him she didn't know. He wasn't sure she really understood what he'd tried to tell her. He found it hard to believe she could love him, want him, or allow him to touch her if she fully understood, but he hadn't lied to her, or hidden anything from her. He'd been as honest as he knew how, and if she chose to ignore certain things, or to pretend he was something better than he was, he wasn't going to argue. He wouldn't allow himself to plan or hope beyond the present, but he was going to enjoy every moment with her he could steal.

He didn't get to see her that evening. Davey had need of his help. A quantity of British wool had arrived unexpectedly, and was waiting in a secluded cove to be exchanged for a small fortune in brandy and tea. They slipped away under cover of darkness, catching the night breeze and cutting silently through the still waters of the bay. Once they were well underway, Gabriel gathered his courage and sought out Davey on the quarterdeck.

"'Tis a fine evening, is it not, lad?" Davey welcomed him with a merry grin. "I smell profit and adventure in the air tonight. You've something else on your mind, though, I think. Spit it out."

"There's a private matter I'd like to discuss with you, Davey, when you have the time."

"No time like the present, my boy. This lovely lady is well underway. Come with me to my cabin. We'll share a brandy and you can tell sweet Davey all your troubles." The fellow looked as skittish as a cat in a roomful of rockers, Davey thought with a grin. He directed him to a comfortable chair in front of his desk, and poured them each a brandy. Amused, expecting some breathless revelation about his feelings for Sarah, he was a little taken aback when Gabriel finally blurted out his business.

"I killed a man, Davey, just over a year ago, almost in front of Jamie. I dream about it all the time. Sarah says . . . she said I should talk to you about it."

"Do tell." Davey sat back in his chair, crossing his ankles on the desk, and sipped his brandy as he watched his pupil intently. *Sarah says. So that's the way of it,* he thought. "Pray continue, lad."

Gabriel told him about the German, his obvious interest in Jamie, and how he'd found him attempting to molest the boy. He was a little more candid with

Davey than he'd been with Sarah about some things, and less so about others. The result was the same. He'd killed a man in the throes of rage, and he'd enjoyed it.

Davey closed his eyes, nodding his head as Gabriel spoke, as if listening to some internal music. He stopped when Gabriel finished his story, and took a sip of brandy, motioning for his protégé to do the same. He considered a moment before responding. "A man may kill for many reasons, Gabriel. To defend himself or his country, to protect that which is his; his holdings, his woman, or those who depend on him; to avenge an injustice . . . some fools even kill to avenge their honor over any slight, real or imagined." He shrugged. "Generally we accept these reasons as just and worthy. Others kill for greed or gain, out of anger or jealousy, even for pleasure or sport. I've been a mercenary, lad, and I've seen men kill and be killed, for all these reasons." He swung his legs down and leaned forward across the desk, one finger absently circling the rim of his glass. "Sometimes it's a cold-blooded business, and other times it's not. Sometimes a man hates. It's easy to kill when you hate, and there's joy in it."

He looked directly into Gabriel's eyes. "You killed to protect your own. There's no shame in that, but if you took pleasure in it, I suspect you must have hated him a great deal." He shrugged his shoulders, still fingering the glass. "Nevertheless, it didn't drive you to kill him until he put his hands on the boy. I wouldn't worry about it overmuch. For what it's worth, I'd have done the same. Still . . . a word to the wise, Gabriel, eh? Hatred is a powerful thing. It crawls up inside a man when he's empty, filling him, pretending to be his only friend, and then it eats him from the inside out, killing every worthy feeling he has, leaving no room for peace or pleasure, happiness or love. If a man has hatred in his heart, it's best not to feed it. Leave it starve, let it loosen its grip, let it die before it kills you." He stood and clapped Gabriel on the shoulder. "Now, that's enough of my blathering, lad. We've a tea party to attend."

A heavily armed contingent of custom men was waiting with the wool, and Lieutenant Brey and the *Hind* skulked in the shadows of the cove. A hasty change of plans precipitated a mad scramble on deck. Davey shouted orders and the *L'Espérance* heeled in the wind as she hove to the right, back toward open waters. Her sails slackened and flapped for a moment as she strained to recapture the breeze, then fluttered, popped, and billowed as she surged forward, running before the wind with Lieutenant Brey in hot pursuit. It was twenty-eight hours before he gave up the chase.

Cursing and laughing, Davey handed Gabriel the wheel and took his glass to watch the cutter disappear over the horizon. "*Bon Dieu*, but he's a tenacious bastard! That was a close one, boys. Discretion being the better part of valor, and as we're already halfway to France, I do believe we shall do our business on a different coast for the next few days. Let that panting cur pick up another scent. I've no mind to skulk home without a profit."

In the end, rough winds, treacherous rocks, and serendipitous opportunities along the French and Irish coasts resulted in an unplanned, but very profitable delay in their return home, and it was almost three weeks before Gabriel saw Sarah again. He was in his element, and gloried in life at sea. Davey gave him the wheel more often than not. He was assigned to one of the watches, required to muster the men at night, and took command of watering parties ashore. It was his first time in a position of leadership. The men accepted it readily, and he performed ably and well.

Sarah had been right about talking with Davey. The older man's straightforward advice and calm analysis acted as a balm. Gabriel had dreamed of the German only once since he'd been at sea. He dreamt of Sarah every night. In his dreams she welcomed him deep into her bed, and there was nothing between them but naked flesh. He missed her terribly. He had watched, wide-eyed, in amazement with half the crew as a magnificent whale almost sixty feet in length surfaced off the bow. Davey identified it as a sperm whale, and Gabriel had turned in delight to share the moment with Sarah, before he realized she wasn't there. Every time he had an exciting thought or saw something worth remarking, it was lessened somehow because she wasn't there to share it.

Aching to hold her, starving for her kisses, his entire being was thrumming with excitement when they finally sighted the harbor, and home. He had so much to tell her. He determinedly banished the creeping anxiety, whispering to him that with time and distance she might have changed her mind, and what had been said in the heat of the moment might now be regretted. He was absurdly pleased to see her waiting for him on the dock, dressed in breeches and boots, her chestnut hair streaming down her back. She stood there waving, with the motley assortment of laborers, tradesmen, sweethearts, and wives who'd come to welcome them home. His heart swelled in his chest and the breath caught in his throat as it occurred to him that *his* sweetheart was waiting for him. By coming to greet him this way she acknowledged it, to him, and to everyone present, putting all his fears to rest.

Sarah devoured him with her eyes. He was waving to her, a dazzling smile on his face. She watched with a huge grin as Davey waved him away and he leapt over the rail and onto the quay, landing catlike and graceful, amidst the laughter of the men. He strode toward her with an eager grin and she rushed into his embrace, flinging her arms around his neck.

Pulling her tight against his hard muscled frame, he hugged her wildly, rocking her back and forth, as the crew cheered their approval. "God, how I've missed you, mignonne!"

"I've missed you, too," she said breathlessly. "I could kill Davey. Where have you been? I was so worried about you!"

"We had a little trouble and ended up off the French coast. Davey had some business there, and then in Ireland, so it turned into a bit more of an adventure than anyone expected," he said with a smile. He let go of her abruptly as he spied Ross making his way down the pier. "I'll tell you about it later, mignonne," he said, giving her a parting squeeze. "Your brother doesn't look pleased." He wasn't sure if Ross had seen them, but he was bound to hear about it soon enough.

Sarah followed his gaze. Ross stalked toward them, his eyes hard, and his face grim.

"Sarah." He gave her a curt nod and turned his attention to her companion. "Gabriel! I have business with Davey. I would like to speak with you immediately after. Meet me in my office within the hour, if you please." That said, he turned on his heel and marched over to Davey's sloop, where the two men were soon deep in a heated exchange.

Shaken, Gabriel turned to look at Sarah. She grimaced, sighed, and wound her arm though his. "He had to find out sooner or later, Gabriel."

He had known that this day would come if he

continued to pursue his feelings for Sarah, but he'd hoped to delay it as long as possible. "You realize if he doesn't throttle me, he'll have me on my way by sunset."

"Nonsense, Gabriel! He's not the ogre you make him out to be, and in any case, you haven't done anything wrong."

Presenting himself in Ross's study exactly one hour later, Gabriel prayed she was right.

Ross stood, arms folded behind his back, clearly agitated. "Come in, Gabriel; sit down." Not wanting to antagonize his beloved's brother any more than he already had, Gabriel did as he was told.

"I'm going to tell you the same thing I told Davey," Ross said, pacing back and forth. "I did not bring you to my home to have you end up swinging at the end of a rope. You are a young man, and doubtless prone to the fancies and foibles most young men share. You wish for adventure and excitement, heedless of the consequences. You look at Davey, and you think him glamorous, romantic, but there's nothing romantic about swinging in the breeze, piss running down your legs as you void your bowels and slowly choke to death. Have you ever watched a man hang, Gabriel?"

"No, sir," Gabriel replied, completely bewildered.

"No? I thought it was a common form of entertainment in most cities. It might have been enlightening for you."

"I doubt I would find such a spectacle entertaining,

my lord."

"You would like it even less, lad, if *you* were the center of attention." Ross stopped pacing and leaned forward, placing both hands on the desk. "You almost sailed into a trap three weeks ago, Gabriel. You would have been hung, had you been captured. It would have been most upsetting to James and Sarah. I suggest you think about that."

"I'm not a child, Huntington."

"No, you're a grown man and I can't order you about. You will make your own decisions. I'm well aware of that. I simply ask that you consider what I am saying."

"I will take it under advisement, my lord."

"Good! See to it you do. Now, to the matter at hand. I've been called away on urgent business. I expect to be gone about two months. I would have left before now, but I didn't wish to leave Sarah and the household unprotected. Davey has his own business to attend to, as you're no doubt aware. He cannot be depended on to be available. Jamie can stay at Sidney's while I'm gone, and I expect, indeed, I insist, that you remain on the estate. I have already informed Davey that you will be helping Sarah with the management of the property, and will not be available to him until my return. She is not to be left unprotected in my absence. Is that clear?"

"Most assuredly. You may rely on it."

Ross gave him a sour look. "And who will protect

her from you?"

Gabriel flushed. "You must know that I care for her deeply, Huntington. I would never harm her."

"Are you telling me your friendship is an innocent one?"

Gabriel took his time and thought carefully before answering, not wanting to lie, or to antagonize him. "If you're asking if we are lovers, then the answer is no," he said, his gaze steady and direct.

Ross nodded. "I don't want to see her hurt."

"Neither do I."

"Good. Then we understand each other. Well, then, I shall be leaving at first light. My bailiff will take care of most of the day-to-day management of the estate, but I will expect you to help Sarah supervise and settle any disputes. I also meant to ask if you wished me to invest your money while I'm in London, as we've discussed in the past."

"I would appreciate it, Huntington. Yes."

"Good." Ross rose and extended his hand. "I would like to discuss some last minute details with both of you after dinner. As of tomorrow, you will be the man of the house."

Gabriel left the study with mixed feelings. He was relieved no mention had been made of his leaving, proud that Ross had placed such confidence in him, and elated that after three weeks apart, he was about to have Sarah to himself. He also felt guilty. He hadn't lied to Ross. He and Sarah were not lovers. Not yet. But they were sweethearts, they were in love, and he'd decided upon seeing her waiting on the dock, that she was a prize he was going to fight for, whether he was worthy of her or not. He fully intended to do everything he could to make her his completely.

Gabriel and Sarah remained closeted with Ross late into the night, reviewing finances, current tenant disputes, and a myriad of other details. It made Gabriel's head spin in a way that being at sea on a heaving deck had never done. Since setting out with Davey, the only thing he'd wanted was to return to Sarah and continue the conversation that had been interrupted three weeks ago, but by the time Ross retired, it was nearly dawn, and it was impossible. He smiled, exhausted, and turned to her. "I'm sorry, Sarah, there's so much I want to tell you."

"You'll tell me tonight. Don't leave yet, Gabriel, there's something I want to give you." She stood in front of him, a tentative smile on her face, her hand outstretched. He shifted his gaze and felt a strange emotion, tender and hesitant, a new kind of aching he couldn't define. It was a pair of wrist guards. Made of black leather, with silver buckles in the shape of the quarter moon, they were intricately tooled with a Celtic serpent design, and inlaid with silver stars. He looked up.

"They're for—"

"I know what they're for, Sarah. Thank you." He caught her lower lip with his thumb, gently pulling her down to his kiss, sighing soft against her mouth. "Good night, *ma chère.*"

"Good night, Gabriel. Welcome home."

He slept late the next day. It was a welcome relief not to have to practice or report to Davey. As much as he enjoyed the other man's company, the past eight months had been a marathon of grueling activity, little sleep, and always something new to learn. It was a guilty, but undoubted pleasure to lie abed, anticipating the night ahead. He saw Sarah at dinner and told her about the whale he'd seen, longer than their ship, and about his talk with Davey. He told her how happy it had made him to find her waiting for him on the docks. They went to the music room after dinner, speaking to each other through tempo, cadence, and gentle harmony, and when the big house quieted for the night, she retired to her chamber, and he walked restlessly along the cliff's edge, waiting until all was dark, so he could climb the big oak into her arms again.

CHAPTER
17

Sarah waited, anxious and eager to have Gabriel to herself. He had said he loved her, she'd replied in kind, and now everything had changed. There was no pretending they were only friends anymore. She had missed him, missed his body, warm and solid beside her at night. She had missed his voice, tender and seductive as he teased her, and she had missed his lazy kisses, sweet and deep, curling her toes and melting her insides. She longed for, and dreaded, his touch, knowing it would take her past all restraint, to a place from which there was no turning back.

It was becoming harder and harder for her to tell the difference between right and wrong, what she feared and what she desired. The more she wanted him, the more she feared that if they crossed that tempting border, there would be heartache on the other side. She worried that what he needed was a friend, not a lover, and feared he would come to see her as another in a long line of people who had used him. She feared their friendship would be destroyed, and where there'd been something lovely, there would be only bitterness, disillusionment, and regret.

She'd also been struck, seeing him at the docks, tanned and fit, his dark hair streaked with sunlight and his eyes sparkling with excitement, at how beautiful he was. He could have any woman he wanted. If his life had been different, would he have ever chosen someone like her; a disreputable, opinionated, eccentric widow; large boned, far too tall, and careless of her appearance? It hardly seemed likely.

Her musings were interrupted by his appearance on her balcony. He stood, framed in the moonlight. An early spring breeze teased his hair, and his eyes sparked with heat and hunger. His shirt was open and her gaze traveled from his eyes, to his mouth, to his torso, taut and sleek, his stomach ridged with muscle, his skin alabaster in the moonlight. He looked like a Greek statue brought to life. She groaned in frustration. No woman should be so tempted. No woman could resist. He grinned, and stepped into the room. Seeing that his sleeves were rolled up and he wore the wrist guards, she returned his grin with a happy one of her own.

He crossed to her bed without a word, and slid in beside her, gathering her into his arms. He'd meant to tell her he loved her. He'd meant to thank her for the gift, but the moment her arms reached around his neck he forgot all his carefully planned words, and lowered his mouth to hers in a feverish kiss. Growling with pleasure and need, he grasped her bottom, pulling her hard against his length. He rolled on top of her, his knee deep between her thighs as his tongue sucked and stroked, thrusting against hers in a dance as ancient as time.

Sarah clutched his hair, pulling him close, deepening her kiss, as he swept her into a whirlwind of passion and pleasure. She moaned when he pulled his lips away, then shivered in anticipation as his fingertips began to trace her collarbone, sending delicious frissons of pleasure singing along her nerves, swelling her breasts, stiffening her nipples, and making her feel swollen and moist between her thighs. She gasped in white-hot pleasure when his lazy tongue rasped wet and hot against her nipple, moistening it through the cotton of her nightdress, sending waves of sensation thrilling to her core. He looked straight into her eyes, the question clear.

She closed her eyes, trying to gather her tattered wits, stunned by the riotous feelings coursing through her. She'd known no pleasure from her husband, and felt overwhelmed by the wild sensations she was experiencing now. It was too powerful. It was happening too fast. Shifting her weight, she pushed him away. "Enough, Gabriel, please. We . . . I . . . I think we should stop."

"I'm sorry," he said, drawing back. "I thought . . .

clearly, I misunderstood."

Stricken by the look of hurt in his eyes, she reached out to pull him back, but he was already up, preparing to leave. "Gabriel, don't!"

"Don't what? Don't kiss you? Don't touch you? I can't help it, Sarah. I think about it all the time. Christ! I can't keep doing this!"

"Please, just listen. Try to understand."

"I *do* understand. I've just reminded you of what I am, a jaded, greedy whore. You've been kind to me, indulged me, though I cannot imagine why, but there are limits. The idea of being touched by me that way, knowing what I am, must disgust you."

"Stop it! I hate when you speak like that! That's not at all what I meant!"

"My apologies," he said, his voice flat and cold. He turned to go, but she leapt from the bed, blocking his path.

"Gabriel, wait, please! For all the times I've listened to you, will you not hear me out?"

The look he gave her was resentful and cold, but he ceded her the door and went to sprawl ungraciously on the window seat. "I am listening, mignonne," he said, his voice remote.

"I'm just so confused, Gabriel. I'm trying to do the right thing, and I don't know what that is anymore. It's not that I don't want you. I do! I dream about you. I imagine . . . Look, you call yourself a whore, as if that's who you are. How can I show you how wrong you are? How can I truly be your friend if I use you as everyone else has? Damn it, Gabe, you're such an innocent!"

"Innocent!" He was so shocked his mouth hung slack and open.

"And now you look just like Ross," she snapped.

"How can you call me that, Sarah? You know me better than anyone does. You're the only one who really knows."

"But you are, you know. You've known nothing of love, Gabriel. How could you? You have no way of arming or protecting yourself. You know how to deal with physical pain," her gaze flicked toward his wrists, "but I'm so afraid that I might hurt you, Gabe, and I never want to do that."

"Jesus," he said with a shaky laugh, "one would never have guessed. You seem to delight in torturing me."

"I'm also afraid that you might hurt me."

He felt as if he'd been punched in the gut. How could she think that of him? Didn't she know him at all? "It's been very foolish of you to have me alone in your room this way then, hasn't it, mignonne?" he said coolly.

"Oh, hush! You know I don't mean it like that! But I've watched you with Davey and his crew. You're one of them. Anyone can see it. The sea will call you and you'll answer. You'll go adventuring. You won't be content to stay here, even if you think so now, nor should you. You'll meet people. You don't seem to realize it yet, but you could have any woman you wanted."

"I've *had* many women, Sarah. The only one I've wanted is you."

She lifted her gaze to his, struck dumb by the torment in his eyes. Loneliness, uncertainty, and stark need were there for her to see, but what broke her heart was the tentative, desperate hope. It was impossible not to love him, impossible not to want him, and to hurt him was unthinkable. She knew what she wanted. Her resistance evaporated and a slow smile lit her face. She held out her hand. "Come, then."

It was salvation. He was a greedy fool, a selfish fool, indeed an unworthy and witless fool, but not fool enough to refuse.

She pulled him up, stronger than she looked, and led him back to the warm bed he'd spent so many nights imagining, the past three weeks at sea. She brushed back his hair with her fingers and trailing soft kisses down his jaw pushed him gently back onto her bed. Following him down, she lowered herself against him, enveloping him in softness, warmth, and Sarah. "There," she sighed contentedly, kissing his brow and giving him a possessive hug, "you're back where you belong. "Now tell me, Gabe, do you truly believe I think so little of you?"

"I know you care, Sarah. I'm not a fool. You could have any man you wanted, but you choose me. You've given me your trust and friendship. You've welcomed me into your home, your life, even your bed." He curled alongside her, cradling her in his arms. "You breathe life into me. I go to sleep wanting to know what will happen tomorrow. I look at the sky and see mystery and magic. I feel the sword dance in my hand and I feel alive. It's all you, Sarah. When I'm with you, I feel like I've been born into another life, where I have friends and a future, and a sweetheart who makes me drunk and wild with kisses she saves only for me. I feel healthy and happy and at peace. I never dared dream of such things. I know I act the fool at times and try your patience. It's just that, every time I look in your eyes, I can see the man that you see, and I can't believe he's really me. I'm so afraid of disappointing you."

"Oh, Gabe!" she murmured, tears in her eyes. "Trust me. You *are* the man I see. You've lived inside yourself so long you've lost perspective. I know you're not perfect. Neither am I. You can be very arrogant and difficult, particularly when you're angry." Warming to the topic, she began to enumerate with her fingers. "Sometimes, when you drink too much, you lie snoring with your mouth agape. It's very unattractive. Sometimes you can be positively missish—"

"Missish!"

"Oh, yes, you're as bad as Ross sometimes. You can also be prickly, and you're over-quick to take offense. Sometimes you're *very* rude, and Lord knows you can be moody. You use very bad, very foul language, and I swear— mmmphhh—"

He held his fingers over her mouth to stop her. "Enough," he said dryly, "I take your point."

"Well, I'm certain there are things about me that you must find annoying."

"Nothing comes to mind."

"Come now, Gabe, there's no need to be diplomatic. I will survive it. Do try. There must be something."

He furrowed his brow, honestly flummoxed. "I swear, Sarah . . . no . . . wait . . . Yes! Your nightgown! I hate that god-awful thing! It's horrendous, frightful, appalling."

"What? But it's very comfortable!"

"It looks like something an ancient crone would wear. When I see you in it and find myself lusting after you, it makes me decidedly uncomfortable. It should be burned!"

"Hmph!"

"Well, you insisted. Now you know." He lay back, gazing at the ceiling with her head nestled against his shoulder. Caught up in his own worries, fears, and desires, he hadn't spared a thought for how the changes in their relationship might be affecting her. She must be as anxious and as confused as he was. He'd been a selfish idiot, and he was fortunate, indeed, she was such a patient woman.

"Better now?"

He gifted her with a lazy smile, his eyes warm and tender. "Much . . . go to sleep now, Sarah."

"But I don't want to go to sleep," she protested, her fingers tracing his lips.

He pulled her close. "Nothing needs to change, mignonne. I'm sorry. I behaved like a child, a selfish ass. As you said, arrogant, and quick to take offense, and—"

"Shhh! Gabriel," she interrupted. "Kiss me, please."

He looked into eyes filled with invitation, warm with promise. "Sarah, no, sweetheart. So much has happened . . . Christ, I—"

Sarah leaned forward, breathing soft against his skin, trailing fluttering kisses, hungry and sweet along his bristled jaw, his cheekbones, and the lobe of his ear. Her fingers trailed through his hair, untangling it, and then curled around the back of his neck, drawing him forward into a searching kiss. "Let me love you, Gabe," she whispered.

He gasped as she trailed her fingers across his chest, brushing his nipples as she reached for his shirt, tugging at it.

"I want to touch you."

He moaned low in his throat, and shifted awkwardly, heart hammering, as she pulled it off his shoulders.

Her hands roamed his chest as she'd been longing to do for months, soft smooth skin stretched taut over iron-hard bands of muscle. "I want to taste you." She kissed his shoulder and ran her tongue along his collarbone and throat as he shuddered beneath her. "I want to please you." When she brushed his abdomen, his whole body jerked beneath her.

"Enough, mignonne," he said hoarsely, reaching for her hands and shifting her to his side. He was raging with need, erect and throbbing, aching for her touch. "Jesus, sweetheart, have mercy. I'm only a man. We can't play this game. *I* can't play this game."

"It's not a game, Gabriel. I love you. I want you, and I want to make love with you. I thought you wanted that, too."

"I did . . . I do . . . You don't know. You don't understand . . . Jesus, Sarah! I've never made *love* with a woman. I just . . . I have sex . . . It's not the same. You deserve so much better than that."

"Well, I expect it will come to you, much like kissing did. You turned out to be wonderful at that."

"I don't know if I want to do this with you, mignonne." Christ, what a hypocrite he was! He'd lusted after her for months, taking her in his dreams over and over again. He'd practically begged her earlier, thrown a tantrum when she'd hesitated, and now the moment was here, he was afraid. All of his sexual interactions had been forced, or bought and paid for. He was afraid she would finally see him for the whore he really was. Afraid he would become one, right in front of her eyes. "Sarah, I don't know how."

"Then let me show you, Gabriel. Trust me as I trust you." Cool fingers traced his jaw, soothing, stroking, and turning him toward her kiss. He shuddered as she moved her hot mouth over the column of his throat, her tongue feeling his pulse as her curious fingers skimmed featherlight across his chest, brushing his nipples. Lips followed fingers. Using the same principles she'd earlier applied to kissing, Sarah tugged gently at his nipple with her teeth, and then stroked it with her tongue.

He'd been trained to give exquisite pleasure to others. No one had ever paid to pleasure him, and Sarah was introducing him to feelings and sensations he'd not known he possessed. He struggled to stay still, struggled not to weep as her exploration continued with teeth and tongue, silken lips and wicked fingers, stroking and soothing, teasing and gentle. He hissed when her fingers brushed against his belly, and almost jerked off the bed when, clumsy and uncertain, they brushed the erection straining against his breeches as she sought to work on the fastenings.

"*Merde*, woman, you will unman me," he snapped, hurriedly twisting and tugging to release himself.

Her eyes widened when his organ sprang free. It was huge, potent, nestled in a thicket of dark wiry hair, veined and bulging and straining wildly. She had only seen her husband's, flaccid and puny, but still capable of causing her humiliation and pain. She held her hand out to touch it, looking into his eyes, asking permission. He nodded, his breath held tight. She tapped it experimentally and smiled when it leapt to her touch. She ran her fingers along its length, up and down, stroking and squeezing, feeling him shudder beneath her hands. He moaned as if in pain.

"It's beautiful," she whispered shyly, "soft and strong, smooth and hard, all at the same time." She bent to kiss him.

Gabriel felt as if he would shatter under her touch. It thrilled him with an intensity he'd never known. He jerked his pelvis, desperate for contact, wanting her lips and tongue, at the same time remembering other hands, other mouths, other nights. He felt a sharp and acrid twist of shame before he mastered himself, prepared to perform. She would not find him lacking.

"Take off your gown, mignonne," he ordered, voice low and seductive, eyes glazed with lust. She looked at him, wary of something in his voice, but she reached down and pulled her much-maligned nightgown over her head, blushing as she knelt on the bed, naked between his legs. He captured her head between his hands and pulled her to him, guiding her back to his swollen penis. Uncomfortable, sensing something different about him, she pulled away.

Letting her go with a knowing smile, he lowered his hands, a predatory glint in his eyes, and brushed her nipples with his fingers. Catching them between fingers and palm he began to roll them gently, squeezing and tugging as she leaned into him, moaning with pleasure. "You like that, chère, do you not? You are hot and wet and for me, yes?" He moved a hand between her legs, stroking the throbbing entrance between her thighs with skillful fingers as she writhed and squirmed, blushing in embarrassment and pleasure. She cried out when he gripped her nub between his thumb and forefinger, tugging it with one hand as his other continued to tug at her nipple. "Tell me what you want, *chère*," he whispered. "Tell me what to do. I'm here to please you."

She sensed his absence, knew he was far away. She had felt the metamorphosis when he had changed, no longer her Gabriel, but the other. She wanted to reach into him somehow, find him and pull him back. Pushing his hands away, she trapped his jaw and leaned in for a kiss. When his lips touched hers, she grasped a hank of his hair and tugged. "Stay with me, Gabriel! I can feel it when you leave." His eyes cleared and he pulled her close. He didn't pretend not to understand.

"If you're going to make love to me, you have to stay with me, Gabe," she said gently.

"I don't know if I can, Sarah. I told you, I know how to fuck, not how to make love."

"Well, you were doing just fine until a moment ago. If you don't like what I'm doing, just tell me to stop. Don't leave me there all by myself."

"I'm sorry," he sighed. "Did I . . . was I . . . Did I offend you?"

"No, you were wicked and wonderful. It's just that your voice was odd, and your eyes were . . . well, you just seemed so far away."

Relieved, he sank back into the pillows, then clutched for the covers, red-faced as he realized that he was more than half-naked, shirtless, with his still-erect member bulging from his open breeches.

She reached out quickly and snatched the blanket away from him. "Come now, Gabriel, that's not fair! I'm here naked as the day I was born. If I am, you should be, as well."

"Or you could dress yourself, mignonne."

"I don't want to dress myself." she said with a playful pout, trailing her fingers back and forth across his chest. "I'm curious. I've never seen a man completely naked. If you truly cared for me you would satisfy my curiosity."

"Not even your husband, chère?"

"No, thank God, he always kept his bedclothes on." She leaned over and kissed his cheek. "But you are very dear to me, Gabriel. I love you, and I love your body, too. I want to get to know it. Won't you let me?"

Rising on his heels, he lifted his hips and slid out of his breeches, feeling shy and strangely vulnerable. When he had sex, working sex, he always oiled and insulated himself with generous amounts of alcohol, until he could distance himself enough to perform, until he became the sensual automaton his clients required. There was no alcohol easing him tonight, just Sarah, but she felt like life itself. She didn't want to be left alone. If he was going to make love with her, he needed to stay with her. He would do his best.

She resumed her exploration, mapping his body, front and back, with gentle caresses and honeyed kisses. She kissed his scars, one by one, hiding her tears when she saw how many, his back, his buttocks, his arms and legs, marks of whip, and blade, and fire. She kissed each in turn, as he trembled beneath her. He shuddered, teeth gritted, violently aroused as her smooth hands caressed his back and buttocks and her soft lips tenderly kissed the back of his thighs.

Cursing, he rolled over, pulling her up and gripping her tight, shifting her onto her back. "Sarah," he moaned, *"mon ange, ma belle amie, mon amour."* He wanted, above all else, to be gentle with her, but her slow and thorough exploration, with velvet touch and dulcet kisses, had driven him half-mad with desire. Aching with a driving need to possess her and make her his, he forgot art, and artifice, and the slow dance of seduction. Panting and moaning he ground against her as he plundered her mouth. Supporting his weight with one arm, he reached down and parted her thighs. Feeling her moist and hot against his palm he pressed against her with his thumb, touching her as he had earlier, sending waves of desire coursing through her body as she stretched her legs wider, pushing up against him, whimpering with need. He moved his hips, his heavy straining shaft rubbing, bouncing, and sliding against her. "Please, Sarah," he rasped.

Oh, God, yes! Yes, Gabriel, please!" She reached

down to pull him toward her, cupping his aching testicles, caressing his engorged penis, guiding him to the heated center where she waited for him.

With a guttural cry, he plunged himself into her slick, tight, heat. Oh, Christ, he was in heaven! Unable to contain himself, desperate for relief, he pumped and thrust savagely as she held him tight in her arms, tight inside her. His frenzied mouth sought hers, and starving for her, thirsty for her, he drank her, consumed her, his tongue stroking and plunging wildly in rhythm with his bucking, pounding, twisting hips. When her muscles began to contract, squeezing and releasing him repeatedly in wave after wave of white-hot sensation, he felt it deep inside, through muscle and sinew, skin and bone, through rapturous nerve and singing blood, deep into his heart and soul. Shouting her name, he clutched her to him as he pumped, one, two, three, and surrendered to waves of ecstasy that transported him beyond anything he'd ever felt, or knew, or imagined. Wild, exultant, his head fell to the pillow. *This must be what heaven feels like*, he thought lazily, awash in peace and pleasure, as he floated in her arms.

Sprawled atop her, coming back to himself, to the room, he shifted his weight, afraid of crushing her, but she tightened her grasp, keeping him close. He dropped his head to her shoulder, nuzzling under her ear as her fingers played through his hair, and her lips explored his face, tasting his tears, kissing his eyes, his nose, and his mouth. Lifting and holding her tight by her shoulders and bottom, he rolled over in one smooth motion, so she lay on top of him, their bodies still joined. Gently he pulled her head down to his shoulder, next to his heart.

"I'm so sorry, Sarah," he murmured into her hair.

"Whatever for?" she asked, bewildered.

"I jumped on you, like a fucking animal."

"Hah!" she chuckled, ruffling his hair, and kissing his nose. "I always thought I could drive a man wild if I cared to try, and right now I'm inordinately proud of myself. Oh, Gabe, I never knew! I had no idea! I never knew anything could feel so wonderful!"

"Neither did I," he said honestly.

Cupping his face in her hands, she whispered against his lips, "Thank you, my love."

"Thank you, *ma chère*." He lay, sated and at ease in a totally unfamiliar way, amazed and wonder-struck. He had pleased his woman, and his own pleasure had been overwhelming, and for once, free of guilt. Hugging her tight he rocked her in his arms until exhausted, warm breath intermingling, they fell asleep in a tangle of loose limbs, silken sheets, and soft words of love.

Sarah was the first to wake. She took the opportunity to feast her eyes on him, as he nestled, lanky and disheveled, in her big bed. His face was relaxed, unguarded and boyish, his sensuous lips curled in a contented smile. He looked adorable. A stray lock of hair tumbled over his brow and she longed to fondle it and tuck it back, but she hesitated. She knew he found sleep elusive and she didn't want to disturb him when he looked so peaceful.

Rising from the bed, she reached for her night-dress where it lay, discarded, in an undignified heap on the cold floor. About to slip into it, she recalled his rather strong opinions about it last evening, and with a playful grin, laid claim to his shirt instead. It was far too big, reaching midthigh, hanging loose and open around her shoulders, but it warmed her, and it smelled like him. Chilled, she moved to the hearth to lay a fire, barring the door on the way against any un-wanted early morning intrusion from one of the maids. Let them think what they would. She knew, deep in-side, that what had happened between her and Gabriel was right, inevitable, fated from their first meeting, and she wasn't going to diminish it by hiding.

CHAPTER
18

When Gabriel awoke, he was alone in the bed. The light spilling through the window suggested midmorning. Sarah was sitting on the window seat, reading, knees curled into her chest, her chestnut hair tumbling loose down her back, wearing only a shirt . . . his shirt. He noted how pretty her toes were, amazed he had never noticed before. His gaze traveled up to trim ankles and finely shaped calves, supple from long hours of riding and walking. His breath caught in his throat when he reached the border of shirt and thigh, marvelous mysteries there, an entire world to explore. She had beautiful legs, legs a man could wrap around himself and hold onto as the world exploded.

Hardening, breathing heavily, he allowed his gaze to wander higher still. The curve of one breast was visible, creamy, soft, and firm. He knew that from last night. A darkened pointed tip thrust delicately against the linen of his shirt. Her breast reminded him of ripe fruit, something that would slake a man's thirst and still his hunger. His mouth watered as he imagined taking that delicate peak between his lips.

"Ahem!"

His gaze flew to hers. Blushing and wide-eyed, he looked like a naughty schoolboy.

"Enjoying yourself, are you?"

His thoughts flew to last night. "Oh, yes . . . enormously!" he said with a grin.

Closing her book, she rose from the window seat and came toward him. His eyes darkened and sparked as he watched the interesting things she did to his shirt. Her shirt now. She inhabited it, as she inhabited him. The thought pleased him tremendously. As she reached the edge of the bed, he reached for the hem and tugged at it, pulling her closer, pulling it open and pulling her down into the warm blankets. They made love again, and Gabriel used all the skill and subtlety that had eluded him last evening, setting her on fire with molten kisses, and a sure and wicked touch. They surged toward release, joining in a climax that left them both shaken and trembling.

"Good Lord, Gabriel what was that? What's happening to us? It's so powerful it's almost frightening."

"*Are* you frightened, mignonne?" he asked, stroking damp tendrils of hair from her forehead. He knew he was. Things like this weren't meant for him. He couldn't believe it would last.

"A little," she admitted. "I don't know where we

go from here. It's all so overwhelming. Everything has changed, hasn't it?"

"Not if you don't want it to."

She drew back, leaning on her elbows, and looked at him carefully. "What do you mean by that?"

"I mean the choice is yours, whether we go on this way or not. If we do, eventually your brother will know, your family. They won't be pleased."

"Are you suggesting we should pretend it never happened? Are you regretting it already?" She was beginning to get annoyed.

"God, no, Sarah! Of course not. This is as close to heaven as I'm ever likely to come. I love you! I just don't want to see you hurt or embarrassed in front of your family."

"And I love you! Do you think I would have let you into my bed if I didn't? Do you think I would be lying here with you now, like this? Do you think that after deciding to . . . to be intimate with you, I would change my mind because my family might be annoyed? What kind of woman do you think I am?" Sarah was almost in tears, frustrated and hurt that after all they'd been through he would withdraw from her yet again, when she was at her most vulnerable. She jerked away from him and sat up. "I think you should go."

Ignoring her last statement, he moved only so far as his side of the bed. He clasped his hands behind his head and looked up at the ceiling. Alarmed at her anger and sorry to have caused her distress, he tried to explain. "I think you're a fine woman, Sarah, a lady in the truest sense of the word. That's the problem. You're far too fine and good for the likes of me. You're so far above anything I deserve, anything I've dared to dream of, that I have trouble believing this is real. I know you love me. I know I wouldn't be here now if that weren't true. I just . . . I . . . I'm afraid you're mistaken."

"What? What do you mean? Mistaken how?"

"I just don't understand how you *could* love me, Sarah," he said with a sigh. "Not if you really understood the things I've been trying to tell you. I'm afraid you'll wake up one day, maybe tomorrow, maybe a year from now, and realize I'm not who you thought I was, that you've made a terrible mistake, and you'll be horrified knowing what you gave up, what it cost you. I'm afraid you'll start to hate me."

Her anger evaporated. "Gabriel, I could never hate you. Not under any circumstances. And any woman would love you if you'd stopped snarling and growling, and just let her. You're intelligent and kind and you make me laugh. You sing and play like an angel. You're strong and brave, and yes, you're beautiful. When I first saw you at Madame Etienne's, you looked so defiant, so utterly lost and so oddly familiar. I felt like I knew you, like I'd always known you. Since then, the more I get to know you, the more I find to admire. I wish you could see yourself as I do."

"How can you say that? You *know* who I am, Sarah.

You know *what* I am. You know better than anyone does. I'm a fucking whore, for Christ's sake! I sell my body to anyone who wants it. I demean and degrade myself for money. Is that what you want? This fucking shell I walk around in? I thought you were different. I thought you were finer. You like my cock, my ass, my face? I still haven't shown you all I can do with them, Sarah. It gets better."

It was what she'd been afraid of. Uncertain of his own worth, he couldn't believe he was wanted for himself. He thought she mistook lust for love. She feared she'd made a terrible mistake.

"Ah, Christ! I'm sorry! Sarah . . . love . . . I'm sorry. You didn't deserve that. But please don't lie to me. Not you. I couldn't bear it."

She realized then that he couldn't understand how she loved and valued him, because he'd never learned to love or value himself. She needed to explain it to him, carefully and completely, so there could be no misunderstanding. She struggled to find the right words. "Shall I tell you how I see you? Who and what, I see, when I look at you?"

There was a long silence, and when he spoke, his voice was weary. "How then, Sarah? How do you see me, truly? I need to know."

"I see a man who's strong and kind, who fought to stay human under the most hellish circumstances. I look at you and I see . . . a wounded hero, a gallant warrior standing brave in the pit of hell, protecting an innocent child, placing yourself between him and the flames, expecting nothing in return."

He laughed bitterly. "That was self-preservation, Sarah. It gave me a purpose. Something everyone needs to go on living. Suppose I told you, your brave selfless hero hated you, you and your saintly brother, for coming to take him away?"

"I know. I knew. Yet you encouraged him to leave anyway. I fell in love with you then, that night, in that room, before I'd even seen you."

"So . . . gratitude and pity," he rasped.

Finally exasperated with him, she reached over and tugged sharply on his hair, making him wince, then smacked him with a pillow.

"Ouch! *Merde*! Stop that, Sarah!"

"Listen to me, you bloody, big dolt! You asked a question. Now give me leave to answer. Why do I love you? I love you because, in that terrible place, despite all that happened to you, you had compassion for a child. You learned to make beautiful music, and taught yourself to read and write, and opened your mind to books, and when I look at you"—her eyes were bright with tears—"when I look at you, I see someone beautiful and precious, and so very dear to me." She stopped his mouth with her fingers, before he could protest. "Shhh, quiet. I'm not finished."

Smiling, she ruffled his hair and kissed him firmly on the mouth and then whispered in his ear, "I *have* heard what you've been telling me, Gabriel, and I *do* understand, and I know who, and what you are. You're the finest man I know. Now listen to me. You are not the things that were done to you." Feeling him stiffen, beginning to withdraw, she shook him gently. "Look at me." He did. "You were a child, powerless and alone, there was no one to help you the way you helped Jamie. You did what you needed to do to survive, and there's no fault in that, no shame.

"You're *not* what was done to you, Gabe," she repeated softly. "Can't you see? If you were, you'd be just like them. You would use people and hurt them without a thought. You would take pleasure from other people's pain. You would let your anger make you a monster, and you would never, ever have protected or cared for my brother. Not for any reason. You would have used him and abused him and then thrown him away, just like they did to you."

He gasped in protest, shocked and outraged.

"Shhh, I know. I know you would never, *could* never do such a thing. That's what I'm trying to tell you, Gabriel. You're a decent man. A *good* man. Let me finish. This needs to be said. I don't know why these things happened to you, Gabe. Why this child, and not that one? Who can say? I do know that it wasn't your fault, and you didn't deserve it. No more than Jamie would have if you hadn't been there to stop it." Tears were starting down his cheeks now. She was afraid to continue, afraid to stop, afraid this chance might never come again.

She stroked his cheek tenderly. "You aren't like them, Gabriel. Through all the things that happened to you, you fought them. They touched your body—"

He groaned beside her, wishing she would stop, fearing he was going to spew all over her bed.

"You couldn't stop that, Gabriel, any more than Jamie could have if you hadn't been there to protect him, but you fought them, nevertheless, and you never let them steal your soul."

"I could have left, Sarah. I should have run away."

"You tried to, from de Sevigny. Before that, you were too young to survive, and after, you couldn't abandon Jamie. Could you?"

He didn't answer. He trembled, helpless, while her gentle fingers circled his wrists, unbuckling the wrist guards and tenderly tracing the intricate weaving of scar tissue, testament to all he'd survived. "No, don't pull away." She bent and kissed them. "These are battle scars, Gabriel, war wounds, nothing to be ashamed of," and now he *was* weeping. "Shhh, my love," she said, pulling him close and cradling him. "Cry, my sweet angel," she murmured, soft, in his ear. "It's all right, it's over now. You're here with me and I'll never let go of you." Threading her fingers through his hair, she pulled him toward her kiss. Hot tears spilled against her cheek, his, hers, she didn't know; it didn't matter.

"I *do* know who you are, Gabriel, and I love you

for it," she said, hugging him tightly. "I don't pity you, I admire you, and yes, there's gratitude and lust and friendship all mixed in, and sometimes I can't tell where one leaves off and the other begins, but that's what love is. I'm proud to love you, and proud you love me, and I don't regret it, I won't hide it, and I could never be ashamed or embarrassed by it."

So much had happened, in such a short period. Gabriel felt buffeted by forces beyond his control. His world, his prejudices, conceptions, and habitual way of viewing things, had just been overturned. He felt disoriented and desperate to be alone. He needed to think. "I'm so sorry, mignonne, for all this drama. Your patience is . . . astonishing. I . . . I need time, Sarah. I need to think."

"You need to be alone."

"Yes."

"Will you be all right, Gabe?"

"Yes, mignonne, I think I will be."

"Do you promise?"

"I promise, Sarah."

"May I keep the shirt?" He grinned, and she knew it would be all right.

Shirtless, Gabriel left, heading down to the beach. He walked along the sand, lost in thought, oblivious to the shrieks of the seabirds whirling overhead, and the dull roar of rolling breakers, pounding the shore. He'd made love twice, without alcohol or guilt, to a woman he loved passionately, who loved him in return. He'd never known sex could be so rewarding; so innocent and healthy and sweet. He'd challenged her love of him, and she'd responded by stripping him bare, reaching easily past walls that had taken him years to erect. He couldn't doubt her understanding anymore, or her acceptance. She saw him clearly, if in a different light than he saw himself.

He questioned his own experience for the first time. It *had* taken strength and courage to survive, to endure, and to protect Jamie. Moreover, he had accomplished things, things to be proud of. He'd educated himself, learned to play music, and he'd taught Jamie, as well. As he tried to see himself through Sarah's eyes, he realized that at least in part, he *was* the man she described.

The day was unseasonably warm for April, and he found himself a sheltered cove. Lying blissful in the sun, feeling it caressing his body, he imagined he could feel the earth spinning beneath him. Lost in the sounds of surf, seabirds, and the distant voices of men, he felt a moment's regret that he was hardly doing his duty to Ross, by the estate, or by his sister. He would make both things right, somehow. He'd often thought of himself as unlucky, but that was starting to change. It seemed he'd been offered a chance to make a life, and given an opportunity to prove himself. What would a gentleman do in this kind of situation? *Marry the girl, of course!*

Jolted upright with a sudden thrill of alarm, he

realized he'd not taken any precautions with Sarah, and he'd been so drunk with love and lust, that he'd not thought to withdraw. She was a lady. She couldn't be expected to know about such things. He might have left her with child! Hastening back to the manor house, he took the stairs to her room two at a time, and pounded on the door. "Sarah! Open the door."

She opened the door, astonished. He looked extremely agitated. "Come inside, Gabriel. What's wrong?"

"I . . . Sarah, I must tell you that in all the excitement, last night, this morning . . . I failed to take any precautions. I fear I might have left you with child."

She blushed crimson. "You needn't concern yourself, Gabriel. That is most unlikely. I have only just finished my courses." He looked at her, puzzled. "It is the wrong time of the month," she explained.

"Ah," he said, comprehension dawning, "but if we mean to, that is to say, if we happen to do it again, I will try to remember and you must remind me to use more caution." He thought a moment. "You said it was unlikely, Sarah, but it's still possible, isn't it? What if you *are* with child? My child?"

"Why then I suppose you'd have to marry me," she said with a teasing smile.

He gave her a boyish grin. "The idea holds a great deal of charm, mignonne. Would you? If I asked?"

"If I found myself with child, you mean?"

"No, if I asked you now, today, would you marry me?"

"If you asked me today, I would tell you to ask me again in a month, when you weren't so alarmed at the thought of little Gabriel, or Gabrielle, tottering about the halls."

"And suppose there was *no* child, a month from now, and still I asked?"

"Then I would tell you yes," she said without hesitation.

Elated, he picked her up and whirled her around the room before depositing her, laughing, on the bed. He had some doubts. Huntington would be unlikely to grant his permission, and he had no idea how he would support her. He had money, but it was money Ross had given him. It hardly seemed right to use it when he was practically stealing the man's sister. Sarah had money, but he couldn't accept that, either.

But there *was* Davey. His share of the profits from his adventures with Davey was the first money he'd earned doing something he was proud of. Davey had been growing bored lately. He was gripped by wanderlust every spring, and it was past time for him to be on his way. The trade had become so ubiquitous that every man in Cornwall, from the preacher on down, was involved to some extent. Davey spoke often of venturing forth in search of plump and juicy merchant vessels, French ones, overflowing with bounty from Egypt and the Orient. A few such prizes and Gabriel would be able to support Sarah comfortably. Resolutely, pushing all such thoughts aside, he dropped down onto the bed and wrapped her in his arms.

He stopped struggling after that. It was clear that Sarah not only accepted him, she welcomed him in her bed. She'd seen his scars, knew better than most who and what he was, and had decided that he was what she wanted. He had almost proposed, she had almost accepted, and he had every reason to expect that in a month from now, when her pride assured her he acted under no constraint, she would agree to become his wife. They made love often during the soft spring nights, sometimes warm and close in her bed as the breeze fluttered the curtains, sometimes laughing and breathless in hidden coves, and sometimes on her balcony, rocking together on her swing, hands, lips, and hips joining in a mating dance of lust and love.

The next month was idyllic. Ross's bailiff had things well in hand, and there were no pressing matters with the estate. Released from the restrictions of routine and duty, free to enjoy the unseasonably warm weather, free to enjoy each other, they were inseparable. Sarah watched Gabriel practice, naked to the waist except for his wrist guards, admiring his toned and lithe grace as he practiced with rapier, cutlass, and Spanish steel. They went for picnics, thundered down the beach on horseback, played music, and sang.

Gabriel slept in her bed, deep and sound, for the first time in years, eight, sometimes ten hours a night, as if making up for lost time. When Davey returned, they went to see him, dancing and playing around the campfire on the shore with him and his crew, whirling and twirling and reeling under the stars, like happy children. They didn't announce their future plans to Davey, having decided to wait and tell Ross first, as was proper, but their intimacy and excitement were obvious, and if Davey had any misgivings, he didn't let on.

CHAPTER
19

Wearing the shirt she'd claimed from Gabriel, Sarah sat at her desk, trying to gather her thoughts. It was almost June, and the night was fragrant and sultry. Ross would be home soon, bringing Jamie with him. Gabriel seemed to have shaken free from his haunted past, and the last several weeks had been a carefree time in which they'd enjoyed, explored, and delighted one another. They would have to deal with harsh reality soon enough. She loved both her brothers dearly, and didn't want to see them upset, but Gabriel was her future, and she was not prepared to give him up.

She went looking for him late the next morning, to ask if he wished to accompany her on a picnic to a local ruin. She found him in the library, sitting barefoot, with his shirt open and his feet on the desk. He greeted her with a dazzling smile. Tanned and fit, dark hair tangled about his shoulders, he looked every bit the disreputable pirate. Her pirate, she thought with a grin of satisfaction

He held out his arms and she went to him, allowing him to pull her into his lap. She was wearing a skirt and petticoats today. She had discovered there were unexpected advantages to such garb when one had a lusty lover. She bounced her bottom until she found the most comfortable position, causing him to groan and harden beneath her skirts. As he wrapped his arms around her, she folded hers about his neck, and they joined in a languid kiss. She forgot why she'd come, as he deepened his kiss, drawing her tongue into his mouth. She kissed him back enthusiastically, making soft sounds of satisfaction as her hands roaming happily across his broad chest.

"What the hell!"

Oh, Christ, not like this! Gabriel prayed, as Huntington stalked into the library, rigid and bristling, cold with fury.

"Get out of my chair. Move away from my desk. Get your hands off my sister! NOW, St. Croix!"

Gabriel flushed and stiffened, helping Sarah as she struggled to her feet, before rising himself, taking the time to tuck in his shirt and give her shoulder a reassuring squeeze. He stepped in front of her, giving her a little privacy to rearrange her hair and clothes. "I apologize, Huntington. I had not meant you to find out this way." His eyes, wary and guarded, never left Ross's.

"You apologize for what, St. Croix?" the earl

snarled, shaking with anger. "Abusing my trust? Lying to me? Disrespecting my home and my family and treating my sister like a whore? You gave me your word!"

"Ross! That's not fair! It's not what you think."

"Quiet, Sarah! I will deal with you later."

"I didn't lie to you, Huntington. What I told you was true at the time, and it's you who disrespect your sister by speaking that way. If you were any other man, I would kill you for it."

"And if you haven't left my home within the hour, I may well kill you."

Stepping forward, Sarah took Gabriel's arm and pulled him back before things went too far. "Enough, Ross! Gabriel is my fiancé. We are in love, we wish to be married, and I can assure you that we will be, so you had better get used to it. I will remind you that I am of age, a widow, and a countess in my own right, and I don't need your, or anyone else's, permission! If Gabriel leaves here within the hour, be assured that I shall be going with him."

The room subsided into a stunned silence. Gabriel was as shocked as anyone, but pleased, as well. She'd sprung instantly to his defense, casting her lot irrevocably with his in front of her brother, challenging him to make of it what he would. His troubles might be far from over, but he wasn't alone with them anymore.

Ross spoke first. "You are being ridiculous, Sarah!

How can he marry you? He's a . . . well, you *know* what he is. He has no family and no fortune other than the one I gave him, and believe me, that can be taken away. He doesn't even have a real name. He's named after the street that houses the brothel he grew up in, for God's sake! Remember his background, Sarah. Can you not see he's cozening you? Marry him and you'll lose your fortune and your self-respect."

Gabriel had heard enough. He understood the older man's anger, but he had a temper of his own, and if he listened to Huntington's abuse much longer he was likely to say, or do, something that he'd later regret. Tight-lipped and silent, he pulled free of Sarah's grasp and stalked to the door.

Stricken, Sarah watched him go. Things had been going so well between them, and now this! She turned on her brother in fury. "Ross, you're a powerful man. I've never known you to be vicious before. How could you throw his background, his lack of family or money, in his face like that? It's appalling! When did you start thinking that such things measured a man's worth? I'm deeply ashamed of you. I'm going to find him now and I'm going to apologize on behalf of my family, and if you wish us gone from here, tell Simmons to ready my carriage. It *is* my carriage, you know." That being said, she stormed from the room.

Sarah had a fair idea of where to find Gabriel. She saddled her black and made her way down the path to the beach, following his trail to the north. He was sitting, hunched on a rock, looking out to sea. Walking up behind him, she squeezed his shoulder and ran her fingers through his hair.

He leaned back into her, and cocked his head sideways. "That went well, don't you think?" he said, looking up with a grin.

Laughing, she kissed him, relieved and surprised he was taking it so well. "Ross didn't mean what he said, Gabe. He just needs some time to adjust."

"Oh, yes, he did," Gabriel said, with a chuckle. "He meant every word."

"I confess, I thought you'd be more upset." She was amazed at his playful mood. It was most unexpected, given the circumstances.

Leaning his head back to rest against her hip, he closed his eyes and turned his face into the sun. "Mmm, I suppose I was upset for a moment or two, but I find myself in too great charity with the world to sustain it. After all"—he opened his eyes, bright with love and laughter, and hauled her down into his lap— "it's not every day a man gets a proposal of marriage from a desperate, lovesick young lass."

She giggled and pushed his face away. "Ack! You need to shave."

He rubbed his nose between her breasts, taking in her scent. Hugging her tight, he kissed her throat and whispered urgently in her ear, "Tell me you meant it, love."

A huge smile lit her face. "Yes, I meant it." She

kissed his nose. "I meant it." His eyes. "I meant it." His lips.

"I won't let you change your mind, mignonne."

"I take it then, your answer is yes?"

"I love you dearly, Sarah. I only want what's best for you, and I'm not at all sure that would be me, but I'm a bloody selfish bastard where you're concerned, and if you'll have me, I'll move heaven and earth to be the man you deserve."

She laughed with joy. "Well, I feel certain I deserve to keep you after putting up with your foul temper, and fouler language," she said, giggling as he tickled her with the rough stubble on his chin. "And with your leaving sand and crumbs in my bed, and . . . mmphhh"—he kissed her soundly—"your stealing my telescope and not putting it away." He slid down into the sand, tugging her, tripping her, and catching her in his arms as they subsided into a tangle of petticoats and kisses. "Oh, Gabriel, I love you. I love you so much."

"*Je t'aime, je t'adore, ma vie, mon âme, mon cœur.* He took her there, on the sand, in the lea of the rock, to the sounds of seabirds and the rolling surf breaking against the shore. With the sea lifting her skirts and tugging at his breeches, he entered her, gently, lovingly, moving with the motion of the swell as it rocked and lifted them. Nothing existed but the sun, the surf, and each other.

Much later, they sat in the hot sun, trying to dry

their clothing. Gabriel leaned against the big rock, his legs cradling Sarah's waist, his chest supporting her back, his arms wound tight around her. They delayed their return, enjoying the peace and quiet a while longer, but both of them knew that eventually they had to face the future. Resting his chin on her head, Gabriel finally spoke. "It's been well over an hour, mignonne. How will your brother kill me, do you think? With a pistol, I expect. I imagine you'd be terribly vexed if I killed him."

"That's not funny, Gabriel."

"No, chère, but it is a problem. You can't say that he took to the notion very well. I expect I'll have to leave, and soon."

"Then I'll go with you. London, Paris, anywhere, it doesn't matter."

He kissed the top of her head and hugged her. "I can't imagine what I ever did to deserve you, Sarah. You make everything worthwhile. But Ross is right, you know."

"About what?"

"I have no name to give you, and no fortune beyond what he's given me."

"Take one of my names, I have several."

He smiled. "Ah, well, I'll not refuse you for lack of a suitable name, but I won't have you support me."

"You're sounding missish again, Gabriel. It doesn't matter. Why should it?"

"It matters to me, Sarah. I want to support *you*, to

take care of you. I . . . it's important to me. I respect your brother and if possible, I want his approval. I don't want to split you from your family."

"So . . . You don't want to marry me anymore? I'm thoroughly compromised, you know."

"Of course, I want to marry you, but—"

"But what?" She was beginning to feel annoyed.

"You're the best thing that's ever happened to me, Sarah. I want to do it properly. I want to give your brother his money back. I want to prove to him I can take care of you, and I don't want you to have to choose between us."

"It's your money, Gabriel, you've earned it."

"No, Sarah, it's not, and I didn't. I never wanted or expected to be paid for helping Jamie. I only accepted because it gave me a reason to leave Madame's, a reason to go with you. It was an excuse. You know it as well as I. I used to pretend Jamie was my family. When I marry you, he really will be. I can't accept payment for helping him. It's never sat well with me . . . I can't keep the money, mignonne."

"Then forget the damn money. I've more than enough for both of us. We'll go somewhere close, Scotland perhaps. Ross will cool down eventually."

"If we do that, he'll never believe I didn't marry you for your fortune. He'll never accept me. I want to be part of your family, Sarah. I don't want to destroy it."

"I see," she said, and she did. He was a proud man. He didn't want to be beholden, and he didn't want her life to be diminished in anyway by joining it with his. She thought it a particularly irrational and peculiarly male conceit, but it was common to all the best men she knew. "So what do you have in mind then, Gabe?"

"I've been talking to Davey, Sarah. He's been restless lately. He says the profits he's making aren't worth the risks now, with all the customs agents about. He intends to do some privateering. He's been talking about setting sail for the Mediterranean."

The excitement in his voice was unmistakable, and her heart seized and stuttered, in her chest. *Privateering in the Mediterranean!* It was dangerous and he'd be gone a long time, if he made it back at all. Damn Davey to hell, and back!

"He's offered me lieutenant, Sarah, and a healthy share of any prize we take. A few good prizes, and I'll be able to take care of you properly, love. I can build you a home with a fine observatory, return your brother his money, and maybe start a small shipping business of my own."

"It's a dangerous business, Gabe," she said, knowing she'd already lost him.

"No, it's not, *chère*. These big merchant ships are poorly armed and slow to maneuver. They rarely put up a fight."

"And they rarely travel unescorted," she observed dryly.

"You know how careful Davey is, and you've

traveled aboard *L'Espérance*. Nothing can catch her."

"How long have you known about this, Gabriel? Why haven't you told me before?"

"I'm not *telling* you about it, I am discussing it with you," he said carefully. "I've made no decision. Davey mentioned it to me weeks ago and I turned him down, but things are different now, mignonne."

"When will you leave?" she asked dully.

"Sarah, please . . . I don't want to upset you. This is only one possible solution to our troubles. If it grieves you this much, I won't go. We'll think of some other way."

She recognized it was something he had to do. It was independence and strength that had helped him survive his abysmal childhood, and it was the same qualities now that refused to allow him to be dependent on anyone else for his livelihood. "I'm sorry, Gabriel. You're right, of course. It *is* a solution. You will establish yourself, and Ross will have time to calm down. If you must go, I'd rather you be with Davey than anywhere else. I just hate to lose you so soon after . . . I'll miss you. When will you go?"

"Davey leaves this week, Sarah. I'll go and see him this evening and ask to live on the ship until then. Your brother *will* shoot me if he catches me climbing up to your room again. That's done now I'm afraid."

She knew he was right. Their all too brief idyll was over and nothing would ever be the same. Tears were streaming down her cheeks as he rocked her in his arms.

"Shhh, mignonne, don't cry. We'll be together, you'll see. Your brother will grow to accept it, and we'll be married and have many happy years together. I promise."

"How long will you be gone" she asked brokenly.

"I don't know, love," he whispered. "At least six months, more if we have bad weather. No more than a year. Will you wait for me that long?"

"However long it takes. However long you want me to."

"What does that mean, *chère*?"

"It will be a grand adventure for you, Gabriel. You've had little opportunity to travel. You'll be able to see things you've only read about. If you're going to do it, I want you to feel free to experience new things, to meet new . . . people."

He burst out laughing and ruffled her hair. "Don't be absurd, mignonne! Do you really think I would choose to be with any woman but you? I love you, Sarah. I'd never treat you that way!"

"A year is a long time, though, Gabe. A man has needs."

"So does a woman. You're everything I've ever needed, Sarah, the only woman I'll ever want or need. I've waited all my life for you. I'll wait as long as it takes, if you will."

"Of course, I will."

"I wish you could come with me, *chère*."

"I've sailed with Davey before. Perhaps I *should* come with you."

"He would never allow it. He knows Ross would never forgive him."

"How do you know that?"

"Because I asked him, when he first brought it up."

"Thank you for asking." She tried her best to give him a bright smile as he wheeled his mount to ride away toward Davey, and danger, and an uncertain future, but her lower lip quivered and her eyes pricked with tears.

Davey was genuinely dismayed when Gabriel recounted the afternoon's events. "You mean to tell me the man came home to find you sitting in his office, on his chair, with your feet on his desk as you blithely fondled his baby sister?"

Gabriel winced. "It sounds worse the way you tell it, Davey, but yes, essentially that's what happened."

"You're lucky Ross didn't kill you."

"He has threatened to. I'd like to think I could defend myself if the need arose."

"Not a battle a man wants to fight, my boy. Lose it, and you lose your life. Win it, and you lose the girl."

"I'm well aware of that, Davey. He's ordered me out and I've left."

"And what of Sarah?"

"I love her, and I intend to marry her."

"Over Ross's dead body, I should think."

"She's agreed to it, Davey. She's a grown woman and she doesn't need his permission."

"True enough, lad. True enough. Then why aren't you with her now?"

"I can hardly stay at the manor now, and I won't have her choose between me and her brothers."

Nodding his approval, Davey pointed to a chair, and poured two glasses of brandy. "Sit yourself down, man."

"Can I stay here, Davey? Is your offer still open?"

"You mean to be a privateer then, Gabriel?"

"Yes, if you'll have me."

"Oh, I'll be glad enough to have you, though Ross will have my guts for garters, but what does the lass think of it?"

"She's hurt and upset, but I can't think of anything else to do. I hope to make enough money to support her, and I hope that Huntington will have calmed down by the time I return."

"He likely will have. Perhaps he would have already, if you'd been a little more discreet in breaking the news to him."

Gabriel flushed with embarrassment.

"She's got money of her own. What's wrong with

that?"

"I'm not a leech, Davey."

"Well, clearly you were not brought up with the right and proper aristocratic values. Marrying an heiress so you can live comfortably off her fortune is quite the thing these days, my boy. You're sure you don't want to reconsider?"

"I'm certain, Davey. I intend for my wife to live comfortably off of *my* fortune."

"Fair enough, but I've no mind to be in Ross's bad graces on account of you, so we'll leave on the morrow before he can find out you're here. I can finish stocking the ship in Polperro." He stood and offered Gabriel his hand. "Go stow your gear now, lad, and welcome aboard."

CHAPTER
20

Ross sat nursing a stiff drink, finally getting over his initial shock and outrage. The lad hadn't dared show himself since this morning, and a good thing, too. What had gotten into Sarah? What had she been thinking, displaying herself in wanton abandon, in his office, in broad daylight, with that dissipated libertine? It was disgraceful! He took another sip of his drink, then leaned back and massaged his temples with his fingertips.

Well, it was too late for regrets now. He was at least partly to blame, leaving them unsupervised as he'd done. Sighing, he leaned back in his chair, twirling the glass between his fingers. It was obvious they had strong feelings for each other. What to do? Throw Gabriel out of the house? If he did, Sarah might go with him, and he was not prepared to lose her again. He had shown *some* promise, and his intentions were proper, even if his behavior was not. If they truly loved each other, if there was any chance they might make a happy life together, then God bless them. It was rare enough in this world.

He would bow to the inevitable, and try to salvage the thing as best he could. In the morning he'd contact his solicitor and make arrangements to cede the lad a property, perhaps attaching a respectable and relatively obscure name to it. He would give him the opportunity to act as lieutenant on one of his merchant vessels, with a view to making him captain in time. There would be no more smuggling. The lad would do as he was told, if he wanted Ross's permission to marry his sister.

When morning broke, the *L'Espérance* was gone, and Gabriel with it. Sarah was heartbroken. She hadn't expected him to leave so suddenly. She'd thought they would have a day or two. She'd thought he would come, at least one more time, to say goodbye. She was sitting in the breakfast room, listlessly buttering her toast, when Ross came in.

"Good morning, sister."

"Good morning, brother," she said, waving her hand in a tired gesture. "As you can see, I'm still here. You didn't order the carriage, so I assumed I might stay."

"Pray don't be ridiculous this early in the morning, Sarah. It gives me a headache. Where is your . . . fiancé?"

"He has left, with our cousin, for the Mediterranean," she said brokenly, tears welling in her eyes.

"The devil, you say! What on earth possessed him? Oh, Sarah, I'm sorry." He reached across the table to squeeze her hand. "I thought he intended to marry you."

"He did. He does."

"Well, I must say he appears to be rather half-hearted about it, if he scampers off at the first sign of trouble."

"Why do you persist in thinking the worst of him, Ross?"

"If I thought the worst of him, I'd have never allowed him near you, or James. Why do *you* persist in thinking the worst of me? Surely you didn't really think I'd do him an injury, or force you to leave?"

"I didn't know what to believe, Ross. I have never seen you so angry, and if I thought that you might, you can be sure Gabriel did, as well. He couldn't very well stay, under the circumstances. He left because he knew how much it would upset me if you and he harmed each other, and because he didn't want me to have to choose between you."

"Hell and damnation! Sarah, I *am* sorry, but I'm only human. I have a temper and the fellow tried it severely. He was in my office, with his feet on my desk, fondling you! Of course, I was angry. If you'd only

234

given me time to calm down, we would have come to some kind of accommodation. It's why I sought you out this morning. I'm prepared to accept him if you want him that badly, with certain conditions, of course. Come now, girl, stop your crying," he said gently. "It's not too late. They left only this morning. I'll send a clipper after them and fetch him back to you."

Smiling through her tears, Sarah reached out and patted his hand. "Thank you, Ross. I do love you a very great deal. You are the best brother in the world, but I'm afraid it won't do any good. He won't accept your conditions. He means to have me on his own terms. He's quite decided."

"And just how does he propose to do that, my dear?"

"He doesn't wish to be beholden to you, or me, or anyone else for his livelihood. He hopes to make his fortune with Davey, so he can support us both. He hopes that you will have grown more accepting during his absence, and when he returns, he intends us to be married, with or without your permission."

Ross nodded, feeling a grudging respect. He'd underestimated Gabriel, it seemed. The lad intended to prove himself. It was a quaint notion, but one he thoroughly approved of, and it made the idea of him marrying Sarah a damn sight more palatable. "Well, good for him!"

Sarah sighed, and sat up straight. "I suppose. I can't help but wish he'd put his love for me before his pride."

"No, my dear. You misunderstand such things, as women often do. It is *because* he loves you that he wishes to prove his worth. I admire him for it."

"Well, I don't require it of him," she snapped. "I know his worth already. I don't understand why he can't accept that."

"Perhaps it's not you he seeks to prove it to, but himself."

She knew the instant he said it that he was right.

"In any case, my dear, I respect him for it. Doubtless, he will write you when he can, and you may tell him that if he presents himself, with sufficient funds and in an appropriate manner at some time in the future, he can expect my approval of his suit."

"Thank you, Ross," she said, giving him a hug. "That means a great deal."

"Yes, quite," Ross said, feeling decidedly uncomfortable, "and you mustn't worry too much, my dear. Davey will take good care of him and he'll be back before you know it."

CHAPTER
21

Davey observed his newest lieutenant through narrowed eyes. They were less than half a day out of Falmouth, and already Gabriel's dreary demeanor, surly address, and dour looks were souring his mood. Where was the lad's spirit of adventure? He hoped to hell he wasn't going to have to endure the fellow's pining and bad temper for the entire voyage. "Gabriel! Over here! A word with you, man."

"Aye, Davey, what is it?"

"It's a stunning fine day, we've a spanking wind on our tail, and the lads are all primed for adventure. How long do you intend to mope about like a lovesick puppy?"

Stiffening, Gabriel drew himself up to his full height. "If I've been negligent or remiss in my duties, I apologize."

"Of course, you haven't, but you're bad for morale!

My morale, at any rate. The girl told you she loved you. She's agreed to marry you. You're off to seek fame and fortune, and you'll be back between her . . . er . . . in her arms before you know it. You've no reason for brooding."

"You're right, Davey. I apologize. I just wish I'd done a better job of things yesterday. It wasn't right, the way I left her. She was so hurt and unhappy. I never even said good-bye."

"What? You didn't say good-bye to Sarah?"

"No . . . I . . . I thought we'd have more time. I didn't think we'd be leaving so soon."

"Hmm, that's likely to annoy her, lad, and you don't want a woman annoyed with you for months on end, especially when you're not going to be around to remind her of all your good qualities."

Gabriel sighed. "You're not making it any better, Davey."

"Well . . . it's easily enough mended. I'm partial to her myself, Gabriel. I hate to imagine her hurting unnecessarily, and I daresay she'll be angry enough with me for taking you away as it is. We'll turn back if you like. We can anchor offshore tonight and you can slip in and say your farewells."

"You would do that, Davey?"

"I've just said so, haven't I? I'd rather lose a day now than have to put up with your ill temper for the rest of this trip. Just promise me it will put you back in good humor."

"I'll promise you anything. God love you, man!"

"Oh, he does, lad, no doubt he does. Everyone does. Now let's turn this ship around."

"You're a ship's captain, Davey? A real one?"

"No, Gabriel, I'm the cabin boy. What kind of question is that?"

"Can you marry us? As ship's captain?"

"Eh? What?"

"Sarah was so unhappy. I think it might make her feel better about my leaving."

"Well, I don't know about that, lad. I could do it, but I doubt it'd be legal. But my cook now, Master Aubrey, he acts as chaplain when needed. He's one of Christ's vicars as I recall. He might do the trick, but I'm not sure 'tis a good idea, Gabriel. The ladies tend to like flowers and guests and fancy dresses and such. She never had that for her first marriage. That was an unhappy affair. It would be a shame were she to miss it for this one, as well."

"We can do all of that when I return."

"So . . . a secret wedding," Davey mused. "A private affair no one else need know about. You've seen right through me, lad. 'Tis romance that fuels my soul. I expect we can arrange something. But it will never leave this ship and you'll do it proper and official when we get back. Agreed?"

"Agreed!"

"Then let me be the first to congratulate you on your great good fortune!" Davey said, shaking Gabriel's hand vigorously. "And let's hope she's not so annoyed at your hasty departure that she turns you down."

Restless in her sleep, Sarah groaned, rolled over, and opened her eyes. He was sitting in the window seat leaning back on his elbows. She smiled, delighted to see him. He looked almost real. "Will you come like this to see me every night in my dreams?"

"I will do my best, mignonne."

The sound of his voice, hoarse with longing, swept away the last vestiges of sleep. "My God, it *is* you! You're here! How can that be?" She flew from the bed and threw herself in his arms.

He caught her tight and kissed her hungrily, her throat, her cheeks, her brow, her lips. "God, Sarah, I don't know how I'll survive without you. I need you more than food, or water, or air."

"How is it you're here, Gabriel? I thought you'd left with Davey" she asked between fevered kisses.

"I couldn't leave without saying good-bye, without telling you how much I love you."

"Can you stay?"

"No, mignonne, I cannot. Davey waits for me off-shore."

"How much time do we have?"

"There is a boat, Sarah, it waits for me now."

She drew back and touched his cheek. "No time at all then."

"I've come to ask you if you'll marry me, Sarah."

"I've already told you I would. Do you doubt me?"

"I mean now, *chère*. This very night. There's a man aboard *L'Espérance* who will marry us, if you agree, and Davey will give us his cabin for the night. I know it's not what you wanted, and I promise you, we'll do it right, with your family, when I—"

"Yes, yes, yes!" She covered his face with ardent kisses. "I'll marry you, this very night! I can hardly believe we're really going to do it!" She hugged him with joy. "I was so afraid something would happen to prevent it. Oh, Gabriel! Nothing would make me happier!"

He set her down with a happy grin, thankful she'd agreed, overjoyed to think that in a few short hours she would be his wife, and deeply relieved that the sadness he'd put there yesterday had finally left her eyes.

"Oh, my Lord, Gabriel, what shall I wear? I have nothing appropriate," she said, uncharacteristically flustered.

"That's never stopped you before, mignonne. Might I suggest your breeches? It will make it easier getting you there and back. Besides, sweetheart, do you really want to waste time finding something to wear when we have so little of it left, and when I plan to have you naked as soon as I possibly can?" Remembering what Davey had said, he added, "I promise you, Sarah, we'll be married properly when I return, with guests, and flowers, and music. You shall have a beautiful dress and your family will be there. But tonight is just for us."

"Yes, of course," she said with a happy smile, hauling on a pair of breeches and boots. "You're absolutely right." Turning around to look for a shirt, she found him waiting, hand outstretched, holding the shirt she'd pilfered from him a lifetime ago.

"I would be deeply grateful if you'd wear this, mignonne. It . . . moves me to see you in it."

She was about to object, it was far too large for her, suitable only for a bed garment, but the hungry pleading in his eyes stifled her protest. Plucking it from his fingers with a saucy grin, she put it on and carefully tucked it in. "Your men will think I'm a terrible hoyden."

"My men will think me the luckiest man on earth, and they will surely be right." Sweeping her into his arms, he pulled her tight against his length and kissed the top of her head. "Can you manage to climb down the oak if I help you?"

"For heaven's sake, Gabe," she scoffed. "I've been climbing it all by myself since I was seven years old."

"I should have known. Your pardon, *ma belle*."

They scrambled down to the beach, breathless and laughing like naughty children, and tumbled into the waiting boat. Gabriel wrapped her protectively in his cloak and grinned proudly at the men who'd come to row them back to the ship. "Pierre. Antonio. May I have the honor of presenting my fiancée, and soon to be wife, the very lovely and thoroughly charming, Lady Sarah."

"*Enchantée, mademoiselle*, and very welcome you are, too," Pierre responded with a cheeky grin. "Perhaps now the lad will cease growling and fretting, and leave us all in peace."

"We have met before," Antonio said with a warm smile. "It is a very great pleasure to see you again, my lady."

"And you, too, Tony," Sarah said, emerging from under Gabriel's cloak.

"You've made our laddie a very happy man, my lady. We're all most grateful to you for it. And I'm here to tell you that you might have done worse."

"Indeed, gentlemen, thank you for your stirring endorsements," Gabriel said dryly, as Sarah settled back against his chest.

It was a night she would always remember. The winds had died down shortly after sunset, and by the time the *L'Espérance* had anchored, the ocean was as still as glass. The moon was new, barely a sliver, but the sky pulsed with brilliant light as myriad stars flickered and sparked, reflected in the still waters below. The perfume of a late spring night, soft, fresh, and beguiling, was all around her, and as they approached the *L'Espérance* she could sense the muted bustle and excitement onboard the little ship. The men considered

Gabriel one of their own, and they had loved Sarah ever since she'd first sailed with them six years ago. Like many who roamed the sea, they were romantics at heart, and everyone had joined wholeheartedly in the enterprise, eager to see the young couple reunited.

Davey greeted her with a tight hug when she finally clambered up on deck. "Can you forgive me, cousin, for stealing him away?"

"If you bring him back to me safe and sound, Davey," she said, returning his hug.

"I will, lass. He loves you something fierce, you know."

"I know, Davey. I love him something fierce, too."

He regarded her ruefully. He had loved her since the first time he'd seen her, awkward, and gangly and dressed like a boy. He'd been angry, hurt, and lost, grieving his parents and enraged at their meaningless deaths, a stranger in a strange new world. She'd made him laugh, joined him enthusiastically on his adventures, imagined him a great hero, and made him feel welcome when he'd thought himself completely alone. He'd never told her how he felt. He'd been waiting for the right time, and now it would never come.

"I'm happy for you both, cousin. You know how much I care for you. You've chosen well, my girl."

"Thank you, Davey, I know," she whispered, kissing his cheek, "and I love you, too."

Gabriel came up behind her, enfolding her in his arms. "Now is your last chance to change your mind,

Sarah," he whispered in her ear.

Looking back at him over her shoulder, she grinned. "Not a chance, Gabriel. You are well and truly caught and I shan't let you wriggle free."

"Well, then, children, let's go to my cabin, shall we?"

Sarah and Gabriel stood openmouthed in amazement. Davey's cabin had been transformed. The bed had been made with silk coverlets and festooned with rose petals. Flowers were everywhere, in wild profusion, strewn on the floor, spilling from vases, lining the windows, and framing the door. The room was lit with scores of candles, bathing it in a magical glow, and a feast had been set on the table, the proud work of Mr. Aubrey, who was waiting in his cassock to perform the ceremony.

"Oh, Davey, thank you so much," Sarah said, hugging him with tears in her eyes.

"Think nothing of it, cousin." He squeezed her tight, then steered her back toward Gabriel.

All the crew that could be spared were there, crowded into the cabin and the doorway and spilling out into the corridor as Gabriel and Sarah stepped forward to take their vows. Taking a little gold band he'd managed to find in Polperro, Gabriel placed it on Sarah's finger as Mr. Aubrey proudly pronounced them man and wife to the hearty cheers of captain and crew. He kissed her then, passionate and tender, oblivious to the company, the swell of congratulations, or the wild music that swirled around them, until Davey stole her from him, pulling her into a merry swirling dance.

The only awkwardness was when Davey asked them how he was to register them in his logbook. Gabriel hadn't given it any thought, hadn't even thought to discuss it with Sarah. She put a hand on his shoulder and leaned into him, whispering "I'd much rather St. Croix, than Munroe, if you don't mind too terribly." He thought about it a moment, and found that he really didn't mind. He was done with being ashamed of his past. It had made him who he was, and who he was, was the man whom Sarah loved and had chosen to marry. St. Croix was as good a name as any, and he signed it in the register with a flourish.

The next half hour was a mad blend of dancing, feasting, and toasts to the happy couple, until Davey called a halt. "Enough, you scurvy lot. You were invited to the wedding, not the honeymoon! It's time to take it out on deck and let the happy couple sort things out for themselves." This announcement was greeted with good-natured jeers and bawdy jests, but in short order the celebrations had moved down to the lower deck, and Gabriel and Sarah finally found themselves alone.

Gabriel moved to bar the door before turning to face her. She sat cross-legged on the bed, in her breeches and his big shirt, a crown of flowers perched slightly askew atop her head. His heart ached at the sight of her. There was nothing more precious to him in all the world. "I would see you in nothing but my shirt, Madame Wife, if you would be so kind."

She leaned back on her elbows, shimmying her hips, hooking the band of her breeches with her thumbs, and tugging as she slid them to her knees. Sitting up, she peeled them slowly down her calves to her ankles, and then, with a little shake of her leg, she hooked them with her toes and tossed them carelessly to the floor.

He watched her, mesmerized.

"Like so, husband?" she inquired, leaning back on her elbows again, her splendid legs slightly splayed, her look, pure seduction.

"Exactly so, wife," he managed hoarsely, aching all over at the sight of her, his entire being vibrating with carnal excitement. Her fingers twisted and played with the fringes of his shirt, her shirt, *their* shirt—raising it slowly up her thighs, revealing wonderful mysteries. His eyes flared, igniting with pleasure, darkening with passion. He stalked her now, his lips thick and burning, wanting her kisses. His fingertips tingled with the urge to touch her. His arms ached to hold her. His woman. His wife.

Stretching her body with a voluptuous feline grace, she flashed him a wicked grin. He pounced on her, growling, trapping her easily beneath him, his muscular arms keeping him from crushing her. Engulfing her, he claimed her lips in a long, searing, kiss. "I love you," he said into her ear, his voice husky with emotion. "I may yet go mad, for love of you."

The tenderness in his eyes and voice took her breath away.

"Sarah, I never dreamed . . . I never dared hope . . . when I met you, I couldn't have imagined you'd ever be mine, but I wanted you from that very first day. I was barely surviving. When you came, my life began. I love you with every part of me, my heart and my mind, my body and my soul, and I thank you with all my heart, for giving me your love and giving me a life."

He reached up to draw the floral crown from her head, watching as her chestnut curls tumbled and cascaded over her shoulders and down her back in a riotous stream, combing his fingers through it and trapping one long tendril to draw to his lips. His fingers found her chin and eased her mouth to his. He breathed into her, drawing his lips over hers, again and again, touching and teasing, imploring her to open.

"Oh, Gabe," she moaned, hot and dizzy from his kisses, "I was so afraid I'd lose you. When you left without saying good-bye . . . I—"

"I know, mignonne. I'm so sorry."

"No, don't be. You're here now. I only meant . . . I felt as if I'd lost a part of myself. I felt sick and empty inside. I'm so glad you came back! I can hardly believe you did this for me. You're the sweetest man alive, Gabriel. I *adore* you! I will love you until the day I die, and I am so happy and relieved that we're actually married."

"It made you feel better, mignonne, yes?" he said with a happy grin. "I thought it would."

"Oh, yes, my love, much better. Now you're mine, and I won't let anything take you away from me."

He slid a leg over hers, and then she was under him, her hair spilling across the pillow, shimmering in the candlelight. She nuzzled him through his open shirt, her hands sliding sensuously up and down his arms as she kissed his powerful chest, his throat, and then his wicked luscious lips. Lying there wrapped in his strength, she closed her eyes and enjoyed the sensations as his lips brushed her hair, her cheeks, her ear, and he placed feathery kisses against her up-turned nose and jaw. The soft linen of his shirt was warm from his flesh, soft against her cheek, and she gave a soft cry of protest when he withdrew to pull it off, subsiding when he returned, hot and silky smooth, to her arms. She'd always loved touching him, and now she indulged herself, letting her hands roam his sleek, sculpted form, feeling the taut muscle of it, the strength. She caressed the warm skin of his back, feeling the faint ridges of scar tissue, feeling his muscles flex under her touch. She pulled him closer, so her aching breasts pressed tight against his solid chest, and his hard-muscled thigh lay firm and heavy between the heated juncture of hers.

His generous hands explored her slender rib cage and the swell of her breasts, caressing her through the fabric of her shirt, sending frissons of delight wherever they alighted, rubbing and stroking, sliding and petting. He thrust against her, growling deep in his

249

throat, and she moaned and arched her back, shifting her hips and digging her heels into the mattress, grinding against him as she tried to relieve the aching longing between her legs.

He slid his hand under her shirt, grazing her naked skin with his fingertips, teasing her nipples with clever fingers as he continued his fevered kisses, stifling her moans of pleasure with his mouth as she squirmed and strained against him. Lowering his head, he rasped her peak with his wet, sinuous tongue, making her cry out with pleasure. Cupping her breasts with both hands, he moved from one to the other, suckling their ridged tips through the wet material as she groaned in bliss, her hungry cries of passion muted by the distant sounds of music and laughter from the deck below.

"More, please . . . Gabe, more . . . harder." She pushed against him, wanting more, and he obliged her. Pushing aside her shirt, he tugged at her with his teeth, sucking and stroking with lips and tongue as he moved his hand to play gently with her soft curls, separating her nether lips with his fingers, stroking back and forth in a teasing motion, as pleasure and delight coiled and spread within her. Rocking and moaning with need, she pushed against his hand, reaching for his hips, desperate for release.

"Soon, mignonne," he promised huskily, running his hand up and down her legs. He nudged them gently apart, kissing the inside of her thighs, then bent his head to tickle her silky heat with his tongue.

"Gabriel, please, love . . . you're killing me," she moaned, clutching at his shoulders.

"But it's such a sweet way to die, my love," he murmured, looking up at her, his eyes smoky with passion and desire. He parted her with his tongue and began hungrily kissing her core. Frantic, aching, raging with desire, she tugged and pulled against his head, making primitive sounds of surrender, urging him on until she was drowning in hot, rolling waves of ecstasy, drowning in love, crying out his name.

Drawing himself up her length, he captured her lips with his own. *"Je t'aime, mignonne. Je t'adore.* I love you so much, Sarah."

"Oh, God! I love you, too, Gabe." She wrapped her arms around him, shifting her weight, spreading her legs to accommodate him. "Come, love. Come to me."

Feeling near to bursting, raw with wanting, he gritted his teeth, telling himself to be gentle with her. As he slowly eased into her, she clamped her legs around his hips and pulled him deeper, closing around him, encompassing him as their bodies joined, on fire for each other. Lifting her, he claimed her as his own, his love, his life, his wife, thrusting deep within her as she raked her nails across his back.

Their groans and cries echoed wildly about the cabin as they consumed one another, ecstatic, eager, and unrestrained. It was rapture when her tight hot muscles began to contract around him, tightening and clenching, spurring him to his own blissful release. His head snapped back and a deep growl tore from his throat as his hot seed spilled into her body. Breathless, unable to speak, their bodies slick with sweat, they lay tangled together amongst the disordered bedclothes. They had so little time, neither of them wanted to waste it, but nature demanded her due, and exhausted, cuddled together, they drifted helplessly to sleep.

Sarah woke halfway through the night. The ship had quieted and Gabriel's warm body was wrapped around her, holding her at waist and thigh, his chest moving rhythmically at her back. She turned on her side to look at him, resting her head on the inside of her arm. He was a magnificent lover, this husband of hers. He looked so boyish and vulnerable that her heart squeezed with pain. He moaned, anxious in his sleep, muttering under his breath; another dream, and she did what she'd done so many times before. She cradled him in her arms and drew him down to rest, one last time, before he left. She didn't know why she was crying, or why such joy should bring such pain.

Davey came for them well before dawn. "It's time, children. Two of the lads will row you to the beach, and there you must say your good-byes."

"Thank you, Davey, for everything. You will take care of him? You'll bring him back to me?"

"Aye, cousin, I'll do my best. Make haste now, Gabriel. We sail with the tide."

The wind had risen, and the boat rose and fell

on the waves as he cradled her in his lap, holding her close against the chill that permeated the air and both their hearts. They had nothing they wished to say in front of others, and they made the trip to the beach in silence, hands clasped tightly together. He insisted on accompanying her up the path to the foot of the great old tree, not knowing how to say good-bye. Taking her hand in his, he raised it to his mouth, his breath warming her fingers as he kissed each one in turn. His eyes held hers, bright with love and tenderness. "Please don't cry, mignonne," he murmured, drawing her close. "I can't bear it when you do."

"I'm sorry," she whispered, putting her hands around his waist and pressing her cheek into his shoulder. "It's not like me at all."

"Indeed, it's not," he said, laughter rumbling in his chest. Burrowing his head against her neck, he took in her scent, and kissed away her tears. "I will always love you, Sarah. I'll write you every day, and I will come back to you as soon as I'm able. I'm your husband now, and you're my wife, and no one can keep us apart. You believe me, do you not?"

"Yes, my love. I believe you." She threw her arms around his neck and plundered his mouth in a hungry, soul-searing kiss. "You will miss me terribly."

"Yes, mignonne, I will. I'm not sure how I'll survive without you."

"My thoughts will be with you all the time, Gabriel. I'll think of you every night. Pick a star and show it to me, and when you look at it, you'll know I'm looking at it, too."

Delighted with the idea, he lifted her off the ground and twirled her around. Setting her down, he pointed to a lambent glow flickering low on the horizon. "That one, Sarah."

"That is Venus."

"The planet of love, yes. She will help us spend some time together, *chère*. Watch her when she's risen in the sky, and know that I'm watching her, too, thinking of you, loving you, and trying to get home to you."

She smiled. "And what if the sky is clouded over?"

"Then I'll come to you in your dreams." Pulling her close, he enfolded her in his arms, hugging her so tight she couldn't breathe. "I have to go now, wife. Know that I love you and I live to be back in your arms, and when I return we shall marry in front your family and the whole damned world, and nothing will ever part us again." Helping her up into the branches of the oak, he waited until she was safe on the balcony before waving good-bye. He was gone an instant later, knowing the men would be anxious, and Davey, fretting to leave.

Sarah watched his tall form as he loped down the path. She'd lain down to sleep, drowning in sorrow, and he had come in wonderful surprise, with his sweet smile and generous heart, taking away her pain, warming her in his arms, and making her his wife. He loved her, and she was certain now that he intended to return. It was enough. It would have to be.

CHAPTER
22

Two years earlier, Napoleon Bonaparte had amassed a huge force in the Mediterranean port of Toulon, sending shivers throughout Europe and the Ottoman Empire. England, Spain, Sicily, and Portugal, all potential targets, had breathed a sigh of relief when he had turned his attention to the east, setting the French flag over the pyramids of Egypt. Days later, the battleships that accompanied his transport fleet were caught at anchor by the British at Aboukir Bay, and all but two of them were lost in the Battle of the Nile. The Egyptian debacle had given the British strategic control of the Mediterranean, and handed Napoleon his first defeat, leaving his troops stranded, cut off by sea from rescue or reinforcement.

French merchant ships still darted in and out, eager to reap profits, their country greedy for plunder and wonders from the Orient and the Middle East, but they were no longer well protected. It was a circumstance that presented interesting opportunities for men of skill and daring. With the right ship and crew, there was a fortune to be made. Davey was of indifferent, somewhat opportunistic, nationality, and he'd held letters of marquee at different times, from various nations. His family had been harassed and evicted from France in the sixteenth and seventeenth centuries on religious grounds; and he gave a nominal nod to Protestant England, which had been one of the first nations to shelter his Huguenot forbears. For that reason, out of deference to Ross's sensibilities, and in the interest of having a safe port of call, he'd always avoided preying on British ships. It was his intention now to prey on French and Spanish ones, reaping the harvest sown by failed ambition and rampant greed.

They stopped first in Calais. An edict of tolerance passed a little over a decade ago, had partly restored the religious and civil rights of Huguenots in France, and it was amongst this community Davey intended to arrange financial backing, and provision the *L'Espérance,* and fit her with a new copper bottom that would dramatically increase her speed. Leaving the ship there, they continued inland to Paris. It was Davey's intention to take care of some personal business, see to his protégé's introduction to polite society, and once his ship was ready, set sail for plunder and adventure. It caused him no discomfort at all to know he would be soon preying upon his host.

Davey insisted Gabriel accompany him as he went about his business, and the two of them made a striking pair. Gabriel was accepted wherever they went as a minor French nobleman and adventurer. His eagerness to see the sights made Davey laugh, and compare him to an English lordling on the Grande Tour. They received a great deal of attention, and were avidly pursued by eligible young ladies, disreputable widows, married women, and females of far less respectable origins. Davey enjoyed himself immensely, falling in and out of love at least three times over the course of a month, and in and out of welcoming beds far more often than that.

Gabriel found the interest tiresome, and although he was always scrupulously polite he didn't encourage intimacy, coolly rebuffing those who solicited his attention, including males of a certain variety. He was casually dismissive of all who hungered for him, and his disinterest only heightened his appeal. The only person he had any sexual interest in was Sarah. He missed her terribly and wrote her as often as he was able.

His first letter didn't reach her until a good three weeks after his departure. Sitting in the library, going through her correspondence, she was debating attending an upcoming scientific lecture at the Royal Institute. She was in desperate need of diversion, and a trip to London might be just what she needed to lift her from the doldrums. Shuffling her papers haphazardly across the desk, she cast her mind back to her last night with Gabriel. The whole evening had a fairy-tale quality to it that sometimes made her wonder if it had ever happened at all. Lost in reverie, she was so startled when Jamie burst into the room that she almost fell from her chair.

He ran to her, grinning with excitement, waving a thick white packet in his hand. "Look, Sarah! A parcel from Gabriel! It's from France and it's addressed to you. Open it, please. Read it to me. How is he?" Hopping onto the desk, Jamie peered over her shoulder as she ripped open the bindings and several letters spilled out. "Maybe one is for me," he said hopefully.

"I do believe you're right, Jamie; it looks like two are for you," Sarah said, scooping them up and handing them to him. "Now why don't you go and read yours, and I'll read mine, and when we've both finished, we can share from them what we wish?"

"Oh, yes, of course, I understand. He will have written you private things, I suppose," Jamie said with a disappointed sigh.

"You might be right!" Laughing, face flushed, she ruffled his hair and gathered her letters. Her heart was pounding so hard she was half surprised Jamie couldn't hear it. "I believe I'd like to read these in my room, Jamie. Will you forgive me?"

"I think he may have written you some very private things," Jamie said with a laugh. Bowing, he clutched his letters and practically skipped out the door,

The moment he left, Sarah rushed to her room, giddy as a schoolgirl. Throwing herself onto the window seat, she tore open an envelope and began to read.

Mon amour, chère amie, Madame Wife,

We are settled in Paris now, and I finally have some solitude to write. My head is crowded with you, mignonne, your voice, your image, your scent. You plague my thoughts and dreams, both day and night, and in revenge I shall plague you with letters. I miss you terribly, and have so many things to tell you.

The L'Espérance remains in harbor at Calais with most of the crew, loading provisions and preparing for several months at sea. Davey and I have rented quarters in St. Germaine. Our lodgings are situated very near the Luxembourg Garden, which much resembles an enormous English garden but for the statues and the little men bent head-to-head, playing chess. We tarry here so that we may purchase navigational equipment and various other necessities best found in Paris, and so that Davey may take care of some financial matters as well as business of a personal nature.

He seems to know everyone, in high places and in low, including the Charge d'affaires. He had no difficulty acquiring French citizen papers for us both, and it seems to cause him no discomfort whatsoever that we are soon to be preying on French and Spanish ships, It is curious how such an essentially amiable man, the wisest, truest, and most trustworthy of friends, can be so cheerfully amoral! I confess to feeling a great deal of admiration for him in this regard.

I am uncertain as to why he insisted I accompany him, but so he has, and so I do, not without much disquiet and unease. I can tell you and you alone, that I have no desire to *encounter anyone that might remind me of my past, which is still too recent for comfort. Although I have a dread of it, it weakens day by day as I become evermore convinced that people see only what they expect to see. I introduce myself by the name St. Croix, and we are everywhere welcomed as gentlemen. Your acceptance of me as I am, and your choice to take that name as my wife, has served to take the sting from it. If it is acceptable to you, then how can it be otherwise for me?*

In truth, my love, I am finding this entire experience passing strange. My life has been so circumscribed by the events and circumstances of my youth, that I find myself a stranger here in this country of my birth, with no sense of home or belonging, or even recognition. I have never known this city beyond a few confining blocks, never felt this as my country, never thought of any place as my home, until I met you, and now you are my only country, and my only home.

I am seeing much of this city for the first time, as a tourist might, which seems to provide your cousin with much amusement. at my expense. Let me tell you first of the mood of the place. Bonaparte, the Little General, has come up in the world. He managed to slip past the British and his own troops, and has returned to Paris in glory, abandoning his fleet in Egypt to accept the great honor of being named First Counsel of France. A sense of excitement and a macabre gaiety have gripped the city. Everywhere, people from all classes join in the new craze from Germany, the waltz, at les bals publics that spring up throughout the city, and those aristocrats who managed to escape the revolution's fury have begun to emerge once more. You may not credit it, but many of the relatives of the guillotined find it smart and stylish to sport a thin bloodred ribbon around their necks, in a ghoulish fashion they call à la victime.

More than a few young men have found their inheritance available to them sooner than expected, and possessing more money than experience or wit, they seem in a very great hurry to lose it. We are constantly invited to parties and to play at cards, and consequently I have developed a more-than-passing acquaintance with the gaming tables, both at the dens situated in the Palais Royale, which Davey loves to frequent, and in private homes. The habit of gambling gives one entrée into the beau monde; and it seems there is no other requirement to recommend one to the finest company in France.

I find myself much intrigued with a game called vingt-et-un. While most games appear to have nothing to do with skill, it seems to me that this one does, and a person who pays careful attention to the cards can greatly improve his chances of winning. My research of this theory has proven most fruitful to date, and despite, or because of my successes, I am somewhat sought-after wherever the play is deep.

Davey had asked me to accompany him to a gathering tonight, but I assured him that I would be useless at company or at cards, as I can think of nothing but you. Everywhere, I hear your voice, and I am constantly annoyed when I turn my head to see some painted creature clutching at my arm and prattling in my ear. It is your conversation I want, not theirs. I confess that the pleasure of your company has made *me rather difficult to please.*

Now that I have relieved my conscience by confessing my newest vice, I pray and trust you will forgive me, though I've no intention of renouncing this particular sin. It is far too profitable and may, in itself, absolve me of the obligation I have to your brother. I pray you indulge me further by allowing me to share some observations I've made as a tourist. It's a lonely pastime, as Davey is supremely disinterested and far more inclined to visit friends of his amongst the fairer sex. He maintains that he has seen it all before and is far more concerned with investigating the charms of the locals rather than the locale.

As I ramble about by myself, I'm certain that I'm often mistook for a madman, for I am constantly looking over my shoulder to remark upon some wondrous sight to you, and of course, you aren't there. Yet, I have promised myself that I will share this experience with you, in as much as I can, and so I wonder what you're doing as you read this now. Are you warm in your bed, or do you sit wrapped in my best shirt, with a candle in the window seat? Maybe you're out on the balcony, under the stars. Accompany me in spirit then, my love, as I walk the streets of Paris.

The city is in a state of flux. Beggars are everywhere to be seen and much of the city has been vandalized. There are headless statues, streets running raw with sewage, and much bustle, chaos, and confusion. The façade of the Tuileries is ridden with bullet holes, and Louis IX's priceless Saint-Chapelle sports a fine sign saying "National Property for sale." Notre Dame has been sadly plundered and neglected, and is currently being used as a grain warehouse. She reminds one of an ancient grande dame, destitute, fallen on hard times but still magnificent and proud.

One needn't travel to Italy to see the fine sculptures and artwork of ancient Greece and Rome. Napoleon, the art lover, has raped those poor countries and brought their treasures to the Louvre, along with plunder from Egypt, the Orient, and most of the noble houses of France. It is magnificent to the point of being overwhelming, and one would need to stay a month at least to do it any justice.

There is a place I know you would particularly enjoy, mignonne. We shall have to visit it together someday. I speak of the Observatoire de Paris, which has a splendid view of the city from its rooftop. They claim it to be the first modern observatory built in the world. I expect you would know the truth of it. You will be pleased to know they possess a refracting telescope made by your Mr. James Short. I had the good fortune, while there, of meeting the current director, a Monsieur Pierre Mechain, who has discovered no less than seven comets in the past twenty years! I took the liberty of telling him about your interest in such things and your exquisite taste in telescopes. My learned new friend did not believe me at first, but at my insistence he was much intrigued, and he has humbly begged you to correspond, if you so desire. I hope this pleases you.

Well, there now, it has started to rain. I can hear it drumming on the roof, tapping on the pane, and splashing in the street below. Alone here by myself, I find it a melancholy sound. With you by my side it would be a sweet song of peace and contentment, a prelude to warmth and comfort and secret delights. Damn, mignonne, this writing business is a double-edged sword! I feel both infinitely closer to you and infinitely forlorn and far away.

Lord, how I miss you, Sarah! You pervade my entire being. I miss the feel of your head on my shoulder at night, the soft caress of your breath against my cheek, and the soothing comfort of your heart, beating strong and steady next to mine. I leave a space for you beside me, even though you're far away. I watch the night sky, and when I see Venus, I imagine your arms wrapped round me as you lean against my back. I smell your scent and crave your touch.

They say that time and distance teach perspective. Well, it has taught me this. Fortune, adventure, discovery, these are hollow things without your presence to bring them to life. I am determined that when this adventure is completed, I will not part from you again. I confess to a love for the sea, but her charms are insipid and pallid things compared to yours. I will spend my life at sea only insofar as you may wish to accompany me.

I am serious, mignonne. I hope to gain enough from this adventure to have a vessel and a crew of my own. If you will have it, we will adventure together as man and wife. If you will not, then I shall hire a captain and spend my days doting upon you until I am so much underfoot and such a nuisance that you will indulge me, and we shall run away to sea together. Think what a marvelous observatory we might fashion on the quarterdeck at night.

Ah, mon amie, you've become a habit with me, much

like breathing, and God's truth, it seems as hard to do with-
out you as to do without air. If I were there with you now,
or you here with me, I would pull you close in my arms,
bury my face in your hair, and give you a thousand kiss-
es, starting with your pretty shell toes and the magnificent
arch of your dainty foot, which, I assure you, is far lovelier
and more inspiring than any of the tracery or architecture
in all the cathedrals and palaces I have seen here in Paris.

I shall wish you a good night now, love. I'm going to
slip between the sheets and close my eyes so that I may imag-
ine you beside me and visit you in my dreams. Until I can
take you in my arms again, know that I hold you close in my
mind, in my heart, and in my soul.

Forever Yours,
Gabriel

CHAPTER
23

It was mid-June when they finally returned to Calais. The newly fitted *L'Espérance* stood at anchor in the harbor, riding high in the water, pennants flapping in the breeze. She'd been captured from the French in 1784. French warship design and construction was far superior to that of the English, and she was sleeker, faster, and more powerful than anything Davey might have bought from an English shipyard. Square sailed, she was fitted with twelve nine-pound cannon, Davey having chosen to sacrifice some of her original firepower for maneuverability and speed. She was no longer a warship after all, but a privateer, and her prey was merchant ships, her goal, to catch and board them, not to sink them. As it was, she combined a formidable capacity for attack and defense with agility and lightning speed. She was Davey's first love, his pride and joy.

As they were rowed out to join her, the bustle and frenetic activity, which from shore had resembled a swarming anthill, became sharper, distinguishing it-self into human form. Gabriel could see busy sailors passing casks of salt pork and beef, cheese and ship's biscuit, beer and rum, into the hold from the boats hove to alongside. They also loaded powder and solid shot, for bringing down masts and smashing through hulls; chain shot, to take down sails and rigging; and bags of sand, to act as ballast. When their cutter bumped to a halt against the starboard side, the waterman caught the main chains with a hook, holding it steady along-side as they climbed, hand over hand, up the ladder and onto the deck.

Early the next morning, Gabriel stood on the quarterdeck, skin pricking with excitement, seized by the spirit of adventure and the thrill of the unknown. The *L'Espérance* was rolling a little, but she slid along smoothly, the only sounds the gurgling of the sea green waves frothing past her hull, and the rhythmic creak-ing of her spars and joints. As she surged forward, the coastline faded and disappeared, and only the deep blue sea and azure sky stretched on the horizon. Taking a deep breath he raised his face into the sea breeze and called out a course for Gibraltar. They were underway.

Davey managed his ship and crew with far more organization and discipline than would be found on a pirate vessel, and far more freedom and flexibility than would be found in His Majesty's Navy. There were no floggings or hangings, and no drunkenness or deser-tions aboard his ship. His men were a tight-knit group of highly skilled, highly trained professionals, and he treated them as such. He respected his men and made them rich, and they loved him for it.

It took three weeks to sight Gibraltar. The language spoken in the Mediterranean ports was the *lingua Franca*, a bastardized vernacular parsed together from the many tongues spoken throughout the region by natives, traders, and captives from many nations. Since leaving Calais, Davey had insisted the crew converse in it so as to accustom them to its use. Its many Latin derivatives made it familiar to Gabriel, and with his facility for languages he picked it up quickly.

Mornings were taken up with gunnery drill and the putting on and the taking off of sail. A well-trained gun crew could get off three shots in two minutes, and they practiced over and over again until that standard was as easy to them as breathing. They were also repeatedly exercised in the use of small arms, cutlasses, and boarding pikes. Gabriel was the only member of the crew who had never traversed these seas before, and as was his habit, he shared his discoveries with Sarah.

> *Ma chère, mignonne,*
> *It is now seventy days since last I held you in my arms. Somehow, I have survived, though I curse each day that takes me farther away from you, and pray for swift winds to bring me home. With luck that will be before Christmas. I have many wonderful things to tell you! We have made*

Gibraltar our base of operations as it is the major English settlement in the area, its fort controlling the entrance to the Atlantic, and its trading post a conduit to and from the Iberian Peninsula to the north, Africa to the south, and the Mediterranean and the Orient to the east.

I was much impressed when we first caught sight of her. The rock itself, one of the Pillars of Hercules, is an impressive limestone formation with fortified caves and tunnels towering one thousand feet above the surrounding countryside. The fort is said to be impregnable. The strait it only thirteen kilometers across at its narrowest point, and sailing through this passage can be dangerous at any time of year. We will make one last pass to the east before setting sail for home. Our intent is to leave by early October, just ahead of the storm season, when even the Barbary corsairs put their galleys into port for the winter.

We've had very good hunting since our arrival, Sarah, taking several French and Spanish ships, generally without so much as a shot being fired. With twelve cannon and our new copper bottom, we're fast enough to catch them, light enough to follow them into coastal waters, and formidable enough to frighten them into submission. They are always relieved to find that we are not Barbary pirates, a breed of men who roam the waters hereabouts looking for plunder, mostly in the form of captives to hold for ransom or take as slaves.

Many of these pirates are European renegades, or renegados as they're called, men who've forsaken their religion and accepted the Muslim faith. Much like Davey, they refer to themselves as privateers. Britain has a treaty with them and we have a pass from the Algerian Dey, but Davey knows them well and he's not inclined to trust them. Nimble and quick, we stay out of their way.

So far we have "liberated," as Davey likes to call it, large quantities of silks, jewels, and wool carpets. Two of the vessels we've taken have given us good battle, both of them military ships. Much to our delight, one of them, a pretty little Spanish frigate returning home from the Caribbean and riding suspiciously low in the water, proved to be carrying sixty thousand pounds worth of gold and silver coin! To be honest, I'm not certain we are at war with them, but Davey says it makes little difference, as the Spaniards are a lawless bunch who hang honest privateers with their letters of marquee strung around their necks in any case. I petitioned to have the frigate calculated as part of my share in lieu of gold, and no one objected, so I have a vessel of my own and a way to make a livelihood, waiting for me in Gibraltar.

I account myself a wealthy man now, my love, first and foremost because I have you. I also have a ship of my own at harbor, and my share of the profits from this very lucrative adventure looks to be close to twenty thousand pounds, God bless your cousin's larcenous soul! Upon my homecoming, I'll be able to return your brother his money and support us both in comfort. When I cast my mind back to where I was two years ago, I can scarce believe my good fortune. You have opened a door to a brand new world for me, ma chère, and I can never thank you enough.

Your letters have reached me in Gibraltar, ma belle.

I kiss them and keep them under my pillow, knowing your thoughts and your dear hands have touched them. I know how you enjoy attending your lectures and such, and the plans you have for your stables, yet you say it would please you greatly to travel the world with me. I would not wish you to sacrifice your interests and pleasures any more than you wish me to sacrifice mine, but I believe they are easily reconciled. We shall do as Davey does, my dear, enjoying the pleasures of terra firma throughout the fall and winter, and taking sail in the spring. I leave it to you to plan our first adventure. My only request is that it be a honeymoon.

I am greatly relieved to hear that your brother has softened toward me. Beyond the fact that he is your brother, and dear to you, I am very much aware of how good he's been to me, and other than for the want and need of you I would never have willingly chosen to anger or upset him. I hold him in the greatest esteem, not only for your sake, but also my own. Tell him I will present myself to him upon my return, and if it pleases you, tell him we will be married in the spring. It will be a great relief for me to do this openly and properly, as I'm not altogether convinced that our marriage by Davey's cook was entirely legal in the eyes of the world. The sooner we are joined by respectable means, in front of your family, the better.

I'm delighted to hear that you've begun a correspondence with Pierre Mechain, and no I'm not the least bit jealous. Remember that I have seen him and you have not. As for your concerns regarding Jamie, he has written to tell me that he is very much looking forward to attending school in Truro, come the fall. He seems to know his own mind and I wouldn't worry overmuch about it, if I were you. He will have comrades in arms in Sidney's brood, and I expect he'll do very well.

I don't know that I'll be able to write again before we return, my love. We plan a sweep across the eastern Mediterranean as far as Alexandria, through what is essentially hostile territory. As such, we are not likely to make port again until we return to Gibraltar, at which point I am likely to reach you before a letter does.

You will note that I have kept this missive friendly and informative, and have avoided any excess of emotion or sentiment. It's not from want of passion, but rather from an excess. I find our separation increasingly unbearable, and if I allowed myself the indulgence of fully expressing my feelings to you, I fear it would open the floodgates, inundating you with a deluge of dreadful poesy and self-pitying ramblings, and leaving me sore, hungry, and dissatisfied.

We leave in the morning, our last hunt, God willing, and I hope to have you in my arms again by mid-November. Despite my fine words and noble intent, I am now haunted by flashing images of trim ankles and snowy white thighs and plump, luscious lips. What a fool I was to leave you. Wait for me. There is only you.

Gabriel

With strong winds and easy sailing, they made Alexandria in twenty-three days, stopping along the way to relieve two French merchantmen of their cargo, swelling their coffers with African diamonds, gold, and Mediterranean coral. The return trip was more difficult and less lucrative, but no one complained. With the hold stuffed full of riches and plunder, no one was interested in risking battle. The weather was getting rougher, and it looked like an early autumn. It was time to go home.

Greeting several British warships, dodging a few French ones, and keeping clear of any Barbary corsairs, they fought against strong headwinds all the way, and it was the end of September before they approached the North Algerian coast. Five days out of Gibraltar, the lookout called down from the crosstree, having sighted a sail just over the horizon. It was a large French three-decker in hot pursuit of a smaller vessel. She was a formidable-looking ship with two rows of cannon bristling from her sides, and three masts towering close to two hundred feet in the air. Maintaining a respectful distance, they came about to watch the chase.

"You are watching alarming inexperience or gross stupidity, Gabriel, or perhaps just the tragic result of years of French inbreeding. Tell me why," Davey asked, leaning back against the rail.

"Because he's following her into the shallows

where he doesn't belong, making a good eight knots under full sail, and he will very likely run aground."

"Aye, that he will. It's not well charted here. What should he be doing?"

"He should put about and head for open water," Gabriel said with a snort. "Failing that, he should have leadsmen in the bow, calling out the depth as he goes."

Davey nodded, satisfied, and then leaned forward, poking Gabriel in the shoulder, suddenly alert, "Look close then, lad. There she goes." They watched with interest as the giant ship shuddered and ground to a stop, stuck atop an uncharted reef. The little ship she'd been chasing came about and darted away, quickly disappearing over the horizon. "Now I wonder what cargo she'll be carrying, cousin," Davey mused with a wicked grin. "She smells like a pay ship to me."

Gabriel smiled, pleased and surprised as he realized Davey *was* his cousin now, by marriage. The thought had never occurred to him before. "I shouldn't think it would be wise to annoy her, Davey. She looks to have upwards of sixty guns."

"Oh, no doubt she does, my boy. She'd blow us clear out of the water. But observe carefully. What do you think her captain, and I use the term lightly, is up to now?"

Gabriel took the glass and surveyed the activity aboard the trapped vessel for several moments. "He's crowding on sail, hoping to push her over the shoal no doubt, but he only seems to be driving her farther onto the rocks."

"Indeed, indeed," said Davey, with a grin. "And next, my child, if he proves true to form, he will try to lighten her. He will order his fresh water pumped out, and if that doesn't work he's likely to cut away his foremast and—"

"Jettison his guns," Gabriel finished for him.

"Precisely, my dear. And there he'll sit, unable to fight or flee. It's worth the wait to see, don't you think?"

The next morning brought a sirocco wind from the Libyan Desert to the southeast. Warm, moist, and oppressive, it was accompanied by a fog so thick they couldn't see past two miles. "There's something wicked coming our way," Davey said to his lieutenants. "See that everything's stowed tight and prepare for rough weather."

By midmorning the fog had lifted, dispersed by the steadily mounting winds, revealing a lowering slate-gray sky. The French warship was still visible, hung up on the reef, but she'd kept her cannon, and it looked like the wind and mounting waves would soon have her free. "Well, lads," Davey shouted. "It was a nice thought, but the good Lord protects drunkards and fools, and doubtless her captain is both. There'll be no sport for us here, and I'm not liking what's in the wind. There's a storm coming and we're going to need some sailing room. Turn her about, reef the main, and mount the trysails, gentlemen. It's time for us to go home."

By late morning, the wind had grown stronger on the port side, and the *L'Espérance* was lurching and swaying amidst tremendous breakers, listing dangerously to starboard. They were making painfully slow headway against the wind when the lookout spotted four more ships to the south, heading fast toward the grounded ship.

"Looks like two gunboats, a frigate, and a galley, Davey," Gabriel said, fighting to maintain his balance on the heaving deck as he examined them through the glass. He watched as three of the ships continued steadily toward the man-of-war, while the galley lingered in the rear. They could hear shouting now, and the distant thunder of cannon fire and the whistling of shot as the gunboats closed in on the beleaguered French vessel.

Nudging Davey, Gabriel passed him the glass as the galley slowed, stopped, and then gradually came about. She flew a broad black pennant emblazoned with a silver crescent and scimitar, off the main masthead. Mainsails reefed, using her topsails and two banks of oars, she was moving through the water at an amazing speed, heading straight toward them, the sound of steady drumming, faint, but discernable through the din.

"Algerine pirates," Davey announced. "Let's hope the rest stay busy with our French brethren, and see if we can't raise a little more sail."

"We're at peace with them, are we not?" asked Willy McMaster, the second lieutenant. "We have a pass."

"Oh, aye, lad. That we do, but yon galley does not appear to be friendly. I doubt her captain is braving the storm to come for tea and a chat. Alliances shift as quickly as the wind in these parts. Who's to say if it's still any good, or if their captain will care to read or respect it, particularly if he sees what's in our hold? I've no taste for slavery. We'll run, and if we're outpaced, then we'll fight, and if we lose and any survive, why then we will take a very great snit, wave our papers, and sternly demand an apology."

By midafternoon they were battling gale-force winds and monstrous waves, and they had hardly moved at all. Creaking, groaning, and heaving like a living thing, the *L'Espérance* sank beneath the long swells only to rise again, white foam exploding, erupting over her bow as the sky ripped open and the howling wind drove squalling sheets of blinding rain in black swathes across the deck.

The galley still followed them, tossing precariously, but steadily gaining ground. The French warship, battered, limping, and listing badly to one side, had finally broken free. Clumsy at the best of times, she was in far too close, leaving her little room to maneuver, and the seas were now so high she was unable to open her lower gun ports. The vigorous cannonading continued back and forth, rumbling in the distance. She'd just fired off two broadsides from her upper decks when the sky was rent by a deafening roar and a brilliant flash of light. She shuddered from stem to stern and exploded, sending masts and spars and splintered timbers, cannon and burning bodies, hurtling through the air.

The guns fell silent, and the roar of the storm faded into insignificance. The preternatural quiet that followed was split only by the agonized screams of those few who'd survived the explosion. What was left of the mangled warship was still visible, flames and oily black smoke roiling from its blackened hull, licking against the turbulent sky as if fed by the winds and the driving rain. It was a hellish scene. "Poor bastards," Davey said. "They must have lost their magazine."

"Shall we go back? Look for survivors?"

"There's no point, Gabriel, even if we could safely turn around. The corsairs will fish out any survivors. They're worth more to them alive than dead. Our main concern now is to weather this storm and pull away from that galley. Gather the officers on the quarterdeck, if you please. We have work to do."

The officers assembled quickly, faces grim. Many of the crew were still stunned, awed by the force of the blast and horrified at the tremendous loss of life. "We have a problem, gentlemen," Davey said, raising his voice to be heard above the tempest, pointing to the galley still making its way determinedly in their direction. "As you will have noticed, yon galley has been gaining on us all day. They have the advantage of movement in this blasted storm. They have the use of their oars and can row directly into it. *We* are forced to tack before the wind, each time chancing that a strong gust might heel us over. Their captain cares not if his oarsmen drown. They are slaves and expendable. He will keep after us. They want our cargo, they want our ship, and they want our asses on those benches."

"I've heard they have other uses for our asses, if we be comely enough," one of the men shouted, prompting loud guffaws and lewd remarks.

"Aye, well, I've often thought that your ass is your best feature, Robbie, my love. You're welcome to launch over the side and try to arrange an assignation. No doubt, you'd have better luck with them than you do with the ladies, but here's the thing," Davey said, serious now, waving down their laughter. "As things stand, I calculate she'll be upon us within the next two hours. We're beset by pirates *and* this bloody storm. The cannon are no use to us now. That galley's too low in the water for them to do any damage to her decks. I reckon they outnumber us, two to one. Not impossible odds, but discretion is the better part of valor, gentlemen, so here's what we're going to do. We're going to lighten this ship and raise more speed, and we're going to prepare for battle. I want six of our cannon jettisoned immediately. I want every man armed and prepared to fight, with muskets, cutlass, and boarding pikes at the ready, and I want our best sharpshooters stationed at the top and the crosstrees, lashed in tight, mind. Look sharp now, men. Let's get it done!"

Gabriel made his way to the lower deck to supervise and help with the cannon. Bent low and struggling to maintain his balance on the slippery planking, his attention was caught by Carlos Estaban, a grizzled Portuguese petty officer who'd joined them at Calais. Garrulous and affable, he was bent over the portside, heaving up the contents of his breakfast. In the next moment the ship, battered by the storm, heeled to the left. A wave of foaming water flooded across the deck, and Carlos was gone.

Gabriel blinked, blinded by the salt spray, and then he saw him, clinging desperately to the rail. Sliding and scrambling across the tilted deck, he lunged for the terrified man, grasping his sodden collar, bracing against the rail to hold him as the water swirled waist-deep around them, knowing that if he let him go, there'd be no way to go back for him in the storm. He'd be lost.

As the *L'Espérance* struggled gamely to right herself, Gabriel gripped his sodden companion tighter, and began hauling him back over the rail, but the sea was not about to let loose what she had claimed as her own. As the ballast shifted to the right in the mountainous swells, they were pummeled by a mighty wave that flooded the decks again, tearing loose one of the cannon from the men who were struggling to control it. It careened down the steeply tilted deck toward them, stopping with a sickening crunch, pinning Gabriel, snapping his forearm, crushing his ribs, and snatching at his coat, before crashing through the rail into the treacherous waters below, taking both of them with it.

Gabriel struggled frantically to free himself as the cannon plummeted into the inky depths. Ignoring the grinding pain, he struggled free of his coat. Escaping the deadly anchor that was pulling him to his death, he struck for what he prayed was the surface, suffocating, retching, and straining to hold his breath as his lungs rebelled and painful lights sparked and flickered at the edge of his vision.

He broke the surface, disoriented, lungs heaving, gasping for air, sickening pain jolting through him with each precious breath. He couldn't see a thing. He was completely alone, adrift among the swells. Carlos was gone, and so was the ship, and the world seemed eerily peaceful and silent. Then he caught a glimpse of her in the distance, surging up from a trough gushing water from all sides. He'd feared that she'd been wrecked and he felt a wave of relief that she hadn't gone under. It was followed by a stab of panic as he realized that even if they knew he was gone, there wasn't a thing they could do to help him.

Gripped by intense, raw-edged pain, he fought against the black despair threatening to engulf him, focusing all his concentration on staying afloat and surviving from one moment to the next. He caught sight of *L'Espérance* again, about three hundred meters off now, fading into the horizon, still battling the swells. There was no sign of the galley that had been chasing her. He continued to watch her; he had no idea how long, plunging into the abyss and somehow rising, until eventually she disappeared from sight.

He was tiring now, every movement, every breath, an exquisite torture as his broken ribs ground ragged in his chest. His arm was bent at an obscene angle, jagged bone exposed, sending sharp thrills of agony coursing through him as he paddled to stay afloat. He hoped there were no sharks about. That would be a damned unpleasant way to go. He had thought himself inured to pain, long since, but his hubris was being strictly adjusted. Well, at least, it was keeping him awake. If he fell asleep, he would slip between the waves within moments. It amused him, somewhat, that after fighting most of his life to get to sleep, he would spend what little of it was left trying to stay awake.

It was full dark, and a chill had seized him. The sky had cleared and the storm had disappeared without a trace, as had the *L'Espérance* and her pursuers. The swells were tamed now, rocking him gently. He'd been doing his best to move as little as possible, but he was still wearing his clothes and boots, and there were two swords strapped to him, weighing him down. A comforting lassitude had gripped him some time ago, and the task of removing them seemed unbearably complicated, but he wouldn't last long at this rate. He was barely managing to keep his head above water as it was. Biting back a groan of pain, he was struggling to loosen his sword belt when he was knocked under the water by a powerful thump to the head. Spitting and coughing, barely alive, he struggled instinctively for the surface.

It was a charred and shattered spar. Fighting to remain conscious, the only sound the wheezing and whining of air in his lungs, he struggled to pull himself onto it. In some fevered part of his brain he imagined that Carlos was there with him, helping to pull him out, clutching him tight just as Gabriel had done for him before they had both been tossed, like broken toys, into the raging storm. He was dimly aware of the sky turning a deep violet, and then, despite pain and thirst, and his own determination, he slept.

He drifted in and out of consciousness. Sometimes he was lying in a leafy meadow, a soft-voiced woman cradling his head in her arms, whispering warm in his ear. At other times, he imagined that his broken spar was crowded with Davey, Carlos, Robbie, and others of the crew, annoying him by their jostling, and incessant questions that he was too tired to understand, or to answer.

The excruciating pain receded to a rhythmic throbbing. At some point, you no longer feel pain, he thought dully, a lesson he was familiar with, and no immediate cause for alarm. Trying reflexively to strengthen his grip, he *was* vaguely alarmed when his body refused to respond. He knew then that he was dying. He felt peaceful. He loved the sea. He need only let go to slip into her soothing embrace. Still… there was something nagging at him, insistent, something he needed to remember. Someone. Sarah! He was flooded with memory, her scent, her sweet voice. She called to him and she wouldn't let him go. He managed to tighten his grip, pulling himself up a little farther before fading into blackness once again.

At first, the voices were far away, indistinct, and he listened to their vague babble and hubbub with sublime indifference, but that was quickly turning to annoyance. He willed them to go away and leave him in peace. As if to spite him, the chatter grew steadily in volume and excitement. It was a foreign tongue, one he didn't recognize. No, wait, yes, he did. It was … Arabic, and the *lingua Franca*. Even as he realized it, rough hands seized him, hauling him up, smashing his shoulder and his arm against something hard and unforgiving, sending searing waves of pain knifing through his body, and sending him back to blessed oblivion.

CHAPTER
24

Gabriel woke coughing and retching. A strong grip braced his shoulders, steadying him and holding him still. Jagged shards of pain assailed every movement, every breath, and he struggled to contain a moan of pain, grateful for whatever force it was that restrained him.

"Easy, *mon ami*," a cultured voice reproved him as a tin cup was pressed to his lips. "You want to keep as still as you can. You've broken some ribs, it seems. You need to drink. It's a vile witch's brew, I know, but you're badly dehydrated and we're given very little water. If you hope to survive, you need to take whatever's offered."

Gabriel struggled to get his bearings. His head was pounding and an insistent throbbing radiated up and down the length of his left arm, which seemed to be in some sort of splint. It was torture to breath. It was dank, dark, and suffocatingly hot, and the stink of sweat and fear was overwhelming. It took him a moment before he recognized the sounds he was hearing, the slapping of oars as they hit the water, the creaking and moaning of wood, stressed by wind and sea, and the muffled thudding of canvas, beaten by the wind.

He was on a ship, and he was in the hold. Memory came to him suddenly, in a flood of images. The stricken warship hung up on the reef, the sky bloodred with flame and smoke, the angry sea littered with bodies and debris, and Carlos's eyes, changing from wild hope to terror and despair, as the tumbling cannon swept them both into the sea.

"You were aboard the French ship," he croaked.

"I was, indeed," the stranger agreed. "You must have been aboard that little privateer that played about us for a while. Fell off her then, did you? Rather clumsy of you, if you don't mind my saying."

Gabriel grunted in reply.

"Please allow me to introduce myself. I am Jacques Louis David, Chevalier de Valmont, at your service. I would offer you a bow, but there just isn't the space, you see, and I'm currently occupied striving heroically to give you a drink. Do be a good fellow and make an effort to cooperate."

Gabriel's lips were cracked and bleeding, his throat raw and sore, and he was in desperate need of water. He did his best to drink the fetid swill the Frenchman was trying to give him, struggling not to retch as he swallowed it.

"There now, that wasn't so bad, was it?"

"Why are you helping me?" Gabriel asked dully, exhausted from even these minor exertions.

"You wound me, sir! We are old friends and traveling companions. Do you not remember?"

Gabriel's brow furrowed, then cleared as a thought struck him. "You were on the spar that struck me."

"Quite unintentionally, I assure you."

"I thought there was someone else."

"Yes, I know. You kept calling me Sarah. I was most affronted."

"You pulled me from the water. You saved my life."

"Well, I was bored, you see, and I felt somewhat obliged after knocking you unconscious. You proved to be very poor company, though."

"I'm not sure you did me any favors," Gabriel said. His sigh made his ribs grate inside his chest. Wincing, he turned his head and peered through the gloom. There was a faint light from a grate overhead and his eyes were adjusting to the dark. The hold was filthy, filled with huddled forms crowded close together, some of them weeping and moaning. Chained, naked or in rags, there must have been upwards of fifty of them, leaving little air to breathe. The heat and stench were overpowering.

"Well, you needn't thank me, then, but there's a belief in these parts, that if one is so impertinent as to interfere with fate by saving another man's life, he becomes bound to him, their fates entwined."

"You must not feel any such obligation, Chevalier. I assure you that I do not."

"Nevertheless, monsieur, we are chained together. It gives one pause. Who knows? Perhaps we are fated to spend the rest of our lives shackled together on a bench, closer than any husband or wife. You might at least tell me your name."

"St. Croix . . . Gabriel St. Croix."

"Ah, a fellow Frenchman! How is it, sir, that you were serving on an English privateer?"

"My cousin was the owner and captain. How is it that you are serving the French Republic, Chevalier?"

"Oh, well, it's not much of a republic anymore. More of a dictatorship now, really. Much like the *ancien régime*, although it *was* republican leanings and military skill that saw me safely through the revolution. I do it for the adventure, for the money, to spite my father, and to survive. These are interesting times, are they not? Fortune makes strange bedfellows of us all."

A hatch opened above them, causing a sudden commotion of cursing and shouting and the rattling and clanking of chains. Desperate men leapt up, contorting themselves, tearing their skin against their chains as they struggled to catch the small, missile-hard loaves of black bread that were thrown in all directions, many of them landing in the slop and filth that coated the floor. The *chevalier* held out a hand almost negligently, and retrieved a loaf from midair, calling something out to their captors before handing it to Gabriel and plucking another for himself.

The feeble daylight from the open hatch offered Gabriel his first good look at his new companion. He was fine-boned, tall and well-made. Refined features were marred by several fist-sized bruises, and offset by sharp and penetrating ice-gray eyes. His dark hair was tied in a neat queue with a piece of materiel torn from his ragged shirt. He looked surprisingly elegant, despite his chains and filthy rags.

"Tell me of our capture, Valmont. I missed most of it. Do you know where we're headed or what lies ahead? And how is it you speak Arabic like a native?"

"You've been most fortunate in your illness, St. Croix. I would that I had missed most of it. Where to begin? I have the honor of holding a commission as major in Bonaparte's army. I have been on his Egyptian campaign the past three years. I learned the Arab tongue in Alexandria. One can get by with the *lingua Franca*, but one can also get by with interpreters, if one wishes. People of higher rank and more refined social status speak Arabic, and I thought it worth learning. One never knows when it might prove useful. Our ship was carrying treasure, and I was carrying dispatches back to France, when we ran aground."

"Indeed? We were wondering if you were worth the risk. We'd rather hoped your captain would chuck your cannon over the side so we could find out."

"*Bon Dieu*, but he nearly did!" Valmont laughed. "It took myself and three of his lieutenants to dissuade him. The cannon didn't help us, though. I wonder now if tossing them might have made a difference . . . Well . . . there's no point pursuing that chain of thought. You and I were hauled onboard two days ago, and as I've told you, you were lucky to be unconscious. They are slavers, of course, and the hold was already full when we arrived. They rescued, if that's the word, about thirty from the ship I was on from a crew of one hundred and fifty. We were all examined to determine our social standing, profession, and potential for ransom, then stripped, robbed of our clothes, and beaten. Two of the younger, comelier lads, were taken and haven't been seen since," he finished grimly.

Shifting a little, he leaned his shoulder against a bulkhead and continued, "As for you, you were unconscious, badly injured, and half-drowned. They decided you weren't worth the bother and were planning to throw you over the side for the sharks when I took the liberty of telling them you were a very wealthy nobleman, your mother's darling lambkin, and sure to bring a fine ransom. Well, my friend, there was no end of excitement when they took a closer look. A good pistol, two swords, one of them a very fine Toledo blade, rich clothes, and beautiful to boot. They've concluded from your weapons and apparel that I spoke the truth, and you will bring a healthy ransom. Failing that, you are young and handsome enough to do very well at auction. They had their surgeon splint your arm and have left you in peace ever since. They even give me an extra ration of water for you, which has been a great trial to get down your throat."

"And what have they concluded about you, Chevalier?"

"Oh, much the same," he said blithely.

In fact, Jacques Louis David, Chevalier de Valmont, was the dissolute and deadly younger son of a French duke of that name, and was likely to fetch a very fine ransom, indeed.

As they approached the port of Algiers, they were pushed and prodded onto the deck with whip and cudgel. Gabriel was barely able to stand. He was gaunt, pale, and badly dehydrated. The foul water and filthy conditions of his captivity, combined with his weakened state, had given him dysentery. His splinted arm was hot and swollen, and throbbed with a dull pain that exploded in searing jolts of agony whenever it was jostled or touched. Every movement grated in his chest and side, and each breath was a torment. As they shuffled in their rags, chains clanking and clattering at wrist and heel, he was forced to lean on the *chevalier* for support.

Training and force of habit made him observant, and despite his weakened state, he examined the scene before him, searching for information, weakness, and opportunity. The city was built on the side of a very high hill, tapering upward so steeply that from seaward he could see almost every building. The houses were whitewashed, and from a distance the city seemed to float and shimmer, resembling a pristine North Atlantic iceberg gone wildly adrift. It was well fortified, surrounded by two walls about twenty-five feet distant, which looked to rise almost one hundred feet in places. The outer wall was defended by brass cannon and a trench forty feet wide. *Now* that's *going to be Christly difficult to escape*, he thought bleakly.

They were herded down the docks and past the city gates to be paraded through the street. The main thoroughfare was crowded with people of all nations and every imaginable dress. Gabriel could see Turks watching at a distance, sitting on carpets and rugs, smoking tobacco. There were Moors and Janissaries in billowing knee-length drawers, Berbers in hooded cloaks, and *renegados* sporting European fashions that spanned the past fifty years. There was a cacophony of shrieks and curses as they were jostled and pummeled by a crowd hurling imprecations, refuse, and abuse. Occasionally he could hear European voices shouting out questions, begging for news from home.

He was stumbling now; the *chevalier* would have to carry him soon, or leave him at the mercy of the guards and the crowds. A peaceful calm came over him. The voices around him receded to a soothing murmur. The sun seemed brighter, colors more deeply varied and hued, and time seemed suspended. The buildings around him were impossibly lovely. Built around delightful courtyards, bedecked with galleries supported by elegantly arching pillars, their flat roofs and terraces were joined by ladders and bridges and capped with rooftop gardens that were much as he'd imagined them from Sarah's balcony. His reverie was interrupted by a particularly vicious kick that sent him stumbling sideways, only to be righted by Valmont.

"Careful, *mon vieux*, if you fall here, you may never get up."

Seized by a spirit of perversity, Gabriel stopped and turned to the mob, bowing and giving them a mock salute followed by a rude gesture as men stumbled into him from behind. The crowd roared with indignation. A whip cracked, laying a stinging stripe across his back just moments before a cudgel struck his head, sending him crumpling to the ground.

CHAPTER
25

Gabriel was lying down, his face pressed against clean fresh linen. Relief flooded him. It had all been a terrible dream. He could hear a soft voice, murmuring close by, and felt a cool hand against his brow. *Sarah*, he thought, smiling contentedly; come as always to rescue him from his nightmares. He reached for her, but the hand withdrew. He thought he could hear the roaring of wild beasts in the distance. That was strange. The bed creaked and his weight shifted as someone sat down beside him.

"*Bienvenue, mon frère*, you have returned from the Elysian Fields at last. I am greatly distressed that you would go to such lengths to avoid me. I assure you, most sincerely, that in some quarters I am accounted an agreeable companion."

Gabriel turned and looked into concerned gray eyes. "Valmont," he croaked.

"Indeed, it is, my friend. You have been in a delirium these past few days. Ever since you were rude to our hosts and they tapped you on your very hard head."

Groaning, Gabriel raised his head and looked around. He was lying on a simple cot in a clean and spacious room. There were worktables along the wall, and busy men in European and Arab dress conversed earnestly in hushed voices in the corner. There were several other cots, but only three of them were occupied. He heard the unmistakable roar of a lion. Surprisingly, he was feeling little pain. Certainly his circumstances seemed to have improved. "Where are we?"

"We are in the *bagnio* of the Dey of Algiers, along with his menagerie, about three hundred other slaves, and various denizens of the criminal sort. Fortunately, we are housed in the infirmary. You are here because you are ill, they fear you will die, and you are considered valuable. I am here because I am thought to be eminently redeemable, though my family and several ladies of my acquaintance might disagree. Whatever were you thinking, provoking the crowd and our guards that way? I was certain it was the end of you. I was amazed when they picked you up and carried you here. Someone has marked you as a sound investment."

"I don't know," Gabriel answered ruefully. "I find myself seized by a spirit of perversity at the most inconvenient times."

"Ah, yes, I know that feeling well," the *chevalier* said with a grin.

"Things seem to have improved, though. The accommodations are better and I'm feeling no pain."

"I should hope not! You've been plied with enough laudanum to fell an elephant. You are still gravely ill, though, you may yet die, and the accommodations beyond this room are nearly as bad as they were on the ship. It's filthy. Men are in chains, beaten and whipped, and most sleep in the open on bare ground. Those who have not been sold at auction are driven out to work at hard labor from dawn to dusk, and fed little better than we were in the hold. When your health improves, if we have failed to secure a prompt and healthy ransom, we will find ourselves joining them soon enough."

"Thank you for your comforting words, Valmont."

"You are most welcome, St. Croix. I confess, though, that I *am* somewhat troubled."

"Truly? There is something that troubles you in our present circumstances, Chevalier?"

"Yes," he answered, ignoring the sarcasm. "Consider that we were never brought before the Dey. The practice is to parade the new slaves before him, so he may choose those he wishes to keep or ransom. If we are sold clandestinely, we will not be listed, and therefore not protected or brought to the notice of any European embassy. It also means that that the buyer is taking a very great risk and must be expecting a worthy return. I know that I'm not worth such an extraordinary risk, so it must be you, St. Croix. Who are you?"

"I am nothing, and no one, Chevalier," Gabriel

said, genuinely perplexed.

"That's unfortunate. It would appear our new master may be in for a severe disappointment, which he will be more than likely to visit upon us."

Gabriel moved restlessly as the effects of the laudanum began to wear off. Fatigued by the effort of conversing, burdened anew by the familiar pain in his arm and chest, he allowed himself to drift again, flitting in and out of consciousness. *Sarah, where are you? I'm so lonely here, so tired,* but no matter how hard he tried, he couldn't find her again. The voice of the *chevalier* hummed steadily in the background until the nurses came and shooed him away. Exhausted, he drifted to sleep.

Suffering from massive infection, Gabriel hovered near death for several days. The chief surgeon had been promised a hefty purse of gold should his patient recover, and he applied all his knowledge and considerable attention to winning it. Dysentery and dehydration were treated with medicinal salts and copious amounts of liquid. He was sedated with laudanum to reduce his movement and his pain, and his chest was bound tightly to keep the ribs from grating when he coughed. His arm was broken and reset properly and the dead tissue was cut away from the wound before it was treated with salt, stitched closed, then splinted and wrapped again. Fortunately, he remained insensate through it all. Young and strong, he slowly began to respond.

As his fever abated and his condition improved, the dosage of laudanum was gradually reduced. When he finally awoke, he was surprised to find that more than two weeks had passed. Concerned to see no sign of the *chevalier*, he managed to reach out a hand and catch the sleeve of one of the nurses. When he stopped, he asked him what had become of his companion.

"Gone, gone," the man replied somewhat nervously. "Your friend has been sold. He has left the city."

Exhausted by the effort, Gabriel closed his eyes again. In the short time he'd known him, he'd come to rely on the *chevalier*'s vitality and relentless good humor. He'd been an amiable companion under trying circumstances, and he was going to miss him. He wished him well, wherever he might be.

Gabriel drifted in and out of sleep over the course of the next few weeks as his bones slowly knit and his body healed. Onions and oranges, white bread, raisins and figs, had all been added to his diet. Someone wanted him to get better, but after more than two months, he still had no idea who or why. It was early December now by his crude calculations, and the days were cool and wet. He was certain he had enough money to buy his own freedom, but he wasn't allowed pen or paper, and was given no opportunity to write.

Sarah and Ross would be decorating for Christmas, expecting Jamie home from Truro, expecting him and Davey to arrive at any moment. Davey would tell them he was dead, drowned, and he couldn't tell them otherwise. Sarah would . . . his heart clenched in dread and anguish, and he pushed all thoughts of home away.

A commotion at the doorway drew his attention. Several men had entered the infirmary, bearing a litter and talking excitedly in Arabic. From what little he could understand, the Dey was coming to inspect the *bagnio*. Money changed hands, a large purse was given to the surgeon, and then they came for him.

"Hurry, hurry," the surgeon prodded, "you must leave immediately." Gabriel resisted, struggling to climb to his feet, but the surgeon pushed him back. "No, no. You have been sold. You can no longer stay here. You must go to your new home. To your new master. Maybe he will let you write. Maybe he will ransom you. Go now. These men are here to take you to him."

Feeling the first stirrings of hope since the beginning of his captivity, Gabriel offered no further resistance. They were hurried through the courtyard and out onto the street. Gabriel had been feeling much better over the past two weeks, and as his strength returned, he'd taken every opportunity to move about the infirmary, clutching onto tables and walls until he could manage on his own. He'd been careful to appear dangerously fatigued, feigning collapse on occasion, thinking it prudent to appear as ill and weak as he could for as long as he was able. Now, as they moved through the city, he was watchful and alert. It wasn't his intention to escape. Not yet. It would be far wiser to wait and see if he might arrange a ransom.

He was delighted nonetheless, when his escort made their way to the western gate and out of the city. With the walls behind him, his chances of escape had increased dramatically. He asked in broken Arabic where they were going, and was cuffed for his troubles, but he did receive a surly reply.

"We go to Bilda, slave, twelve miles to the west. We must carry you all the way when it is you who should be carrying us. Now shut your mouth before I shut it for you."

Gabriel suppressed a grin. Things were definitely improving.

Bilda proved to be better than he had dared hope. Nestled beneath the snowy heights of the Atlas Mountains, peaceful, lovely, and close to Algiers, it had become the preferred home of so many of the ruling Turks that it had no need for the garrison and fortifications that many other towns had.

They approached a large rectangular house that enclosed a tiled courtyard with two fountains, a beautiful trellised garden, and a lush grove of fruit trees. Gabriel noted two well-armed men guarding the entrance. Two more guards were stationed on the flat roof. The northern wall was given over to stables, and he caught a glimpse of delicately shaped muzzles and flashing eyes, no doubt belonging to the Barbary steeds Sarah so much admired. It seemed that his patron—he refused to use the word *owner*—was a wealthy man.

"You are here now, slave. Walk." The litter was tipped over, spilling Gabriel into the dust. He rose quickly to his feet, brushing dust from his hands, smiling dangerously.

"You think to look me in the eyes, slave? You have much to learn." The guard struck him a blow across the face, splitting his lip and drawing blood. "The master will soon have you begging and wagging your tail like the dog you are."

Unable to help himself, Gabriel looked him in the eyes again, his own glittering and hard, and spat blood at his feet.

"You dare!" the guard roared. Throwing him down he pulled out his whip and began flailing away at him as the others joined in, kicking, and punching him as he lay on the ground, knees drawn to his chest, trying to protect his newly healed ribs. He suppressed a scream when his bandaged arm was struck with a vicious boot. Fighting nausea, he reflected that Davey might be right when he said discretion was the better part of valor. His vision began to dim and he surrendered gratefully to the black wave that tugged at him, as an angry voice in the distance snapped commands.

"Leave him be! What are you about, you fools? How dare you! You will pay for this. You will all be very sorry. Now lift him and follow me."

The voice was vaguely familiar and he struggled to place it, but before he could, the darkness pulled him under.

CHAPTER
26

Gabriel opened his eyes and heaved a long sigh. This was becoming a bad habit. He'd taken to fainting like an insipid society miss, and each time he did, he woke, battered and confused, somewhere new. He didn't need to move or turn his head to see he was locked in a cell. The dreary little room was about eight feet in width and contained a cot, a stool, and a jug for water, and he seemed to be chained by the ankle to the wall. A tiny window with iron gratings, close to the ceiling and too high to look out, afforded a little light. Frustrated, he kicked out his leg, rattling the chain.

"That can be most annoying, St. Croix, when a fellow's trying to get some sleep."

"Valmont!" Gabriel sprang from his cot, only to be brought up short when he reached the end of his chain. The *chevalier* was in the cell facing him, sitting cross-legged on his cot, saluting him with a grin and a wave. His face was bruised and swollen, and he appeared to have been badly beaten.

Gabriel grinned as well, and gave him a deep bow. "My apologies, monsieur. And might I say, I did not truly appreciate what agreeable company you afforded, until I was deprived of it. It is very good to see you, *mon amie*."

"Sadly, that's always the way, St. Croix. No one seems to appreciate me until I'm gone. It might give a more introspective fellow pause. I am very pleased to see you, as well. You were so ill when I left, that I did not expect you to survive."

"I'm not that easy to kill, Chevalier. Do you know what we're doing here? And what's happened to you? You look a bloody pulp!"

"I have some idea. As to the bruises, I have met our master, and he's been urging me to convert, well, in a manner of speaking, anyway. I have proved uncooperative so far, and so he punishes me," he said with a shrug.

"You don't strike me as a religious martyr, Valmont."

"I'm not, dear boy. It's not *that* kind of conversion he seeks," he answered with a slight smile.

"Ah, I see. I had hoped you would be ransomed by now, Jacques. How long have you been here? Have you contacted your family yet?"

"I've been here two months now, Gabriel, and yes, I wrote my family and received a very prompt reply."

"And so? Do they redeem you?"

"Alas, no, they have refused. My father explained

it to me quite succinctly in his reply. It seems that my views are too republican, my taste in women too ill advised, and my sense of duty and humility to my father nonexistent. He disowned me in writing, with a great deal of satisfaction. He has done so in the past, of course, but I had rather thought it metaphorical, something to be taken back one day over heartfelt tears, et cetera. I had forgotten how heartily he detests me. He has always doubted that I am truly his son, you see. One can hardly blame him. My mother has always delighted in acting the whore, and he has always been a vicious and vindictive bastard.

"I am abandoned to my fate, and it will be most convenient and not the least displeasing to him if I never find my way home. He may content himself that his less-than-dutiful, and less-than-certain second son, is deservedly suffering for his many sins. His final words were, 'May your slavery teach you the submission and humility you would never learn from me. It will be good for your soul.'"

"*Ma foi*! He sounds like an unnatural father and a sadistic tyrant."

"Ah, you've met him then. Pay me no heed, though, I beg you. It has been a trying week, else I would never have burdened you with such maudlin nonsense. And what of you, friend Gabriel? Have you any news of ransom?"

"No," Gabriel answered shortly. "I've not been given the opportunity to write or contact anyone."

"That is troubling. I've heard disturbing things

about our patron, and after meeting him I don't doubt them to be true. He is said to have established a flourishing trade buying and selling to a certain type of client. Although it's not acknowledged, such practices are widespread. No doubt he will seek to sell me to some lusty sodomite now that I am useless for ransom. I have no talent for humility or submission, as my dear father has already noted. I am not long for this world, I expect. No doubt he intends to do the same with you once you are fully recovered."

"Then we must apply ourselves diligently to our own rescue, Chevalier."

They were left in peace over the next week as they recovered from their respective beatings. Their only visitor was a mute, elderly slave of undeterminable origins, who never looked up. He came once a day to bring them food, fresh water, and remove the slop bucket. The food was passable and plentiful, and Gabriel was recovering quickly, exercising as best he could in his cell, and practicing the deadly steps that Davey had taught him with imaginary sword and cutlass, working to regain his strength.

The *chevalier* was teaching him Arabic, and they spent much of their time conversing in that language, discussing what they had seen of the compound, and how they might plan an escape. Gabriel continued to exaggerate his frailty, even in the presence of the old slave, but in truth he did feel dizzy and disoriented some of the time, and his sleep was like that of the dead.

It was almost Christmas, and Jamie was back for the holidays. They'd feasted and feted and now he lay content, stretched on his stomach, lazily watching the fire as it crackled merrily in the grate, chasing away the December chill. He shifted his position to make room for her, as she came to sit beside him on the bed, both of them hypnotized by the flames. He grinned and purred when she began running her hand gently up and down his back, caressing his buttocks. She leaned in close to whisper in his ear.

"Réveille tois, mon ange."

A bolt of ice ripped through him, stopping his heart, chilling his blood, and freezing his soul. His eyes flew open and met Valmont's, watching silently from across the corridor. His breathing was harsh and ragged, and he was turned to stone, unable to move as those hateful hands rested on the small of his back. Deliberately, he slowed his breathing and strove to armor himself, to find that hard, chill space that none save he could enter. He knew he would need to if he were going to survive. When he'd found it, he was able to answer.

"I'm awake, de Sevigny."

"Good, good! I'm so very pleased you remember me, Gabriel! I've gone to a great deal of trouble to acquire you. I suspected it was you as soon as that rascally corsair described you to me. He always lets me know when a beauty arrives so I might purchase him first. You're as lovely as I remember. You should really call me 'master,' though, you know, and I should punish you for your disrespect. But I do want us to be friends, as we were in the past. Do you remember? So in the future you may call me 'Monsieur le Comte.'" He patted Gabriel on the back and rose to leave.

"I didn't mean to disturb your rest, my dear. I just came to see how you were progressing, and to renew our acquaintance. Rest now. I've had laudanum put in your food to help you sleep. I want to see you better. I have plans for you." He turned to look at Valmont. "*He's* very handsome, isn't he, Gabriel? Is he your lover? No? Well, no matter, I have plans for him, too. I have plans for you both."

Gabriel lay there, his eyes black with rage, his heart twisted with hatred, his soul cold and still, as something long dormant stirred to life.

"How is it that you know this man, St. Croix? How is it that you know him so well?"

"I was forcibly converted as a child," he said flatly. And after that there was nothing else to say.

Monsieur le Comte de Sevigny fairly skipped up the stairs. He was very pleased. Very pleased, indeed! He had done well for himself in Algiers. He'd had contacts here for many years, and it had seemed an ideal home when The Terror had swept across France in the wake of the revolution. He had converted to Islam willingly. Accepting circumcision and remembering in which direction Mecca lay seemed a small price to pay for the social advantages it gave him. He had enthusiastically entered the slave trade and was now far wealthier than he had ever been in France. He specialized in providing beautiful, well-trained men and boys for private sale to discriminating buyers.

It had been his intention to ransom Valmont. His blood was a bit too blue for him to have easily disappeared, but surprisingly, his family hadn't wanted him. Well-made and strikingly handsome, he would fetch a small fortune once he was properly instructed. Gabriel was another matter entirely. He had thought never to see him again. He had been enraged when he'd dared to run away, punishing him and sending him back to the cesspool he'd found him in. But there had been a quality about him, something untouchable and proud, a distant reserve he had never been able to breach. He had thought about him often over the years, and had realized that he'd never really possessed the boy. But now he owned the man. His body, at least. And he wouldn't be satisfied until he owned his soul.

Gabriel remained locked inside himself. He didn't eat or drink, knowing his food was drugged. He said nothing to Valmont, was hardly aware of his presence as he struggled to restore the defenses that Sarah had made him abandon. He'd let himself relax, become weak and unwary, but that was over now. This was war, and if he was to be the victor he needed to focus. He needed to hold himself remote, detached, and above all, to rid himself of feeling—and think!

He paced his cell all day, restless, almost eager for the battle to begin. When the key rattled at the top of the stairs he was prepared. When the Comte reached his cell with two guards in tow, he was stretched on his cot pretending to sleep. He let de Sevigny shake him awake, feigning confusion and fear, looking at him with sullen eyes as the guards waited, blank faced in the hall.

"I've been very patient with you, Gabriel. I have paid well to restore your health, and I've given you time to heal, but my patience is at an end. There's no need for you to live in these conditions. I can change them like that," de Sevigny said, snapping his fingers. "If you submit to me, I will remove those chains and you will live in comfort." He sat beside him, snaking an arm around his waist and drawing him close. "You would like that, Gabriel, wouldn't you? I could give you gold, a fine horse, beautiful clothes . . . and a bath." He wrinkled his nose and let go of him with a laugh.

"Yes."

"Yes, what? Speak up, my dear."

"Yes, I would like it. To have clean clothes and a bath . . . to be free," Gabriel said, his voice a blend of pleading and defiance.

De Sevigny smiled, running a finger down his cheek, and then gripped his jaw, forcing him to look directly into his eyes. "Then I shall tell you how. Here. Now. Tonight. You will show the other one how it's done." He looked pointedly in Valmont's direction. "You will endeavor to please me, Gabriel, and you will acknowledge me as your master. Until then you will be treated as a slave. Prove to me your devotion, make yourself worthy of my favor, and I will reward you. I may even free you. If you fail, or if you dare to defy me, I won't kill you, nor will I return you to the *bagnio* or sell you to the Dey. I will have you hamstrung, and then make a private sale. There are many here who share my vice, Gabriel. I will ensure that your life becomes a living hell."

"I would not like that, Monsieur le Comte. I would prefer to stay with you. I can obey."

"Can you? You've lied to me before. I think you

will have to prove it, my dear," he said, tugging open Gabriel's shirt and running his hand across his chest.

Gabriel winced, drawing away. "Your men . . . my ribs . . . I need more time. I . . . I beg you."

"You beg me? That's good, Gabriel. That's very good! My men hurt you, I know. They weren't supposed to, and they have been severely chastised, I assure you. I shall give you all the time you need. Do you see how pleasant it can be when we are nice to each other? But first you must give me a kiss, to show me how you love me. You do love me, don't you, Gabriel?"

"No, Monsieur le Comte."

De Sevigny burst into delighted laughter. "Then you must pretend, until you do. Show me, Gabriel, and show your friend. He needs to learn. Kiss me, and then I will leave you in peace."

He hadn't expected that. It had never been asked of him before. His kisses were for Sarah. No one else. But that life was fading now, almost gone. It had started the moment he'd fallen, battered and torn into an angry sea. Monsieur needed convincing. Let the games begin. Leaning forward, he took de Sevigny's face between his palms and pulled him gently into a kiss. He touched his lips, featherlight against the count's, pretending it was Sarah he was kissing, his heart breaking as he knowingly defiled the purest thing they'd shared between them, knowing that by doing so, he was saying good-bye to her forever. He deepened the kiss, almost sobbing, and then pulled away. "Like so, Master?"

Dazed, de Sevigny pulled himself to his feet. Gripping the wall for support, he stumbled from the cell as if drunk. The guards locked the door after him, and followed him up the stairs. The *chevalier* coughed, but said not a word.

Gabriel lay motionless, staring at the ceiling. He had wanted to kill de Sevigny when he'd dared put his hands on him. He'd almost choked on his hatred, and his hands had clenched in anticipation, reaching for the chain. He had imagined himself wrapping it around his neck and twisting, breaking Monsieur le Comte's vertebrae with a satisfying crack. If he'd done so, he would have died. The guards would have killed him, or the Dey's justice would have.

Two months ago he'd been a rich man. He had a wife he loved, who loved him in return. Blithe and carefree, trusting in himself and his future, he'd reveled in it. Now fate was punishing him for challenging her, and daring to take for himself what he was never meant to have. It was a harsh lesson, a costly and painful one.

He remembered something Davey had told him a lifetime ago. It had resonated with him, because he'd always known it to be true. *Your best armor, is your mind.* He needed to steel himself, to kill every weakness including hope. All that was left was revenge. Fate might have taken everything else from him, the vicious bitch, but he wouldn't let her rob him of that. The seed was planted. De Sevigny was going to die.

CHAPTER
27

The next evening, two guards came to remove Gabriel from his cell. Valmont sat, staring pointedly at the wall. They hadn't talked to each other since the day before, and they didn't speak now. The door slammed shut and Gabriel was escorted down the hall, up the stairs, and out into the night. There were three men at a post in the corridor, guarding the courtyard and the access to the second floor and cellars. Two more were posted on the roof. He took everything in as he was led, dirty and bedraggled, through the house. Cooling fountains, rich carpets, lush gardens, all the accoutrements a connoisseur like de Sevigny might require, but he had not neglected security.

He was brought to an area with two luxurious tiled rooms, one housing a steamy, rectangular bath, and the other a cool refreshing pool. Stripping off his vermin-infested rags, he allowed the attendant to wash his hair and shave him as he sank blissfully into the heated water. Its warmth was a welcome balm that soothed his aching muscles and abraded skin. Who would have thought such a simple thing could give such pleasure? When he was done with his bath, he was handed clean clothes and fitted with a chain around his ankle attached to a five-pound weight he would have to carry or drag behind him. It seemed to serve no purpose other than to humiliate and remind, but it had potential as a weapon.

Feeling greatly restored, he followed meekly as he was led down another corridor and brought to a halt in front of a large, ornately carved door. Two more men were stationed here. The door opened onto a suite of opulent rooms, flanked by a long gallery that took up the entire south wing of the building and offered a commanding view of the courtyard, gardens, and stables below. Another guard was stationed in front of an imposing door etched with a crest Gabriel recognized from years ago. This must be de Sevigny's private suite, and that was his sleeping quarters. So far he had counted ten guards in all. The man tapped on the door and de Sevigny opened it, smiling in appreciation.

"Oh, my, you've cleaned up very nicely, my dear," he said, caressing Gabriel's shoulder and stroking his arm. "You've grown into a very handsome young man. Do you feel better, now that you are clean?"

"Yes, Monsieur le Compte, thank you. I am hungry, though. I haven't eaten since yesterday."

"Ah, because of the laudanum. It was for your

own good, you know. To ease your pain and help you sleep. Nevertheless, if you don't want it, I will order it stopped. You've pleased me, Gabriel, and you will find that I am generous when I'm pleased. You will sleep in my suite from now on. I've had a small room prepared for you next to mine. It is not luxurious, but a great improvement from where you were. When I know I can trust you, your situation will improve. Rest now. I'll order food sent, and we'll speak again tomorrow."

Gabriel was shown to a small closet adjoining de Sevigny's bedchamber. It was fitted with a trunk, a stool, and a comfortable mattress, but it offered no privacy. It lacked a door and was positioned in full view of the sentry. De Sevigny might want him, but he didn't trust him. He was brought a meal of aromatic lamb stew, soft white bread, lemon sherbet, grapes, and wine. He tore into it, wolfing it down and savoring the wine. It had been more than half a year since he'd eaten anything nearly as good. Clean, sated, and comfortable for the first time in months, he settled down on the soft pallet and fell into a dreamless sleep.

Early the next afternoon the count had Gabriel brought to his chamber. He was dressed in the Turkish fashion, much as Gabriel was, and wore a magnificent jeweled dagger tucked in his waistband. The guard took up a position by the open door. The room was sumptuous to the point of being excessive, but there were several interesting features. The far wall held a collection of swords and other weapons, and Gabriel's eyes sparked when he saw his own Toledo blade there. The count must have acquired it from the corsair captain.

He turned quickly to scan the rest of the room, praying that de Sevigny hadn't noted his interest. There was a piano that seemed strangely incongruous in the corner, an ornate fountain splashing against geometric tiles in the center of the room, and a long window seat that overlooked the gallery and the courtyard below. He studied the room, he studied his surroundings, and he studied the count, as a predator studies its prey.

They played chess, and de Sevigny ordered him to play the piano. He did as he was told, somewhat surprised that after a few rough notes, the music flew from his fingers as light and effortless as it ever had. Tiring of it, without asking permission, he rose and went to lounge by the window, gazing out to the courtyard below. No guards there, just grooms and stable boys, likely all slaves.

De Sevigny rose and came to join him, and Gabriel closed his eyes, steeling himself, suffering the kisses, the insistent caresses, remaining mute as his heart roiled with hatred. He couldn't tolerate much more. He needed to kill Monsieur le Comte the first time they were alone, and he needed to get him alone soon. He'd learned much from Madame after he'd left de Sevigny, and he used it now, pushing him away with hooded lids and a knowing look. "You promised to give me time . . . Master." His voice was seductive, beguiling. "You promised to let me heal."

"I didn't promise to let you play me for a fool,

though, my dear. I think I shall have you examined by my own physician. If I find you've been playing games with me, I will punish you, Gabriel. Do you understand?"

"Yes, Monsieur le Compte. I understand," he whispered against de Sevigny's lips, then turned his head away and returned his attention to the courtyard below.

"Leave me now, Gabriel. Go to your room. I shall send my physician to attend you directly."

Gabriel rose, bowed low to the ground, and returned to his room to wait. He'd recognized the look in de Sevigny's eyes. He'd deliberately provoked it. Lust and greed and wanting. He'd seen it a thousand times before. It would override caution and good sense. The physician would come, he would examine Gabriel and pronounce him healthy, and the count would delight in the opportunity to chastise him for his lies. He would want privacy to do so. The trap was set. Gabriel was a grown man, powerful, deadly, trained to kill, not the defenseless child the count remembered, but de Sevigny couldn't see it. Blinded by habit and hubris, he imagined himself all-powerful, and Gabriel well schooled in obedience. His hunger would rule him. It shouldn't be long now.

The physician came and went, and Gabriel awaited the summons. It came just before midnight. He had fallen into a light sleep. The guard stepped into his chamber and kicked at his pallet.

"The master wants you. Be quick about it."

Gabriel entered the chamber with the same mix of

anticipation and dread he felt before battle. De Sevigny was waiting, cloaked in a long white silk *djellaba*, a jeweled belt cinched around his waist, his dagger thrust through it. He was tapping a rod against his boot. "Leave us," he snapped at the guard. Hurriedly the man bowed and backed from the room, pulling the door closed behind him. "I am very disappointed in you, Gabriel. You lied to me. My physician says there is nothing wrong with you. Nothing at all." He flicked the rod against his boot, making it whistle and snap. "I so wanted us to get along. But you force me to punish you."

"I am sorry, Monsieur le Compte. It was only a game. I thought to amuse you."

"Come here."

Gabriel moved forward, eyeing the rod warily.

"Remove your clothing."

"I have said that I was sorry. I did not understand the game we were playing."

"Do as I say!" de Sevigny snapped. "I would see that you are unarmed," he added evenly.

Gabriel removed his clothing, spread his arms wide, and turned around in a circle. "I carry no weapon . . . Master."

"I don't wish to punish you, Gabriel. If you show me your loyalty and your devotion, I will spare you this." De Sevigny twirled the rod in his hands.

"What must I do, Master?" he rasped.

"Come here," de Sevigny said, pointing to the floor in front of him. "Kneel."

Judith James

Heart racing, breathing heavily, Gabriel knelt in the soft carpet.

"That's right. Oh, my, such fire and passion in your eyes!" Placing one hand on top of Gabriel's bent head, the count swept his robe aside with the other, and leaning over, whispered, "Now, offer me your submission, Gabriel. Show me that you love me. You know how."

And so he showed him. Wrenching the jeweled dagger from its gem-encrusted scabbard, he plunged it into the soft underside of Monsieur le Comte's belly, turning and twisting it with one hand as the other reached up to stop his mouth, stifling his anguished screams. Rising to his feet in one fluid movement, he sliced him from pubic bone to breastbone, castrating him, gutting him, and laying him open. Dropping the dagger, he hugged him close, holding him upright as he gazed into his eyes, watching his shock and terror. "Now you know how much I love you," he whispered, fierce against his cheek. Taking his hand from his mouth, he grasped the back of his head and kissed him savagely as the life fled from his eyes. "Know that I give you this kiss freely, de Sevigny. It's the kiss of death. Now go to hell!" He let go of the body, pushing it away, and watched dispassionately as it crumpled, lifeless, to the floor.

Stepping calmly around the body and its widening pool of blood, Gabriel barred the door and went to immerse himself in the fountain. He spent several minutes scrubbing away all trace of de Sevigny, his touch, his scent, his blood. When he was done, he began rifling through the count's trunks, throwing the treasures he found there haphazardly onto the silk-covered bed. A pair of leather riding boots, a finely made burnoose, and copper-plated leather gloves. He opened another trunk and smiled slightly, pulling from it a sword belt and a cuirass ornamented with gold calligraphy, made of black steel plates and chain.

Retrieving the dagger, he sat on the edge of the bed and began working at the iron around his ankle. Loose fitting and flimsy, it had been meant for decoration, a sign of ownership, and he was able to pry it open with little difficulty. He put on gloves, trousers, boots, and cuirass, and cinched the burnoose with the sword belt, before going to examine the weapons that decorated the wall. He hadn't felt naked without his clothes, but he had without a weapon, and now he equipped himself with short sword and pistol, as well as his Toledo blade. Drawing the blade with a lightning flourish, he whirled it about in a dazzling sequence of maneuvers before sheathing it. It felt good to be armed again.

Scooping gold and jewelry from a casket beside de Sevigny's bed, he wrapped them in a silk cloth, tying them into a small purse and tucking it under his robe. People saw what they expected to see, and he was no longer a slave. Now he was a wealthy *renegado*. All was quiet. He needed a moment to plan and gather his thoughts. Peeling an orange, he sat back in the window seat, one leg dangling down, and gazed out into the night.

CHAPTER
28

The guards would have to be killed. There could be no one left to identify him or raise an alarm. His freedom and his life depended on it. He had managed to avoid bloodshed in the past, except for the German, and de Sevigny, of course. It hadn't been necessary. Now he was pumped with energy, still fueled by his hatred, and Davey had trained him well. He supposed he would accustom himself to it. He drew the Spanish steel from its scabbard with a metallic hiss, tossing and catching it contemplatively, pondering his first move. The only real advantage he had was surprise. He would need to be silent and quick.

Retrieving the chain from where he'd dropped it on the bed, he wrapped it loosely around his left forearm and strode to the door, sword drawn. Lifting the bar, he kicked it open and stepped out into the corridor. The startled guard hesitated a moment, blinking, surprised and confused, not recognizing him in his warrior's garb. That split second of indecision was his last, as the silver blue blade sliced down, cutting through artery and bone. His lips were still twitching as Gabriel stalked down the hall.

He loosened the chain as he went, unwrapping a three-foot length and swinging it, gathering momentum. The doors to the suite opened outward. The guards stationed on the other side of the door were conditioned to prevent entry, not exit. They were sitting at a table rolling dice when he burst upon them. The chain whooshed and swooped through the air catching one on the temple, felling him instantly. The second man gave a shout of anger and leapt at him, his scimitar cutting downward in a death stroke. Gabriel threw himself flat and the sword whistled above him, slashing through empty air. Lashing out with the chain, he caught the man around the throat, strangling the breath from him and jerking him down to the floor. Cursing, praying no one had heard the cry, Gabriel gripped the chain with both hands and twisted as his opponent struggled for his life, kicking and heaving, his hands desperately scrabbling to loosen it. A jerk, a sudden snap, and he lay still.

Panting for breath, Gabriel leaned back against the wall and slid to the floor. He'd been months without proper practice, his ribs were still tender, his arm ached, and he had yet to fully regain his strength. He was fortunate no one had heard. The hardest part was before him. At last count, there were at least three men at the guard post on the lower floor.

Edging stealthily down the staircase, he kept his back to the wall, sword drawn and chain at the ready, hiding in shadow as he surveyed the area. One man was lounging back in his chair, his feet resting on a battered desk, eyes closed. Another had his back to Gabriel, and was leaning against a pillar smoking a long Turkish pipe and looking out onto the courtyard. He couldn't see the third.

Bursting into the hall, he sent the chain snaking through the air, felling the sleeping guard so quickly he never woke up. He let go of the chain as the second man jumped him from behind, shouting for help as he grabbed him by the hair, jerking his head back to cut his throat. Gabriel managed to grab his wrist before the blade descended. Turning into him, he tripped him and threw him to the ground, kneeling on his chest to slice his throat. Catching a glimpse of movement reflected in the dying man's eyes, he whirled to his feet, wheeling to strike, catching the last man through the heart.

Chest heaving, rasping for breath, he stumbled to the desk and rifled through the drawers, finding two sets of keys. Hooking a lantern with his fingers, he opened the door to the cellar, starting down the stairs. "Valmont? Chevalier?"

Le Chevalier de Valmont sat up, blinking with surprise. "St. Croix? Is it you?"

"*Oui, c'est moi.*"

"*Bon Dieu*! What's happened to you? You look

like a desert prince!"

"Never mind that now. I'm leaving, Valmont. There's not much time, and I want to be as far from here as possible before daybreak. Do you come with me?"

"Yes. Yes, of course!"

"Good. Try your chains with these while I work at the door." Gabriel tossed him a set of keys.

"What . . . how . . . what's become of our guards?" the *chevalier* asked as he worked at the lock. "Ah, there, I have it!"

"They're dead."

"All of them?" he asked incredulously.

"No, there should be two more on the roof, and two at the front gate."

"What is your plan, and what of our . . . patron?"

"De Sevigny is no more, and my plan is to escape," Gabriel grunted, giving the cell door a shove with his shoulder and forcing it open. "Come, follow me."

"How do you know him? Was he your lover?"

"I wouldn't call it that," Gabriel said sourly. "I was little more than a child, Valmont."

"You are not his catamite, then?"

"No! Leave off, Chevalier," he said dangerously, "or remain behind. I do not care to discuss it."

Chastened, but still curious, the *chevalier* followed Gabriel up the stairs. Surveying the carnage in the hall, he eyed his companion with newfound respect. Stepping fastidiously over the two dead bodies on the second floor, he was surprised to see yet another corpse as they entered the luxurious apartments at the end of the hall.

"*Bon Dieu, mon ami*, you frighten me! Where did you learn to fight like that?"

"My cousin taught me."

"The privateer captain? Who is this cousin of yours?"

"He's called Gypsy Davey."

"Is it so? I have heard of him. He is a famed captain of mercenary. They say none can best him. How fortunate for you to have such a man as your teacher!"

"Yes, very. Shall we take our leave now, Valmont?"

"Yes, indeed, my dear."

"Come," Gabriel motioned, "you can equip yourself in here."

Two things caught the *chevalier*'s immediate attention as he entered their former patron's bedchamber. One was the bubbling fountain splashing against the tiles, and the other was their former patron's corpse, lying splayed on the floor in a pool of blood. "You've been terribly busy, I see. And very . . . efficient. In fact, St. Croix, I would have to say that you are one of the most efficient men I have ever met."

"Hurry up please, Valmont. Take what you need and let's go."

"Yes, of course, after I have availed myself of a bath."

"We haven't the time."

326

"J'y suis, j'y reste. Go without me if you must, Gabriel. You smell sweet as sin, but it's been six months since I've felt clean and I am covered in filth. I *will* bathe."

"Hurry, then," Gabriel said, pulling out clothes for him.

The *chevalier* happily immersed himself in the fountain, scrubbing away months of filth and grime before contentedly dressing himself.

"Et bien, mon frère. What is our plan from here?"

"We will remove the sentries on the roof, slip down to the stables and take some horses, remove the guards at the front gate, and quietly leave town as two wealthy *renegados*. You speak their language fluently, we both speak the *lingua Franca*, and if we are well armed and mounted, no one will question that we are what we seem."

With Valmont's help, Gabriel's plan unfolded exactly as he'd hoped. Well before dawn, they slipped out of the gate and moved quietly through the town, and by sunrise they had left Bilda well behind and were approaching the Atlas Mountains. The night's adventures had eased the awkwardness between them, and they grinned at each other, intoxicated with their success and the taste of freedom. At midmorning, they sighted a large caravan ahead of them, and a party of horsemen approaching fast from the east. Gabriel reached for his sword, but Valmont grasped his arm, staying him.

"They are not from Bilda. They come from the wrong direction, *mon vieux*, and there are too many of them to fight. We must brazen it out, or flee."

Wheeling to face them, Gabriel let his horse dance beneath him, and threw back his cloak, displaying his weapons and armor. *We are not runaway slaves. I am a* renegade, *a wealthy and dangerous man, and it will be as Allah wills*, he thought with a grim smile.

They rode up in a cloud of dust, a motley collection of hard-eyed Turks, Moors, and Europeans, milling around Gabriel and Valmont, horses snorting and prancing, bridles jingling, encircling them and crowding them together. Gabriel eyed them impassively, steadying his mount while the *chevalier* gave them a broad grin. "Good day, brothers," he said in flawless Arabic. "May Allah, peace be upon him, guide you and keep you safe. Is there so little room on this wide plain that you must inconvenience us with your dust?"

Good, Gabriel thought. *He knows how to play this game.*

The one who appeared to be their leader, a blond, blue-eyed, bearded giant in a combination of Turkish garb and Spanish armor, motioned the other men back. "Your pardon, friend. We protect yon caravan and could not help but be curious as to why two strangers with swords and pistols should follow so close."

"Why? Do you take us for thieves?" Valmont said with rising indignation, placing his hand on his sword hilt as Gabriel did the same.

"I mean no offense, brother. We are merely doing our job. I would simply know who, and what you are, and why you are here."

"We are *renegados*, just as you. Our formal employer has angered the Dey, and we thought it prudent to seek employment in Morocco, at least through the winter months while the ships are in port."

The blond man nodded, and then turned to look at Gabriel. "And you, brother. What's your story?"

Gabriel shrugged. "Mohammed pays better than Jesus does, friend."

Everyone broke into laughter, and the tension eased. "Serve with us then, brothers. The mountains are dangerous, and we travel the same route. You can help us protect the caravan, and you will be safer with us than alone. My employer is a wise and generous man. We go to meet him in Meknes. He will pay you. He may even offer you further employment."

They had little choice but to accept. It was a generous offer given their supposed circumstances, and they would have surely aroused suspicion had they refused.

Trained to fight, intrepid and used to the company of rough men, Gabriel and Valmont fit easily into the mercenary troop, and they were always careful to prostrate themselves in the dust, heads toward Mecca where the prophet lay entombed, whenever everyone else did.

The rough and desolate mountain passages were home to numerous bandits and robbers, mostly poor and desperate Berber or Kabyles tribesmen, and ambush was a constant threat. Some days they rode ahead with the vanguard, checking each hill and pass, exposed, vulnerable, and alert for danger. At other times they traveled in the rearguard, shaking dust from their robes and spitting grit from their teeth, guarding the caravan from being waylaid from behind. On good days they rode along the flanks. There were several skirmishes along the way. They lost two of their men and slaughtered upwards of a score of bandits, bows and arrows being no match for muskets. Gabriel supposed he should have felt some pity, but he didn't have any left.

Crossing the frontier into Morocco, they traded ragged bandits for garrisons of soldiers, and snow-capped mountains for fortresses capped with severed heads on pikes. There were well-marked roads now, olive groves and farms, and vultures lazily circling overhead. The current sultan, Mulai Slimane, had been fighting a civil war for control of the country with factions from Fez and Marrakech. It resulted in a poor harvest for simple folk trying to raise their crops and families, and a bountiful one for mercenaries and other agents of war.

They arrived in Meknes at sunset as the plaintive call of the *muezzins* drifted over the city, summoning the faithful to prayer. They prostrated twenty times before Mecca, and entered the city. Gabriel and the *chevalier* had decided they would take their leave here, and head for the coast. They hoped to attach themselves to a corsair crew for the spring, so that they might find a way to slip across the sea to Europe. Unfortunately, el Inglezi, their captain, had other ideas.

"I cannot allow you to leave, brothers. You have been very helpful, it is true, but your circumstances trouble me. Two Europeans, leaving Algiers in somewhat of a hurry, and now in a great rush to head for the coast. I would be lax in my duties if I did not investigate further. What if you are not who you say? What if you are slaves, trying to escape? I have only your word. Show me that you are circumcised, and I may believe you." He motioned to his men. "Hold them, and we shall see, eh?"

Eyes flashing, Gabriel threw back his cloak and drew his sword so quickly it sparked. "You are welcome to try . . . brothers."

The *chevalier* had drawn his scimitar and stood behind Gabriel so that they were back to back. "This should prove interesting, *mon frère.*"

"Now, now," el Inglezi laughed, raising his hands placatingly, motioning his men back with a shake of his head, "there's no need for that. Not every convert is circumcised. It is the custom, surely, but not an absolute

331

requirement. Perhaps you are just who you say you are. I will present you to my employer, as we have already agreed. He needs good fighting men. There is much opportunity. He is a great and important man. If you serve him, none will dare to question you, yes? I shall introduce you tomorrow. Now go and take your ease, gentlemen. You've earned it."

They were escorted to an agreeable little house complete with pleasant furnishings, three timid servants, and a cook. They could not fail but notice the guard posted pointedly outside the only exit. After a bath, a shave, and an excellent meal of lamb, wine, and honeyed apricots, Valmont turned lazily to Gabriel and belched. "Pardon me, dear fellow. I do believe, Gabriel, that we have just met the civilized version of a Mohammedan press-gang."

"I believe you are correct, Jacques. It is far superior to slavery or impalement, though. I propose we bow gracefully to the inevitable for now."

"I agree, my friend. Oh, look! How delightful!" The *chevalier* sprang to his feet with even more alacrity than he'd shown in battle, as two nubile, giggling young women were ushered into the room. *"Mais c'est charmant!"* Performing a courtly bow and grinning from ear to ear, he escorted them gallantly to the pile of cushions that served as their fauteuil. "God in heaven, St. Croix, but these Mohammedans put a lot more effort into recruiting a fellow than your British friends do! I am quite overcome. Have you a preference, or shall we share?"

"I leave it to you to carry the day, Chevalier."

"But there are two, St. Croix, one for each of us."

"I feel certain you will rise to the challenge," Gabriel said, gathering his pallet and retreating to the covered gallery.

"*A votre santé*," the *chevalier* said, raising his glass in a toast and watching Gabriel's retreat with puzzlement. What was wrong with the fellow? Understanding dawned, and he gave a slight shrug. *Chacun à son gout.* It wasn't to his taste, but St. Croix was a solid enough fellow otherwise, quick-witted, and coolheaded, and damned good with a sword. *Dieu,* but it had been over six months! With a playful growl, he scooped up his female companions, one under each arm, and they dropped together in a giggling, groaning heap amongst the cushions.

Gabriel sat on the gallery sipping his wine. It was not uncommon for *renegados* to drink alcohol, despite the Muslim prohibition against it. They would do without pork, even their foreskin, but they would not do without their liquor. The stars were brilliant. Venus was rising over the horizon, and for a moment he thought of Sarah and their last moments beneath the ancient oak. Pain clutched at his heart, worse than anything he'd endured through blows or broken bones, and he winced and shuddered before taking a deep breath and willing it away.

He didn't deserve her anymore. Perhaps he never

had. His sins had multiplied in this seductive, alien land. He killed for pay, he'd murdered a man in his own bedchamber with his own knife, he'd sold his soul for revenge with a single kiss, and he regretted none of it. He frightened even himself. He had promised to love, honor, and protect her; but that promise had been made by someone else. All he could do for her now was protect her from the man he'd become. He couldn't afford anything soft, anywhere inside him. He pushed her firmly from his thoughts.

El Inglezi came the next morning to take them before Meshouda Murad Reis, a Scottish adventurer and corsair captain of some renown, formally known as Peter Lisle.

"Well, gentlemen, here you are, converts both of you, sons of the Prophet, or so my captain tells me," he greeted them. "What's more to the point, he tells me you can find the pointy end of a sword. I'm no fool, gentlemen, but I *am* short of soldiers, and I'll be needing crew in Algiers when I return in the spring. So . . ." he said, steepling his fingers, "I can send you back to your master, to do with as he sees fit. I can turn you over to the authorities here, which might be most unpleasant . . . or . . . you can serve me and be well paid for it."

He pointed to Valmont. "You, I will take. You look like a soldier and I'm told you are fluent in Arabic, but I'm not sure about the other one." Murad Reis motioned Gabriel forward and examined him carefully. "You appear far too young and slight to be an experienced soldier. You look more like a pretty child. No matter, I'm sure I could find other uses for you. Perhaps I will find your master and purchase you from him."

"I have been ill, and I'm older than I look," Gabriel replied coolly, "and I *have* no master. He who thought to call himself that, now lies dead and gutted."

"Indeed? Then you are a very dangerous man, I suppose. You must think yourself so if you dare to threaten me. Perhaps you will demonstrate." He turned to his men. "Who among you would like to teach this dog a lesson in manners?" The men were laughing now, eager for sport, and several stepped forward. "You," Murad Reis said, pointing to a Turkish giant brandishing a long, wickedly curved blade, "and you have my permission to kill him."

El Inglezi looked at the *chevalier* regretfully, and shrugged his shoulders. He had thought Gabriel an able man from what he'd seen in the mountains, but there was nothing he could do.

The giant stood over six and a half feet, wore chain, and must have weighed a good twenty stone, most of it muscle. He had the brawny arms of a swordsman and the feral glint of one who took pleasure in dealing death. He roared and beat his chest, to the delight of the growing crowd, then played with his blade, weaving intricate patterns in the air, ending with a dramatic flourish.

Valmont stepped next to Gabriel and put a hand on his shoulder. "How are you going to fight that?"

"I'm not going to fight him. I'm just going to kill him."

El Inglezi pulled the *chevalier* aside before he could do anything foolish and anger the Reis further.

Laughing and beckoning Gabriel forward, the giant cooed, "Come, beardless one. I would have some sport of you. I will take your ears first, child, and then your arms, next your manhood, and only then your head."

"I'm a very well-trained child, my dear, but you are welcome to try." It was hot, his opponent was better protected and had a longer reach, but he was also overconfident and the heat would slow him down. Gabriel would be much faster. Best to strike quick and clean. The giant held his sword out in front of him with both hands, in a theatrical attack stance, playing to the crowd. Gabriel waited, unmoving, until the big man took a step forward. Taking three quick steps of his own, he drew his sword screaming from its scabbard, whirling it back one-handed, and whipping it around in an arc so quick it was only a blur.

The giant stood motionless, a look of stunned surprise on his face. His eyes rolled upward, the sword slipped from his grasp with a dull thud, and then he toppled to the ground, his head rolling along the floor to stop, almost at the feet of Murad Reis. The shocked silence was broken by the sound of the *chevalier* clearing his throat.

"Ahem . . . Yes . . . well . . . I have said it before, St. Croix. You are very efficient."

Murad Reis stepped forward with a hearty laugh, slapping Gabriel on the back. "Welcome to my employ!"

And so their disguise consumed them and they became mercenaries in truth. They fought throughout the rest of the winter and into the spring, for Meshouda Murad Reis, who fought for the Sultan Mulai Slimane, who fought for control of Morocco, and they were paid handsomely for it. They returned to Algiers in the late spring as Murad Reis's men, and no one gave them a second glance.

CHAPTER
29

Gabriel and the *chevalier* cruised the coast throughout the summer and into the fall, alert for any opportunity to seize a boat or take passage on a ship and escape, but Murad Reis kept them busy, and he kept them close. They were both his lieutenants now, but they were always watched and surrounded by others of the Reis's men. *Renegados* caught attempting to escape could expect to be dealt with harshly. At best they would be severely bastinadoed and returned to slavery at hard labor, in heavy chains. They might also be burnt alive, crucified, or impaled. The unlucky ones were thrown from a tower on the battlements. It was equipped with iron hooks to catch them on their way down, holding them as they writhed and screamed in agony, slowly consumed by carrion birds as they prayed for death. It was a fate a fellow would much rather avoid.

The Reis preferred to use ruse and deception when stalking his prey. Disguising themselves as a merchant ship, they would lure their victims in close by masquerading as friendly countrymen, flying the flag of whichever nation's ship they stalked, and hailing them in their own language. Once their unwary quarry came within range, they would terrify them with a thundering broadside and a hail of musket fire, grappling their ship and swarming onto the deck in a screaming horde, waving pistols, knives, pikes, and swords, in a ferocious display that usually resulted in a quick and terrified surrender.

The summer passed without any viable opportunity for escape, and they resigned themselves to another winter campaign. Murad Reis kept his favorites richly supplied with gold, horses, and women, and Jacques Valmont, who was particularly fond of women, availed himself of all three. He no longer expected Gabriel to share his interest in wenching, but was somewhat surprised that he seemed to have no interest in fornicating with anyone at all. He decided that he might have been mistaken about St. Croix. As attractive as he might seem to either sex, he himself seemed attracted to neither. If not for his lithe and muscular frame, he might have been a eunuch. It was certain, in any case, that he was an enigma.

They spent the rest of the year on campaign, protecting caravans, punishing the enemies of the Dey, and skirmishing with the enemies of the sultan, traveling back and forth from Algiers to Morocco and from one commission to the next, until they lost track of who they were fighting or why. It no longer mattered to them as long as they were paid. Gabriel had seen so much brutality and death that it no longer seemed real to him. Tragic scenes of mayhem and cruelty, the disjointed scrambling and hacking, the cursing and pleading and agonized screams, it had all taken on a cartoonish quality, and the dead and dying reminded him of nothing more than puppets with their wires cut, sprawled in ungainly heaps upon the ground.

The spring of 1802 found them in the Atlas Mountains again, fighting for their lives. Several local chieftains, organized, armed, and led by Moroccan insurgents based in Fez, had caught them in a coordinated pincer attack, trapping them in a steep defile with no avenue of retreat. Their captain, guilty of a gross underestimation of his enemy's ferocity, organization, and numbers, paid for it with his life. The vanguard had been ambushed and slaughtered, and the rearguard was struggling to join the caravan, paying dearly in blood and death each step of the way.

The battle had raged, savage and unchecked, for over three hours, coalescing into a slashing, hacking melee. Gabriel was fighting off two attackers, swinging with his Spanish blade and parrying with his short sword. A mounted Berber, screaming curses, charged him from the rear, driving his sword straight at the back of his neck. Valmont swung round to deflect it. Metal screamed against metal and sparks flew. Drawing back his sword, he slashed at the horseman's legs. The Berber swung his sword down as Valmont thrust up, catching him in the throat and spilling him from his horse. He floated to the ground, his snowy robes billowing, like a cloud.

Gabriel shouted a warning, and the *chevalier* jumped back, barely dodging a stroke that would have cut him in half. They edged closer together, fighting back to back, surrounded by a circle of mutilated, dead, and dying. Still they kept coming. *We die here today,* Gabriel thought, as the sun began its quick and early descent behind the mountains. The ebb and flow of the battle had pushed them closer to their pack animals when he saw an opening. Grabbing the *chevalier* by the sleeve, he jerked him in among the panicked animals, and began slaughtering the camels, forming a bulwark around them.

Seeing what he was about, those who still survived from the rearguard and the flanks did their best to join him. Reorganized, they rallied, some of them holding the barricade while others rifled frantically through packs and supplies, searching for more ammunition, and praise Allah, finding it. Muskets were loaded, shots rang out, and men spun through the air in lazy pirouettes to fall broken on the ground.

A bloody dawn found them alone in a silent field of corpses. The mountain raiders had vanished, leaving only their dead behind. The only things that moved were the ungainly vultures that hopped and strutted, necks bent and twisted as they pecked and tore at cloth, and leather, and flesh. Of a hundred-man caravan, only seventeen mercenaries and a few horses were left alive.

Ashen-faced, chest heaving, covered in gore, Valmont grimaced as he surveyed the carnage. Sighing, he threw an arm around Gabriel's shoulders and gave him a slight hug. "We need to leave this godforsaken place, Gabriel," he rasped. "Soon, before there's nothing human left in either one of us."

It was decided. No matter the risk, no matter the consequence, they would make good their escape before another summer had passed.

Limping into Algiers in early April, they were greeted with the news that a treaty had been signed in March, at Amiens, between France, England, Holland, and Spain. It was a matter of indifference to Gabriel, as were most things these days. His unexpected encounter with de Sevigny had changed him. That, and the nightmare existence he'd known over the past eighteen months as a mercenary, had tempered him in the same way fire and forge tempered steel, burning away everything extraneous to survival. It had honed him into something cold, hard, and deadly. The old Gabriel, the one who knew fear and pity, love and sorrow, had been immolated in the heat of battle, hatred, and revenge. No trace of the eager young lover, the curious scholar, or the sensitive romantic remained.

Gabriel's training in combat, sailing, and command served him well with Murad Reis. As they launched their summer campaign, he found himself promoted to second in command aboard the Reis's flagship. Early June saw them roving the Ionian Sea between Italy and Greece, after a particularly lucrative sweep of the eastern Mediterranean. They had already sent two prize crews hurrying back to Algiers, when they chanced upon a small Spanish trader heading for home. Too wily to be taken in by false colors and hearty greetings, her captain raised sail and tried to flee, but hampered by strong headwinds and burdened with a full hold, he was caught within the hour. A ferocious battle ensued in which a dozen Spaniards and twenty corsairs were killed, but inevitably, overwhelmed by superior numbers and firepower, the Spanish ship was taken.

Sullen and defiant, the survivors were stripped down to their drawers, disarmed, and herded roughly to the upper deck where they were held under guard, chastened with whip and cudgel if they dared to move or speak. Murad Reis conferred with his lieutenants. The corsair hold was full, there was no more room for cargo or slaves, and the merchantman's sister ship had been spotted slipping into a cove to the north. The Reis ordered Gabriel to take command of a prize crew, giving him three other *renegados*, ten Algerians, and orders to make haste for Algiers. Gabriel caught Valmont's eyes, signaling him to join them, and amidst the bustle of men and movement, and the excitement of a new chase, no one thought to question it.

An hour later Gabriel sat at the Spanish captain's table, his feet on the desk, a study in arrogance and cruelty. Valmont stood to one side of him, paring his fingernails with a wicked dagger, looking up with mild boredom and distaste as two of the Algerian corsairs kicked open the door and threw the battered captain down at his feet. Still defiant, the young captain, with more courage than sense, pushed himself up off the floor and spat in Gabriel's direction, causing the corsairs to roar and jerk him around by his hair. Throwing him back to the ground, they lashed him vigorously with the short leather straps they carried at their sides.

Interrupting with a slight cough, Gabriel waved his fingers, and motioned the men to step away. "That really wasn't wise, *signor*. It serves no purpose other than to annoy," he said mildly, in perfect English.

The captain's head snapped up and he examined Gabriel closely. Bronzed skin, dark hair, and the pitiless eyes of a predator, he looked every inch the vicious pirate. It was astonishing to hear a cultured voice and civilized tongue coming from his lips.

"You understand English? Good. The two gentlemen who escort you do not. You will look down at the floor like a good slave, and speak only when spoken to."

The young captain, guilty of all the excessive pride his countrymen were known for, raised his head defiantly. Staring Gabriel full in the face, he spat again, provoking a flurry of punches and kicks and prompting one of the corsairs to declare that he should be severely bastinadoed, then thrown over the side as an example to the rest.

"No," Gabriel said decisively in Arabic. "He's worth gold alive, and nothing dead, and he can give us information about the rest of the crew. Give him a taste of the whip, and I will continue to question him." Already battered, the recalcitrant captain was whipped until he was bloody, then forced to his knees in front of what used to be his desk.

"I did warn you," Gabriel said pleasantly. "You bring it upon yourself. Let us try this again, shall we? Keep your head down and your eyes to the floor and listen carefully. It will be best if you show nothing other than fear and respect, although you may be sullen if you feel you must. I am going to assume, by the way you fought, and the way you defy us now, that you are not inclined to a life of slavery. Am I correct? Answer me!"

"No, *signor*!" the Spaniard responded, looking up and hastily looking down again as the strap was laid smartly across his shoulders. "I mean, yes. You are correct. I do not wish to be a slave. My family has money. They can pay you a ransom."

"How nice for you! But I'm not interested in ransom.

I'm interested in your ship. My good friend and I find ourselves weary of these climes and desirous of returning to Europe." The captain raised his head, startled and excited, a gleam of hope in his eyes. "Recollect yourself, *signor*!" Gabriel snapped, nodding at the guards who stepped forward and applied the strap again. "Really, Captain," he sighed, "courage serves best when seasoned with common sense. I require that you use your head. There are thirteen of them, and two of us. If our plan is to succeed, they must not suspect what we're about."

"You will have thirty-five if you wish it," the captain whispered, head bent submissively and finally, behaving as he ought.

"We do wish it, Captain. Will you follow my orders exactly?"

"I will, *signor*."

"Very well. We will continue to interrogate your men. Some of them will be needed to help crew the ship, and will remain above deck. Tell them to be docile and cooperate. The rest, yourself included, will be locked in the hold and shackled. The *chevalier*, he is the handsome fellow to my left, don't look at him, will supervise. You will be rude to him, you seem skilled at that, and in the course of chastising you he will leave you a key. Unlock the shackles but have your men continue the appearance of being fettered. Four men will come, two to feed you, and two guards. Your men will start a fight over the food. When the guards step in to restore order, you will subdue them, fighting your way up to the deck where my friend, your other men, and I, will be engaged in subduing the others."

"What of our weapons, *signor*?"

"There is no way to get them to you without arousing suspicion. You will have to rely on force of numbers. No doubt it will be a circumstance in which your courage will finally prove useful." They continued to speak a while longer, Gabriel barking out questions and the captain meekly responding, before he was waved away and taken, apparently much chastened, to be locked in the hold.

Gabriel finished the interrogations while Valmont inspected the ship and the hold, managing to pull aside the three *renegados*, one British and two Portuguese, and inquire as to whether they would be inclined to return home if the opportunity presented itself. All three confirmed that they would be very much so inclined, and the *chevalier* encouraged them to pay attention lest such an occasion should arise.

Later that afternoon, the *chevalier* checked the prisoners, tugging on a shackle here and there, to make sure they were held tight. The temperamental Spanish captain objected by tugging back. He was hauled up by the hair and punched in the stomach, sinking back to the floor with a moan, and an iron key stuck in the band of his ragged drawers. The rest of the plan unfolded later that night. It went as smoothly as any could have hoped, and was over within twenty minutes.

The crew's fury resulted in the deaths of four of

the Algerians. The rest were locked in a storeroom. Gabriel's insistence that the weapons remain under his, and the *chevalier*'s control, ensured that the Spaniards couldn't act on any lingering resentments they might have harbored over their initial treatment. Despite strenuous objections, they pulled in close to the coast and let the six remaining Algerians jump the rail and swim to shore. Four of them had been in the rearguard of the mountain massacre, and neither Gabriel nor Valmont would countenance sending men who had fought shoulder to shoulder with them, against impossible odds, to be sold as Spanish slaves, or hung. They arrived in Barcelona, Spain, midway through June, and were back in Paris by July.

CHAPTER
30

Sarah walked listlessly along the shore. The days were getting shorter now, and dusk was crowding in. The sullen sky was laced with soot-tinted wisps. Leaden pillars of cloud towered on the horizon. The water, thick, gelid, and lashed to a frenzy by the wind, spit wintry foam as it battered the coast. There was ice in it. The weather matched her mood.

It was November. The Yule would be upon them soon, and Jamie would be home for the holidays in a few more weeks. Next year he would be at Oxford. It should have been a happy time, but it was two years now, almost to the day, since Davey had come home bringing news of Gabriel's death. Drowned, he said, swept from the deck of the *L'Espérance* in a heavy gale, while trying to pull another man to safety. She had fainted, the first time she'd ever succumbed to such weakness. The world had gone black, and she had slumped to the ground as Ross and Jamie rushed to support her. Davey had just stood there, dumb with sorrow and stricken with guilt.

It was a terrible storm. It claimed at least two other ships and a great many lives, Davey told her later. Gabriel could never have survived it. She'd refused to believe it at first, certain that if he were dead she would have known it, felt it somehow, deep within her being. But Davey had been thorough. He had been to all the great slaving capitals, Salé in Morocco, and Tunis, Algiers, and Tripoli along the northern coast. He'd checked with all his contacts, spoken with merchants and traders, every embassy, and even representatives of the Sultan and the Dey. After two years of searching there was no trace of him, no record of him or anyone resembling him having ever been a captive anywhere on the Barbary Coast.

The world had seemed colorless and grim since then. She'd lost interest in everything around her, spending her days walking along the beach or sitting in her room, arms wrapped around her knees, tears running down her cheeks, cursing the ocean she'd once loved, for stealing him away. They were all worried about her, Ross, and Jamie, and Davey. They didn't really know, any of them, the depths of the bond between her and Gabriel, how close they'd been, how much they'd shared, though Davey must have guessed. Ross blamed himself for sending him away, Davey blamed himself for taking him, and although she blamed neither of them, she found she had nothing left with which to offer comfort.

They were adults, but Jamie would be coming in another six weeks, and she refused to abandon him to her grief. She had done so once before, with disastrous results. His visits home had been one of the few bright spots in her life over the past two years. They had grown closer since Gabriel had left, sharing his letters and a special bond, and she always managed to find some semblance of her old self whenever he was with them.

Between times, Ross kept encouraging her to do something, anything, strewing the breakfast table and her desk with newspapers, invitations, and articles on upcoming lectures and talks. There was a French astronomer she had once been eager to meet, coming to London to give a Royal Society lecture. A friend had written with an invitation to visit her salon, and she'd been wanting to commission a new telescope with a long focus lens.

Just this past week, Ross had asked her if she couldn't visit an old acquaintance of his in Hampshire, a half-Irish peer named Killigrew, related to their shipping neighbors in Falmouth. He was ill, it seemed, and interested in selling some of his stud. The earl was a highly successful racehorse breeder, and both Ross and Sarah had talked in the past of crossing Sarah's stallion and their Arab mares, with English-bred hunters and racers. Ross claimed he hadn't the time to go, citing urgent business with his shipping interests, and begged Sarah to go in his place. She had as good an eye for horseflesh as he did, and was better at bargaining, besides.

Well, then, she thought, shivering and pulling her shawl tighter, why *not* go to London? She was sick of sorrow and sick of herself. She was young and alive, and as hard as it was to accept, Gabriel was gone, and he had been for over two years. She owed it to herself and her family to move on. She could travel to London and spend a week or two, attend Monsieur Doucette's lecture and visit Mary's salon, and perhaps do a little Christmas shopping. If she left this week, she would have time to visit Ross's Irish earl on the way, and still be back for Christmas.

Chilled now, she quickened her pace, striving to warm herself and eager to speak with Ross. He was delighted and deeply relieved to see her taking an interest in something at last. That night at dinner, she felt the first stirrings of excitement as they discussed arrangements for the trip, her plans in London, and the Killigrew stud. Even so, when she went to her room her gaze was drawn to the empty window seat, and tears pricked at the corner of her eyes. Despite her best intentions and all her new resolutions, she cried herself to sleep, and she dreamed of Gabriel.

She left two days later, accompanied by John Wells, the coachman, and William Towers, one of their senior grooms. Both men were burly ex-soldiers who had served under Ross on campaign, and were as skilled with fists, pistol, or sword, as they were with horses. Ross watched her leave with a satisfied smile. He'd sent ahead to London to open the town house for her, and his lads would make certain no harm befell her on the trip. He smiled as he wondered what she'd make of Killigrew.

Sarah arrived at the old earl's estate just before sunset. Located close to Winchester, the house was an impressive stone edifice, perched on a slight rise and surrounded by lush wooded parkland that sloped down to a lazily meandering river. To her left, she could see a great arched roof topping a sizable stable built of dressed stone and surrounded by white fenced paddocks. It was cool for November, and there was a damp metallic taste in the air.

The butler greeted her with a look of disdain. She ought to have worn something other than breeches and boots, she supposed, but it was her habit to choose comfort over style, particularly when traveling. She was here on business rather than pleasure, and Ross's friends were not usually sticklers for protocol. Ross had certainly made no complaint regarding her attire when he saw her off, although he may have been so relieved to see her active again that he simply hadn't noticed. If the earl was offended, it was likely to be a short visit, and at the moment that suited her. She would prefer to be well-settled in the London town house if a storm hit.

"What is . . . madam's business?" the man inquired, his voice dripping with distaste.

"My business is no concern of yours. It is with the earl," she replied crisply, looking about the spacious entrance hall. Really, one would think she wasn't expected! Indeed, the butler's manner bordered on outright hostility! She had hoped to avoid bad food and bedbugs, and the discomfort of sleeping in an inn, but it wasn't looking very promising. Looking down the hall through a gilt-framed arch, she could just see into the dining room. It appeared to be filled with a merry and boisterous company. There were loud bursts of raucous laughter, and high-pitched feminine shrieks and squeals. Sarah blinked in surprise. The old earl seemed to be recovering. He certainly seemed to enjoy his revelry.

"Please, my good man, simply tell his lordship the Coun—"

"Barstow, what seems to be the problem?"

"This . . . *person*, claims to be expected, my lord."

Sarah glanced back and forth between the walls, hung with numerous equestrian pictures, and the man who had emerged from the dining room and was sauntering toward her. She seemed to be in the right place, but this couldn't possibly be the old earl. He had chiseled features, a full cruel mouth, and tousled blond hair curling about his ears. His coat was unbuttoned in glorious disarray, and a half-naked woman was wrapped around his waist. Leaning tipsily against his bountiful companion, one hand absently caressing a naked breast, he tilted his head and looked at her askance.

"Well, my fair Cyprian, what manner of gift are you? Who sent you, my love?" He eyed her slowly up and down with an appreciative smile.

She should have been outraged, or at least deeply offended, but she found herself responding to the spark of humor and mischief in his laughing blue eyes. "My parents and my nurse used to tell me I was a gift from God, my lord, but, of course, parents are notably partial to such fancies."

"Are they? I don't recollect so myself. Have you come to grace our company, my dear? Because I do believe I should prefer to keep you for myself. You'll find I'm generously proportioned in both my purse and my parts," he added with a wicked grin.

"How wonderful for you, my lord, and for your lovely companion," Sarah said with a laugh, glancing pointedly at his pouting mistress. "But, in fact, I came to see your stud. I seem to have come at an inconvenient time however, I do beg your pardon."

Killigrew, if that's who he was, grinned broadly and waved toward the dining room, where sounds of revelry continued unabated. "Not at all my dear, your timing is impeccable. They are all gathered here to dine. Won't you join us?"

"I think not, my lord. That was not the stud I had in mind," she said with a slight smile. "I will find an inn in town. Would it be convenient were I to call upon you sometime tomorrow?"

He regarded her with some puzzlement now. "I begin to fear there's been some misunderstanding. You are not one of my Falmouth relatives come to call, are you? An aunt or a cousin, perchance?"

"No, my lord," she said, bursting into laughter. "I am Sarah, Lady Munroe. My brother Ross, the Earl of Huntington, received a correspondence inviting him to visit your stables. He asked me to come in his stead. Were you not expecting me?"

"Huntington's little sister? Good Lord, you're the one they call the Gypsy Countess! Indeed, no, you are most unexpected," he said, pulling free of his blowsy *inamorata*, and waving the sulky armful away.

"And you, I assume, are not the old earl."

"Good heavens no, Countess. I am the notorious earl, the one they all whisper about."

"Ah! The cursed Killigrew."

"You have heard of me!"

"You are the favorite topic to be avoided when visiting in Falmouth."

"How amusing that two such infamous people should meet only now. I beg you to accept my most humble apologies, Countess. Barstow, whatever possessed you to leave Lady Munroe standing about? Call a footman for her bags, and make arrangements for the comfort of her servants at once."

A voice rose above the din from the dining room,

as the flustered butler made haste to redeem himself. "I say! Killigrew! What the devil's keeping you?" A head poked out into the hall. "Ah, a new ladybird! Should have known. Do share. Bring your fancy skirt to the party so we all may enjoy her charms."

"Barstow!"

"My lord?"

"Do go and shut that lot up. Immediately, if you please."

"Of course, my lord, my lady." He bowed to each of them in turn and walked purposely down the hall, bowing to the company in the dining room, before firmly closing the doors.

"Again, my apologies, Lady Munroe," the earl said, eyeing her clothing with thinly veiled appreciation. "But you were not expected, and not quite what one expects."

"Neither are you, my lord. You needn't trouble your man. Winchester is but four miles away."

"I wouldn't hear of it, my dear!. It's full dark now, and the roads are no longer safe. Your brother would have my head should any harm befall you. This evening's company is unfit for a lady, but you happen upon the last evening of carousing, I assure you. They are helping me celebrate the old bas—the old fellow's death, and my new inheritance, you see." He gave her a charming grin. "They will all drink themselves to sleep and depart for London in the morning. If you will indulge me this evening, I will see to my guests and have Barstow make you and your servants comfortable, and I'll be delighted to meet with you tomorrow and show you the stables."

"Very well," Sarah said, too tired after ten hours of knocking about in a coach to argue. "I thank you for your hospitality."

"*De rien, Madame*," he said, buttoning his coat, and gallantly offering her his arm.

He escorted her to a comfortably furnished salon. A fire cracked merrily in the hearth, and he waited with her as a maid prepared her a room. They exchanging pleasantries about her trip and the weather, and he watched with interest as she hungrily devoured the meal Barstow had brought her. *The Gypsy Countess!* It was true that she dressed as man, and a very fetching little gamine she made, indeed. The style was most becoming.

What else might be true? Her lusty appreciation of her food gave rise to the hope she was lusty in her other appetites, as well. He had every intention of finding out. Bored and jaded, no woman had stirred his interest so keenly in quite some time. Chuckling in appreciation, he bade her good evening, and returned to his guests. The vicious old bastard dead, a title and a prosperous estate, and an uncommon beauty fetched up on his doorstep, ripe for the plucking. Things were looking up. He should really try his hand at cards.

Sarah slept late, had breakfast, and went to find the library. The new earl had come as quite a surprise. She'd been expecting his grandfather! She had heard of William Killigrew, of course. A notorious rake, he was said to be a dedicated voluptuary who had once cheated on his mistress, the Countess of Strafford, with both her sister *and* her aunt. It was even rumored that he'd bedded all three of them at the same time! Well, he'd certainly seemed to be enjoying himself last evening. She had to admit though, that despite her better judgment she'd found his charming grin and mischievous eyes quite appealing. Sought after as a lover, he was shunned as potential husband due to his poor financial prospects, and some unfortunate Irish ancestry on his mother's side. With a title and a fortune, all that was about to change. She almost felt sorry for him.

The earl found her in the late afternoon, curled up in a comfortable chair by the fire, reading. "I am very sorry to have kept you waiting, my dear. The last of my guests has just departed. It was beastly difficult getting them to leave. I had to tell them the cook's taken ill and the wine's gone sour, before they'd bestir themselves back to London. What are you reading?" Sarah held up the book she was holding in her hands.

"Ah, *Robinson Crusoe*! Rather an adventurous story for a lady, isn't it? I had thought the fairer sex generally more inclined to the gossip and fashion journals."

"Did you, indeed? Perhaps your knowledge of the fairer sex is more limited than you imagined, my lord."

"*Touché*, my dear. Please call me William."

"As you wish, William," she said with a sweet smile. "And you may call me, *Lady* Munroe."

"Indeed, Lady Munroe," he said, grinning and offering her his arm. "Shall I show you the stables now?"

As they toured the stables, Sarah was amazed at the opulence around her. The stalls were made from teak, with polished brass posts, and the names of the horses were engraved on marble plaques.

"Very impressive, is it not, my lady?"

"Indeed so, William, although it seems a trifle . . . excessive. What will you do with it all?"

"Why, I intend to throw it all away in an extended orgy of debauch and dissipation."

"Ah! I see. I wonder if you might consider selling some of your horses, to fund these projected works, my lord."

"Do you know, my dear, I hadn't really thought about it. The stud is the only part of the estate that holds any interest for me, and the only thing about my late grandfather I admired."

They continued to talk as they wandered the stable and paddock. It soon became clear to Sarah that Killigrew was no mere dilettante. He knew his way around horses, and his appreciation of the old earl's discernment in matters of horseflesh was equal to her own. "You were not fond of your grandfather?"

"Our relationship had warmed over the years to a cordial hatred. He must be spinning in his grave now that I've inherited. It was all supposed to go to my cousin, you see, but he failed in his duty and died not three weeks after my grandfather, leaving me as the only surviving heir."

They continued touring the property, talking easily about horses and breeding principals and the relative merits of the more popular London racehorses and jockeys. Killigrew was surprised at how knowledgeable the countess was in such matters, and the ease with which he found himself discussing things of more personal nature. Ambling about in easy camaraderie, they lost track of time, and it wasn't until the wind had picked up, the sky was darkening, and fat, wet, sloppy flakes of snow were tapping against their faces and hair, that they hurried back to the house.

Sarah felt a sense of anticipation as she went down to meet him for dinner at eight. She had chosen to wear a becoming redingote of hunter green velvet. The dress was out of fashion, but very flattering. It occurred to her that she had been flirting outrageously all afternoon, and that she was without a chaperone, alone in the home of a notorious rake. Oh, well, *she* was a notorious widow, and despite his lurid reputation, he'd certainly behaved as a gentleman ever since he'd learned her identity. In any case, she was enjoying herself for the first time in a very long while. She'd be on her way in the morning, and she saw nothing wrong with enjoying the company of a handsome and charming man tonight.

William's eyes gleamed with appreciation across the table. He dared to hope the dress was in honor of him. The color was most becoming, setting off her amber eyes and honeyed complexion to perfection. Her chestnut hair tumbled around her shoulders and spilled down her back in glorious disarray, catching the flame from candlelight and hearth, suffusing her with a warm, alluring glow. He swallowed and clenched his hand around his glass. She was magnificent! She had a bold freedom of spirit, and easy laughter that put a man at his ease. By the end of dinner he was smitten. He'd intended to sample her briefly and add her to his long list of conquests, but his plans had changed. The Gypsy Countess was going to be his mistress.

They stayed at table talking, until close to eleven. Outside, the snow and wind battered against the windows, rattling the windowpanes, and encompassing the house in an impenetrable blanket of stinging white pellets. Warm and cozy inside, they made their way to the comfortably appointed library to share a brandy, and play a hand of whist.

"I'm very much afraid you'll have to abandon your travel plans for tomorrow, my dear," the earl said, sincerely thanking Dame Fortune as he tried his best to look sympathetic and concerned. "It looks very much as if we're about to be snowed in."

"Ah, well, *c'est la vie*. I do hope you won't find me too great an imposition."

"In truth, my dear, I'm unable to recall when I've enjoyed anyone's company as much."

"How charming! You know, you're not at all what I was led to expect."

"Old and decrepit, you mean?"

"That too, but I was referring to the curse of the Killigrews. The terror and bane, and dare I say, delight, of your relatives in Falmouth."

"Mmm, yes. I really must go and visit them sometime. I've been told they never speak of me, rather in the manner one doesn't speak of the devil."

"But they do, my lord, with a shudder and a slight flush, and avid looks all around. You are a delicious shock to them, sir."

"Rather hypocritical, wouldn't you say? They seem to have forgotten they are descended from pirates."

"What a pity! My family is inordinately fond of their piratical connections."

"So one hears, Lady Munroe. Indeed 'tis said that you have an . . . intimate acquaintance with the piratical sort. Is it true?"

"One hears that you have an intimate acquaintance with dancers, opera singers, cheats, and three generations of the same family," she replied with asperity. "One hears a great many things, my lord. My cousin is a privateer, and my brother, Lord Huntington, has been known to dabble on occasion, so yes, I suppose it *is* true."

"I am sorry, Sarah . . . Lady Munroe. Please forgive my clumsiness. You interest and unsettle me, and I find myself curious as to whether you have any significant attachments. It was impertinent and I apologize." If he'd expected an answer to that, he didn't get one. The lady appeared to be gripped by a sudden melancholy, and shortly thereafter, she excused herself to go to bed. Alone.

Killigrew was confused. She was unlike any female he'd ever met. She was far freer in her speech, dress, and manner than any of the respectable women he knew, but she had a genuineness and grace that belied her being a strumpet, aristocratic or otherwise. To add to the confusion, her conversation, education, and sense of humor were more like a man's than a woman's. To a jaded rake, she presented a novel and intensely appealing challenge.

The next morning the house shuddered as angry gusts of wind howled and shrieked outside, as if furious at being denied entry. Drifts piled deep against the walls, burying the driveway, and Sarah knew she wasn't going anywhere.

Over the next three days, Killigrew waged a tireless campaign of charm and seduction. They bantered over chess and cards, their conversations wide-ranging and delightful, both of them surprised at the breadth of the other's interests, and depth of knowledge. Killigrew found himself laughing more than he'd ever done, while Sarah found herself laughing for the first time in a very long while.

Intent on the hunt, the earl failed to notice, that the more he exerted himself to entice and capture, the more securely he was caught. On the third day of the storm, he tracked her to the library. She was in breeches again. He tilted his head sideways, enjoying the view and trying to see her book. "Still reading *Robinson Crusoe*?" he asked, crossing the room to sprawl on the settee beside her.

"Yes, William, I'm almost done. The weather looks to be clearing, and I hope to finish it before I leave to-morrow," she said, marking her page with her finger and closing the book in her lap. "Have you read it?"

"Yes, and I shan't tell you the end. Unless you beg me prettily, of course."

"Do you think it possible for a man to disappear that way? To be alive somewhere when everyone else has given him up for dead?"

"I suppose it must be. The book is said to be based on a true story. Some Scotsman, Alexander Selkirk, got himself in trouble while playing at pirates, and was marooned for four and a half years."

Sarah nodded thoughtfully and leaned back against the cushions. He lifted his arm carefully, reaching it tentatively around her shoulders, and almost without thought, she sighed and leaned back into him. She'd been sad and alone for such a long time. It had been over two years since she'd felt the warmth and the strength of a man pressed against her. She'd forgotten how wonderful it felt.

Easing the book from her grasp, he placed a hand on her shoulder, drawing her closer, leaning forward until his lips brushed hers.

It had been so long! Flooded with sensation, Sarah turned fully into his embrace, but as he deepened the kiss, the memory of other arms and other lips intruded. *Good God! What's wrong with me?* she thought in despair, blinking back tears and pulling away.

"I had not thought you to be coy, madam," Killigrew said, letting her go. "Surely I did not mistake your interest?" *So we're to play this tired old game,* he thought. *How very disappointing.*

"No, my lord, you did not," she said, surprising him. "I just . . . I'm really very sorry. I thought that I could . . . that is, I wanted . . . Oh hell and damnation! I'm so sick of this!" she cried, bursting into tears.

Nonplussed, he searched for a handkerchief. Her tears were clearly genuine, but he had no idea what he'd done to provoke them. "Take this, my dear. I do apologize if I've caused you distress. I assumed you were as eager as I."

"It's not you, my lord, and I suppose you might call me Sarah now that you've kissed me," she said, drying her eyes. "You asked me a few days ago if I had any significant attachments and I didn't answer you. I really didn't know how. There is someone . . . was someone . . . I don't know! Someone I love very much. I haven't seen him for a very long time. Two years ago he simply vanished, swept into the sea."

"Ah. I'm so sorry."

"He . . . My brother and my cousin tell me that he's dead, but I find it very hard to believe. There is no proof of it, you see, and I promised him that I'd wait for him as long as it takes. Lately I've been so confused. I'm really very sorry, William. It was not my intent to lead you on. I'm just so tired of being alone and I find you so amusing and appealing. I thought maybe . . ."

"Please don't apologize, my dear," he said, patting her hand and rising to fetch her a brandy. "I don't deserve it. I'm a conscienceless rogue, bent on seduction, and deserved a good set down. It must be deuced awkward for you," he continued, returning with two drinks and lounging alongside her again, this time keeping his hands to himself. "If you accept that he's dead, you betray your promise to him if he's yet alive."

"Yes, exactly! No one seems to understand that. And I don't feel that he *is* dead. Do you see?"

"I do. But what if you're wrong? If you spend

your life waiting for a dead man, you deny yourself the future and spend your life in sorrow. Would he expect that of you, my dear?" he asked gently.

"No, he wouldn't. I'm certain of it. But then he's never really expected anything much from anyone."

"So . . . you will wait?"

"I will wait. But I will continue on with my life and stop being such a bloody martyr about it."

"How long *does* one wait in such circumstances?"

"It's a very good question, William. I don't know the answer, but I expect that somehow I'll recognize when it's been long enough."

"And what of me, fair Gypsy? Was I to be a purely medicinal diversion, a cure for the melancholy, or do you like me, if only a little?"

"False humility ill becomes you, Killigrew. You are well aware that I like you rather a lot."

Grinning broadly, he took her hand and raised it to his lips. "Then perhaps you would allow me to call upon you, should my affairs bring me to Cornwall in the future."

"I should be most delighted," she said with an answering grin.

The snow had changed to rain overnight, followed

by mild winds, and by morning the roads were rapidly drying out. Sarah spent part of the morning negotiating an exchange of broodmares with the new earl, and the rest of it getting ready to resume her journey. She was dressed in breeches and boots, and just about to take her leave when two carriages came rolling up the drive. They stopped in a commotion of hooves and greetings and flouncing petticoats, and spilled a glittering assortment of lords and ladies into the courtyard.

"Are you certain you can't stay another day?" Killigrew asked her mischievously.

"Quite certain, my lord," she said, climbing into her carriage and offering him her hand.

"'Pon my word, I do believe that's the Gypsy Countess, and dressed as a lad!" one of the gentleman remarked. "Wonder what she's doing here?"

"I should think that would be obvious," a glacial blonde responded, to amused titters.

"Oh, dear me! Have I annoyed your mistress, William?" Sarah asked sweetly.

"What? Do you mean Barbara? Lady Wilmont? You wound me, dear girl! I am known for my good taste and fondness for a challenge."

Sarah's eyes lit with amusement as Killigrew kissed her hand. "Well, in any case, I am publicly accounted one of your discards now, my lord. The least you can do is offer me a mare, as compensation for accepting my *congé* with such dignity."

"And so I shall, Countess, if you promise not

to disclose that 'twas you who rejected me," he said, walking alongside her coach.

"Well, my reputation is already ruined. I see no point in damaging yours. Your secret is safe with me. Till we meet again, sir."

"Till we meet again, Sarah," he said with a laugh, rapping on the side of the coach and stepping back. He stood in the drive watching her leave, even as his company clamored for his attention. So . . . his rival was a dead man. He would have to be, to leave such a jewel unattended. It presented some interesting difficulties, but nothing insurmountable. With a satisfied smile, the Earl of Falmouth returned to his guests.

Sarah loved approaching London after dark. From eight miles out, the roads were bordered by lamps lit with crystal balls, providing a beautiful glow that transformed the squalid and mundane into something magical, and full of promise. One never knew what adventure might await. The town house was situated in the west end overlooking a pleasant square. The skeleton staff, forewarned by Ross, had managed to open and air it and fill it with the welcoming odor of roast beef and baked bread. Sarah unpacked, had her dinner, and tumbled into bed, exhausted.

The next few days were busy ones. She visited the circulating library on Bond Street, and bought Christmas presents for Jamie, Ross, and Davey. Going through her mail, she found several interesting invitations. Her family had kept up a lively correspondence with many of the leading thinkers of the age, and though she was not welcomed by the best society, she was warmly received by the most interesting.

She visited galleries and museums and attended the salon of Lady Webster, a semirespectable friend from before her marriage, who was now a writer. Sarah found these evenings in the company of writers, scientists, musicians, and others from the demimonde, far more interesting than any she might have spent in the stifling bosom of the ton. The night she enjoyed the most, however, was one she spent at William Herschel's, an astronomer friend and music teacher who had constructed a large telescope with the aid of his brother and sister, from which they had discovered two satellites of Saturn.

Heading home, she realized that she'd crowded more living in the past three weeks than she'd done in the last two years. It was a grand day. The air was crisp, the sky was clear, and she was glad and grateful to be alive. She'd really only had a year with Gabriel, and come the spring it would be two and a half years since he'd left her. She thought about what William Killigrew had said, and knew that he was right. Gabriel would never expect her to wait.

She wondered what life might have been like had he returned home with Davey, as he was supposed to do. She'd thought never to marry again. Her own experience, and what she'd witnessed amongst her friends and acquaintances, had convinced her that she would never let any man rule her body, her fortune, or her life, but Gabriel had been different. She knew he'd been faithful to her, much against the fashion, and much to the disappointment of the maids and village girls. He'd had no thought of ruling her, content to be friend and lover, and he'd been far more concerned about leaving her fortune to her own use than she was. Above all, he'd taught her the joy and pleasure a man could give a woman. Her lips and toes curled as she remembered his heated kisses. She'd not hesitated an instant when he'd come to her in the night asking her to marry him, and she didn't regret it now. At least she'd had that time with him.

The problem was that he had taught her to appreciate a man in a way she never had before, and to be lonely in a way she had never imagined. She thought of Killigrew, and wondered for the first time, if Ross hadn't known damn well what he was about, hadn't put him deliberately in her path. The thought should have made her angry, but it didn't. He was a challenge that any sensible woman would stay well clear of. Charming, handsome, and very wicked, he was a licentious rake, but she'd sensed something more, and his cynical good humor held great appeal. Sensible, or not, she found herself interested in someone for the first time in years.

Arriving home two days before Jamie did, she was immediately caught up in the bustle of holiday preparations. Her good cheer communicated itself to the rest of the household, and although they passed a quiet Christmas, it was a very pleasant one. When Davey came, tentative and careful around her, as he always was these days, she threw her arms around him and gave him a great hug, knowing he'd taken her silence for blame. "I'm so sorry, Davey. I've been unforgivably selfish. I don't blame you for it, you know. It wasn't your fault. Not at all. It's just been so hard."

He hugged her back, relieved, and thankful for the return of the easy camaraderie and deep affection that had always been between them.

Sarah greeted the New Year with excitement. She'd received several letters from London, including one from her old friend Lady Webster, inviting her to go mountain climbing in Italy with her and Lady Spenser in the spring. There was also a very charming letter from the Earl of Falmouth, thanking her for her visit and inviting her to call upon him in London should she find herself so inclined. She thought that she might take him up on it. Perhaps she would write and invite him to visit her in Cornwall. But not yet. She felt as if she'd finally woken from a deep sleep, and she had no intention of losing herself in it again, but every night she dreamed of Gabriel, and she supposed, even though he'd not expect it, she would wait a while longer.

The coming of spring found Sarah in the stables helping Simmons with the foaling. She was expecting to leave for Italy within the month, after a quick stop in London to renew old acquaintances. The thought made her grin. Ross had gone to Holland on business and was expected back anytime, and when a servant came to inform her of his return, and his request to see her immediately, she hurried to the house. He greeted her with a warm hug, but he was clearly uneasy, eyeing her with a mixture of trepidation and solicitude that he hadn't shown in months.

"Good God, Ross, whatever's the matter? You're making me nervous."

Sighing, he poured them both a drink. "Sarah, I've recently had some information from a fellow who served under me almost ten years ago. I'm not sure how reliable it is, and I've debated telling you. I want you to understand that I put very little credence in it, but I feel you have a right to know."

"Tell me what, Ross? What information?" Sarah asked, her heart pounding.

"Well, my dear, the fellow claims to have been taken prisoner off the Barbary Coast a few years back.

He had recently escaped his captivity you see, and he came to me, as his former commander, to see if I might help him back on his feet. He claims to have served some corsair captain, as a *renegado*, a fellow who's turned Turk, as they say. He says he escaped with two Frenchmen and some other crew members, when they were placed on a prize ship. One of them was the second in command. The thing is, Sarah . . . it seems most unlikely, but from the way he described this man, he sounded somewhat like Gabriel."

"Oh, my God!" Sarah threw herself at Ross, hugging him excitedly, laughing and crying at the same time. "He's alive! I knew it. Oh, I knew it. Oh, thank God! Where is he, Ross? Surely you asked the fellow where he is?"

"Calm yourself, Sarah," Ross said, gently detaching himself and guiding her back to her chair. "You mustn't get your hopes up. As I told you, I doubt very much it could be him. Surely if it were, Davey would have found him long before now. The man I spoke with made good his escape ten months ago. He says the Frenchmen went to Paris, and then on to London. Surely if one of them were Gabriel he would have contacted you immediately. I tell you this not because I believe it. I simply felt it was something you needed to know."

"You're quite right, Ross," Sarah said, stunned and elated. "I most certainly needed to know."

CHAPTER
31

Napoleon, upon his triumphant return to Paris, had proclaimed a general amnesty for most classes of French exiles, and within the first year of the consulate over forty thousand families had been permitted to return, the *chevalier*'s among them. By the time Gabriel and Jacques arrived in Paris, the city was thriving, teeming with soldiers, citizens, returning old guard, and eager British tourists who'd swarmed across the channel shortly after the treaty was signed. It was a cosmopolitan city, particularly in the summer of 1802. Even so, they created somewhat of a stir as they strode down the streets of Paris in flowing burnooses, armed to the teeth.

"*Il faut d'argent*," were the *chevalier*'s first words upon entering the city.

"What do you propose, Jacques? We left a bloody fortune behind us. That's two I've lost now. We do have this, though." Gabriel reached under his burnoose and pulled out the purse he'd pilfered from de Sevigny, tossing it to his companion.

"But this is very nice, indeed, Gabriel! I propose we invest it at the Palais Royale."

"Are you suggesting we apply ourselves to vice, Chevalier?"

"Most assiduously, yes. I have led *une vie manquée* until now. It's hardly the time to stop. I assure you I'm very well suited to it."

"I don't doubt it. I have had some small success at the gaming tables myself. I've noted that with the proper skill and attitude one can reliably turn the play to one's advantage."

Well, then, my friend," Valmont said, tossing Gabriel back the purse, "I suggest we prepare our offensive. We must divert and distract. We must shimmer, dazzle, and shine, and above all, we must not appear *à la bourgeois*."

The Palais Royale was the center of Parisian political and amorous intrigue, and one of the most celebrated gambling dens in the world. It was here they launched their campaign of gambling and gallantry, with an eye to replenishing their lost fortunes. The society of professional gamblers that roamed the major courts and cities of Europe had largely forgone the distinctions of birth, the willingness and ability to play deep, being the great equalizer. It was a mobile society of cynical, cold-blooded, hard-eyed men and women, that lived by their own rules, and Gabriel and Valmont fit right in.

They implemented a strategy that quickly elevated them to the top rank of predators in Paris at the time. They didn't cheat. They didn't need to. Pooling their resources and sharing their winnings they played only those games where skill, attitude, and a cool head, gave them an advantage over their opponents and the odds. Affecting the flamboyant mannerisms and dress of the *ancien régime*, wearing velvets, silks, jewels, and high heels, tall men both, they towered above most gatherings. Outrageously beautiful, glittering, and painted in powder and kohl, they were always the center of attention.

Gabriel found himself a cousin again, claimed as the *chevalier*'s not so distant kin. They were widely rumored to be lovers. It was nothing obvious, a smile across the room, a touch on the arm, an unguarded look, and a certain *je ne sais quoi* of style and manner. Pederasty *and* incest. Even the most *laissez faire* of their dissolute society was enthralled by the gossip, which suited them both. The *chevalier*'s family, trying to reestablish themselves and their fortune, were uncharitably dismayed at the prodigal's return, loudly and publicly disowning him. They were dead to him, but their shocked outrage at his scandalous behavior fueled gleefully malicious gossip that both the *chevalier* and Gabriel welcomed. By drawing attention to themselves, they diverted their opponents from the play.

A player who was adept at identifying situations where he had the advantage over the casino, could make a good deal of money at *vingt-et-un*, and Gabriel taught a delighted Valmont his system for counting the cards. Choosing their games, remaining relentlessly sober while those around them surrendered to excess, they pitted *sang-froid*, knowledge, and experience, against ignorance and reckless self-abandon. Within three short months they had recovered all the fortune they'd left behind in Algiers, and were well on their way to doubling it.

Gabriel's return to Paris revived feelings and memories he had long thought dead and buried. His nightmares had returned with a vengeance. His sleep was filled with grisly horrors of blood and death; towering waves and snapping bones, and sweet kisses that ended in twisting hatred. Awake, he was plagued with thoughts of Sarah, constantly aware that she was now within his reach, three, maybe four days away. He wondered how she had taken the news of his death, what she was doing now, and if she ever thought of him. He wondered if she'd married again, properly this time, to someone whom her brother would gladly accept, someone worthy of her.

The thought of her with someone else twisted through him like a knife in the belly. He no longer harbored any illusions though, about who or what he was. He'd come to understand what Sarah had tried to tell him, that as a youth, and even later, he'd never really had a chance to choose for himself. What de Sevigny had done to him years ago was not of his choice, or his making, and when he'd been given the chance it was Sarah that he'd chosen. He'd even started to believe that maybe she was right. Maybe he deserved to love and be loved as much as anyone else did, but he couldn't believe it anymore.

He'd been given the opportunity to know something better. He'd been given Sarah, and he'd betrayed her with the most intimate gift he had to give. It hadn't been taken, or forced. He'd given it freely, deliberately, to de Sevigny. One kiss, followed by others, to charm, to seduce, to destroy. He'd finally become the whore that de Sevigny and others had always thought him, not for money, not for favors, but for revenge.

He'd betrayed her, and he'd betrayed himself, and for that alone he'd be too ashamed to look her in the eyes, but there was more. Nothing had mattered after that. He had killed, cold, mechanical, and merciless, dealing death and being paid for it. Even now he preyed on the weak and the pathetic. He was familiar enough with the rituals of self-destruction and despair to recognize them in others. He saw it in the faces of the foolish boys and desperate men who haunted the casinos, seeking the perverted solace of debasement and ruin. He knew them intimately, and he preyed on them, using their weakness to his advantage, and helping them along their way.

The best thing he could do for Sarah was to stay away from her, let her think he was dead, and let her start her life anew. Even though she was just a few miles away, a few days distant, it was an impossible distance, an insurmountable chasm to cross. He couldn't find his way back. He just didn't know how. He was well and truly lost. At least de Sevigny had taught him one useful lesson. He had taught him not to feel. All he need do was remember that, and he'd be fine.

Telling himself that a man who had money had at least some control of his fate, he drowned his turmoil in the ruthless pursuit of perfecting his game, and increasing his and the *chevalier's* winnings. Their strategy was not without flaws. The *chevalier* was inordinately fond of women. Tall women, short women, young or old, strumpet or lady, he felt supremely dissatisfied if he didn't have at least one to charm, and one more for a grand *affair d'amour*. Having gone far too long without, he availed himself of the discreet services of a local courtesan, until he hit upon the happy discovery that many ladies were fascinated by his androgynous appearance and enigmatic sexuality. They vied to seduce him, delighting to think that they might have the power to sway him. He delighted in hesitantly allowing them to try.

"*Ma foi*, Gabriel! *C'est un embarras de richesses*! They find that though I am not inclined to be willing, I am ever so willing to be weak. They pursue me unmercifully, beauties each and every one of them!"

"I am delighted for you, of course, Valmont."

"Yes, but how is a man to choose? Which one should I allow to seduce me first?"

Unlike the chevalier, Gabriel was not willing to be weak. Beautiful and ice cold, there were few who dared challenge his reserve He was not kind to those who did, flaying them with a frigid disdain and an acid wit that frightened others from approaching.

"Does it really matter, Valmont?" Gabriel asked tiredly. "They seem somewhat interchangeable."

"But of course it matters, *mon vieux!* Great honor will go to the Diana, Hecate, or Artemis who succeeds. More importantly, there appears to be a great deal wagered on the outcome."

Gabriel burst out laughing, so unaccustomed to it, it actually hurt. He thanked God, not for the first time, for putting the *chevalier* in his path. "You are incorrigible, Jacques! By all means, you must choose the one with the longest odds."

In the end it was Madame Mercier, a statuesque Diana with a pert nose, golden locks, and pouting lips, who carried the day. What her conversation lacked in depth, she more than made up for in quantity and volume. Gabriel found her company annoying in the extreme, but the *chevalier* didn't seem to mind in the least. She accompanied him everywhere, clutching her prize tightly by the arm, preening in front of her rivals and reveling in Gabriel's obvious distaste, which she mistook for jealousy.

Intelligence and good conversation were not among the qualities Valmont found necessary, or expected in a lover, and what he *did* prefer she had in ample abundance. It was most unfortunate then, that her husband, a major stationed just outside of Paris, had the bad manners to object to her affairs. The *chevalier* soon found himself challenged to a duel.

"*Croix de Dieu*! I have no wish to kill a man over such a trifling affair, Gabriel. What on earth is the matter with him?"

"Mmm, perhaps he doesn't love or appreciate you as I do, Jacques."

"I'm sure that you find yourself very droll, St. Croix, but I do not."

"I apologize, Chevalier. It is a serious matter, of course, an *affair d'honneur* after all. What says your paramour? Perhaps you might allow her to convince you to spare him. *Noblesse oblige*, and all that."

"Unfortunately not, she's proving to be rather bloodthirsty. She wants me to kill him and marry her, or at least give her a house and an allowance and a carriage. She says he's been most unkind to her, threatened to throw her out on the street without a *sou*."

"The monster!"

"Blast you, man, it's not amusing! She's threatening to sue me. It's all becoming very tedious."

"I'm not at all surprised. I found her tedious from the moment you introduced her. She is vapid, shallow, and lacking in understanding of anything beyond her own needs. I'm perplexed at what you saw in her."

"Yes, well, there are things that *most* men appreciate in a woman, and I assure you she has them in abundance, and wit and beauty besides."

"If she has wit, Chevalier, I can assure you that I have lacked the wit to discover it."

"You are being too harsh, Gabriel! You expect too much of her. Women don't think as we do. Most of them are charming, silly creatures, and meant to be enjoyed as such. One mustn't blame them for things that are foreign to their nature, or beyond their abilities and comprehension."

"That's arrant nonsense, Valmont. I know a woman whose understanding is as great as any man's, and superior to most."

"Do you really? Who is she? Have I met her?" Valmont was surprised and keenly interested. The only time he'd heard Gabriel speak of a woman was when he'd been delirious.

"Leave it be, Jacques. It's of no importance."

There was a note of finality to the statement that told the *chevalier* the subject was closed. He knew Gabriel well enough by now, not to press. Still, he was fascinated by the inadvertent revelation. Apparently there *was* a woman in his inscrutable friend's past.

"Perhaps it's time we leave Paris," Gabriel ventured. "There's talk the peace won't hold, and I've a mind to try London rather than get caught up in Napoleon's latest madness."

"Really, my friend? Do you imagine I would just abandon my lover? Am I so cold? Is my love such a timorous and superficial thing?"

"Yes. It is,"

"You do not believe that I love her?"

"I believe it's the adventure you love, Jacques, not the woman."

"Your pardon, *mon vieux*, but what would you know of such things? From what I've seen, you love women not at all."

Gabriel shrugged his shoulders. "Stay then, Valmont. Murder the poor major and marry your trollop if you feel you must."

Two days later they took the packet boat from Calais to Dover, and a few days after that they were settled in comfortable bachelor's lodgings on St. James Street.

Despite decades of fairly constant warfare, and recent concerns about Napoleon's buildup of forces along the coast, the British aristocracy's love affair with gambling and all things French continued unabated. Gabriel and the *chevalier* found themselves welcomed, just two more Frenchmen lost in the crowd who had emigrated from Paris over the past decade.

Their new lodgings placed them in the immediate vicinity of three of the most prominent men's clubs in London. Establishing themselves quickly at Brooks, chosen for its wealthy members and reputation for sensational gambling, they applied the same principles that had served them so well in France. It was even more effective in London, as the British were more enamored of their drink. By the start of the New Year, they were well enough situated to purchase a house on Chesterfield Street. With the house came dinner invitations, a mere trickle at first, mostly from expatriate acquaintances of the *chevalier's*. These were rapidly followed by a stream of others, as their flamboyant dress, flagrant good looks, and blatant wealth made them irresistibly appealing to a bored and jaded ton, eager for novelty and gossip.

"We are accepted everywhere, *mon vieux*," The *chevalier* remarked triumphantly a month after their move.

"*Veni vidi vici*," Gabriel said with a tired smile.

"Perhaps I shall marry one of these pretty little English heiresses and settle here. What do you think, St. Croix?"

"I think they invite interesting foreigners to their parties and balls as a form of entertainment, Chevalier. They don't marry them, particularly when they are the focus of the kind of rumors attached to you and me."

"I am not some *arriviste*, Gabriel! My family's lines can be traced back to Charlemagne. I am extremely well bred and very wealthy, and as my cousin, so are you. It is more than enough to ensure that any youthful indiscretions will be forgiven," he added with a grin.

"I am not extremely well bred, Jacques. My lines can be traced back to the gutter."

"What nonsense, *mon cher*! How droll you are at times. You are all that remains of the ancient line of St. Croix, and our families have been intermarrying for generations."

Despite their respectable fortunes and ancient lineages, the scions of the families Valmont and St. Croix found themselves welcome at the clubs as guests, but not as members. Rather than ingratiate, placate, and graciously lose in the hopes of smoothing the path to membership, they chose to start holding their own informal card parties, inviting the outrageous, the witty, the wealthy, and the wild.

The house on Chesterfield Street was large, comfortable, and tastefully decorated, backing onto an elegant square. They equipped an upstairs room with a magnificent billiard table, and the drawing room and salon were furnished in the style of Louis XIV. The library and a number of smaller private rooms were furnished with inviting armchairs and sofas for those who preferred comfort to elegance. Valmont was able to secure the services of a Monsieur Villeneuve, a superb French chef. When all was ready, they began holding court, plying their guests with sumptuous food, the best wines, most entertaining conversation, and more to the point, the deepest play in all of London.

Unlike the clubs on St. James, women were welcome, and many came, some accompanying their lovers, and some to enjoy the company and to play. Although most were *demimondaine*, there was more than a sprinkling of adventuresome society ladies amongst the mix. It was a dissolute and jaded crowd, wealthy, bored, and addicted to alcohol, gambling, and sex. They enjoyed their own company, they enjoyed the women, and they lost their money. The barbed and vicious wit, lavish meals, and plentiful alcohol kept them coming back.

To Gabriel it quickly became a hollow farce. Sometimes he could detach himself and watch it with a cool curiosity, similar to what he experienced in battle. His wit was at its sharpest then, acid and corrosive, flaying whichever unfortunate drew his attention, to the delighted amusement of the rest. At other times he was gripped with an emptiness and despair so profound that he could hardly move or speak. He would withdraw then, usually to the library, and try his best to lose himself in drink.

Jacques was becoming concerned. Throughout their adventures on the Barbary Coast, slavery, warfare, escape, and whatever had happened with de Sevigny, Gabriel had shown little or no emotion. It had seemed unnatural at the time, but he'd come to accept it as simply a part of the man's nature. Now he wasn't as sure. Ever since their arrival in England, St.

Croix had become increasingly moody and edgy. He was drinking more, though never when he played, and he had found him on occasion, staring into space with a grim and haunted look in his eyes.

Jacques knew all too well, that it did a man little good to reflect on the past, particularly when it was a violent and a bloody one. When such moods over-came him, he sought his comfort in warm and willing women, losing himself in an ecstasy of sex and plea-sure. He had yet to see Gabriel do either, and it worried him. He found him in the library, drink in hand, star-ing vacantly into the fire. "*Bon soir, mon ami.* Our guests have sent me to track you to your lair. There is one in particular, a golden-haired Amaterasu, who pines for you mightily."

"You are referring to Lady Wilmont? That raven-ous bitch won't leave me alone."

"Forbidden fruit, spiced with sin and malice. Who can blame her? You have no interest in her, then?"

"None, Valmont. Do as you wish. Who else is with us this evening?"

"We are graced by the usual, *mon cher*, various knaves, whores, sluts, and bitches, and then there are the women. Will you join us?"

"Not right now, Jacques, perhaps later."

It was much later before Gabriel finally stirred. The house was quiet at last, and the pale light of dawn was edging through the drawn curtains. He started down the hall to his room, not expecting to sleep, but the ritual would at least pass some time, when he heard moaning from one of the private rooms. Damn it, it was past time for guests to leave! Didn't they have their own homes to go to? Gabriel stalked down the hall and flung opened the door. The *chevalier* lounged in a comfortable overstuffed armchair, a drink in one hand, his other resting on the lustrous crown of Lady Wilmont's head as she knelt between his thighs, applying herself to his pleasure. They both looked up at his entry.

"*Pardonnez moi*," he said, bowing and turning to go.

The lady smiled provocatively, an icy blonde with blue eyes as cold as his own. "Perhaps you would care to join us, St. Croix?"

"*No, merci, madame. Je suis de trop*," he said, withdrawing from the room and closing the door.

"What is wrong with him, Valmont?"

"Nothing for you to worry your pretty little head about, mon chéri," Jacques whispered, groaning with pleasure as he guided her back to the task at hand.

Despite Gabriel's pointed disinterest, Lady Wilmont would not leave him be. Surprisingly, the women of the ton were far more persistent than their hot-blooded French counterparts, they refused to take no for an answer. Beautiful, cold, and emotionally detached, he was considered somewhat of a rare trophy. All the women who frequented their establishment wanted him, and some of the men, as well. His contempt and rejection served only to pique their interest, and as he grew increasingly weary, his refusals grew evermore cruel.

Tempted to take a lover if only to put an end to it, he cynically considered telling the *chevalier* first, so that he might lay a wager on the timing and the gender. In the end, he chose Barbara, with her ice-cold eyes, because it kept them all guessing, including Valmont, because they were able to come to an arrangement that suited them both, and because they were both whores.

CHAPTER
32

Gabriel hated the coming of spring. It was a time of hope and new beginnings, and its cheerful fecundity seemed to mock him, emphasizing all that was sterile, barren, and crumbling in his own life. It was when he had first met Sarah. If anyone had told him four years ago that he would travel the world, accumulate riches, own a fine home, and be welcomed in the highest reaches of society, he would have named them lunatic or fool. Yet here he was, and none of it meant a thing. Sick of his home and the company he kept, sick to death of his mistress, he left the gathering and made his way to Brooks, hoping to read the paper and have a coffee in peace.

It was more crowded than he would have expected this early in the evening. William Killigrew, now the Earl of Falmouth, was holding court. Gabriel returned the man's nod with a curt one of his own. Notorious for his womanizing and reckless disregard for protocol and danger, the earl's vices did not extend to excess in gambling or in drink. He had attended a few of their soirees; indeed, it was he who had first brought Barbara Wilmont, but he was not a regular. There was an intelligence and civility to the man that Gabriel liked.

Glancing through the paper with disinterest, he debated heading to the gaming tables when Sir Charles Seymour entered, loud, obnoxious, and out of breath.

"Killigrew! It's been a while. One hears you are to be congratulated!"

"Thank you, Seymour, although it's ancient news by now. The old bastard met his maker more than six months ago."

"Oh, yes. That, too. I was alluding, however, to your latest conquest. The word about the *ton* is that you bagged the Gypsy countess. She's arrived back in town, you know."

Gabriel stiffened and rose to his feet.

Killigrew laughed and motioned the footman to bring him another drink. "Has she, indeed? I must pay her a call. As for the rest, I wish it were true, Seymour. I certainly tried hard enough. Unfortunately, the lady actually *was* a lady you see, and although I enjoyed her company in some ways, she was not of a mind to allow me to enjoy her in others." Every one burst into laughter except Gabriel, who stood watching, intent and still as stone. Killigrew noticed his interest and was perplexed. The man was said to be indifferent to gossip, whether it was about him or anyone else.

"Upon my word, Killigrew, you're slipping then,

don't you know. I had the use of her when she was gadding about London just before Christmas, and a hot little piece she was, I assure you."

"Did you indeed, Seymour? Permit me to say that I find it *most* unlikely. She was at pains to inform me that she was waiting for some fellow she'd made a promise to. I can scarcely credit that a woman of such exquisite taste could have been referring to you." There was another burst of laughter and a heightened sense of anticipation. A duel seemed likely, and wagers were being laid.

"Are you calling me a liar, sir?"

"Indeed, sir. I am, sir."

Flustered, acutely embarrassed, and deathly afraid, Seymour tried to bluster his way out. "This is preposterous, Killigrew! You are being absurd! There's no need to protect her honor. Everyone knows she's little better than a whore."

The Earl of Falmouth sprang from his chair to issue a challenge, but before he could, the deceptively languid Monsieur St. Croix leapt across the room and one-handed, lifted Seymour off the floor by his throat and slammed him against the wall. It seemed there was a great deal of strength hidden underneath the flamboyant clothes and face powder.

"You offend me, Seymour. Dare speak of her again and I'll kill you," he said in a pleasant, conversational tone.

Gasping for breath, his feet struggling to find

purchase, Lord Seymour disgraced himself by wetting his breeches. Gabriel lowered him to the floor and stepped back, his eyes glittering with deadly promise. Catlike and lethal, every inch the hardened mercenary, he strode from the room, oblivious to the astonished babble of voices, and the amazed looks that followed him.

The Earl of Falmouth narrowed his eyes and sat back down, reaching for his paper. How extraordinary! St. Croix was known for his detachment and icy reserve. One certainly didn't expect strong reactions from him of any sort, let alone in regard to a woman. Nor did one expect him to possess such strength and speed. It appeared that more than his tongue was dangerous. It was worth remembering. He speculated as to whether the man might be Lady Munroe's misplaced paramour. It seemed unlikely that such a cold and distant chap could have ever been the lover of a woman as warm and vibrant as Sarah Munroe. Still, there were clearly some hidden depths. He wondered briefly if he was morally obliged to write and tell her of his suspicions. He shook out his paper and began to read, deciding that he was not.

Gabriel walked home, to all outward appearances a model of calm indifference, but his heart slammed inside his chest and the blood was roaring in his ears. He had no awareness of crossing the busy street, or brushing coolly by those who sought to greet him. She had been here, in London, just before Christmas! He might have walked right past her on the street. While he and Valmont were presiding over the debauchery on St. James Street, she'd been shopping, going to her lectures . . . waiting . . . for him. She was here, in London, now!

He'd been certain she would think him dead, that she'd be long since remarried. There was nothing to stop her, no record of their marriage besides a note in Davey's logbook, but she'd told Killigrew that she was waiting for someone, that she'd made a promise. It seemed that she'd kept it, even after three long years. *As long as it takes*, she'd said. He should have known. Sarah always kept her word.

He felt like weeping. What folly had possessed him to come here? It was a small world and they both existed on the fringes of it. If he stayed they would be bound to meet. How could he possibly face her? The thought filled him with joy and dread. He knew if he saw her he'd lack the strength to do what he must. Shaken, he sought out the library and poured himself a stiff drink. He was tossing back his third when the *chevalier* found him.

"*Bon soir, mon vieux*. You are the talk of the *ton* this evening. They say that you frightened the piss out of George Seymour. Literally!"

"He was annoying me, Valmont. What of it? I did him no permanent harm."

"You seem a great deal on edge these days, my friend. I had hoped *la belle, Barbara*, would soothe your nerves. Is there some problem? Something you wish to discuss?"

"As a matter of fact, there is. I've been thinking of returning to the continent."

"*Mais non, mon ami!* I like it here, very much. There is nothing left for me in France. I have no desire to leave. How can you even consider it? You are rich! You have a beautiful mistress and a magnificent home! What more could you possibly want?"

"You needn't come with me. This life doesn't suit me. I have a mind to acquire a ship. I will be happy, of course, to leave you my share of the house."

"You would return to piracy? Have you taken leave of your senses, Gabriel? Do you not recollect what we went through to escape such a life?"

"Do not lecture me!" Gabriel snapped, and instantly regretted it. "Your pardon, Jacques. I'm sorry to be so churlish, but as you've noted, I've been somewhat distracted as of late. This life is destroying me. I am far more comfortable with the wind at my back. I envision becoming a merchant captain, not a privateer."

"Well, you don't have to decide it all this evening, do you? I will pardon you if you come and join me for dinner. We have a full house tonight, and Monsieur Villeneuve has outdone himself. If you are tired of Barbara, there are plenty of others to choose from. After your heroics at Brooks, there are several young women, and one or two young men, eager to swoon at your feet. And you needn't feel guilty. I will do my very best to console her."

"Yes, Jacques," Gabriel sighed, "I am sure that you will." He followed Valmont to the dining room. Half of Brooks was there, curious and vicious, tittering as they recounted Seymour's humiliation and eager to see if St. Croix would provide any further entertainment. Lady Wilmont was quick to lay claim to him, gripping his arm and guarding him jealously, hissing if anyone, male or female came too close. For once he was grateful for her cloying possessiveness.. At least it kept them all at bay.

CHAPTER
33

Sarah stood outside the magnificent house, watching the carriages pull up, watching their glittering occupants mount the stairs and go inside. Her first reaction upon hearing Ross's news had been a stunned elation. She'd recognized instantly that it was true. Somehow, Gabriel had survived. She'd never been able to accept that he was dead. It was more than the denial typical of those who grieved. It was the connection she had felt from the first moment she'd met him in Madame Etienne's library. It continued to hum and pulse deep inside her. She hadn't known where he was, but she knew *that* he was, and so she'd searched, and she'd waited.

Her joy, however, was mixed with confusion, hurt, and a steadily mounting anger. A few discreet inquiries through Ross's London factotum, had turned up a Monsieur St. Croix, new to London since last autumn, and currently residing in an opulent home on Chesterfield Street. It had to be him. He'd been in

London, just a few blocks away, while she'd shopped and visited, completely unaware. Before that he'd been in Paris. He'd been no more than a few days away from her for almost a year, and he'd never once come to see her, to tell her that he loved her, or let her know he was alive. He'd not even written. Anger and pride told her to seek out William Killigrew, or to turn around and go home, but she needed to see for herself. She needed to be sure. Unexpected, uninvited, she mounted the stairs and stepped inside.

It started with whispers and continued in a rustling of silk and lace, as elegantly attired dinner guests craned their necks to see. Gabriel blanched and stiffened, white with shock, and rose unsteadily from his chair.

Lady Wilmont, sensing a rival, rose with him, still clutching his arm. "Goodness me, look whose come to call. It's the Gypsy countess! Killigrew's latest discard.."

"I would like you to leave. Now!" Gabriel commanded, his voice clipped and cold.

"You heard him," the woman draped on his arm gloated. "This is a private gathering and you were not invited."

"I meant you, Barbara," he said, removing his arm from her grasp, ignoring her gasp of outrage. He met Sarah's eyes. He couldn't look away. He could hardly stand. Her look was assessing, questioning, guarded. There was no trace of the warm smile he remembered from his dreams. It took a tremendous effort of will to keep his voice even. "Good evening, Sarah. You've tracked me to my lair." He stretched his arms wide, an amused smile on his face, but his eyes were hard and dangerous. "Well, my dear, have at me. It's what you came for, isn't it?"

There were snickers throughout the room, but neither of them was aware of anything but the other.

Sarah's heart squeezed painfully, her throat and chest were aching, and she fought to hold back tears. Whether she felt joy, hurt, or dismay, she couldn't say. His gaze was cold, with no hint of welcome. He was the elegant, disdainful stranger she remembered from Madame Etienne's. She wondered if her Gabriel was any part of him now. How could he be, and have left her to suffer as she had? How could he be, and not take her in his arms? How could he be, and stand there now, beside his mistress?

"What I came for, is best discussed in private."

He was known for the cruelty of his wit, and his guests waited, breath bated, to see her humiliated for her effrontery. But whatever faults he had, however angry he was with her for invading his carefully constructed fortress and forcing this confrontation, there was never any question. He would never show her the slightest disrespect. Nor would he allow anyone else to do so. Although a flash of bitterness showed clear in his eyes, his voice was cool and courteous as he gravely offered her his arm.

"As you wish, my lady. Come."

She nodded curtly, and rested her ungloved hand on his forearm. He closed his eyes a moment, fighting to stay on his feet, fighting to stay on his guard, as her touch shattered every nerve in his body. He walked her out onto the veranda, away from prying eyes and listening ears.

Sarah's heart ached with such pain it felt as if it would burst. It was difficult to breathe, let alone speak. She'd been overjoyed to see him alive, and devastated to see him with his mistress. She wanted to throw her arms around him, hug him and kiss him and never let him go. She wanted to slap him and shake him and rake her fingers down his cheek. She wanted to wound him, as he had wounded her. After all they'd been to each other, how *could* he?

"Why are you here, Sarah? This is no place for you."

"I'm here . . . I'm here for you. I came here to find you and . . . to bring you home."

Her words almost staggered him. A wild longing pierced his heart, and he almost reached for her, but the last three years had honed his control. He gestured coolly to the open doors behind them, instead. "Well, my dear, you've found me, and I *am* home, as you can see. Say what you have to say, quickly please. I have guests."

He was so detached, so remote. Somehow, she remembered how to breathe, and when she spoke her voice was almost as cold as his. "I will come straight to the point then, Gabriel. Where have you been? Why haven't you contacted us? We thought you were dead! How could you have let us go on believing such a thing? How could you be so cruel, Gabriel? You have no idea what it felt like, what we've been through. Davey has been consumed with guilt. Jamie and I . . . we . . . I just can't understand it! Why would you leave us to mourn you? All it would have taken was a letter."

"But I am dead, *chère*," he said with a faint smile. "I'm just not buried yet."

She took a step closer and he backed away. "What's happened to you, Gabe, to make you act this way?" she whispered, reaching her hand out to him, then letting it drop.

"Please don't think me ungrateful, my dear, to you, or to your family. But the deed was done, the secret out, and the miscreant whipped to the curb. What else was there to stay for?"

She looked carefully into his eyes, searching for the truth, something, anything, but they were lifeless and empty, like his voice. "I don't believe you," she snapped. "I don't understand why you insist on this charade. If you haven't the courtesy or the courage to tell me the truth, pray say nothing at all."

She considered for the first time that he was truly lost, forever beyond her reach. He was alive, though, and there was great comfort in that. It was time to go. She would leave him to his mistress and mourn him in a different way. At least now she could move on with her life. Moderating her tone, she continued, "My coming here has been a mistake. I am sorry for having intruded, Gabriel. Please don't let me keep you from your guests."

He'd never meant to cause her pain. He'd seen the wounded look in her eyes when he stood, with Barbara clutching his arm. He would never have purposely flaunted her that way, but Sarah had come upon him unexpected, taking him by surprise. The hurt and disappointment he saw in her eyes now almost unmanned him, flooding him with a wave of desolation worse than any he'd experienced in all his dark life. But for once, the gods were merciful, and nothing, not his face, or his eyes, or his voice, betrayed him. "I am very sorry to have disappointed you, my dear," he said, and turning on his heel he walked away. Her parting words were carried to him on the breeze, barely audible as he stood on the threshold, poised to leave her and return to the cruel gaiety within.

"Stay safe, Gabriel, and welcome home."

Gabriel moved through the dining room, grim-faced and silent, and left, closing the door firmly behind him. The *chevalier* knew where to find him, and minutes later, he cornered him in the library. "You let her walk away? Are you mad? She is your Sarah, is she not? The one you spoke to while we drifted about the Mediterranean. The woman you spoke about in Paris? She is *sans pareille!* So lovely, so cool, so hurt!"

"Mind your own damn business, Jacques! You understand nothing, and it's none of your affair! If you place any value on our friendship, you will never speak of it again." Hurling his glass into the fire, Gabriel stalked from the room, slamming the door behind him.

CHAPTER
34

Sarah returned to the town house and lay awake in bed, blanketed in a deep sadness that was oddly comforting. She was done with weeping, and just wanted to go home. The man she had known, however briefly, had been ruthlessly murdered, replaced by the stone-faced stranger who stood in his place. No . . . she reflected, that wasn't fair. The hard-eyed warrior was no stranger. He had always been a part of Gabriel. He would never have survived without him. But where was her joyful, tenderhearted lover, the passionate adventurer, her beloved friend? *I am dead,* he'd said, and walked away from her, leaving her little choice but to believe it. What had happened to him? She hurt just to think of it. He had suffered and survived so much in his short life.

"Oh, my poor, dear, wounded angel, may the Goddess find you. May she love you, and protect you, and keep you safe from harm," she whispered into the dark.

"Ah! So that's been my mistake," a soft voice drawled. "I've been praying to the other fellow, cold-hearted bastard."

She shrieked and sprang from the bed, her heart pounding. He was sitting on the floor, a half-empty wineglass dangling from his fingers, moonlight and shadow tangling his hair. She shrieked again, in anger this time, and threw a pillow at him. "You bastard! You scared me half to death!"

Shifting the wineglass to his left hand, he deftly caught the pillow and tucked it behind his back. "Tsk-tsk, mignonne, temper."

She searched for a candle, found and lit the lamp, and climbed back into her bed, pulling the covers up to her chin. "You're sotted!"

"Mercy no, not yet, *chère*. But if I apply myself diligently."

"Why are you here? What do you want?"

Why *was* he here? Because she'd waited. Because he'd been lost in a world of nightmares and she'd come to find him, as she always did. Because she had reached out as far as she could, had done all that she could, and he knew it was up to him to do the rest. As hard as it was, he had to trust, he had to hope, he had to believe. God help him, he had to try.

"I . . . I came to apologize, Sarah. I owe you that much at least. Earlier at the house, I wasn't prepared to see you. It took me by surprise. You deserved better from me than that."

"So . . . you're here to tell me you're sorry you let me think you were dead? You're sorry you never bothered to write me, to let me know you were alive?"

" . . . Yes."

"Well, there you are, then. It's done. Now you can go."

"Would you have me beg then, Sarah? Do you want me to crawl? I've never done it before, but I would . . . for you," he said softly.

"Good God, no! What do you take me for? I'm angry with you as I've every right to be! I cried for months, fearing you were lost somewhere, imprisoned or hurt. I couldn't believe you were dead. I made Davey keep searching for you even though it broke his heart. He felt so guilty, Gabriel! And now! Here you are! Look at you! Healthy as a horse, surrounded by your new . . . *friends*, and only a few days' journey away. I don't want you to crawl, or to beg. I want you to explain." She stopped, drew a deep breath, and let it out in a sigh. "I want you to tell me why. I haven't the slightest idea what you want anymore. Why are you here, Gabe, and what do you want from me?"

"I want to be there beside you Sarah . . . warm in your bed," he said brokenly. "I want to talk, like we used to. I only wish—"

"Well?" she snapped. "You've made it across town and up three floors, all without spilling a drop, I might add. Why stop three feet from your goal?"

"Do you invite me?" he asked carefully.

She refused to answer and he chose to make of it what he would. It wasn't the alcohol that made him unsteady as he rose to his feet. Moving to the bed, he sat down cross-legged on the far side. They were both breathless, remembering other nights. His heart was hammering. *Praise God, she still wore his shirt!* He felt like weeping. He had only to reach his hand out to touch her, but the distance between them was much wider than that. He took a sip of his wine, offered her the glass, and she shook her head no.

"I'm not sure how to begin."

She refused to help him.

"I could not have contacted you at first, Sarah. I would have, had I been able. There was a storm on our way back to Gibraltar. I'm sure Davey told you. I was lost overboard. I don't know how I survived. There was another man, Jacques Valmont, whose ship was destroyed. He pulled me up beside him on a broken piece of lumber. I can't remember much about it. I had broken my arm, and some ribs, and taken a knock to the head. I was delirious much of the time. For some reason, Valmont decided to take care of me. I would never have survived without him."

"He is the man who lives with you?"

"Yes, he was the tall, dark-haired fellow who watched you so closely at dinner tonight. We were taken captive by slavers and moved to a prison in Algiers. I was there several weeks recovering."

"Why didn't you send to us for ransom? Why couldn't Davey find you? He searched all those places."

"I wasn't permitted to write and we weren't meant to be found. We'd been sold to a private buyer, and he had no intention of letting me go."

"But I thought that's what they do? Davey said they would ransom anyone who had the money to pay."

"It was de Sevigny, Sarah."

"Oh, my God!" she moaned. Her heart froze, then filled with pity. It explained so much!

His eyes met hers, despairing and bleak. "Yes. He remembered me well." He could still hear de Sevigny's voice, malevolent, amused, *rèveille toi, mon ange*. He supposed he would hear it always. "I was his slave, Sarah. He kept me in a cell, drugged and chained. He was prepared to sell or ransom Valmont, but he wanted something more from me. I . . . he . . . he came to me when I was asleep. He started touching me. I knew what he wanted. I pretended to want it, too. I kissed him, Sarah. To prove it. The same way that I kissed you. Christ! I pretended he *was* you." He closed his eyes, sickened by the memory, and wondered if it wouldn't have been better to be raped. At least it would have been against his will.

"Poor Jacques didn't know what to make of it all. He was too well bred to pursue it, but I know he was confused. He must be even more so, after seeing you."

Sarah felt a rush of protective rage, remembering what he'd told her before their first real kiss. How it was something meant for lovers, far too intimate and personal a gift for anyone else. He'd been so happy to have kept his kisses for her, to have something between them that was theirs alone, unsullied by the horrors of his past. She could guess what it must have cost him. "I had to kiss my husband, Gabe, and I hated it, but it didn't take any magic away from the kisses between you and me. If anything, it made them all the more precious. If I'd known you then, believe me, I'd have done my best to pretend it was you I was kissing."

He looked at her intently, wishing he had nothing more to tell, wishing she would reach out and wrap her arms around him and hold him close. But there had always been honesty between them, and so he continued. "It's not the same, mignonne," he said quietly. "I *chose* to do what I did. I knew it wouldn't stop there. I knew it wouldn't be enough. He had me moved to his private suite, a reward for my cooperation. He was beginning to trust me and he wanted me very much. I used everything I'd learnt at Madame Etienne's to make certain of it. The first night he had me brought to him alone in his room, I was ready. I took the knife from his belt and I gutted him and cut his throat. I watched his eyes as he died, Sarah. I wanted him to know. I kissed him, one last time, and I didn't feel a thing."

Sarah blinked, startled and caught off guard.

He watched the confusion in her eyes, the play of muscle and skin over her throat as she struggled to find something to say, finally lapsing into silence. The clatter of hooves and the drunken shouts of late night revelers rose from the street below. He stared at his hands, folded in his lap. "I've done so much in my life, so little that I'm proud of, but I . . . I never deliberately set out to harm anyone, Sarah. Not even the German. But I meant to kill de Sevigny. I set a trap. I baited it with a kiss, and then I murdered him. It . . . I . . . I sold my soul. I acted the whore so I could have my revenge. I betrayed myself and I betrayed you, Sarah," he whispered, "and I would do so again."

"No, Gabriel," she said gently. "There was no betrayal. You didn't go after him. He came after you. He stole your childhood, your life. He degraded and abused you and when you'd finally got free of him he tried to drag you back."

"He did drag me back."

"No! He didn't! He tried to and you killed him for it." She was becoming angry and her words grew more heated. "He would have destroyed you! What other choice did you have? You did what you had to do to escape him. It wasn't a betrayal, it was self-preservation. It wasn't murder it was self-defense. Did you think I would blame you for that, or want you to do any differently? I would have kissed him for you if I could. I would have killed him for you, and done it gladly. You're only human, Gabe, not some plaster saint. So what, if you don't regret it? I'm glad if you got some satisfaction from it after all he put you through. But you have to find a way to let it go now, to put it all behind you, or he wins."

"Do you really think it's that simple, mignonne?"

"It has to be. What other choice is there? He's taken far too much of your life already. Don't allow him to take any more. He's not worth it!" Noticing the shocked look on his face, she took a breath and calmed herself. "I'm sorry, Gabriel. The thought of him . . . it just makes me very angry. I don't care *what* you did. All I care is that you survived him, and he can't ever hurt you again. I'm glad of it, and I won't apologize for it. He would have killed your soul."

"He did, Sarah. Or, I did. I let him."

"Nonsense, Gabe! If that was true, you wouldn't have come here tonight."

"There's more, though, Sarah. Things I . . ." He shivered and wrapped his arms around his knees, a haunted look in his eyes.

"Tell me then, Gabriel. Tell me the rest."

"We disguised ourselves as mercenaries, Jacques and I. We . . . I . . . *became* a mercenary. We spent the next eighteen months fighting for a *renegado* commander before finding an opportunity to make good our escape last summer. We killed for money, Sarah, for profit. I saw terrible things. I did terrible things."

"And did you enjoy that, as well?"

"No," he said, his voice devoid of all emotion, "by then I was dead. I didn't feel a thing."

"I can't believe you would have killed the innocent, Gabriel. Women or children."

"No, God, no! We were mercenaries, Sarah, not butchers. It was paid warfare. But they were men who'd done me no harm."

"But they would have killed you if they could."

"I'm hard to kill, mignonne. Davey's seen to that."

"And I'm deeply grateful for it, Gabe. And while I can't say I approve or understand it, it seems that a good portion of the adult males in Europe fight and kill each other, and whether they fight for commerce, king, or country, they all get paid."

He gave a short bitter laugh. "Will you absolve me of all my sins, then? Hail Sarah full of grace, mother, sister, and dearest friend." He reached out his hand to take hers, but she withdrew it from his reach.

"You've been free for almost a year now, Gabriel. Why didn't you come back to me, or write me when you were able?"

"I knew you would think me dead, and the man that I was, the man that you loved, *was* dead. I thought you would have grieved him and moved on with your life. I never expected that you'd wait. I thought you'd be married. I thought it was too late, and even if it wasn't . . . I didn't realize how much hatred I had, Sarah, how dangerous I could be, though Davey warned me.

"After de Sevigny, after all that I'd done, I felt unclean. I didn't feel I had the right to seek you out. I was ashamed, Sarah, and afraid of the disappointment I'd see in your eyes. I didn't think I could bear it. It's

413

how you looked at me tonight. I . . . it was for all those reasons. I felt you'd be better off without me. I still do, but after I saw you tonight, I just didn't have the strength to stay away. I don't know what else to say."

"Why would you think I'd remarry? I *am* married! To you! When did you stop believing in us, Gabriel? When did you stop believing in me? You *are* the man I love. Even with hate in your heart and blood on your hands. How could you think I would judge you? How could you think I would not want you back, alive and safe with me?"

"You've never judged me harshly, mignonne. You've always been too kind for you own good. I sought to protect you. I never stopped believing in you. I stopped believing in me. I . . . I was too afraid to hope, Sarah. I just couldn't believe that I deserved you. We stayed in Paris and I was miserable. I thought about you all day and dreamt of you every night. We continued our partnership, Valmont and I, gambling at the Palais Royale. We have done very well for ourselves. You saw the house. I'm a wealthy man now."

"They whisper about you. They say you and he are lovers."

His laugh was bitter. "Yes, I know. It suits us both. He wanted to spite his father and I wanted to be left alone, and when he blinks at me, besotted, everyone watches him while I watch the cards. It's proven very profitable. He's become a true friend, Sarah, and those are rare in my life. You would like him very much. I have so few friends. I hope you still consider us . . . I . . .

"What of your mistress? Lady Wilmont? She has comforted you in your misery, has she not? It seems to me you've made many new friends. It's no great wonder you have difficulty finding time for your old ones."

Dismayed at the sudden welling of tears in her eyes, he reached out to offer comfort, but she stiffened and pulled away. "She's not my mistress, Sarah," he offered hesitantly. "She only appears to be."

"Is that so?" she replied acidly.

Relieved, far more comfortable with her anger than her tears, he tried to explain. "Yes, Sarah. That *is* so. Barbara is a highborn slut. She's probably been with every man who was in that room tonight. She means nothing to me, nor I to her. No doubt she's playing with Valmont as we speak. I was tired of being pursued. It was growing very awkward. Women . . . men, they were worse here than in Paris."

"I see. So you were really left with little choice."

He winced. "Sarah, please, let me finish."

She looked at him expectantly.

"Thank you. She waylaid me in the library one night. Don't look at me like that! She wouldn't leave me alone, and I was tired of being chased, so I told her that while I was in Algiers I had been converted, and there had been an unfortunate accident during my circumcision."

"You told her *what*?"

"That I had been unmanned, mignonne," he sighed, "that I was incapable of satisfying her needs. I begged her to tell no one. It delighted her, as I knew it would. She wanted me as a sort of trophy, and she assumed she had me in her power. She promised to tell no one if I'd pretend to be her lover, and I agreed. It was a mutually satisfying arrangement that has served both our needs."

It had hurt. Far more than she'd been willing to admit, even to herself. Something deep inside her began to relax. "She is not your lover, then?"

"No, Sarah," he said gently. "She is not my lover. Valmont is not my lover. And there was no one in Paris. There's been no one since my last night with you."

A thrill of elation and wild hope spread through her, warming her like fire, and she edged closer to him on the bed. "You were cruel to her in front of all those people."

"She was rude to you. Don't fret, mignonne, that is one sin I don't feel guilty about."

"And what now, Gabriel? What happens next? You didn't seem happy to see me. You looked like you wanted to wring my neck."

"Good God, woman! What did you expect? The world I built crumpled into dust the moment you set your dainty boot into London. They whisper about you, too, my love. They whispered that you were here, that you waited for someone. Ever since I heard it I've been in an agony of suspense."

He reached for her hand again, and this time she let him take it. A familiar jolt of longing sizzled through her body.

"I couldn't return to you, mignonne. I didn't know how. But you will admit, I hope, that for a man who didn't wish to be found I've made quite a spectacle of myself. I wanted you to hear of me. It's why I came from France. I couldn't stop myself. I've waited in dread, wondering if you'd come. I've been terrified you would, and terrified you wouldn't. When I saw you tonight I wanted to weep. I was so grateful you came, but I hated you for it, too, because you made me hope again, as you always have, as you always do. It would have killed me if . . . Ah, Christ, love! You were so angry, so disappointed but you'd waited. I had to know. I had to come because without you I have nothing to believe in, nothing to hope for, and . . . Oh, God, Sarah, when I got here you were wearing my shirt! I've thought of you, and ached for you, and missed you with every breath. All I know of loving, wanting or need, begins and ends with you. I'm so sorry I hurt you and disappointed you. I pray you can forgive me, Sarah. I need you to hold onto. Without you I find this business of living so very lonely and so very hard."

She threw herself into his arms and he clasped her to him, sobbing with relief and need. "God, how I've missed you, Sarah," he moaned, sliding his cheek up and down against hers, mingling their tears. I'm sorry

417

. . . so sorry . . . please forgive me, I . . ."

"No, Gabriel, shhh . . . stop . . . don't, I beg you," she soothed, bracketing his cheeks with her palms, kissing his eyes, kissing his tears. "There's nothing to forgive. It wasn't your fault. It doesn't matter, not any of it. All that matters is that you're safe, and well, and back in my arms. Don't be sorry, just hold me, love me." She wrapped him so tightly he could hardly breathe, and he held her tighter still, pulling her into his lap and rocking her back and forth. They stayed like that a long while, murmuring words of love and joy, comfort and forgiveness.

Slowly, steadily, the soothing cadence of comfort and relief, pulsed and quickened into passion. Sliding his fingers through her hair, Gabriel bent his head and drew her into a kiss. He tried to be gentle, courteous, and careful, but his body raged with longing, overwhelming all restraint, desperate to join hers, to feel and to touch. Growling his need, he pushed her back against the pillows, kissing her wildly.

Swept along with him, consumed by a craving and joy as deep as his own, Sarah kissed his eyes, his lips, his throat, writhing and straining against him. She pulled frantically at his shirt and breeches, desperate to feel his skin, his warmth, his heartbeat, close against her own. Cursing softly, moaning, and laughing, they struggled with their clothes as he murmured sweet endearments in French, and Latin, and Arabic.

"Forgive me, mignonne. I don't think I can be

gentle. It's been too long."

She didn't expect him to be, she didn't need him to be, and he wasn't. He held her too tightly, bruising her skin. His kisses were frenzied and rough, leaving her sore and abraded. But when he entered her, it was with exquisite care, and though their clothes and limbs were tangled, she rose to meet him, and for a private eternity they lost themselves, in love, in ecstasy, and in each other.

Sated for the moment, deeply content and enormously pleased with themselves and each other, they lay side by side, holding hands. "What did you say to me before, Gabriel? It was Arabic, wasn't it?"

"I said that your eyes were lovely, sultry, and lambent, and soft as those of a she-camel."

"You didn't!" she said, laughing and shoving his shoulder.

He caught her hand before she could hit him again, and held it flat against his heart. "I said that every part of me is yours, mignonne, to do with as you wish. I place myself freely, completely, and most gratefully, under your governance. My heart, my soul, my body, my breath, and whatever other parts you might have a use for," he finished with a grin.

She wrapped herself around him, burrowing her head against his shoulder and tracing her fingers absently back and forth across his chest. "Joke if you must. I'm sure I can find out for myself."

"I wasn't joking, Sarah," he said, suddenly serious.

"I meant every word. I thought I'd lost you forever. I had to force myself to keep going from one day to the next. It was hell. Dark, and cold, and empty, stretching out before me the rest of my life. I can hardly believe you waited for me, love, but I'm deeply grateful you did. It would have killed me if you'd married again, if you'd found someone else."

"I know. "I've felt much the same. When I saw . . . never mind. Don't you understand by now that there could never be anyone else? I wanted there to be. It hurt so bad that I wanted to forget you, but I couldn't. You've ruined me for other men. I never believed you were dead, you know. I felt you. I knew you were alive. I knew you were hurting, and lonely, and lost, but I couldn't find you. It broke my heart."

He gathered her in his arms and rested his chin on the top of her head. "I suppose we were meant for each other, and no one else."

"Of course we were, you fool! Are you realizing it only now?"

"Forgive me, mignonne. I am not as quick about these things as you are."

"Well, now that you've grasped it, see that you don't ever forget," she said, snuggling closer.

"I promise you, I will never forget it again, Sarah," he said, his voice sleepy and tender. Warm in her arms, lulled by the steady beat of her heart and her soft breath against his cheek, he fell into the sweetest sleep he'd known in years. He slept all night and well into the next day, still and quiet in her embrace, at peace in a way he hadn't been since they'd parted.

Sarah woke first, grimacing as a shaft of light pierced through the edge of the curtains, hurting her eyes and snatching her rudely from her sleep. Despairing, she turned her head and burrowed under the covers, desperately trying to recapture the lovely dream that had soothed the ragged edges of her grief. It had been so real, and it pained her to leave it behind to face another lonely day. The mattress shifted beside her and she started, coming fully awake.

He lay stretched out beside her in all his glory, one arm flung back above his head, the other clutching the sheet about his waist. He looked boyish and vulnerable. His hair was tousled, a sweet smile curled his lips, and his jaw was rough with early morning shadow. She blushed and feasted her eyes. He had the broad shoulders, muscled chest, and rippling abdomen of a swordsman. Licking her lips, she reached out to touch him, to make sure he was real, and wanting to see the rest. Catching the sheet with her fingertips she tugged gently, gasping in surprise when he woke, and with one flowing motion, flipped her onto her back.

"What a naughty wench you are, mignonne!"

"I was attempting to ascertain if you were real. I feared I might be dreaming."

"If you are, my love, then so am I. It's a lovely dream and we are caught in it together." He placed his hand against her breast, feeling the nipple tickling the palm of his hand, keeping his touch light and gentle, even though he was raging inside. "You feel real to me," he murmured, capturing her lips.

"How like a winter hath my absence been,
What freezing have I felt, what dark days seen,
For summer and his pleasures wait on thee."

They made love again, unhurried, and tender. He employed all the art and grace at his command, dedicating himself to her delight, weaving a spell of tender words and delicate sensation. Heedless of the world outside, the servants, or the passage of time, they satisfied their hunger, feeding each other with passionate caresses, poetry, and words of love. After, held close in each other's arms, they shared the moments they'd missed from one another's lives.

Sarah told him about Jamie, how much he'd grown, and how close they had become. She told him about Davey and Ross, and Killigrew. He told her about the *chevalier*, what he owed him, and how he loved and valued him as a friend. He described Algiers and Morocco for her, and all the things he'd seen in Africa, the fantastical, and the horrific. He described the battles, the dead bodies, and his own strange detachment. She couldn't find any words to help him with it, but she listened, her arms wrapped tight around him while he relived it, and he wasn't alone with it anymore. It was three days before they finally stirred from her room.

"I have no clothes, Sarah."

"That is how I like you, Gabriel. I've decided to keep you this way."

He laughed and tickled her, lying across her back and capturing an ankle, contenting himself by caressing her calf and playing with her toes as they talked. "I should go back, though, to collect some belongings and let Valmont know I'm still alive."

"I'm afraid to let you out of my sight. I'm afraid I might lose you again."

"Fear not, mignonne, we shall be as Castor and Pollux, 'united by the warmest affection, and inseparable in all our enterprises.' *Wither thou goest, I will go, and where thou lodgest, I will lodge.* Where *do* you want to live, Sarah? Here in London? We can stay wherever you like. I have more money than I could ever spend. We are rich."

"We are richer than you think. Your ship, the one you left in Gibraltar, is waiting at anchor in Falmouth Harbor. Davey sailed it back, and Ross had your shares put in the bank, in case you should be found someday."

"God bless them both! Did you see her, Sarah?" he asked excitedly. "Is she not a quick and lively little thing?"

"She truly is. She's beautiful, Gabe. I'd rather hoped we'd go sailing together. In the last letter you sent you promised me travel and adventure."

"Would it please you, mignonne?"

"It would please me very much, indeed. I would love to travel the world with you. We could go to the Sandwich Islands, and Japan, and visit the Americas, and I've always dreamed of going to China."

Laughing, he kissed her toes, and reluctantly let her go. "If we're to do all that, mignonne, I really must get dressed."

Not ready to explain themselves, to leave their own private world, or to converse with anyone but each other, they snuck out late that night, whispering, laughing, and shushing each other like a pair of naughty schoolboys. Sarah, dressed in breeches and boots, looked every inch the part. Any fears, doubts, pains, or sorrows that might have stood between them, had been forever washed away in a torrent of lovemaking and sweet communion, and they were inseparable now.

Although the hour was late, there was a still a steady stream of traffic in and out the house on Chesterfield Street. They stole through the garden, and stopped under a balcony adjoining Gabriel's private suite. "Here we are, my girl. Up you go." Making a foothold with his clasped hands, Gabriel boosted Sarah easily up to the railing. She scrambled over, laughing and panting.

"Be careful, Gabe," she whispered, reaching down to him. "You're a lot heavier than I am."

"I'm a sailor, my love," he said, waving her hand away disdainfully. Leaping up, he caught the rail, one-handed, and pulled himself easily onto the balcony beside her. Flushed with the excitement of clandestine escapades in the dark of night, they forgot their purpose, and tumbled happily into his bed, kissing, squeezing, and struggling with their clothes.

"You ripped my shirt," she complained, sometime later.

"You can use one of mine, mignonne. You wear them so much better than I." He found her a shirt in one of his chests, grinning appreciatively when she put it on.

"Should we go and see your friend now?"

"No, he'll be with his guests, and a woman after that. Tomorrow will do well enough."

"Mmm. You know this room doesn't seem like you at all, except for those," she said, pointing to several instruments that took up most of the far wall.

"I don't suppose I've really thought of it as my room. It's just a place to sleep, if I can. Those? I don't know . . . I thought it might . . ." He shrugged and made a helpless gesture with his hands.

"Do you still play?"

"No, Sarah. Not for some time now."

Absently caressing her new shirt, she ambled over to the wall for a closer look.

The *chevalier* entertained his guests, making sure that the wine and the conversation flowed smoothly, but his mind was somewhere else. It had been four days since St. Croix had stormed from the library. Gabriel's reaction to Lady Munroe had been astonishing. He was well aware the man wasn't the callous libertine most people thought him, but he'd always found him to be cool, verging on cold-blooded. He'd never seen him truly upset before. He wondered if he might have left for France, if he might have done himself an injury, or if Lady Munroe might know what had upset him so. Weary, worried, and increasingly perplexed, he pushed away Barbara's grasping hands, stepped around a pretty raven-haired doxy, and set off for his bed, alone. He would visit the widow Munroe and make some inquiries of her tomorrow.

He stopped suddenly, turning to look down the hall. There was light spilling from under the door to Gabriel's rooms, and he could hear the unmistakable sounds of merriment within. Damn the impertinence! These were private quarters and no one was allowed to enter here without express invitation. *Nom de Dieu*, they weren't operating a brothel! He stood outside the door, collecting himself. Quiet laughter, the murmur of soft voices, and the discordant notes of piano and fiddle drifted from the room out into the hall. He was about to enter when notes turned into chords, and chords turned into music. Piano and fiddle coaxed and caressed each other, engaging and coalescing into a hauntingly lovely melody that spoke of yearning, pathos, and joy. His anger evaporated. He couldn't recollect the last time he had been so moved. Curious, spellbound, he opened the door.

They were oblivious to everything but each other. St. Croix, barefoot and bare-chested bent over the keyboard, his fingers weaving an exquisite spell, his eyes warm and intent on his lady. She sat cross-legged on top of the piano wearing nothing but a shirt. Stunned, Valmont watched them, completely captivated. Gabriel was a virtuoso! His lady was enchanting! He waited until the last notes rolled, slowed, and stopped, then exclaimed into the silence, "Oh, well done, *mes enfants!* Well done, indeed!"

Sarah shrieked in surprise and slid hastily off the piano as Gabriel jumped to his feet, pushing her behind him. "Damn you, Jacques! Have you no manners? Has no one taught you how to knock?"

"*Je suis désolé, mon vieux*. Your pardon, Madame la Comtesse," the *chevalier* said with a deep bow. "I was so enchanted, transported, in fact, that I quite forgot myself. Gabriel, dear friend, will you not introduce me to your lovely lady?" he asked with a disarming grin.

"Sarah, may I present to you Jacques Louis David, Chevalier de Valmont."

"It's a great pleasure, Chevalier! Gabriel speaks very highly of you," Sarah said, smiling warmly from behind Gabriel's shoulder.

"Does he really, my dear?" the *chevalier* asked, delighted. "I've always assumed I annoyed him terribly."

"You do!" Gabriel snapped.

"He tells me you are his dearest friend. I am most grateful to you for your care of him."

"It seems that I might say the same of you, *mademoiselle*."

"She is to be called *madame*, Valmont!" Gabriel growled. Damn Jacques! He was trying to ogle her bare legs! It was time to set him straight. "Chevalier, allow me to introduce my *wife*, Sarah St. Croix, *Madame* St. Croix to you. Sarah? Perhaps you would like to retreat to the dressing room and find something a little warmer to wear."

"Yes, Gabe," Sarah said meekly, kissing his shoulder, slightly ashamed of herself for enjoying his jealous snit. She slipped quickly into the adjoining dressing room.

"Your wife! I am *bouleversé, mon ami*! Shocked! I never imagined!"

"I know you didn't, Jacques," Gabriel said with a wicked smile, relaxing now that Sarah's legs were no longer on display. They both turned as she reentered the room a moment later, lost in one of Gabriel's dressing gowns.

"Madame St. Croix," the *chevalier* said, clicking his heels and making a formal bow. "It is a very great delight to meet you! Gabriel, *mon ami*, when you refused all the women who threw themselves at you, here and in Paris, I felt certain that . . . well, never mind. Clearly, you had a *grande passion*. And to think, she is your wife! How unusual! I am delighted for you both! Come now, *mes enfants*. We shall share some wine and celebrate and you will tell me of your *grand amour*."

Gabriel and Sarah spent another month in London finishing up their affairs, moving back and forth between the town house and the house on Chesterfield Street. Gabriel ceded his share of the property to Valmont, refusing any compensation other than the *chevalier*'s agreement to come to his aid if ever he was needed, which they both knew either would happily do for the other, in any case.

Within days, it was common knowledge they were lovers, and that a startling transformation had come over St. Croix. Gone was the glittering disguise. The man who emerged from underneath was virile, powerful, and intensely alive. He doted on his lady in a way that was unfashionable, entirely unexpected, and the envy of all the ladies of the *ton*. His hard-planed features gentled and warmed, his cruel mouth softened and smiled, and his eyes glowed with a proprietary flame whenever he looked at her. They were inseparable. Wherever one was, there was the other, always touching, hand in hand, leaning in to each other to speak, and walking with arms linked or wrapped around each other's waist. It was disgraceful, and they didn't care. They were sought after everywhere, receiving many invitations, and accepting none. They enjoyed themselves with Valmont, whom Sarah quickly came to know and love, almost as much as Gabriel did, and when their business was done, they went home.

They were married in June, in front of Sarah's family. There were flowers, and music, and Sarah wore a beautiful dress. Only Davey and the *chevalier* knew it wasn't the first time. Things were a little awkward. Sarah's family rejoiced in her obvious happiness and Gabriel's safe return, but they were wary, too, unable to understand why he'd stayed away so long. He had no intention of explaining anything so private. It was enough that Sarah knew and understood. He hoped that things would improve and smooth with time, but it didn't concern him unduly.

After the ceremony, they made their way down to the docks, accompanied by a merry throng of well-wishers. Gabriel's ship, *La Mignonne*, strained and pulled at her ropes. Crisp and clean, newly outfitted and painted, flags flapping and snapping in the breeze, she was decorated stem to stern with bright ribbons and garlands of flowers. They bid farewell to friends and family with hugs, and tears. Gabriel surprised Valmont by pulling him into a fierce embrace

"I didn't think I could live without her, Jacques. It was you who kept me alive so I could find my way back to her again. I love you, *mon frère*. Stay safe."

The *chevalier* hugged him back. "I seem to recall you saving my skin a time or two. I love you, too. You and your Sarah are the only family I have now. You're a lucky bastard, Gabriel. I envy you what you've found."

"Perhaps one day we can find the same for you, *mon ami*, we'll see you in a sixth month."

Turning to Sarah, he smiled, all the joy and hope she gave him shining in his eyes, as he held out his hand. *"Arise my love, my fair one, and come away, for lo, the winter is past, the rain is over and gone."*

EPILOGUE

Sarah sat in the captain's quarters, checking the charts. It had rained for nearly three days, and she could still hear a gentle patter tapping against the skylight. It was a warm and cozy stateroom, furnished with solid armchairs, a settee, and a piano. A large and comfortable double berth was built into the wall. Gabriel had been giving her lessons in navigation, teaching her how to work out the position of the ship, sighting by the sun in daytime, and using the stars at night.

Pushing the papers aside, she crossed to where he sat, sprawled in an armchair, writing in his logbook. She pushed his long legs apart, kneeling between them, and hugged him by the waist, laying her head in his lap and nuzzling him.

"Mignonne, you are a naughty wench," he said, setting his work aside and pulling her into his lap, kissing her soundly.

"What shall you do with me then, Lord Husband?"

she whispered in his ear, biting his tender lobe.

"I'll show you, wicked child!" Growling, he gathered her in his arms and dropped her unceremoniously into the bunk, diving in after her.

Much later, drowsy and content, she realized that she couldn't hear the rain anymore. "Gabe?"

"Mmm?"

"I think the rain has stopped."

"Shall we head out and see?"

There was nothing Sarah liked better than walking the deck under the moon and stars, with Gabriel's arms wrapped around her. They poured some wine, and then barefoot and wrapped in blankets, they stepped out on the deck. They looked up in awe. The sky had cleared, and the stars glittered above them, diamond bright and impossibly lovely. The air was crisp and cool against their faces, and glowing wisps of silver mist skimmed and curled against the flat surface of the sea.

"Oh, Gabe. It's beautiful!" she whispered, leaning back into the cradle of his arms.

"Sarah, look! Over there!" She followed his gaze and gasped in wonder as an orange plume of fire hurtled across the sky. It was followed by another, and then another. They could hear excited whispers and amazed exclamations as men in other parts of the ship stopped to watch the show. Enchanted and eager, like little children, they lay back on the deck. Wrapped in blankets and each other, bundled together against the cold, they watched in amazed delight as arcing trails of light streaked overhead, and the heavens danced before them.

"Do you remember, Gabriel?"

"Oh, yes, mignonne! I will never forget. We were on your balcony, sailing together under the stars. You shared your world with me. It was the first time I held your hand, the first time I held you in my arms, the first time I dared to dream. It was the night my life began."

Alone, lost inside a nightmare world, all Gabriel had ever wanted was companionship and a place to belong, but Sarah had given him so much more. She had taught him to trust in friendship and in love, and by believing in him, she had taught him to believe in himself. He had faced his demons, and with her help, he'd survived them. He would always carry scars, but the wounds had healed and the adventure was just beginning. They sailed together, under the stars, fellow journeyers in life, and love. He was a man with an enormous capacity for love, and Sarah had released it. Forgetting the stars, the ship, and his men, he adored her with its full measure. There was only Sarah, and he kissed her with all the ardor in his soul.

AFTERWORD

I've always been drawn to independent people who rebel against stereotypes and challenge the conventions and norms of their times. There's a tendency sometimes, to think such behaviors, particularly among women, are unique to our modern age, but anyone who reads the works of historian Antonia Fraser will find accounts of women who led troops, went to war, ran their own business, wrote books and plays, dressed and lived as men, secured divorces, abandoned husbands, and didn't die of shame. Although some of Sarah's behaviors are unconventional for the time, they are by no means unique. A century earlier, Hortense Mancini, Duchess of Mazarin, made a practice of wearing men's clothing, and was soon the mistress of a smitten King Charles II. Thirty years after this story takes place, the novelist George Sands, a French Baroness who counted among her lovers Chopin and Jules Sandeau, lived her life in men's clothes and traveled about Paris smoking a pipe. Dekker and van de Pol, in their study **The Tradition of Female Transvestism in Early Modern Europe** give several examples of women who lived their lives disguised as men. They go on to say there were several circumstances in which it was considered acceptable for women to "cross-dress" giving the examples of flight or escape from dangerous circumstance, sexual play, during travel, and 'while carousing.'

Women also traveled, often alone, sometimes together, and some made a name for themselves as travel writers. Brian Dolan's **Ladies of the Grand Tour** gives a fascinating account of these accomplished ladies (who included bluestockings, divorcees, great ladies, and courtesans) and their adventures on the fringes of society and the fringes of Europe. Among them was Mary Wollstonecraft, writer, philosopher, and feminist, who in 1792 wrote what is now considered one of the first major feminist treatises **A Vindication of the Rights of Women**.

Contrary to popular belief, women also went to sea with their men. Ships with women living, as opposed to traveling, on them, were referred to as Hen Frigates. Cordingly's fascinating **Seafaring Women** is filled with stories of the 'surprising number of women who went to sea, some as the wives or mistresses of captains, and some dressed in men's clothing." Perhaps most interesting of all, according to **Life At Sea in the Age of Nelson**, by Steven Pope, women travelled aboard warships and were present in numbers at all the major battles of the era, usually as assistants to the surgeon. Most were the wives of officers, but the rules governing soldiers allowed each company of marines to travel with five women. It could be argued that Sarah's travels with her cousin Davey, and later Gabriel, were not terribly unusual for the time.

These women weren't stereotypical and they didn't fit the norm, but they were real flesh and blood people. Like Sarah, many of them, particularly those in the upper classes, paid a price, facing ostracism and social disapproval, but they also lived adventures and lives forever closed to their more timid sisters.

Sarah would have had to be unconventional and far from timid to become involved with someone like Gabriel. This book is in large part his story. Brothels like Madam Etienne's, frequented by men, and even some women of quality, were not unusual in Europe, and young boys and girls were sometimes taken from the streets and sold into prostitution, a practice, unfortunately, that persists to this day. Although it might be shocking for some readers, I've attempted to deal honestly with the after effects of childhood abuse as well as battlefield trauma. *The Age of Illusion*, by James Laver gives a gritty, entertaining, and sometimes shocking account of the manners and morals of the period, including the darker aspects.

In regards to language, Gabriel's isn't always appropriate or polite, but neither is his background, and he spends much of his life in the company of mercenaries and soldiers. Several words we sometimes assume to be common only since the twentieth century, have in fact been in wide use for a very long time. The writings of the seventeenth century court poet, the Earl of Rochester would put some modern rappers to shame, as would the ode Horace Walpole wrote to the Earl of Lincoln in 1743. You can find it in *The British Abroad*, by Jeremy Black.

Bohemia, which now forms the core of Czechoslovakia, was home to nomadic populations of Roma (gypsies) and also provided refuge for Huguenots fleeing France. Kali Sara, also know as the Black Madonna, is by some accounts Patron Saint of the Romany people, and was said to be an Egyptian maid who accompanied the three Marys as they escaped Palestine for France after Christ's crucifixion. It was said she begged alms for the Marys and spread her cloak over the water to save them when their boat was sinking. To others she is a Romany Goddess, one of the faces of Kali, whose worship predated Christianity and was later incorporated by the Christian church. The origin of her statue in France is lost in antiquity, and the latter explanation seems most likely.

Vingt-et-un was a precursor to the card game blackjack, one of the few games where attentive statisticians and card counters can have an advantage over the odds. Although there are many accounts of card counters making a fortune and being banned from casinos today, I can find none from the late eighteenth and early nineteenth century. Perhaps Gabriel was the first to recognize and profit from this method.

Several prominent Cornwall families made fortunes from smuggling (or free trading, as it was called at the time), piracy, and privateering, including the Killigrew family who established Falmouth. There was an upswing of privateering during the Napoleonic wars. Although most of the characters in this story are fictional, Lieutenant Gabriel Brey did scour the coast of Cornwall at the time in the revenue cutter the *Hind*, leading raids by land and sea and in one instance catching his man after a chase lasting twenty-eight hours. There was increased pressure to curtail the trade after the murder of a customs officer on the *Lottery* in 1798.

The turmoil and shifting alliances in Europe at the time resulted in an increased number of Europeans being taken captive and held for slavery and ransom in the Mediterranean. The practice was at its peak in the seventeenth and eighteenth centuries, but still flourished well into the nineteenth; indeed, the words from the United States Marine Corp anthem "to the shores of Tripoli" refer to a campaign instigated by Thomas Jefferson to suppress the Barbary pirates and free American slaves in 1804. There were still 120 European slaves in the *bagnio* in Algiers when the French took it over in 1830. Sultan Mulai Slimane ruled Morocco from 1792 to 1822 and had to put down several rebellions in the early years. The Scottish renegado Peter Lisle, known as Murad Reis, was also active at this time, eventually becoming admiral of Tripoli's navy and marrying a daughter of Yusuf, the *bashaw*. Galleys had been largely replaced for use in warfare in Europe by the early 1700s but were used in the Mediterranean in an auxiliary capacity until the advent of steam propulsion. Chain mail was worn in the Barbary states until well into the nineteenth century.

The quotations and snippets of poetry are borrowed from Thomas Bullfinch, William Shakespeare, and the Bible. For those who are interested, I have included a glossary and loose translation of the foreign phrases used in this story.

GLOSSARY OF FOREIGN TERMS

French words and phrases (in order of appearance)

Maison de Joie: House of Joy.

Non? C'est bien: No? That's fine.

Au contraire, monsieur: On the contrary, sir.

Les Anglais sont ici: The English are here.

On-dit: The gossip, what everyone's discussing.

S'il vous plait: If you please.

Mon vieux: Older French phrase, my old friend, old man, old boy.

Mignonne: Small and pretty, dainty, cute, a term of endearment.

Et bien: And so, it's good, all right, ok (depends on the context used).

Au revoir: Until next time, until we meet again, good-bye.

Ma belle: My beauty, my pretty.

Réveille toi, mon ange: Wake up my angel.

Bon Dieu: Good God!

Ma chère: My dear

Mon chèri: My darling.

Mon ange, ma belle amie, mon amour: My angel, my beautiful friend, my love.

Merde: Shit.

Je t'aime, je t'adore, ma vie, mon âme, mon cœur : I love you, I adore you, my life, my soul, my heart.

Salut, mon vieux: Hello, old friend.

Enchantée, mademoiselle: Enchanted, miss.

Mon amour, chère amie : My love, dear friend.

À la victime: In the style of a victim (refers to those who were guillotined during the revolution*)*.

Entrée into the beau monde: Entry into fashionable society.

Vingt-et-un: Twenty-one (card game similar to and pre-dating blackjack).

Mon ami: My friend (masculine).

Mon amie: (feminine).

Ancien régime: The old order of pre-revolutionary France.

Bienvenue, mon frère: Welcome, my brother.

Chevalier: Literally a horseman or knight. A rank within the French nobility including members of families of ancient nobility, even when untitled.

Ma fois: An exclamation of great surprise. My faith!

Oui, c'est moi: Yes, it's me.

J'y suis, j'y reste: French saying 'here I am, here I stay.

Et bien, mon frère: All right, my brother.

Mais c'est charmant!: But how charming!

A votre santé: To your health (a toast).

Chacun à son gout: Each according to his taste.

De rien, madame: It is nothing, madame.

Touché: Touched, a term from fencing, acknowledging a point was scored.

C'est la vie: That's life.

Congé: Leave, permission to depart, term sometimes used in French and English when a lover has been discarded and told they aren't wanted anymore.

Il faut d'argent: Money is required, one must have money, it takes money.

Une vie manquée: A misspent life.

À la bourgeois: In the style of the middle classes, conventional etc.

Je ne sais quoi: An indescribable something, I don't know what.

Laissez faire: Easy going, non interfering.

Sang-froid: Cold blood, cold-blooded.

Affair d'amour: Love affair.

C'est un embarras de richesses: French expression "It's an embarrassment of riches".

Croix de Dieu: Cross of God! Sacrilegious French expression.

Affair d'honneur: A matter of honour.

Noblesse oblige: Expression meaning those in high positions are obliged to act responsibly.

Sou: A penny.

Arriviste: Social climber, a person with money but no ancient gentility.

Demimondaine: Woman who lives on the fringes of society, a women of questionable repute.

Bon soir: Good evening.

Pardonnez moi: Excuse me, pardon me.

No, merci: No thank you.

Je suis de trop: French expression meaning I am one too many, superfluous, not needed, sometimes unwanted.

Sans pareille: Matchless, without match, without parallel.

Nom de Dieu: In God's name, Name of God.

Mes enfants: My children.

Je suis désolé: I am sorry, desolate, heart broken.

Bouleversé: Overwhelmed, staggered, deeply moved, bowled over, etc.

Grande passion: Overwhelming passion, all consuming love affair.

Grande amour: Great love, (a person) love of one's life.

Latin words and phrases

Veni, vedi, vici: I came, I saw, I conquered (attributed to Caesar)

Spanish

Querida: My dear, my love.

For more information
about other great titles from
Medallion Press, visit

www.medallionpress.com